DENIAL.
IT ISN'T JUST A RIVER IN EGYPT.

It means that you *retain the puca powers, Daphne,* his voice said in her head. *Those powers are now loosed from the stone… and tied to you.*

Daphne whirled to glare at Tremayne, who stood unmoving off to the side. "Are you insane?"

No. And before you ask, neither are you. Mindspeak is a puca power, as is shape-shifting. It's apparent you have a strong natural talent for both. His lips never moved, apart from a small twitch. He thought this was funny?

"Oh, no. That's all on you." She pointed a finger at him. "*You're* the freak around here, not me. I'm human. I don't 'mindspeak' and I don't turn into a wolf after dark. The only 'powers' I wield involve math, taxes and the IRS. So why don't you go find more of your kind and loiter somewhere… metaphysical. But leave me out of it. I have a flight to catch."

BETWEEN a Rock

AND A

Heart Place

Natale Stenzel

LOVE SPELL NEW YORK CITY

LOVE SPELL®

March 2009

Published by

Dorchester Publishing Co., Inc.
200 Madison Avenue
New York, NY 10016

ISBN 10: 0-505-52783-9
ISBN 13: 978-0-505-52783-7
E-ISBN: 1-4285-0616-0

The name "Love Spell" and its logo are trademarks of Dorchester Publishing Co., Inc.

Printed in the United States of America.

10 9 8 7 6 5 4 3 2 1

Visit us on the web at www.dorchesterpub.com.

*To Carolyn M-P, Audie A² and Renee W H, for memories.
I miss you guys.*

*Special thanks to Chris Keeslar for introducing the goat and
cheering Phil; to Michelle Grajkowski, who deeply understands
priorities; and to my Duetter/Deadline Hellion buddies for
unwavering support, advice and hilarity.*

BETWEEN a Rock AND A Heart Place

Two thousand years ago, I was little more than dust and spirit. And then I Became. The Archdruid Akker summoned me, out of anger, out of vengeance. I would be his soldier—a slave, really—a jailer to a condemned puca and responsible for containing that puca's powers. Many centuries have passed since the Druid's death, yet still I soldier on. Why? Because once these powers are contained, once they can no longer threaten anyone of human or faerie blood . . . then I will be free.

—Tremayne

Yesterday, I was an independent woman with career ambitions, great shoes and a one-way ticket to a new life. Today, I'm under house arrest. And sometimes a cat.

—Daphne Forbes

Chapter One

So close. So damned close. But it was not to be. Not yet. Tremayne had felt the violent shift in power as a rare opportunity eluded his grasp. Seeking patience, he tried to focus on the woman's words.

"What? So petty theft, greed, conspiracy and assault aren't enough for you?" Daphne Forbes, who gripped the cornerstone that had nearly fallen into Tremayne's welcoming hands, glared down at her father lying sprawled in the dirt. "Obviously not. I've read your damn journals, which brought me all the way over here, today of all days." She gestured widely at their rustic surroundings. They were, in fact, all standing in a clearing in the middle of Albemarle State Park in suburban central Virginia—an absurd location for an official Druid grove. "But did you also have to ruin my shoes?" Daphne swept that same hand downward to point at said shoes. The toe of one of the deep red, patent-leather stilettos was badly scuffed, courtesy of a badly aimed cornerstone. "Damn it, these were my going-away present to myself, and not exactly chea—"

She broke off as a blinding light seemed to emanate from her center and radiate outward. Her eyes glazed, rolling back in her head as her knees buckled.

And then it happened, just as he'd expected. Tremayne restrained himself from moving forward into the light, wanting nothing more than to get his hands on—

A crackle of energy, a wash of sparks, and heavy smoke obliterated all view of Daphne and the stone. Tremayne heard gasps and alarmed muttering from behind him, from all the other assembled players in this drama, but he ignored them and just waited in silence. He knew he could not interrupt the process, much as he might wish to do so.

As the smoke dissipated, he stepped forward to peer carefully into its foggy depths to locate first the cornerstone. He grabbed it from the ground and shoved it into the pack he carried over one shoulder. Then he cast his gaze beyond, to address whatever disaster had befallen the woman.

And that's when he saw. Taken completely aback, he couldn't help but smile, in spite of the circumstances, in spite of all he'd just lost. There, where Daphne once stood, was a pretty, cream-colored cat, eyes spitting rage and terror. She'd left one scuffed red shoe behind. That would plague her with every shape-shift, he predicted. At least, until she learned control.

Gently, expecting claws, he plucked the cat from its perch atop the shoe and lifted it high so he could peer into the familiar, crystal blue depths of Daphne's eyes. "So. It appears my work here is not yet done." That should piss her off completely.

Her eyes flared, proving him correct.

Stifling his amusement, he cradled the cat close, felt Daphne's growing indignation even through her silky feline fur. "Easy, sweetheart. I will help." He murmured the words for her alone, letting his lips drift gently over the delicate tip of one ear. Then he closed his eyes and let his powers consume him.

His was a dampening force. A walking power vacuum, he could undo magic and nullify it. Druids called upon his kind only as a last resort. He was dangerous to them and to all magical creatures.

But not to Daphne. Not yet.

Traces of puca magic crackled against his skin, intensifying as he worked on Daphne. He experienced a wavering of time, space and matter, all shifting and reforming. Then he felt the definite dig of human fingernails—not kitty claws— as Daphne pinched and scratched at him, seeking release. He felt her heart racing like a trapped wild thing, and she shoved herself free to pat herself up and down her clothed and again-human form.

Allowing the retreat, he watched closely as she strove to collect every scrap of her usual composure. She managed, too. Although she sometimes underestimated herself, Daphne Forbes was every bit as formidable as anyone or anything he'd ever encountered. Until now she'd been merely an untutored hereditary Druid, a human female who didn't want—didn't even know how to use—her inborn powers.

Probably a good thing, he decided as she glared at him. "You just watch where you put those hands. Got it?" she snapped. Pivoting on the pointy toe of one elegantly shod foot, she hobbled off into the trees.

He wondered what she made of her missing shoe.

Still shaking, Daphne forced one foot in front of the other. The path. Where was the freaking path? She was so completely out of here, both shoes or not—

"Ms. Forbes." A commanding voice from behind. Not Tremayne's. Yeah, and speaking of *freak*ing things, what the hell was Tremayne? Obviously he was not simply the mysterious private detective her mother had hired to tail her philandering and apparently criminal father. Daphne should have known there was more to him than what first met the eye. After all, she'd never been drawn so compulsively to anyone before in her life. Not to Warren, her one-time boyfriend and almost fiancé, and not to any man before or since then. She'd ignored them. Easily. Once burned, twelve times shy.

But since she'd first spotted him a couple months before, Tremayne had proven to be completely, disturbingly un-ignorable. Not only was she constantly aware of him on an elemental level, but it seemed there was no avoiding the man, period. He was everywhere, either one step ahead of her or almost on her heels, watching her, watching her parents. He drew her eye, her thoughts, her near obsession, in spite of her well-founded mistrust of interfering types. She hated feeling that way about any man. The lack of control galled and stunned her. It struck her as unnatural—and shouldn't that have been a tip-off? Where was her head? No doubt about it, Tremayne had a whole lot more going on than a simple private detective would. Even a stunningly good-looking one.

"Daphne Forbes. Please. I realize you're unsettled by what just happened here. Let us help you."

She slowed and turned to look over her shoulder. It was that Druid guy her father hated, Phil something. He was also the High Druid, which would make him, in her opinion, the cult leader. If the crowd thought she was getting naked and submissive with *that*, they were as nutty as white-robed fruitcakes. Which they were, actually.

Well, the Druids were white robed. The puca and the faeries were dressed like any other schmoes on the street. *Pucas and faeries.* She felt like an idiot even silently acknowledging—Okay, sure, she'd read of the existence of such . . . *beings* . . . in her father's journals, and she'd actually met two guys who claimed to be pucas, but *faeries*? *Tinkerbell*? She'd probably be doubting still—a smart girl didn't believe everything she read—if she hadn't just now watched a man who called himself faerie king summon others of his kind with a simple snap of his fingers. Just *poof*, and two women had appeared out of nowhere.

To think that most people had no idea they coexisted with beings like this. Other than model-perfect faces and bodies, these pucas and faeries looked *human*. That was so wrong! Where were the pointy ears and magic wands and slanting, googly eyes? Was a tail or pair of hooves too much to ask? The fact that freaks could walk among humans, controlling them, manipulating them, when humans were completely unaware of their existence or interference . . . It was intolerable. Daphne backed away from them all.

"Oh, no. I'm done with you weirdos. Do what you will with Daddy Dearest and his conniving and violent ways. He asked for every bit of justice you want to drop on his power-hungry head. Just count me out." She turned and kept walking. Where had the path disappeared to? It was here, right here, just a moment earlier.

"We will deal with Duncan Forbes," Phil said. "I am not asking you to intercede for him. I am concerned, however, that you might spontaneously shift-shape again."

She froze. *Spontaneously . . .* "You're kidding me." So, the cat thing could happen again?

But she hadn't really changed into a cat. How could she have? Sure, she knew of the existence of shape-shifters—in myth and legend and, well, hearsay—but she was human. Humans did not change shape. So, obviously she'd just . . . had an episode. Or something. Maybe it was something she'd eaten. Or maybe that stupid cornerstone had really bounced off her head and done cerebral damage before landing on her foot. That would explain much. Like the zinging she still felt along her nerve endings, as though they were all conversing energetically. What would nerve endings have to discuss anyway? She could just imagine: *Hey, how's the weather on your side of her ass? Kind of chilly over here.*

I would say that there's nothing remotely chilly about that ass of yours, said a voice out of nowhere.

She caught her breath. Tremayne's voice? She was thinking about her own ass in Tremayne's voice? That was just wrong.

So you did hear me. That answers all questions.

What did *that* mean? Maybe she was in shock. Or dealing with aftereffects from her episode. Was it an aneurysm? A stroke?

It means that you retain the puca powers that were discarded by the former puca Riordan, used by your father for foul purposes and then bound so temporarily inside that cornerstone. Those powers are now loosed from the stone . . . and tied to you. You wield the puca powers.

She whirled to glare at Tremayne, who stood unmoving, off to the side. "Are you insane?"

No. And before you ask, neither are you. Mindspeak is a puca power, as is shape-shifting. It's apparent you have a strong natural talent for both. His lips never moved.

"Oh, no. That's all on you." She pointed a finger at him. "*You're* the freak around here, not me. I'm human. I don't 'mindspeak' and I don't turn into a wolf after dark. The only 'powers' I wield involve math, taxes and the IRS. So why don't you go find more of your kind and loiter somewhere . . . metaphysical. But leave me out of it. I have a flight to catch."

"I'm afraid we can't let you do that, Ms. Forbes." It was High Druid Phil again, his calm almost exaggerated.

Daphne scowled. "Funny, how you have absolutely no say in the matter. I'm outta here. Now, where the hell did the path go?"

"It will return when the time is right."

She whipped around to face Phil. "Return? What, the path is gone? *You* made it go away? Oh, but of course. You're a Druid. Your type can do stuff like that. Guess that means I'll have to strike out on my own. Cross-country and all."

Steeling herself, she made a sharp left, kicking aside brush and ignoring the sharp edges of rocks and sticks beneath her bare foot. Stupid missing shoe. Had the cat eaten it? Her thoughts stumbled clear of that mental sidetrack.

Shoving through branches and brush that seemed to grow thicker, she felt perspiration dampening the material between her breasts. A drop of moisture slid down her spine. It was winter in Virginia—albeit a mild one—and here she was sweating all over her silk blouse, thanks to a misguided and badly timed attack of conscience.

She would smell utterly rank by the time she set foot in the airport. And oh, look, a fresh stain on the sleeve of her blazer. Damn it! So much for getting her seat upgraded to first class.

She reached up with both hands to grasp a particularly thick grouping of branches obscuring her view and . . . pushed right back into the Druids' circle?

They all patiently looked at her, thirty or so assorted males and females, all dressed in white robes and representing probably every walk of life, not to mention every brand and style of footwear. Also present were that handful of supposed faeries, a puca and a few non-Druid humans. All were staring at her. It was like Halloween, except scarier and with no candy to make her feel better. And they were all standing in that damn circle, right where she'd left them.

Which she would do again. Stoic, she turned her back on the group and raised a hand to shove at another branch.

"It won't do you any good." Phil spoke quietly. "Every path you take into the trees will lead back to this circle until I give you permission to leave."

Daphne's temper flared. Great. Another damn control freak of

a Druid. Like she hadn't seen enough of that as the daughter
of Duncan and Violet Forbes as they acted out the Druid version of *War of the Roses*. But didn't the warring spouses in that
movie end up mercifully broken and forced to stare at each
other as they expired? Like she could possibly get so lucky. No,
if there was dying to be done in the Forbes household, her parents would undoubtedly crush Daphne between Mommy and
Daddy so all three could expire simultaneously. On their terms.
Never hers. She was so done with possessive control freaks, that
right now she felt capable of—

*Careful, Daphne. Your temper. You have undisciplined powers. If
you hurt the Druid, even by accident, the penalty will be very high.*

She glared at Tremayne. "Do you think invading my mind
will make me any less inclined toward violence?"

Amusement glittered in his eyes.

He thought this was funny? *Funny?*

"Well, it is really refreshing to see someone as composed as
you completely lose your temper. I imagine you can count on
one hand the number of times you've made a scene like this in
front of anyone," he replied.

She narrowed her eyes. "If that's your way of suggesting I
take it easy and be a nice girl, I'm very much afraid your efforts
are backfiring." Very afraid. Very, very—Her breath hitched.
Oh, god. She felt it again, the zings racing along her spine and
veering outward to pelt various nerve endings.

Tremayne abruptly strode toward her. Unnerved by the force
of his presence and her usual reaction to it, she backed up a step.
But he kept coming until he stood just a pace away. His face expressionless and his manner calm, he gripped her shoulders with
both hands. The zinging, which had accelerated to a mind-
robbing frenzy, slowed and then dissipated. Daphne exhaled shakily, gazing sightlessly around the clearing. She wouldn't meet his
eyes.

"Daphne." Tremayne murmured her name. "Look at me."

Gritting her teeth, she peered through her lashes at him.
"I'm looking. What should I see?"

Dark, nearly black eyes, fathomless depths she'd always found so unnervingly compelling, stared down at her. Calm overtook her. *Oh.* She inhaled deeply, drinking it in, and let her breath out slowly.

"Better?"

Strangely enough, it was. She eyed him warily. "What happened? Why is . . ." She gestured shakily at him and her and their silent audience. Everyone else seemed willing to let Tremayne deal with her, crazy as she was.

He smiled. "You're not crazy. You just have a lot to accept. Including the powers Duncan Forbes batted at you."

"My father?" She gritted her teeth as shattering confusion realigned into insane logic. In a charged game of keep-away with a brick-sized cornerstone, her errant father had made a grab for it but managed only to swat it toward a clump of bushes. Those bushes had concealed an eavesdropping but well-meaning Daphne. Her foot would never be the same.

"It's all because of that stupid cornerstone—the one he stole from those puca brothers and chucked at me. *He's* the reason I did the cat thing. All because he thought he could use the trapped powers to replace Phil as head of this weirdo glee club." She glared at her father.

"Take it easy, Daphne. It's not that he doesn't deserve your anger, or that karma would object to a little vengeance against him. But if you lost your temper completely, well . . ." Tremayne's words dwindled, as though he were still in search of ones that wouldn't completely blow her mind.

"Will I spontaneously combust? Channel my inner feline? Turn the Druid grove into a smoking crater?" she asked.

Tremayne tipped his head thoughtfully. "Maybe."

He could only be referring to all of the above. She licked her lips and could feel her heart racing again.

"The puca powers, when combined with your Druid heritage . . ." Tremayne shrugged. "Let's just say it's a volatile mix. Unpredictable. Anyone who gains powers such as these, especially with the background you have . . ."

"You mean psycho parents?"

"That would be it, yes. Basically, we need to keep an eye on you and contain potential damage. That will be my job. As it has always been." Tremayne cast a less-than-friendly glance at High Druid Phil.

"What do you mean, 'as it has always been'?" Daphne eyed him with suspicion. "Have you been spying on me?"

"Not you, but what you now possess. Oversight of these dis-embodied puca powers is part of my responsibility."

"You mean, you're the keeper of whatever is wrong with me?" She stared at him, disbelieving.

"Keeper of the puca powers. Yes. This particular set, anyway. A Druid saddled me with the duty a very long time ago. So . . . you'll be seeing a lot more of me."

"Oh, neat. I'll have a freak of a probation officer following me around." She glanced between Phil and Tremayne. "And a hostile one at that. Just what I needed. Well, if the plan is to fol-low me, let's make tracks, Mr. Probation Officer. Because I have a plane to catch. Just expect to spring for your own ticket and other expenses. I'm on a budget until I start my new job."

"Not so fast, Miss Forbes." Phil again, still calm. It was really, really getting on her nerves.

She stared at the High Druid. "Look, Phil. I'm an innocent bystander, both to my father's stupidity and to everything about these proceedings. Sure, I followed my father to this grove and hid and listened in, but only so I could bust him for his crimes if you guys didn't. As it turns out, my presence was totally un-necessary. You guys figured everything out on your own and didn't need me at all. If my father had surrendered gracefully instead of making a grab for the rock, I could have left with no one the wiser and nobody hurt as a result."

Daphne glanced around, hopeful. "So. Since he's busted and I'm innocent, how about just pointing the way back to the yel-low brick road so I can get on with my new life? I've waited for this . . ." Her voice caught unexpectedly. She was breathless, a little, and emotional, a lot. She inhaled deeply. "I've been wait-ing for this a long time."

A big hand gripped her shoulder, and she looked up. Into

dark, dark eyes that were anything but cold. No, that was impassioned fellow feeling she saw. "You understand," she murmured without thinking.

Tremayne nodded. "But you still can't go free. Any more than I can."

She studied him. "So you're stuck, too. With me."

"Yes. And you thought *you* had it bad." He shook his head, lips quirking at the corners.

A thought occurred to her. "Back up, buddy. Just how stuck with me are you? What's going on? Why me, and how much will this really suck?"

"Your answers are basically variations of 'a lot' and 'you already know'—or should know, if you trust your senses."

He seemed perfectly satisfied giving these answers and no other.

Dismissing the unhelpful jerk completely, Daphne turned back to the guy who seemed to be running this farce. "Look, Phil. I'm willing to cut a deal. You just undo whatever poofie thing happened when that brick clobbered me. That way you can be sure that I'm no threat to anyone and I can cheerfully go about my business. See how this works out for everyone? So, go ahead. Whatever you have to do, I'm ready. Do you need to conk me with it? That's fine. I can take it." She braced herself, arms out, hands fisted, and closed her eyes. "Just do it quick, okay?"

"You're inviting him to hit you with the cornerstone?" Tremayne sounded amused.

Daphne opened her eyes and responded with a look of exasperation. "Well, it worked for Mina and Riordan, didn't it? Or haven't you heard about their showdown with these Druids?"

Thanks to an ancient curse, half of a puca named Riordan—his eternal, shape-shifting, glamouring, faerie half—had once been caged inside the very rock that had just struck Daphne. Mina, after reading an ancient script, had come to believe that clubbing the head of his reincarnated human half with that particular rock would free him of his curse and captivity. Riordan had been made whole again, but his puca powers were transferred to the blasted cornerstone. Then they had been transferred to Daphne. To her way of thinking, the same logic should apply now: one slug to the noggin should free her. If a blow to the foot could invest her with puca magic, couldn't a second blow reverse the action?

"Not exactly," Phil interceded. "What really worked for Mina and Riordan was the truth."

Daphne threw her arms upward. "Well, that's easy enough. I'm not lying to anybody. You want truth? Ask me questions. I'll tell the truth. Yes, I had cookies for breakfast this morning. I confess. The cupboard was bare and I felt like celebrating my escape from this damn town. So I'm a bad, bad girl. Can I go get on a plane now? Please?" Folding her hands beseechingly, she cast a desperate look at Phil and then Tremayne. "It leaves the gate in little over an hour. I want to be on that plane. I've waited to be on that plane. I'm ready. I'm packed. I'm honest. Let me go."

"It's not as simple as that, I'm afraid," Phil responded quietly, and not without sympathy. "Your situation is different from the puca's. His was a trial of guilt or innocence. Your situation . . . is more a judgment of fitness. Are you fit in mind and spirit for the powers bestowed upon you?"

Daphne lowered her voice, but it throbbed with frustration. "See, that's the thing. I don't *want* any powers. I just want to leave. Take the powers back. Then I won't have to be judged fit for anything, right?"

Phil was already shaking his head, his expression rueful. "It doesn't work that way. Fate ruled that you should have the powers. We can't take them from you unless you're dangerously unfit, and slugging you with the cornerstone will just give you a headache."

"But fate didn't rule this. My father's poor coordination and bad judgment did." She glared at her sire.

In fact, Duncan was still prone on the ground under the weight of the puca who'd tackled him. The puca—Riordan's half brother, Kane—seemed to be enjoying himself there, all poking elbows and knees and heavy bulk. Given that her father had framed Kane for crimes Duncan himself had committed, Daphne supposed she couldn't blame the puca for such minor retaliation.

She wouldn't mind getting a few pokes in, herself. "You know, Dad, if you were going to make a grab for that stone when What's-her-face the faerie chick tossed it to Tremayne, why didn't you hold on to the damn thing?" The 'faerie chick,' who looked more like an overblown girlie-magazine centerfold than any waiflike sprite, merely raised an amused eyebrow as Daphne continued. "What did batting at the damn rock do for you, other than get your face in the mud and me in a fix?"

Duncan Forbes, his cheek smooshed against the dirt, eyed his daughter broodingly. "You don't even realize. You don't even know what you have."

"Oh, no, I think I get it just fine. Everything you wanted, I now have. Oooh, lucky me." She eyed him with distrust. "I guess you'll be making nice with your daughter now?"

"It's not like that, Daphne."

"Yes, it is." She turned back to Tremayne. "Spell it out for me. My life. It's screwed up permanently?"

"That depends on your definition. Some would be willing to kill for what you have gained so effortlessly."

"Yeah, I heard. But are these powers permanently mine?"

"Probably." Tremayne's face was inscrutable.

She ground her teeth. "What would make them not permanent?"

"The intervention of a powerful Druid."

Naturally. And the most powerful Druid in this circle was unlikely to intervene. "What else?"

"Death."

She flinched. "So, not exactly a solution for me."

"Not an attractive one, no."

With strained patience, Daphne turned to High Druid Phil. "You say fate insists that I keep these powers. When will you— or, rather, *fate*—say I can have my life back?"

The Druid smiled slightly. "When we decide the powers will not destabilize you. Like they did your father while he possessed them."

Daphne focused on the most important part of that information. "*Destabilize* me?"

"Drive you nuts and encourage you to steal, assault and kill." Phil's voice was matter-of-fact; his expression remained pleasant.

"Oh." Daphne glanced briefly at her father. "So it was the puca powers that . . . ?"

"Drove him insane?" Tremayne finished for her. "Yes. I've been watching your father for some time now, and I'm convinced that's exactly what happened. From what I've heard, Duncan was never a stellar example of humanity. And of course he did steal the cornerstone after Riordan's trial with every intent of using the powers to frame an innocent man and gain political power for himself here in the grove. But once he possessed those powers, his crimes escalated from fraud and deception to outright violence. He assaulted and nearly killed an innocent woman. And he didn't do it out of panic or necessity; she was no threat to him. It was a random, vicious attack. He was simply and completely out of control. Do you see how dangerous this could be for you and for innocents around you?"

"You think I might go crazy, too?" Surely not. The idea was intolerable. She wasn't nuts, damn it. That's what she was trying to avoid. She had to escape this town peopled with nuts so she damn well wouldn't become one of them. But even she could hear the tremor in her voice.

"You seem like a decent human being, which is a miracle in itself, given the examples set for you by your parents." Tremayne spoke quietly. "But the combination of puca and Druid powers, while a rarity, is just inherently risky. It's a volatile combination of idealistic yet powerful diplomat and mischievous—equally powerful—faerie. Forging the two . . . It's unnatural. Totally incompatible. The conflict between two such contradictory magics would strain even a sane, usually moral person's mind."

She looked to the Druid next. "Is that your verdict, too? Dad couldn't handle the two sets of powers, so he lost his mind, and that's why he did all those things?" The concept was both alarming and reassuring. Her father wasn't a soulless killer; he'd just gone nuts for a while. But she was stronger than that. No way would she lose control of her own mind, and she couldn't fathom killing anyone, especially an innocent. It was unacceptable. Inconceivable.

"I tend to agree with Tremayne." The Druid shrugged. "But you tell me. Did your father try anything so horrible before a month or so ago?"

She thought about everything Duncan had done recently and in the past. "To my knowledge? No, nothing so nasty. Not that my father's been an angel. Far from it, in fact. Just ask Mina . . . the daughter he doesn't claim." She raised her voice, deliberately, for her father's benefit. "My sister. Whom I *do* claim."

Daphne had only recently gained the chance to know her half sister, whom Duncan had conceived with another woman within weeks of getting his wife pregnant. Mina and Daphne were born less than a month apart. Duncan had acted the proud, if controlling and interfering, papa to Daphne for her entire life, but he continued to deny Mina's paternity. He was an irresponsible, cowardly weasel.

"So, you're saying you're a little angry with your father?" Druid Phil said.

"More than a little. One needs to search far and wide for a single redeeming quality in the man."

"I love you." This from Duncan, in a low voice.

Daphne stared at him. "But somehow your brand of love makes me want to run, not stick around for the warm fuzzies. You're a little alarming, especially given the recent instability Phil here mentioned."

"Sometimes instability, or a tendency toward it, is hereditary," Phil commented. "Like the Druid powers themselves."

"I've heard that," Daphne murmured.

The High Druid folded his hands and regarded her quietly. "So, what we see in you is an angry, untrained Druid wielding undisciplined puca powers, and who may very well inherit her father's instability. Do you see why we can't just wish you well and send you off?"

Daphne shook her head helplessly as she felt the trap—a trap she'd helped set with her own absent agreement—quietly deploy. "You're kidding me. But I'm nothing like him."

"And then there's the incident with a Druid neophyte you dated," Phil interrupted quietly. "A young man named Warren?"

Daphne stared. "How did you know about Warren?" Her gaze drifted to her father.

"*He* didn't tell me," Phil assured her. "We discovered it on our own some time ago. We've been investigating your father and acts he's committed."

She frowned. "What's your point?"

"As I understand it, Warren never saw fit to tell you he was seeking favor from your father and hoping for a little magical power boost from him. In the form of a spell or charm, I don't know. Silly boy. But he used you to get to Duncan?"

Daphne shuddered inwardly at the memory. It had been another freak encounter, and one she'd choose not to relive. "That's ancient history. And long past the time when my father should have been capable of boosting anyone's power."

"Oh, we all knew he was capable. His expulsion from the position of High Druid in the grove didn't remove his powers. We assumed he wouldn't abuse them to the extent that he has, but that's another issue altogether. At issue now is your reaction to the situation with Warren."

She felt her face flame. "And how should I have reacted?"

"Maybe by *not* driving his car into a brick wall? I understand you'd been attending some function at a country club restaurant with Warren when the situation became known to you?"

Warren had prized that car almost as much as he'd prized Druid power—and a great deal more than he'd respected Daphne. "He drove me there but then had too much to drink, so I had to drive myself home. But it was an unfamiliar car, and with me already upset . . ." She shrugged. "What can I say? I thought I'd already put the car in reverse. It was an accident."

"Did you really believe the car was in reverse?" Phil asked her quietly. "Or did you just tell yourself you did? You smashed the nose of that Beemer like an accordion. Nobody reverses with that much force. I understand there were no skid marks beneath the tires to indicate that you tried to brake, either. The police were interested in that."

"I couldn't brake. There wasn't time—"

"Maybe. Or maybe it points to a genetic tendency. Once you prove to our satisfaction that you can control Druid and puca powers, as well as your temper, you will be free to go." Phil smiled. "And you'll take with you a few neat tricks to pull out when you need them and when karma deems it appropriate."

Daphne didn't return his smile. "You think I'm a psychopath like my father."

"No, but it would be irresponsible to ignore the possibility."

"But I'm not like him. I don't use people."

"I would really like to believe that," Phil replied. "Maybe you could consider this your opportunity to show everyone, once and for all, that you're not like your father. That you can wield great powers responsibly and for the purpose of good, not evil."

"But like I told you, I came here to expose my father in order to help Janelle and Kane—two people totally unrelated to me, but who I thought deserved better than what he had in mind for them. Doesn't that shed just a little light on my character? I'm not my father."

"It does speak in your favor." Phil smiled. "That's why we're not eliminating you immediately."

"Elimin—"

"Don't mind me. Just a little joke." Phil chuckled a little and pushed his purple-framed glasses back up his nose.

Daphne had the feeling it wasn't really a joke. And the glance Phil cast Tremayne suggested exactly who would be called upon if they needed to 'eliminate' one nutty, hereditary Druid girl wielding walkabout puca powers. A girl could easily get hysterical if she thought about it too much.

"It wasn't a joke. You need to be careful," Tremayne murmured to her. "You know, this isn't a disaster unless you make it into one."

"Spoken like a guy who didn't just drop hundreds of dollars on a plane ticket he wouldn't use, accept a new job he probably will now lose, and rent a very nice apartment that will now remain empty while my current lease expires today." Her voice grew louder with each frustrating fact.

"Stay with me, then."

Chapter Two

"Stay with *you*?" Daphne stared at Tremayne in disbelief. "You can't be serious. Hello? Remember me? I'm the woman who claims not to be insane. I can't stay with you. I hardly know you."

And what little she did know of Tremayne wasn't reassuring. Her typical encounters with the man before now had been incidental sightings of him obviously spying on her father. At first she'd assumed he was a detective her mother hired to report on her father's sexual stupidities. But only an incompetent or a cheat would have taken longer than a month to accumulate enough evidence for a court of law. Tremayne had taken longer than a month and, as she could see now, wasn't a bumbling idiot or ruthless swindler. He was simply after bigger game. And he'd found it. Just her amazing luck that he'd shifted his focus to her. And now he wanted her to move in with him? Even temporarily? Bad idea. Especially given that unnatural allure of his. He was a powerful, unknown quantity who could control her more easily than her own father could—and one look into his fathomless, thrall-inducing eyes could probably convince her to enjoy submitting. She'd be a fool to put herself further under his thumb by moving in with him.

"I have friends in town. I'm sure I could stay with them."

But Phil was already shaking his head. "That would be unwise. You have powers you can't control and that you can't explain to the human world. Not without exposing us all."

Honestly, Daphne couldn't imagine morphing into a cat and then trying to explain herself to her peers. Conservative professionals, though well-meaning, they tended to steer clear of weirdo antics. Shape-changing would qualify, no question, and it wasn't like she'd cultivated confidantes she could trust with information this wild. She tended to naturally resist such close connections out of self-preservation; it wasn't easy maintaining secrets as big as her weirdo, hyper-controlling and occasionally criminal parents. After enduring scrapes over rumors of her parents' escapades in grade school—to which her parents had responded by criticizing Daphne for choosing judgmental and probably hypocritical friends—she'd learned to lie and conceal and keep her distance. Her grandmother had served as trusted confidante for a while. After her grandmother's death . . . no one, really. Maybe Warren, a little. But look where that had gotten her. Even if she could somehow conceal the shape-shifting fun, she'd already said all of her good-byes. The idea of doing it all over again—and this time ending matters on a wishy-washy note, while trying not to shape-shift—just made her cringe. Much better to let her peers and acquaintances think she'd left town.

"I still can't move in with a man I don't know or trust."

Tremayne eyed her thoughtfully. "I guess there's always the other option available to you: you can sleep under the moon with a contingent of armed Druids serving in my stead."

Can anyone say overkill? "A contingent of armed Druids or one unarmed . . . er, weird guy? Why all the firepower?"

"Your new talents. Unexplored. Powerful. Wielded by an angry woman with the potential for going ballistic. If that happens, somebody will need to take you out. Either them or me."

Daphne took a long step backward. "I really think one of my choices should be 'Daphne, go get a room at a five-star hotel and Druids, Inc., will pick up the tab. Help yourself to room service, pedicures and deep tissue massage sessions.'"

Tremayne grinned. "I can give you a massage."

His shift of mood completely disarming her, Daphne took another cautious step back. "Not in the cards, buddy." But neither was a contingent of Druids or, for that matter, sleeping under the moon. "If I stay with you, can I at least have mace or pepper spray or a sturdy club at my disposal? You know, in case you get the overwhelming urge to massage me or, well, eliminate me. It seems only sporting."

Phil laughed as if she'd been joking. "Well, it looks like you've made your decision, Daphne. I wish you well. Tremayne will be your mentor. Make your choices wisely and overcome your obstacles with a cool head and a clean conscience."

Almost noiselessly, everyone in a white robe drifted into the forest. Glancing to the side, Daphne saw the elusive path right where she'd thought it should be. "But . . ."

A whispering of footsteps and another man's voice spoke from behind her. "Daphne."

"Kane?" She turned back to the man—er, puca—who'd tackled her father a few life-altering minutes previously. "Where did everyone else go?"

"I'm here." Janelle moved forward, sympathy shining in her eyes.

As another woman who'd been tied to a magical being against her will, Janelle could undoubtedly relate to Daphne's current frustration. Not too long ago, Janelle had been named guardian to Kane, a puca charged to make amends for his past offenses. Considering that Kane's offense against Janelle herself had been steep and overwhelmingly personal, no doubt it had been doubly galling for her to be tied so closely to him. But the two had actually fallen in love. As of today's trial before the Druid Council, with Kane officially forgiven his past crimes and ruled innocent of more recent offenses, they'd overcome what had seemed overwhelming odds against their future.

She gave Daphne a rueful look. "I'm so sorry you got wrapped up in our drama. Especially since the only reason you showed up was to help us. Some thanks, huh?"

"No kidding. Not that any of this is your fault." Daphne was still peering around. "But where . . . I mean, there were Druids and faeries and my father—"

Kane cleared his throat. "I can only guess, but I suspect your father will be having his inborn Druid powers stripped from him. As a precautionary measure to protect the rest of us."

Daphne wavered. "Will it hurt?" She inhaled sharply, hating that she cared. "Will he be okay?"

"He'll be fine," Tremayne spoke up. "His humanity saved him. After what he did, were he of faerie lineage, King Oberon would have taken him out on the spot. When someone from the human world is executed, there are human police and courts to be handled, not to mention family and friends and paperwork. . . ." He shook his head.

Daphne folded her arms. "There's a shocker. The Druids seemed darn willing to eliminate me."

Tremayne responded quietly. "That should tell you something about your situation. Take it seriously."

Kane cleared his throat and addressed Daphne. "I don't blame you for being leery about moving in with Tremayne here." He gave the other man an assessing look before turning back to Daphne. "You don't know him. I'll admit I've never had any heart-to-heart chats with him, either. But I've known of him and his kind. I'll vouch for his integrity. I think you can count on him wielding justice . . . maybe even to a fault. Any innocent person is safe in his care." And Kane sounded adamant about that part. "I would even trust him with Janelle's safety."

Daphne eyed him a moment, then Janelle, who nodded agreement and support of Kane's judgment, then turned back to Tremayne. "That's pretty high praise," she reluctantly allowed but then scowled. "Just remember that there are lines I will not cross. Regardless of Druid expectations and whatever you think it might take for me to satisfy them, understand that I am *not* joining any cult. You pagan and magicky types can just conduct your little naked rites in private and without me. I'm doing the bare minimum to get all of you off my back."

"Naked rites?" Tremayne regarded her with exaggerated interest. "Nobody told me about these. And you're sure you won't participate? Or is that what you meant when you volunteered to do the bare minimum? As in, stripping down to . . ."

"One more word about naked or rites and I'm walking, buddy. I don't care what Phil said," she warned, attempting to keep some long-ago pictures out of her head. Once upon a time, her parents had participated in those supposed "rites" (read *orgies*) with some of the more out-there members of another grove, and they'd been careless enough to get busted in the act(s) by their adolescent daughter. Thank god her grandmother had been so normal—not to mention adamant that Daphne never associate with the sickos.

"Hey, just don't ever accuse me of being closed-minded." Tremayne's voice was eminently reasonable. "You want to get naked, I'm more than willing to accommodate it. Any rites you want to perform while naked are also welcome and encouraged."

Kane, who seemed to be biting back a grin now, wrapped an arm around Janelle. "Well, if we've reached a relative accord, Janelle and I should go. She's had a rough night and, honestly, I think we need to celebrate a little."

Freedom. Kane had gained his freedom, Daphne mused silently. As had Riordan before him. Both natural-born pucas wielding puca powers. And both, from what she'd gathered in the past, disliked by Tremayne. Come to think of it, the puca-hater didn't seem to cherish any warm feelings for Druids, either.

So where did that leave her? If Freaks & Co. were to be believed, she was a hereditary but nonpracticing Druid who now wielded puca powers. As luck would have it, she would now be living with the mysterious yet powerful guy who wouldn't mind getting naked with her, but who also freely admitted he might have to eliminate her.

So, this would be the new life she'd promised herself? She would be jobless and living under house arrest in a city infested with her parents and similar weirdness? Gee. A veritable utopia.

Studying the face of the old brick warehouse that had only recently been renovated into apartments, Daphne released her seat belt. Tremayne had insisted that she leave her car in the parking lot near the grove and let him drive her to his downtown Richmond dwelling. No doubt he'd worried that she would cut out and make a run for the airport. Hey, the man had reason to be concerned; that's exactly what she would have done if left to her own devices. But faced with little choice, she'd climbed into his snazzy toy sports car.

Given the trendy apartment and pricy car, she couldn't help thinking the guy was raking in money somehow.

"Daphne? We're here." Tremayne had opened the passenger door and was now offering her a hand. The fact that she hadn't even noticed the car door opening betrayed her state of mind. Apparently she was already nuts. Absolutely bonkers.

"You are not nuts, as I've already told you." Tremayne spoke calmly as he gently but insistently reached for her hand. "You have every right to feel unsettled, given this morning's events. Any sane woman would. Cut yourself some slack."

"And suddenly you're Mr. Sensitive?" Scowling, she let him tug her out of the car and retain a grip on her hand, but she stepped sideways to avoid additional contact. Personal space—the man loved to invade hers for some reason. And how she wished he'd keep his pheromone-drenched scent to himself. She would become a chronic mouth breather purely in self-defense.

His lips quirked. "Nobody's called me sensitive before."

"Sarcasm, buddy. Like I'd ever accuse an 'eliminator' of sensitivity. But I guess everybody has their softer side, huh? And that, for your information, is another example of sarcasm. It might be an alien concept for something as . . . alien as you are."

Now he full-out grinned at her. "You claw and scratch at me with every word. No wonder your first shift was to a cat. I'm told the first form bespeaks personality."

"Really." Her heart pounded, her mind rejecting every bit of what he was suggesting.

"Later you learn to control the shift and can consciously choose your form, but the first one is uncontrolled, unaffected by environment and specific to the individual. That makes it an intimate thing to witness." His gaze felt like a caress.

"Oooh, nice. So I'm naturally catty. How original." She yanked, finally managing to free the hand he'd held with such persistence, then took a step away from him. "I'm sure it gave you wonderful insight into all the nooks and crannies of my character. Produce a litter box, however, and I will shove it where the sun doesn't shine."

He took a step toward her. "You blame me for everything that's happened to you. That's not logical, you know. I didn't throw the stone at you. Your father did. More to the point, fate determined the outcome. My job now is to help you grow accustomed to your powers and help you learn to control them. For your sake and for mine."

He'd taken another step, completely unnerving her, and she backed up two, hands outstretched and protesting. "Will you please just keep your distance? I hardly know you, and I really am a big fan of personal space. I need my bubble of comfort. Stay outside of the bubble, and we'll get along just fine." She eyed him doubtfully. "Maybe."

"Maybe I'm still concerned that you might 'cut out and make a run for the airport.'" He gave her a pointed look while casually shifting closer.

Heart skipping along at a betraying, way-too-girlie beat, she not-so-casually shifted away. "There you go, privy to my thoughts again. I don't like it. It's not fair."

He smiled. "You actually have an advantage over me, if you'd only learn to use it."

"Oh, really." She gave him a narrow-eyed look. "The mind-reading thing you mentioned? Ha. I'll believe it when I see it."

"Then I guess you'll need to see it. Come." Turning, he strode toward his apartment building, obviously just expecting that she would follow. Like a dog.

She glared at his back, pondering contrary maneuvers.

"You don't have keys to my car or access to your own. It's also been a long and trying morning. Wouldn't you like to rest?"

She didn't move. "What about my car? What about my things?"

"I told you a Druid would drop the car off. You gave him your keys, remember?" He opened the door to the lobby and held it for her. "And I assume your luggage was in the trunk, since you were headed toward the airport?"

"Yes." Her response grudging, she strode past him, absorbing her surroundings with interest. Vaulted ceilings, brick walls, exposed beams, newly tiled floors . . . They likely charged a mint for rent here.

"What were you going to do with your car, anyway?" he asked her, almost as an afterthought.

"Um, drive it? To the airport?"

"And then what? Leave it?"

She stared, feeling as though half of her brain cells were just imposters pretending to contribute to her IQ. Then what, indeed? She'd wanted to be rid of that car so badly, just one more chain linking her to her parents, but she hadn't even addressed its disposal. What would she have done with it once she'd reached the airport? Would she have abandoned it? She honestly didn't know. Lord, maybe she needed a keeper after all. Maybe her parents were right to dominate her incompetent self.

Not that she needed to admit as much to a guy who'd managed to dominate her habitually control-freak parents. She'd suffocate under his brand of domination. "My car is none of your business."

"Suit yourself," he murmured casually. "I'm on the second floor. Stairs okay?"

Still inwardly kicking herself for incompetence, she just nodded. He opened another door and held it, indicating she should follow him. Reluctantly, she did so and trailed him up the stairs, her gait still hobbled by her missing shoe. Much as she hated admitting it, he was right. Her choices *were* limited, and frankly she stood not a chance in hell of making it to the airport in time anyway. Her plane was scheduled to leave ten minutes from now, damn it. She followed him through another door and into a broad hallway. More tile, more brick.

A mint. He must pay a mint.

"I am sorry about your plans being canceled. I really do understand your need to be free." Stopping at a door, he turned to face her. "You were almost there, weren't you?" He met her eyes somberly and steadily, as though searching for something. "I was almost there, too." He glanced around him. "The apartment building's nice, yes. But it's nothing without the other.

Not without freedom." He turned back to her. "For as long as I can remember, my will hasn't been my own. Someone else has directed my actions, my lifestyle, my every purpose. I don't live. I just exist."

Disarmed, she stared up into his eyes. Torment, constant and endless. Had she caused that? No, she'd simply made it worse. "You were almost free. But what happened at the clearing ruined your plans, too," she realized.

"Yes. But you have the ability to put them back in order. For you and for me."

"By . . . ?"

"Proving you have control. Wielding your powers with wisdom, honor and compassionate forethought. Responsibility."

"And if I fail? Or if someone else *decides* I fail?"

Tremayne shrugged. "Then you lose."

"I lose." So simple. "What about you? Do you lose, too?"

"Maybe. Probably. But I do need a resolution to your situation, one way or the other, before I know how to proceed."

"Tell me about me losing and how you would proceed."

He seemed reluctant, but answered. "That would be the uncomfortable solution we discussed earlier."

She swallowed hard. Death?

"Possibly," he conceded.

"You would kill me."

"Only if you were dangerous to others and unable or unwilling to relinquish your powers."

"For the record, just consider me willing to relinquish the powers at any time! Perfectly willing." She raised her eyebrows for emphasis. "Just show me how, and you can have them back, all tied up with a pretty bow. I never wanted this."

"As Phil pointed out before, I can't just take the powers from you. I can neutralize them temporarily . . . or you permanently. You would need Druid intervention to permanently and safely separate yourself from the powers."

"Hey, but what's to keep me from taking a dive? I mean, what if I did something bad enough to suggest I was unfit to wield these powers but not bad enough to justify killing me?

You tell the Druids I'm a bad girl, they ask for the powers back, I pass them off willingly and, boom, I'm free. Isn't that my loophole here?"

Tremayne nodded slowly. "I guess you could try that. I'm not sure it would work. And would you keep trying new things, making yourself worse and worse? And what about what you told Phil? About not being like your father and being sick of people expecting the worst from you because of him? Here's your chance to prove them wrong. Can you pass it up? You haven't even begun to explore what you can do. Power shouldn't be rejected so carelessly. You could do so much good in this world with abilities like yours."

She cast him a suspicious look. "Why do you care whether I keep these powers or relinquish them? If I give them up, you'd be rid of me, right?"

He considered her question. "I might be rid of you, but I wouldn't be rid of whoever assumed those powers in your stead. Or have any say in where they might go or who might wield them next. My duty would change but continue. And . . . to be honest, I'd rather see you with these powers than another. I've seen others like your father with power and no morals. I see you . . . with morals. And power you need to control. I think there's a reason for that. My kind believes in promoting the greater good. I think you could do good things in our world if you learned to control these powers." Before she could interrupt, he continued pointedly: "And then there would be no comparing you to Duncan."

Daphne glanced away. Damn it, had it really been necessary to use *that* argument on her? It just wasn't fair. Why should she have to prove herself? She should be judged on her own merits, regardless of her parents.

"But the world doesn't work that way," Tremayne said. "Not your world and not mine. And can you really bear to prove them right? That might be, as you say, your loophole. But, to prove you're as bad as your father? Could you do that?"

Daphne cringed. No. She couldn't. Period. And it just sucked to realize as much. So much for the loophole. "So, I'm *still* going to be punished for my father's crimes. You know, Dad and I aren't exactly thick as thieves. All I want now—all I've ever wanted—is to live my life on my own terms, completely out from under anybody's thumb."

"I can see the appeal of that. Few of us ever have the luxury of being totally unaccountable, though."

"Yeah, well, try being accountable to Duncan and Violet Forbes. Then we'll talk reasonable and luxury in relation to total control freaks at war with each other." She scowled.

For most of Daphne's life, her parents had insisted on choosing her wardrobe, her schools, her alliances, her beliefs. Often, it had seemed the only place she could breathe was in Gran's library room; the books and the easy company allowed her to be herself. As an adult, she didn't cave as easily, but the pressure was applied all the same—and she no longer had the buffer of Gran's frequent and level-headed presence. These days, her parents preferred to disagree with each other on every matter, and Daphne found herself shoved back and forth between them. She couldn't make any decision for any reason without leaving one parent smug and the other hurt and vengeful. Her only recourse: shove them both away. She'd been headed to California.

"Just because you must stay here to get used to your powers doesn't mean you have to return to your old life with them," Tremayne remarked.

"No. I don't suppose it does," she allowed grudgingly.

"Will you come inside now?" He eyed her with some amusement. He'd been standing with the door open, while she waited in the hall as though afraid she was being propositioned by a vampire. His smile widened. "I'm not."

"Maybe not literally, but I bet you have your own share of joy-sucking weapons to use against me." Like that tyrannical mojo of his. Cautiously inhaling through her mouth, she stepped past him, trying very hard not to make contact. The bubble of comfort. Bubbles were good. She had to maintain the bubble.

As she stepped so carefully past him, Tremayne closed the door and turned to watch Daphne study her surroundings. The brickwork extended inside his apartment, as did the exposed beams, but lush carpeting replaced tiled floor. What he liked most was the sense of space he felt in the apartment. Huge windows opened onto a view of downtown, with the river and canal visible in the distance, if he angled his perspective just right. That, together with vaulted ceilings, exposed hardware, large rooms—it all made this seem bigger, more open. The other places he'd considered had made him feel claustrophobic. Besides, he felt more at home surrounded by brick than by plaster and Sheetrock.

Leaning against the cool surface of the wall, he watched Daphne pace and look around. The woman was almost too perfect, like a doll, with her silky wisps of blonde hair curled across her jawline and cheekbones. Creamy skin highlighted huge eyes as blue and bright as the open sky. Pink lips would curve and part intriguingly with smiles or speech. He'd seen that smile become real and engaging, with flashes of a slightly turned front tooth. That unexpected flaw gave this perfect doll a fascinating gamine edge.

He had to admit he'd spent a lot of time imagining Daphne in his home, although with more personal goals than one commanded by Druids. He motioned her to a chair. "You are welcome in my home."

Daphne jumped and gave him a stern look. "There's that soulless, night-stalker tone again. I know. I've read the stories and seen the movies. What have I let myself in for by staying with you?"

He smiled slowly. If only she knew. Life would get interesting once she mastered the mindwalk. What would she do once she realized he wanted her nearly as much as he wanted his freedom? Very likely she would try to use that information to gain her own. The apple usually did not fall far from the tree, in spite of the apple's best efforts. He would have to approach that angle cautiously.

After seating herself, with obvious bemusement, on one of a handful of metal folding chairs in the living room, she cleared her throat. "So. Now that we've established at least to *your* satisfaction that you're not a creature of the night, suppose you tell me what you really are."

He'd known this question would come up. Maybe it would be best if he didn't tell her everything all at once. He pulled up a chair and straddled it, careful to keep outside of her precious bubble, and rested his forearms on the back. "What am I? In terms you would understand?" He pondered his options. "I guess you might call me a nature spirit. I was summoned by the ancient Archdruid Akker to cage the magical half of a condemned puca inside a Sarsen stone. And guard him."

Her eyes widened. "But that . . . But you . . ." She inhaled deeply and tried again. "Unless I'm mistaken, Riordan was imprisoned inside that stone two thousand years ago. You're that old?"

"Yes. Actually, I existed before then, but wasn't really, um, goal oriented"—an interesting way of phrasing *sentient*—"until Akker summoned me. I've grown and changed since the summoning. Just bided my time."

"Bided . . . ? That's a lot of time to bide."

"Yes."

"And you're not frantic, not dying to resolve your situation once and for all by hacking me off at the neck?"

He smiled at the suspicion and disbelief in her tone. She truly expected him to chop off her head without a fair chance? "But that wouldn't resolve my situation. It would destroy all hope. Karma would turn against me, and I would be at an end."

"Die, you mean?"

"In a way, yes. In my way." He paused thoughtfully. "That brings me to your first lesson. Karma. What do you know of it?"

She eyed him skeptically. "I don't smoke pot and never in my life have I chanted or made love to a sunflower."

He nodded, unmoved by her sarcasm. "That's very interesting. But what do you know of karma?"

She sighed impatiently. "It's . . . kind of a weirdo good vibe/ bad vibe quotient complicated by freaky auras? I don't know. I'm an accountant. Sure, my parents are hereditary Druids, but

I've never known Druidism on an organized level. They kept me out of it. At first it was at my grandmother's insistence. Then, later, Dad didn't get to be the king high ruler god of the nudie bunch, so he picked up his toys and went home. In a rare show of solidarity, Mom went with him. Worked for me. So, no, I never studied karma."

"You should. It's a relentless, time-tested concept, and now that you wield magic, it can decide your life and death."

The impatience seemed to drain from her. "Okay, you have my attention. Tell me about karma and how it could mean life or death to me."

"Karma, in a nutshell, means that good is rewarded and evil is punished. It's a universal justice system. For those who wield magic, karmic determination is crucial, in that a magic-wielder who has bad karma—a debt accrual of bad deeds and offenses against innocents—is completely vulnerable to anyone he or she has harmed with magic. Anyone. Even indirectly. Humans aren't as strictly punished for their deeds. Magic-wielders, as stronger species, are held in check by what amounts to a ruthlessly strict moral code. It keeps them from becoming tyrannical, and protects the weaker species from the stronger."

"So we're talking anti-Darwinism for freaks of nature," Daphne lightly mused, although her voice shook slightly. "What goes around comes around, but tenfold for the magicky types."

"That's a little simplified. It's more that magic-wielders are given no allowance. No tolerance. Any infraction counts. Humans . . . get a little more leeway."

"Like that's fair." She glared at him. "So yesterday karma gave me a break and today it does not? When I didn't even ask to be a shining example of your 'stronger species'?"

Tremayne paused, absolutely shocked. "No. You *never* got a break. Did your father honestly never share this with you? You are a hereditary Druid. You are held accountable. True, you were nonpracticing and certainly not immortal then, so it's possible that you were spared somewhat, but—"

"Then?" Daphne seemed to pounce on the word. "What do

you mean not immortal *then*? As opposed to now? What the hell?"

Tremayne gauged his charge. She seemed shocked, true. Good shocked? Bad shocked? With Daphne, either was possible. "Yes, as long as you retain the full potential of the puca powers, you will live indefinitely."

"But . . . what does that mean? Do I keep getting older until my limbs decay and fall off? Do I have to drink blood?"

He laughed in surprise. "You have a thing about vampires, don't you? No, you don't drink blood. And you don't necessarily live forever. You can be killed. It's just harder to kill you. Your magic automatically sees to its own preservation by helping you regenerate at a cellular level. Consequently, as long as you have your powers, you will not age, you're not vulnerable to disease, and your body will heal quickly. You cannot regenerate limbs or a head, however, and a being without a head . . . well, that's one way of killing you. Burning to ash is another. Frankly, anything that would destroy you in totality would be fatal. If your powers are drained, you are also vulnerable."

Her brow crinkled. "What do you mean, drained?"

"Remember when I helped you shift back to human? I drained you of a measure of your puca powers, and that's how the shift ensued. After the draining, your magic would regenerate, but it would take some time to build up again. There would be a window of time where you were vulnerable. Not long. Maybe a few minutes for a partial draining, half an hour or so for a more extensive draining. Unless your own energy levels were already exhausted, in which case it would take longer."

She stared. "That's what makes you the perfect jailer for a magicky type like Riordan. Or now me. It's your device of elimination. You would drain me, and then whammo, with whatever lethal move or weapon you have. I couldn't heal or repair and would die like any human being as long as I did it quickly."

"That would be one way, yes."

"Okay." She swallowed hard. "What if I give up the powers? Or if they're taken from me? Do I automatically die then?"

"Not necessarily."

"So glad you can be definite about all of this. I feel so reassured." She spoke with mock relief. " 'Pay no attention to the man behind the curtain.' He's just flashing the neighbors."

Tremayne frowned, completely at a loss.

"You know, *The Wizard of Oz* . . ." She waved impatiently. "Never mind. So you're saying I'm immortal now, but if I ever lose the puca powers, it's possible that I could drop dead on the spot."

"If your immortality were formally removed by the Druids, you would live out a normal human life span, beginning with the age at which you attained immortality. If it were wrenched from you, you could die immediately, if your original life span had already expired." He frowned, tapping a finger on the chair back as he flipped through a mental list of more exotic, but fatal, possibilities. "Or in other specific but rarer circumstances."

She made an exasperated noise and slumped in her chair. "Must every answer come with its own set of fine print?"

"Frustrating, isn't it? But we're dealing with faerie magic, so it's harder to define. Very unpredictable. Especially since we've combined it with Druid magic."

Daphne's eyes widened. "Faerie magic?"

"Yes. A puca is half faerie, half human. Very rare."

She looked shaken. "So, tell me—just so I'm not missing out because I neglected to ask some exact, probably outrageous question—is there anything else I don't know that you think you should share with me, say . . . now?"

He considered a moment. "What do you know of pucas?"

"Well, I read about the puca ride. A puca morphs into horse, throws an offensive human onto his back and takes him or her for a wild ride that basically gives him or her a change of heart. Right?"

Tremayne nodded. "That's the puca's signature trick. You should be capable of it."

Daphne raised her eyebrow at him. "Call me crazy, but I think I'd encounter a few logistical problems if I took a human on a kitty-cat ride. Squash the Daphne-cat, anyone?"

He grinned. In his opinion, it would be very hard to squash a Daphne-cat. He'd seen her parents try a few times, at least emotionally, and while she'd done her share of surrendering or fruitlessly lashing out, she'd never lost spirit, never gave up hope. And if *they* couldn't do it . . . well, heaven help whoever else tried. "Obviously, horse is not your most natural form, but you can choose to shift to horse once you master your skills."

"Oh, goody. I can't wait." She rubbed her temples.

"So, what else do you know about pucas?"

"Besides the shape-shifting trick?" She gestured vaguely. "I know that there were two, when legend claims there was always only one. And that November Day is a big deal."

"The Puca's Day, yes. The one day per year—"

Daphne was nodding, and took over the explanation. "—when the puca must behave himself and might be willing to hand out a fortune-telling or two."

"I believe they prefer calling it a prophecy, since charlatans, crystal balls and tarot cards are not involved."

Now Daphne looked intrigued, if scared. "Can I prophecy?"

He thought about it a moment. "It's hard to tell which powers would be transferable and which would not. Obviously, the shape-shifting and mindwalking and probably glamouring transferred. The prophesying . . . We'll have to wait and see. That's a skill that only comes with age and experience. And that's usually only in the case of native-born pucas."

"I see. So what am I, then?" Daphne gripped her arms as if she could anchor herself that way, clearly feeling adrift in what she likely considered magic mumbo jumbo. "A hereditary Druid with adopted puca powers? A Druid wielding faerie magic? That sounds so taboo, so conflict-of-interest. I can't believe it's even legal! You know, in the magicky realm or whatever. Like we're going against nature or creating an imbalance of some kind."

"That's why the Druids are so concerned. There are some who say that combining the two magics would, due to their conflicting natures, automatically lead to the host's destruction. On top of that, it takes incredible strength of mind to control both sets of powers, especially when one set is of an artificial nature. Having the other set be totally untutored . . ." He shook his head. "I'm not sure if that will work for or against you. They might war with each other, as they did with your father. Or they might merge together peacefully, since both are un-formed and still malleable. We'll hope for the latter."

" 'We'll hope for the latter,' he says, as though hoping for a sprinkling of rain. This is my sanity we're talking about! How can you be so cold?" She sounded furious.

Taken completely aback, Tremayne stiffened and eyed her warily. He was answering all her questions as completely as he could. Isn't that what she wanted? "How would you have me be?"

"I don't know. Human, maybe?"

"Human?" He gave her a puzzled look. "But I'm not."

The statement hung solidly between them, and Daphne seemed a little dazed, as though perhaps she'd forgotten, just for a moment. "No, I guess you're not." She hugged her arms around herself again. "Just a little something to remember whenever the question of elimination comes up."

Chapter Three

Tremayne dropped gratefully onto his bed to stare at the ceiling and let the quiet soothe him. It had been a long day. After their return from the grove at dawn, he'd spent hours fielding questions and composing answers that were really just variations of themselves, alternating with intervals of shocked silence as Daphne struggled to absorb. Finally, she'd wound down, and he'd ordered a pizza for them to share for dinner. Since both of them had been awake since well before dawn, he'd shown her the guest bedroom just after sunset and called it a day. A frustrating one, at that. He wasn't even sure he'd made progress with his charge. Okay, maybe he had. Time would tell. She was a smart woman. That was part of her allure for him, after all. Eventually—

A buzzing against the wood of his nightstand had him glancing over at his cell phone. He'd set it to vibrate so as not to alert his new tenant to his every communication. As it buzzed again, he reached over and, glancing at the face of it with a grimace of recognition, flipped it open. "Yes?"

"Sorry to disturb you, Tremayne, but I needed to see you privately. Meet me at the Druid grove."

"What about Daphne?"

"I need to see you alone. Wait until she's asleep and then slip out. I won't take up too much of your time, I promise."

With a resigned sigh, Tremayne shoved the phone into the pocket of his jeans. At least he hadn't undressed yet. When sounds from the extra bedroom stilled and remained so for an hour, he quietly slid off the bed and slipped into his boots.

★ ★ ★

The apartment's front door quietly clicked shut.

Her heart thudding with nervous anticipation, Daphne strained to listen for further, telling noises. She lay in Tremayne's extra bedroom on a twin-sized bed one of the Druids had brought over earlier in the day. It was made up with cotton sheets, a quilt and, actually, not a bad pillow. Tremayne had offered her his bed, no doubt considering it the gallant thing to do, considering its quality, but she'd declined. She knew those sheets would smell like him, feeding into her fantasies and dreams, and that would just wear down her own defenses. Besides, she'd hoped that, in the comfort of his own bed, Tremayne would fall asleep quickly and leave the way clear for her to sneak out.

She'd never expected that *he* would be the one to sneak out. But, fine. No problem. And the apartment door hadn't reopened, so maybe he had a real errand to run, not just a yen for fresh air.

Carefully she slid out of bed, still listening for sounds of his return. Then she quietly repacked her suitcase. Luckily, her car and its contents had also been delivered, as promised. Now she had her luggage and transportation.

And her purse. She'd need credit card and identity info to buy a brand-new—if pricy—plane ticket. Soon she would begin her new life. No misguided Druid, block of rock, or bossy nature spirit would stand in her way this time.

Less than fifteen nerve-jangling minutes later, she was merging onto the interstate and following signs for the airport.

Look out, brave, new world. Here comes Daphne.

"All right, Druid. I'm here." Tremayne studied the darkened grove, aware of High Druid Phil's presence, even if he wasn't yet visible. Only a convincingly dire cause could persuade Tremayne to leave his bed. Sleep was a pleasure long denied him, and one he refused to lightly forego. Phil was aware of this. So apparently tonight's cause was—had better be—dire.

"Ah! Just the nature spirit I was seeking." Phil, wearing a crisp suit and shiny shoes, clipped smartly into the clearing. If anyone could make shoes clip along a packed dirt path, it was someone like this guy. Efficient and deliberately styled from head to foot, he bewildered and amused Tremayne.

"Did you get your charge all settled in? How's it going, do you think? Any progress yet?" Bobbing lightly on his toes and rubbing his hands together, Phil smiled.

"If you mean progress toward dropping into bed unconscious from shock and exhaustion, then yes, she's made amazing progress. The puca powers remain untested, however."

Dropping back onto his heels, Phil nodded, obviously disappointed. He'd expected miracles, perhaps?

"Is this the only reason you wished to speak with me?" With effort, Tremayne kept the annoyance from his voice. Apparently the High Druid intended to be highly involved and highly interfering.

"This? Oh, the progress report? No, gosh no. It's early days yet." More delighted, optimistic bobbing. Maybe the shoes were new and being broken in? "I'm just glad she didn't run from you. She didn't, did she? I fully expect her to try."

"If she does, she won't get far."

Phil nodded and looked sober. "See here, Tremayne. Just to clear the air—I know I'm not your favorite person in the world and that Druids as a whole are only slightly more appealing to you than a cockroach infestation is to me. For what it's worth, I regret the burden my Druid forefather thrust upon you. It was heavier and more enduring than you deserved. And unfortunately, it will only grow more burdensome before your duty is fulfilled."

Tremayne nodded, unsurprised and only slightly moved by Phil's words. Whatever the Druid thought, the man had still made no effort to ease the situation. If anything, he'd made it more complicated, now that Daphne was involved. Not that Tremayne had any choice but to continue his service to the Druids. But . . . Tremayne sighed inwardly. It was possible that Phil didn't have a choice, either. Akker would have seen to that with his long-ago curse.

"So, what did you want to see me about?"

Phil frowned a moment, then started as though suddenly

recalled to his original object. "Yes!" He pointed two jaunty index fingers at Tremayne, who eyed them doubtfully. In his enthusiasm, Phil didn't even notice. "I have news for you! I had some time to kill this afternoon, so I did some divining, and guess whose name came up?" He paused, obviously excited.

Tremayne shook his head. "You tell me."

"Yours!" Phil triumphantly stated.

Tremayne narrowed his eyes. Divination involving him. Should he be concerned?

"Well?" Phil grinned, his teeth a movie-star shade of white. "Want to know what I saw?"

If he said no, the Druid would probably dissolve into tears or something. A sight to avoid. "Sure. Tell me."

Phil leaned in closer, his eyes sparkling behind purple glasses frames. "I saw you . . . *free*."

Tremayne froze, his attention utterly caught. "Tell me more."

"About freedom and whether it can be yours?" Phil queried, his voice low and vibrant. "It is possible. The vision is no guarantee, but it's one hell of a good sign. You can be free. You now have the means."

"What and how?"

Phil shrugged with outspread arms, as though stating the beautifully obvious. "Your new ward, of course. Daphne Forbes. With her intervention, you can be free."

Tremayne frowned. "I understand the puca powers must be contained, and once they are, once Daphne is deemed fit . . ."

Phil was shaking his head. "There's more to gaining your freedom than just playing babysitter. Akker's curse of the puca and summons of you provided for various eventualities. Including your fate. He realized . . ." Phil paused as though seeking proper expression. Delicate expression.

He continued. "When he cursed Riordan and conscripted you to duty, Akker poured some of himself into that rock as well. Part of his soul, if you will. That contribution in turn seeded a new soul, an untainted, expressionless soul needing a life force to become individual. Riordan already had a soul, even if it was fragmented. You, however, did not. But now you do. Isn't that great?" Phil beamed. "That's why you've evolved. I can't believe you were once a simple nature spirit. Just look at you now! I'm amazed."

"I have a soul." Tremayne stared at the Druid, a bit baffled. What did one do with a soul?

"Yes! This is why you grew to have an identity apart from nature, separate from the greater good. You are an individual now."

"A soul makes me . . . an individual, then?" That increasing but undefined restlessness he'd felt. A searching. Was that due to this soul the Druid described?

"Yes! A soul makes one capable of character growth—or decay. You'll begin to absorb more of the world around you, developing personality and individual conscience and increasingly complex emotions as you encounter obstacles that challenge you and change you. You will retain your powers and your immortality, but in every other respect, you will gradually become more and more human."

Tremayne gave him a doubtful look. Souls sounded complicated. If intriguing. He would bet Daphne had a soul. Did she doubt that he had one? Possibly. She had, after all, called him a 'soulless nightstalker.' He frowned, concerned now. Even if she hadn't meant that literally . . . did his soul seem different from hers? Of course he knew *he* was different from her; he just hadn't realized until now that he'd also been lacking in some way. He should have guessed. Other nature spirits had obviously noticed a lack. They'd held themselves apart from him even before he was conscripted into service, though he hadn't really cared, except in retrospect. No doubt Daphne sensed the difference, too, even as she instinctively held herself back from him. "So you're saying this soul is a good thing?"

"Oh, eminently good. Fabulous, in fact. Just, er, one problem." Phil smiled a little sympathetically.

"What would that be? I'm not a clone of Akker, am I?" For Tremayne, it was a repulsive thought.

"Oh, gosh, no. You're you, and as I said, that soul is untainted according to what I foresaw. But that soul of yours . . . Well, it's just like the rest of you. It's still tied to the cornerstone and your duty. It will stay that way until Daphne gains sufficient control of her powers to conduct a ceremony to set the freedom process in motion."

Tremayne latched on to the best news. "But it can be freed? And *I* can be free and whole and individual? Not just some formless spirit?" He'd suspected, hoped, but never had it been verified. Until now.

"Yes. It's possible. That's what I saw for you."

Tremayne fought back his excitement. "Good. What do I do? What does she have to do?"

"It's very simple." Phil smiled. "And yet, not. You see, the bulk of the work is all on her. She'll need you to help her learn to control those powers, and you'll need to do so with patience and kindness. Gradually, you'll gain her trust and perhaps her cooperation in conducting that ceremony I mentioned. Succeed in all of the above, and you will be rewarded with freedom. Cool, huh?"

That's all it would take? Hell, he'd tutor her from now until the end of time for a chance like that.

"But timing is critical. Daphne must conduct the ceremony on the eve of this year's spring equinox—March twentieth—in the place where it all began: the stone circle of Avebury."

"March twentieth. That gives me nearly two months." So, he was on the clock. But two months was potentially doable. Hell, *it would be done*. Whatever was necessary.

"Oh, but one more thing." Now Phil looked hesitant. "Your ward. You have to make sure she's really, really ready for this. If she's not, and she attempts the ceremony to process your release . . . well, it could drive her insane. Especially given her possible genetic tendencies. It's risky." He shrugged. "I hate to say it, but this sort of thing can be debilitating to a strong entity. It'd be devastating to an untried one."

"Does she know of this?" Tremayne asked, although he guessed the answer.

"Nope. Totally clueless. You get to tell her."

And thereby give her yet one more reason to run from him.

Tremayne quietly met the High Druid's eyes. "*Must* I tell her?"

Phil regarded him just as steadily. "About the possible consequences should she fail?" He reluctantly shook his head. "I didn't sense in my dream that telling her was required. I can't speak for your karma, however."

Tremayne nodded, thinking. "So, if she knows nothing of any of this, how will she perform the ceremony? Will you teach her? Will I?"

"Most of it will be instinctual. Automatic. The details have been magically imprinted on the puca powers she wields, to be unlocked by the still-dormant Druid powers she inherited."

"Details composed and imprinted by Akker," Tremayne mused uneasily, "to be unlocked by Druid powers passed down by Akker."

"Yes. I imagine there's genetic memory involved, too, since Daphne is his descendent. He would have made use of that tie."

"But how could he possibly have known—?"

Phil shrugged. "That was one *powerful* Druid. He was a genius at prophecy, and he had a maniacal obsession with detail. To have foreseen so much, planned for so many outcomes . . ." Phil shook his head. "Druids historically have not written down their teachings and experiences, and I can respect that tradition, but sometimes—like now—I find it hugely frustrating. We could have learned so much from him. Well, except on the subject of ethics. The man was seriously morality challenged. And insane." Phil chuckled nervously. "Fascinating, really."

Damn good thing the man was long dead, Tremayne mused. Akker would have made a formidable opponent and questionable ally, given his power and instability.

"So, that's why Daphne's necessary to your release," Phil concluded. "She possesses the secret yet knows nothing consciously." His smile faded. "Understand that this ceremony is a make-or-break event for you, however. If Daphne fails, she goes insane and you . . . well, you revert to unevolved nature spirit. Not a bad thing to be, unless you've known yourself as more. And you already have. Frankly, it would be torture for you to go back. So there's a lot at risk here, even as there's so much to gain. After all, successful execution of this ceremony would mean closure for you on all levels. You would be free of that rock, free of that stone circle at Avebury, free of your duty to Akker and the puca powers." Phil smiled slightly. "You could live your life as a whole man, complete and capable, physically, spiritually, emotionally, intellectually. You would be Mr. Tremayne . . . well, whatever surname you choose for yourself. You'd still be immortal and powerful, but tied to no one but yourself and your choices and pleasures. You could hold a job, pursue hobbies and even fall in love."

"Love?" Tremayne blinked.

"Oh, are you in for a treat." Eyes sparkling in fresh excitement, Phil clapped his hands together, fingers interlacing, and pointed with both index fingers. "And I'm not just talking about the pump and grind. You could do that anyway. But this is more. Sex without love is like . . ." He tapped those index fingers to his lips as he sought words. "Food without flavor. Or sleep without dreams. Television in black and white. A computer, but no Internet service." Phil looked momentarily appalled before he shook it off. "Basically, there's something nice there without it, sure, but once you've had the good stuff . . . there's really no comparison. You'll see. When your evolution is complete, that is. The ability to love would be proof positive that you've fully evolved."

Love. He didn't know much about that, really. He supposed he could research the idea. Especially that combination of sex and love and how it might be with Daphne. Would she want that with a being like him? Perhaps the combination would entice her more than what he had to offer now. Yes, definitely he would research.

As for freedom . . . he could practically taste that already, no embellishment or research necessary. Imagine. To be free! Wholly free! That this mission could end so sweetly . . . Yes, this was what he wished. And yet, part of him wondered at the wisdom of risking a human woman's sanity just to gain that freedom.

Still, pucas and Druids had thought nothing of enslaving him for two millennia. Why should he hesitate to risk Daphne when her kind had not hesitated to risk him?

As she neared the exit for the airport, Daphne pulled out her cell phone and dialed a number she'd cheerfully and only recently added to speed dial. Soon she heard ringing over the connection. Lots of rings.

"Hello?" It was Mina, her half sister, sounding giggly and breathless.

Daphne winced. She hadn't thought—

"Daphne, is that you?" Mina's voice sharpened a little.

"Yeah. Hi, Mina. Look, I'm sorry for disturbing you."

"I . . . No problem." She cleared her throat, leaving Daphne in no doubt what she'd interrupted. "What's up?"

Hating this part, Daphne pursed her lips. Then she sighed. "I wanted to tell you something and then ask you a favor."

"Oh. Are you okay? You sound funny."

"Yes, I'm fine. I'm just . . . leaving. As planned."

"Oh." There was silence. "I was sort of hoping . . . well, I was hoping that since you got caught up in the Druid mess that you'd hang around long enough to go to my wedding. You know, being my sister and all."

Daphne winced. Mina had been so careful not to take her to task over this when she'd first mentioned moving to California, no doubt realizing Daphne had to get out of Dodge before Dodge chewed her up and spit her out. To be perfectly honest, she'd been almost frantic to skip her sister's ceremony. She hated weddings. Hugging strangers, emotional pronouncements, soppy melodrama . . . It was so far outside of her comfort zone. She had firsthand experience of the ugliness a marriage could become; her parents' union was aged roadkill at its best.

So she dealt best in business terms, not white satin, towering cakes, and empty promises. Somehow she didn't think talk of empty promises would adequately appease her sister, though— nor was it appropriate or kind. And, socially uncomfortable or not, she did like Mina and didn't want to hurt her feelings. "I can't. I have to go. It's—Well, you already knew I'd planned on leaving before your big day."

"Yes." And Mina sounded disappointed, but accepting. "And I want you to be happy. You need a change. I guess this is it, huh?"

"Yes."

"So. When exactly are you leaving?"

"Um . . . now?" She rushed to continue before Mina could interrupt with questions. "And I was wondering if you'd do me a favor and get my car out of airport long-term parking tomorrow and just donate it. Somewhere. I don't care where. Just someplace that helps people in trouble. I left cash in the glove box to cover parking fees." See? There, she'd taken care of her damn car.

"You're leaving now? But I thought—Look, maybe Janelle was mistaken, but I thought . . . something about a cat? Was she pulling my leg, or just recovering from her ordeal with Kane?"

Daphne grimaced. "It was an exaggeration, probably. I can deal with it. And I'll call if I need help." No, she wouldn't.

"No, you won't."

Daphne blinked.

"I don't think this is such a good idea. Maybe you should stick around and find out how much effect all of that Druid stuff will have on you," Mina suggested.

"It's not the Druid stuff I'm worried about." The words slipped out before Daphne could halt them. "But I'm not worried. Except about my new life. I don't want to lose my new apartment and my new job. I'll be a management accountant for a Fortune 500 company, instead of a lowly but dutiful public accountant whose doting 'Daddy' hired her to work for him. This is a big step up for me, professionally and personally. A whole new life. I've waited for this and planned for this for so long, Mina. You know what that's like. To have a lifelong dream and be so close?"

Mina sighed. "Yeah, I do. Sure, I'll get your car. Just text me or call me and tell me where it is once you've parked it. And you'd better call me when you get where you're going and check in regularly. I was sort of hoping to get to know my sister better. I don't want to lose touch."

They'd actually been meeting for lunch on a semiregular basis, mostly as uneasy but well-meaning acquaintances who respected each other and wanted to become friends. The emotional baggage of the past was still sort of a big elephant sitting in the corner, but they'd paid the elephant its due and had begun working it toward the door.

"I don't want to lose touch, either. I'll call, you'll call, we'll meet up for wicked weekends. . . ." Daphne paused, feeling a little silly, a little vulnerable, a little elated. "I've never had a sister. I still want to learn how it works."

"Deal. Be safe. I'll be waiting to hear from you."

Daphne hung up the phone. Perhaps it was foolish to give up her car without trying to sell it, given her situation. She just didn't want any part of it. A "professional bonus" from her parents several years earlier, it was little more than a burden and a reminder of her bogeyman: her relationship with them.

As the only child the doctors told Violet Forbes she could bear, Daphne had watched as her unhappy parents took to torturing each other, cheating on each other, growing to hate each other and trying to use their child as a pawn in their happy little war. Gran had sheltered her as much as she could while she was still alive—offering an ear, a shoulder to cry on and levelheaded advice—but that had ended with Gran's death when Daphne was fifteen. As an adult, Daphne realized her parents, in some perverse twist on the usual romance, actually enjoyed their battles. It was all they had left of whatever spark had brought them together so long ago.

Unlike some people, Daphne didn't think Duncan and Violet were wholly evil. But they'd crossed lines along the way, in unacceptable ways, and she was done waging war with her conscience. She would live her own life now.

The exit for the airport arrived, much to Daphne's jittery joy. She turned off, slowing to take the smaller roads and wending her way to long-term parking. She pulled into the building and found, to her dismay, that the garage was nearly full. She spiraled up and up in search of a parking place in the darkened structure, which echoed with the sound of her engine, its low ceiling encouraging claustrophobic feelings.

At last she found an open spot in a darkened corner near the last level available for parking. The elevator was all the way on the opposite side, so she'd be lugging her bags for a distance. But she was here. She'd made it. She just wished it weren't so dark.

Leaving the parking ticket, her keys and cash in the glove box, she opened her car door and popped the trunk. The sounds echoed eerily throughout the structure. As did the memory of her mother's warnings the last time Daphne traveled to a conference, with the intent of returning after dark. She'd insisted that Daphne let her father chauffeur her to and from the airport. That way, she wouldn't have to walk, a lone woman, in the dark. Airport garages were notorious for—

"Oh, stop it, Daphne." And her own words echoed, sounding small to her own ears. What, was she going to chicken out now? That's all this was. She'd flown before. Walked through dark parking structures before. This was no different. She was just nervous about an unknown future and feeling the effects of her parents' disapproval. Not to mention the dire consequences predicted by one purple-spectacled freak and enlarged upon by one overwhelming nature spirit. She was an adult with every right to lead her own life.

And so she would.

After she pulled her bags free of the trunk, she locked all doors and closed them. Once she was inside the terminal, she'd have to text Mina with her car's location and press-button lock combo. But she was abandoning the car. She felt one more burden lift from her shoulders. Now . . . on to the elevator and the ticket counter.

As she rolled her bags toward a row of parked cars and wove between them to get to the next aisle, she heard quick, heavy footsteps behind her. She turned in alarm, had the blurred impression of tall bulk, as she stumbled over her suitcases. A purse strap snapped beneath wrenching hands. When she abandoned

all to try to run from her assailant, she felt a yank on her hair
and her head wrenched backward on her neck. Yelping in surprise and pain, she fell back against a brick wall of a sweaty man.
One beefy arm encircled her waist. A big hand twined in her
hair, pulling her face closer. Hot, stale breath blasted in her ear.

"Hi, Blondie. Wanna party?

Chapter Four

Daphne Forbes. She can free you.

Tremayne again shook his head in slow wonder at Phil's news. If the Druid were to be believed, his skills trusted, then Tremayne stood a decent shot at freedom. All he had to do was convince a human woman that performing the ceremony, whatever it was, was the answer to both their prayers. She didn't need to know the risks. He would just tell her the truth—that the ceremony was the most decisive way to prove her control, to get the Druids off her back and, as a side benefit, make one nature spirit a very happy, very free man.

But what of the threat to her sanity? Could he really risk that? Would his karma withstand that kind of moral compromise? And what of his newfound soul? An unfamiliar heaviness seemed to weigh in his chest. Guilt? One of those emotions Phil mentioned? Probably. So that's what it felt like. No doubt he was further "evolving," which apparently would not always be convenient. Before, a decision like this would have been easy. Do the right thing and to hell with self and unpleasant consequences. But now . . . the nature spirit wanted more. He wanted something for himself, not just the greater good. Even if wanting more meant bending the rules a little. He never used to bend rules. And now the resulting sensation. That emotion. Guilt. It was unpleasant.

Mouth tight, he signaled and merged his car onto the ramp headed for the expressway just as his phone buzzed. Phil again? With another condition regarding his freedom? Perhaps his guilt would grow teeth and bite him in the groin next? Because evolving nature spirits felt emotions on a visceral level? Suddenly he could see the appeal of continuing existence as a simple lima bean. Or kumquat.

Without taking his attention off the road, Tremayne flipped open the phone and held it to his ear. "Yes?"

"Tremayne?" It was a woman's voice, sounding uncertain. "This is Mina Avery. Janelle gave me your number, said you were—" She broke off. "Damn it, I promised or at least implied I wouldn't tell, but I think she's making a mistake. Janelle told me the Druids said Daphne could still shift and that she couldn't control it, that you were watching her. That the powers she's gained might be beyond her control. I'm afraid she'll get hurt, so . . . She can just be mad at me."

"Do you have a point to make, or did you just call to speak to yourself?" he asked. "If it's the latter, I'm not sure anyone's there to take the call."

"Funny guy," Mina replied. "Do you want to know where Daphne is or not?"

Tremayne's attention sharpened. "At my apartment. Or so I thought."

"You can help her, right? Teach her to control her powers?"

"That's my job."

"But she doesn't know how yet—"

"No. She's completely at the mercy of her new powers."

"Oh, no! You need to stop her, then." Mina sounded urgent. "She slipped out on you."

"Damn. Where is she? At your place?"

"I wish. No, she's on her way to the airport, if not already there. She left me instructions for retrieving and disposing of her car from the airport garage, so I know she's planning on leaving for good. She said she'd text me details."

"I'll find her. Call if you hear from her." Grimly, Tremayne slapped his phone shut and floored the gas pedal.

Two of them?!

Daphne opened her mouth to scream and found a big hand clapped over it as she was hauled tight against a body easily twice the size of her own. The bulk was flabby, but he had weight on his side and a buddy to back him up. She had nothing. Nada.

"We're gonna have some fun tonight." Her captor laughed in her ear. The second guy, only a little smaller, but crafty looking, stood in front of her, digging through her purse.

She thought quickly. "Money. There's money inside the wallet. And credit cards. Take all of it. Just let me go." She spoke against her captor's hand. She received no response but his other hand groping roughly for her breast. Flinching, she tried to wrench sideways, but he squeezed painfully until she yelped.

Damn it. She was not going to start her new life getting robbed, raped and murdered. Ramming an elbow into soft flesh garnered no response, but she continued stomping and squirming.

"Cut it out, bitch." Her captor casually yanked her hair. Otherwise he seemed unfazed. So she stomped and kicked harder. At least she was annoying him, damn it. It might make her dead in the end, but she wasn't going to lie back and take it. She'd done that every day of her stupid life, and she wasn't going to spend her stupid death doing the same damn thing. She'd fight and . . .

Consciousness wavered, and a maddening, prickling heat invaded every nerve ending, every limb. Daphne felt her hair stand on end and—

A deafening shout of "What the fuck?!" battered her eardrums. Meanwhile, the guy in front of her backed a step away, babbling wordlessly and staring.

Daphne bit the arm holding her, hard.

Yanking his arm from her teeth, her captor gave a high-pitched shriek and dropped her. She landed hard, all four limbs sprawling and—

Hooves?

"She's a fucking goat!" This from the groping bastard.

"Oh, man, I do *not* do that shit. Do *not*." The smaller guy continued backing away, eyes huge.

And you think I do? You're the perverts around here, not me. Nothing emerged from Daphne's . . . muzzle? But the thought seemed to be conveyed to both men, who gaped at her.

"N-no? Yes?" answered the smaller one, obviously clueless and hoping to hit on whichever answer would save his worthless hide. Bastard. Nothing would have saved her hide from these two animals. And now he expected mercy? From 'a fucking goat'?

In an uncoordinated act of fury, Daphne lunged at the guy in front of her, teeth bared, and caught his leg. He squealed and yanked backward. When she moved to pursue, half tripping over a shoe lying on the floor—hers?—he threw her purse at her. "No! Here. Take it back! Just . . . Holy shit!" Backing away, eyes wide, the guy rounded a car bumper and stumbled off.

Hearing a sound behind her, Daphne whirled in clumsy fury. She stepped quick and instinctively rammed her head—horns! How useful!—into the groin of the jerk who'd left bruises along her torso. He let loose with a sound she'd never heard a human make.

Satisfied, and feeling more empowered than she ever had, Daphne moved forward in anticipation of another round, but her target stumbled sideways. Turning tail, he scrambled away from her in a clumsy weave between cars, his panic lending speed to a hobbling gait. When a rusty sedan skidded to a halt next to him, he jumped in, depriving Daphne of her deserving victim. The car roared off.

Heart racing with lingering fear and shock, and still hungry for vengeance, she looked around. Finding the suitcase that had tripped her up, she lunged to ram a horn into it. She heard a satisfying rip as she wrenched her head up and backward, then stabbed at it over and over until fabric rained down around her.

Still pissed, she wheeled in the other direction, saw the rear end of her blasted car still parked in its spot. Yes, all the way on the other side of the garage from the elevator. She ran awkwardly toward it, then took pleasure in bursting one, two, three and four tires. Horns seemed to come in damn handy! Every girl should come equipped with a pair.

Satisfied, she turned. Now she would just . . . what? She stood there trembling, panting and completely disoriented. She scanned the area. Her assailants were gone. This level of the garage was mercifully devoid of human or other life. Except for her.

A goat.

So, exactly what would she do? Ask the ticket lady to sell airfare to a goat? Using what ID exactly? And would she pay with a credit card? Which she would hand over using which thumbs? And did they even board livestock? She'd take a wild guess and say, *Uh, no!* Security would be babbling and drooling in the corner after dealing with her.

Damn it, she was trapped. What could she do? How the hell would she get out of here? Better yet, how the hell did one morph from goat back to woman?

Breathing heavily from exertion and panic, she eyed her overturned purse, punctured tires, slashed bags, torn and filthy clothing strewn everywhere. She was a mess. She could shift at any time, apparently, and into anything and for any reason. No control. None. As for sanity . . . Look what she'd done! Her possessions. Her car.

Oh, no. Were the Druids and Tremayne right? Was she nuts now?

The blast of a car horn had her turning and ducking. What would airport security do to a goat in the garage? Take it to the pound? Milk it? Eat it?

But she recognized the car. Reluctantly, she stepped forward. The car slowed and halted. The driver side door opened and Tremayne stepped out.

"There you are." He sounded completely unfazed. It infuriated her.

Well, if you had to show up at all, you damn well could have done it ten minutes ago and saved me the scare of my life and this damn shifting-into-goat experience. I'm going to have a headache for days, she snarled at him.

He frowned. "Are you hurt?"

She seethed.

After a once-over that apparently assured him she was as well as could be expected of a girl-turned-goat, he surveyed their surroundings. "What happened to your car? And what's all over the floor? Clothing? Shoes? Luggage?"

He turned back to her, focused, then strode forward and bent close, his hand outstretched. She flinched, still shaken by her last close encounter with a man, but he simply unsnarled a scrap of lace from one of her horns. He held it up to catch the overhead light. A powdery black stain marred the delicate white fabric. Apparently, horns presented a whole new host of personal hygiene demands. Horn brushing? Horn flossing? Not a topic she cared to explore. No, she'd just stand there like a traumatized farm animal and quake for a while.

Tremayne glanced first at the clothing on the garage floor and then at the tires of her car, before turning back to her. "Did somebody get a little frustrated?" he asked.

No. Somebody got downright pissed. Two guys were going to mug, rape and probably kill me. But do you care? No, you're more worried about the mess I made. I'm standing here, humiliated and in goat form, while you make fun of me.

Dropping wordlessly to one knee, Tremayne wrapped big arms around her and gently pulled her close.

Breath hitching, Daphne stumbled forward to lean shamelessly, gratefully, into the sturdy comfort of his strength. She felt a strange drawing sensation, as though her tension were tugged from her and into him. When he pulled back to look into her eyes, she saw her own hands. They were clutching his shirt. She was human again, and sitting on his propped-up knee. She inhaled. Exhaled. Closed her eyes.

"Thank you." It came out as a broken whisper as she ducked her head.

After a few moments, she braced herself and rose up on shaky legs. Tremayne, who rose more easily, but just as cautiously, kept a hand on her arm in offered support. Grateful for the help, but humiliated by the necessity of it, she kept her eyes averted.

"Hey. Look at me."

Reluctantly, she met his eyes. "Why? You want me to admit

you were right? Fine. You were right: I can't go any-freaking-where without morphing into farm animals. What if I'd done this on the plane? Or in the middle of the airport? Or behind the wheel?" She shuddered. "Think of the headlines: DEADLY CAR ACCIDENT ON I-64. GOAT FINED FOR THUMBLESS DRIVING."

But Tremayne didn't smile. "So you'll come back with me now? I can help you with this. You know I can."

He would indeed be the only guy she knew who could undo her shape-shifting lapses. She'd already proven how little control she had over herself or these godforsaken powers. More tempting, he seemed to think he could teach her to control them.

"Honestly, this is not me saying I told you so. It's as simple as this: You need help. I'm the only guy who can help, and I'm offering. Will you accept? Or will you continue to run?"

Closing her eyes, she remembered the terror of helplessness, dizzying lack of control, rising panic as she realized she was trapped. Trapped in another form, another body, an *animal* . . . Did she really have any choice?

"Let's go back to my place." Tremayne wrapped a steadying arm around her and supported her—she was hobbling along with one shoe on and one shoe missing—back to his car. She kept losing her shoes. That made two now, one for each shift. A connection? She supposed it was a minor casualty, given her alternatives. It was better, for example, than permanently losing her humanity. But she still had to wonder . . . He opened the door and settled her in the passenger seat.

As he started to close the door, she reached out to stop him. "I have to get my stuff. Or whatever I can salvage of it."

"I'll get it. You sit."

He closed the door, then headed away, picking up scraps of fabric as he went. Daphne looked on in embarrassment as he managed to gather up most of her belongings, deposit them into what was left of her luggage, and stash all of it in the trunk. A few moments later he slid back into his car, gently set her purse—now bulging awkwardly with the stuff he'd returned to it—on her lap. Her wallet was inside, she noted with relief, as was her cell phone. He seemed to have found everything except—"Did you see my other shoe out there?"

"No." And he sounded supremely unconcerned.

Fine, so it wasn't his problem, damn it. And maybe she owed him for rescuing her from her horned alter ego. She inhaled slowly. "Look, I wouldn't ask, except that makes two shoes I've lost in as many days, so—"

"It's not lost, Daphne."

His calm denial had her blood pressure rising all over again. "Okay, I get that a nature spirit has a different perspective on reality, but this isn't exactly a gray area. The shoe's not on me. You say it's not in the trunk and you didn't see it on the ground out there. That sounds like lost to me."

"It's not lost; it's just not here. You didn't shape-shift completely."

"So, what, did I eat the shoe? Did the cat or goat eat the shoe? Is it in my spleen, my DNA?" She was horrified and not really joking.

He smiled. "There you go, trying to apply the laws of science to magic. No, you don't have a shoe inside of you, not in any form."

"Then why is it that I leave one shoe behind when I shift to beast, and then when I change back to human, the other one's missing? It makes no sense. And I *know* that's what's happening, so don't even try to deny it. Back at the grove, right after I changed into a cat, I remember sitting in that ruined red shoe with that scuff mark right under my nose, taunting me. But then, when you switched me back, I was wearing the unmarked shoe—the other shoe. How is that possible? Shouldn't the shoe that doesn't shift with me just stay where it is, waiting for me, so that when I change back to human I have access to both shoes? Where's the logic?"

"You want logic? How do you account for the dramatic difference in physical mass between you and a cat? Or you and a goat? You can't. This is magic, not science. More to the point, it's faerie magic, which sort of takes on a life of its own, especially if it's undisciplined and uncontrolled as yours is. It's unpredictable, illogical, even unreliable to some extent. It's inherently mischievous. If something like magic can have a sense of humor, then that's what faerie magic has. When pure or given free rein, it"—he smiled a little—"entertains itself to some extent. Often at its wielder's expense. Well, except for royal faerie magic. That's a more potent strain." Tremayne started the engine, obviously considering the subject settled to his satisfaction.

She fought for patience. "Okay. Magic is unexplainable. Let's try this one: where are my shoes right now?"

"It's hard to say. They might be trapped between realms." He shot her an amused glance. "Or sunning on a tropical beach or shrunk down to fit a mouse. The possibilities are endless."

She groaned. "Given the twisted course of this conversation, I will undoubtedly regret asking this, but . . . Will I ever get my missing shoes back?"

"Maybe. They might return with another shape-shift. Or the magic could spontaneously return them to you. Or maybe they'll never come back. It's hard to tell."

Great. She had rogue shoes either on sabbatical or floating somewhere between realms. She supposed it could be worse. She should be grateful that it wasn't her pants the hysterically funny magic decided to withhold from her. She could be sitting here in her underwear right now.

"I'll send someone for your car in the morning," he murmured. When she just nodded without speaking, he glanced at her. "It will be okay, you know."

"I don't know why you think so. I went crazed goat all over everything I own. It doesn't get a lot worse than that, does it?" Well, she supposed she could have been mugged, raped and murdered. That would have been worse. So, maybe she was insane now instead? Was that worse? She concentrated on shifting the contents of her purse into their usual orderly arrangement. "I completely lost it. I guess you saw that, though."

He nodded, his expression grim. "I saw."

She tipped her head back, picturing herself: Daphne Forbes,

the spontaneously shape-shifting accountant. Somehow, the image just didn't portray Employee of the Year. That perfect life she'd planned seemed far out of the realm of possibility now. The new apartment, the new job . . . Just think if she showed up hooved for work on her first day! She shuddered. "Why a goat?"

"Hmm?" Tremayne was carefully rounding a tight spiral down the consecutive levels of the garage.

"Why did I change into a goat? Why not a cat? I'm not complaining, since the goat sufficiently kicked ass when I needed. And these guys looked like they dismembered fluffy kittens as children. But if I have no conscious control of my shift, why did I change into anything but my so-called natural form?"

"Only the first shift is natural. Afterward, any shift that springs spontaneously from intense emotion will usually result in a form that's somewhat consistent with the circumstances and emotion. Money says you weren't just scared when you shifted, but also angry. Maybe feeling a little stubborn? As in, damned if you were going to be victimized just when you were on your way to freedom?"

Daphne slowly nodded.

Tremayne shrugged. "Stubborn as a goat, with mean teeth and a sturdy set of horns. I can see a connection there." His lips twitched. "Useful, too. You probably scared religion into them, didn't you?"

"Before or after I rammed a horn into one guy's crotch?"

Tremayne winced. "I guess I won't feel compelled to seek them out and avenge you. You did that all by yourself."

She recalled, not without grisly pleasure, the unearthly noise her assailant had made as he cupped himself. "The bastard should be physically incapable of rape for at least a week. Shoot, he watched a woman—his intended rape victim, at that—change into a goat right before his eyes. If that doesn't scare him permanently impotent, I don't know what will."

"So . . . there's a part of you that was grateful that you shifted. Even if it was beyond your control."

Daphne pondered her two assailants' intentions and her own

likely fate. "Very grateful, even if it did scare the crap out of me later."

"You felt empowered."

For a brief while, she'd loved those horns. "Yes. I have to admit I did. It is the very best antidote to that horrible feeling of powerlessness: the victim becomes the avenger. And a decent set of horns made that possible. What's not to like? Except for the part where I was a goat stranded in an airport garage with no way of shifting back to human form."

"Okay, supposing you could learn to shift only when you wanted and only into a form of your choosing, then shift back to human form at will." He paused, letting his words register. "Remember what you did with those horns. You saved yourself, you know. I would have arrived too late to help you."

"Look. I see where you're going with this, but honestly, it would be a whole lot easier just to carry a weapon or learn martial arts or something. Shape-shifting carries a brand-new set of risks for the freedom-loving woman. The pound, for example. I could be sharing a cage with some horny border collie."

"Only because you didn't know how to shift back."

"Or some mad scientist's lab. Or I could be blackmailed by some idiot who found me out and threatened to expose my secret unless I paid him off." Probably somebody like the little weasel who'd gone through her purse while his buddy groped her. She could easily see him as a blackmailer. She shuddered.

"And then there's the whole insanity threat. Or is that no longer an issue? I've already shifted a couple of times and . . ." She frowned. "Okay, I did lose it with the suitcase and tires, but damn it, I had just been attacked. Then I'd involuntarily changed into a goat. Acting rationally wouldn't have been rational . . . if you know what I mean. Freaking out was the reasonable response here!"

Tremayne didn't respond, just pulled up to the attendant to pay his parking fee.

As they left, Daphne glanced at him. "Tremayne. You don't

think I'm losing it, do you? You can't judge me bonkers yet. Not based on that incident."

"No, I don't judge you insane yet. I do worry, though. You were so self-destructive in your anger. That bothers me."

"Yeah, but remember the mugging and groping, the prospect of rape and violent death? A girl gets angry. And, when the true targets of her anger take off in their getaway car, it's just possible that she then thinks of the other things that contributed to her situation. Take the luggage, for example."

"Okay. What did the luggage do to you? Trip you?"

"Yes!" She verbally pounced. "I swear it did! It tripped me up so I couldn't get away from the bastards. Ripping it up made me feel a whole lot better."

"And what about your car?" He glanced skeptically at her. "Did it trip you, too?"

"Gee, nobody told me 'goal-oriented' nature spirits were also smart-asses." She made a face. "No, it didn't trip me. I just wanted it gone with all of my heart. For personal reasons I don't feel I need to share with you. But there it was. And"—she raised an index finger, her point suddenly clear again—"it was parked all the way across the garage, which left me easy prey for those clowns. So you see? I wasn't targeting myself. I was venting my feelings on all the secondary culprits. I also didn't hurt anyone that didn't need hurting."

"The level was empty of people when I found you. Once your attackers left, there was nobody here for you to hurt."

"Yeah?" She scowled. "Well I didn't attack *you,* did I? And we both know you've annoyed me recently."

"No, you didn't come after me. In fact, you seemed relieved to see me." He glanced at her. "Does that mean you're ready to cooperate? You'll stay?"

"If it means learning how not to spontaneously shift into a farm animal in public—how to be normal again—then yes, I will cooperate. I won't run." She gave him a dry look. "Unless, of course, a certain nature spirit threatens to eliminate me. Then all bets are off."

★   ★   ★

"You want me to do *what*?"

It was late afternoon the next day, after Daphne had slept late, and her nerves had only just stopped jangling from the airport incident. The memory of her attack and thoughts of what could have happened had kept her awake and scared until almost dawn. Now, in the light of day, all she could think about was being trapped inside a goat's body. The nightmare seemed endless. And he had the nerve to ask her to do *this*?

Damn it, she'd done everything asked—no, demanded—of her since that stupid grove gathering. She'd moved in with this stranger, canceled her trip, placated her future boss and future landlord (for now). She'd basically put her whole damn life on hold. And now she was sitting in a hard metal chair with her butt going numb, and he wanted her to do what?

"Try to change into the cat. Or the goat. Any form, really." He smiled, leaning back in his chair. "Which one strikes your fancy right now?"

"Let's see. How about a man-eating lion? Do they eat nature spirits?" She tapped a fingernail on her chin as she regarded him coolly. All a facade. Somewhere along the line she'd entirely lost her cool. The hours she'd spent in close confines with Pheromone Boy were wearing on her. He'd seen her at her helpless worst and now represented the only lifeline she had. Feeling unbearably vulnerable, she was reduced to a defensive show of hostility. "No? Maybe a king cobra or a black widow spider. Which would do you the most harm?"

"None of those, I'm afraid." He gave her an apologetic look. "I'm not easily destroyed."

Actually, one positive aspect of her situation was the knowledge that she'd trumped her parents' schemes. They'd left multiple messages on her cell phone, no doubt seeking to launch new strategies based on her change in plans . . . and the change in her situation. She could almost feel the waves of frustration emanating from the heart of downtown Richmond. Yep, she was right down the street from them, practically under their damn noses. And she possessed all the powers they'd so fruitlessly coveted.

Yes, she felt comfortable blaming her mother, too, even though her father was the only one busted by the Druids. Her father was a bumbling power addict, no question, but her mother was discreetly covetous right alongside him. Not to mention lethally competitive. Years ago, her mother had even threatened blackmail in an effort to unseat Duncan during his term as High Druid. He'd called her bluff—but not before she'd put a word in Druid Phil's ear, thus launching Phil's own quest for the seat of High Druid. Where her mother had failed to replace Duncan with her own rule, Phil had quietly and—yes, Daphne would admit it—*bloodlessly* unseated Duncan to become High Druid Phil. Duncan had retaliated against his wife's betrayal with random, blatant and deviant infidelity. Typical of her parents' battles. What one wanted, the other desperately required. Just because the other wanted it. Sick and twisted.

And now they both wanted the puca magic Daphne wielded. No doubt they'd each latch onto one of Daphne's arms and rip her in half in the hope that the powers they wanted so badly would spurt out. Then they'd spill their own blood fighting over her mutilated remains.

"That was particularly gruesome." Tremayne sounded amused.

Fighting a flush of embarrassment—she'd been mentally exaggerating her parents' malice for her own entertainment—she narrowed her eyes at him. "You know, it would help if you'd keep your stupid self out of my thoughts. They're private property, and you were never welcomed inside."

"You still think I'm doing this? I promise you I'm not. It's all you. I don't read minds. You're the one with that ability. I can't mindwalk. But I can participate easily enough with you projecting your thoughts like you do."

Daphne pondered projecting something even more substantial. Like her foot into his rear.

"I'm feeling so much hostility from you right now. That's not good. Unstable Druid, unstable powers, unstable temperament."

He shook his head, his dark eyes seeming to laugh at her, though his expression remained sober.

"Tell me. Just what about this situation is so damned funny? The part where you all hijacked my life? Or is it the threat to my sanity and very existence? All hilarious, truly." And the more she thought about it, the more pissed Daphne got. It was all setting in, now that she'd had a few hours' sleep to work past her temporary, dazed acceptance of her situation. "Thanks to my idiot father and his grasping ways, I'm now fighting for my very life. And I'm probably forfeiting any chances in California. New career, new apartment, new lifestyle. And I had to give it all up"—she stood and gestured toward the room at large—"for this?"

Tremayne had folding chairs and a cardboard box for a dining room set. And, yes, he really did eat off of the box. They both had done so earlier; breakfast was cold cereal in plastic bowls, eaten off a freaking cardboard box. And the box looked like a recent addition to the room. It apparently used to contain the brand-new television set propped gracelessly on the kitchen counter, bits of Styrofoam still clinging to its base. In fact, she didn't remember seeing the box or the TV when she arrived here yesterday. He must have bought it while she slept in this morning.

Tremayne followed her gaze as she surveyed the room. "The furniture offends you? It is kind of plain, I guess. Decorating's not my strong suit."

"Like the decor is even half of my problem! How dare you? How dare you laugh at me?"

He stood up from his chair and moved closer as her voice rose to a shrill note. Her nerve endings seeming to scream, itchy and restless and—

God!

What is . . .

. . . happening?

Her reality seemed to warp, her vision blurred and moved sideways as everything within and without shifted and contorted. And then she was staring up—way up—at Tremayne, who watched with a softened expression.

Daphne felt her heart racing and looked down to see paws. Creamy white. *No. Oh, no. Not again.* Her breath came faster. Panic. *I want out. Let me out. Damn it, let me out!* But nothing audible emerged from her mouth.

Chapter Five

"Open your mouth, Daphne. You can still speak," Tremayne murmured. "I can hear you because you speak in my mind, but you can speak aloud as well. I've heard the puca brothers do it."

Daphne just shook her head in slow wonder, her vantage point low and with creamy fur in her peripheral vision. She felt like wannabe roadkill. People roadkill. Or, more to the point, nature spirit and Druidic roadkill, damn it. She tried to step forward and instead stumbled over one of the ballet flats she'd been wearing. She wanted to scream!

"Sssssh." His movements slow and cautious, Tremayne bent low. He slipped a hand beneath her belly, and, cupping her rear legs with his other palm, lifted her carefully to cradle her in the crook of one arm.

In spite of herself, Daphne felt safe tucked against his chest. Comforted. She looked around, found that her senses were all reporting back to her with increased volume and detail. She could see, smell and hear with greater clarity: Tapping of insects careening into the window. Breeze whistle-rattling through the screen. The heavy thump of Tremayne's heartbeat. His smell . . . was earthy, yet crisp and fresh. He wore a clean shirt. Chemicals—

She sneezed, realized she felt woozy, as if her head were inflating from the nose on back. . . .

"Whoops. Sorry. I just bought this, haven't had it washed yet. Hold on."

Setting her carefully on his makeshift table, Tremayne stripped off the button-down shirt. Under, he wore only a thin white cotton T-shirt, half tucked in his jeans but tugged up a little on one side. She could see a strip of hard flesh between white cotton and faded denim. Then, just as carefully, he picked her up again and cradled her against his soft, body-warmed T-shirt. Daphne sighed. This was better.

She heard a car engine whirring in the distance. Then Tremayne's chuckle.

Not a car engine. She was *purring*!

Digging a claw into his side, she arched upward, seeking freedom. Damn it, why hadn't she shifted back already? Wasn't that the nature spirit's job, to fix her when she screwed up? She squirmed hard, nearly gaining her freedom.

"Whoa! Daphne, wait. I was just calming you down the best way I know how. It's all a shock to you, physically and emotionally. I understand. But you need to be calm so you can figure out how all of this works. You don't want to rely on me forever, do you? You want to be able to shift on your own." He juggled her the entire time he spoke, avoiding claws and keeping a grasp on her desperately writhing body. But finally the meaning of his words registered. Reluctantly, everything in her rebelling, she calmed.

"Um," he said. She could hear the tremble of laughter in his voice. "Your hackles are still up."

This time the "engine" was a growl, not a purr.

"If you bite me, I won't help you change back," he warned.

Maybe she'd bite him *after* he helped her change back.

"Afterward? No problem. You can nibble anywhere you like once you're back in human form." His voice had lowered, was still amused, but with a message clear enough for any post-pubescent female to read.

Sick. Sick nature spirit. Quit with the flirting. I'm not feeling real frisky right now . . . so to speak. Except, of course, I can't speak.

"Yes, you can too speak. And I'm serious now. I think you should give it a shot. Talk to me."

Heart racing, Daphne took a deep breath. Then another. She tried to connect her thoughts to physical awareness. She'd avoided it until now, wanting to reside in comfy denial as long as humanly—she winced—possible.

"Look." And Tremayne's voice was low and soothing. "If it helps any, just remember that I can undo this for you, no problem. Any time. You've seen me do it twice now, right? Doesn't hurt you a bit, unless I'm forcibly yanking the magic from you. I don't think you have the focus yet to fight my power drain like that, so it shouldn't be a problem."

His voice grew increasingly mellow. "I'm what they call a dampening force or a power vacuum; I can consciously undo the effects of magic. I can make glamours drop, shift shape-changers back to their base forms. Render the magical powerless. I just think you like control, right? You want to be able to help yourself if this happens. So consider me a safety net. Or training wheels. Just until you figure things out for yourself."

She digested that. A dampening force. How about that? Like some *undo* function on a magical software program.

"That sounds about right. So, let's try speech. Open your mouth—it is still your mouth. A cat didn't eat you." His voice quavered a little with threatening amusement but quickly evened out. "You're still you, just a different form of you. So say something. Anything."

"I really want to bite you." She jumped. The words had popped out all by themselves. Okay, maybe they'd had help. The kind that came straight from a very annoyed gut.

He smiled. "Good. Not good that you want to do me damage. Although, like I said, shift to human and offer to bite and we'll talk. Hey, retract those things! I'm just kidding."

Her claws were out and itchy, and an engine motor whirred poisonously louder.

"I'm just saying speech is good. You performed like a pro. So. Want to explore a little? Try walking, running, climbing, anything catlike. It might be fun. I've heard it's fun, anyway."

Words came pouring out. "Know what would be fun for me? Turning *you* into a freaking cat while *I* hit the road. This is not fun adventure time for Daphne the Cat. It's get this over with, so Daphne—a real, live person—can get on with her life. What do

I need to do? Screw fun, and give me a simple checklist of requirements that would satisfy you and your nudie Druid buds."

"You know, not a single one of them was naked in the grove," Tremayne mused. "I really don't think Phil's Druids strip down for their rituals. He's a guy who seems to appreciate wardrobe over skin."

"Oh, look! It's *Lifestyles of the Bossy and Druidic*. Gee, thanks for enlightening me." The engine whirred furiously under her voice. "Checklist?" she prompted.

"Well, I think you breezed past the first item that would have been on a list like that. Speech is obviously not a problem for you in this form."

"Apparently, pissing off the fake puca makes her shape-shift *and* speak. Neat trick, huh?" She bared her fangs at him. *Fangs. I have fangs. This is—*

"Neat?"

"*Wrong.* I was going to think 'wrong.' Humans don't have fangs. Cats do. Vampires do. Have I seen your teeth lately, by the way?"

He rolled his eyes. "I'm not a vampire."

"Oh yeah? Well, 'nature spirit' sounds like a girly-looking sprite with silvery wings who flies with the singing birdies and buzzing bees as they flit around pretty flowers. You, on the other hand, look like you should be juggling boulders or stripping with Chippendales." She glanced at the white cotton stretched across his ample, very hard chest and straining at the shoulders. "Or did I just miss seeing the pretty wings?"

He grinned. "I'll never say."

She groaned. "The checklist. Just give it to me, okay? What do I have to master or control or whatever? I'm an overachiever. A perfectionist. A task list gauging my progress would make me absolutely giddy, I promise you."

He sighed. "It's not as easy as that. Fine to joke about a checklist, but this is a lot more complicated, a lot more subjective than just checking off accomplishments. That's a good place to start—controlling your powers—but the real test would be controlling your powers and your actions under extreme pressure."

"What, I should try to shift in a hurricane?"

"No. Try, not shifting shape when you desperately want to hurt someone or something. Try forestalling a well-provoked tantrum. Take the high road even when your opponent is belly-crawling all over the low road."

She stared a moment. "I see. This could take some time, then?"

"It could. Yes."

"Would a few hours or so do it for you?"

He smiled without replying. They both knew better.

Daphne sighed and tucked her nose against his chest, wishing she could hide her thoughts as easily. "All right," she muttered into warmed cotton. "Can we start with two things—of *my* choosing?"

"My pleasure." His voice rumbled low in his chest, sending pleasurable tingles twitching her whiskers and racing straight to her belly. "What are they?"

"I want to be able to change back, and I want to keep from sending you my thoughts."

She felt his warm breath ruffle her fur and could swear she felt prickling on the back of her neck. "Those are a couple of biggies," he murmured.

She quelled a shiver and tried to stay on task. "Yes, they are. Big, as in huge priorities for regaining my peace of mind."

"Let's begin with the shape-shifting, then. Returning you to base form. We'll see how that goes and play it by ear. Deal?"

"I guess." She frowned doubtfully. "So, what do I do? Is there a charm? Or magic words? A talisman? What?"

"None of those. Think back to when you shifted on your own, this time and the last one especially, since the first was a special case."

"Right. The intimate and illuminating first shift. I remember."

"Describe what you felt when you shifted these last two times. What do you remember?"

She gritted her teeth. "Lack of control. Period."

"No, lack of control would just be the part that freaked you out the most. Try to set aside that helpless feeling and relive the sensory memories. What do you recall?"

She stared into space a moment, reliving the horror of help-lessness, trying to dig beneath it. "Energy. Sparks of it seemed to leap from nerve ending to nerve ending, then speed up into something approaching a frenzy. That's when it felt like every-thing was beyond my control."

"That's it. The energy. It's magic. It's what's behind the shift. You need to learn to control the speed of this energy frenzy you described. If you can consciously set it in motion or halt it, you can initiate a premeditated shift or halt a spontaneous one."

"I suppose you realize this is all Greek to an accountant. I'm no physicist and certainly no magician. Give me something I can touch or numbers to play with. I understand those."

He hummed a negative. "That won't work in this case. Much of the shift is an emotional experience. A . . . physically pow-erful experience. The magic is like a parasite, in that it likes to hitch a ride with your adrenaline to shoot around your blood-stream. Adrenaline fuels it. So, extreme emotions or reactions—anger, joy, terror . . . sexual arousal, any of it—could send the synapses buzzing into an upward spiral."

"Okay, I hear you going for something, and it's not going to work. I'm not having sex with you every time I need to shift."

"How about just one time? For kicks?" He gave her a grin.

"You want to have sex with a cat?" She reared back awkwardly to peer up at him.

A flush crept up his neck and invaded his cheeks. "Er, no. I meant in the other direction. Or not. I mean . . ." He cleared his throat, a frown creasing his forehead. "Never mind."

She stared, utterly amazed. She'd managed to embarrass a two-thousand-year-old sprite. Was that cool or what? You'd think it would take a lot to embarrass somebody who'd witnessed the world's antics for two millennia. He'd known her for a tiny frac-tion of a percent of that time, and she'd already flustered him. Hey, a girl would take what power she could get, and disarming Tremayne seemed like a rare moment to appreciate.

"It's *nature spirit*, not *sprite*. And you have an unhealthy defi-nition of *cool*," he responded.

"Yeah, I know. Not a big deal to me. After two thousand

years . . . I can't believe anything could still embarrass you. You must have seen and done it all. Everything."

"Yep. Everything." His voice was flat. "What couldn't or wouldn't a man do with an eternity at his disposal?"

"Take out life insurance?" At his blank look, she pawed lightly at the air, waving off her own words. "Never mind. Lame joke." Then, startled, she stared.

Touching a fingertip to her paw, Tremayne eyed her quietly. "It might not be a bad idea to explore a little in this form before we shift you back. See if you can get used to the physical agility and coordination of a cat's body. What if you shifted for a purpose but couldn't accomplish the purpose because you were too uncomfortable in a different form?"

She gave him a baffled look—or as baffled as a cream-puff kitten's face could look, she supposed. Which was plenty baffled, likely. "Why on earth would I deliberately shift to an animal form? I'm an accountant. I work best with thumbs."

"Does it occur to you that you might have other purposes in this life besides your job? That maybe there's a reason you have been given this gift?"

"Yeah, it does occur to me. I think Phil said I might go insane. There's a neat purpose. I can't tell you how much I'm looking forward to fulfilling it. I think I'd look pretty good in white, don't you? With extra-long sleeves? Oh, but wait. If I go insane, you're supposed to put me down like a rabid dog, right? So a straitjacket would never become an issue."

Sighing, Tremayne decided the matter for her, just setting her down. She stumbled a moment, a little at a loss, before cautiously working all four legs in logical tandem. Admittedly curious now, she padded cautiously around the tiled floor of the barren kitchen/dining area before veering off into the carpeted living room.

Ah, now this was nice. Barren the apartment might be, but she had no complaints about the floor coverings and the size and classy makeup of the place. The apartment was expensive and downright luxurious. It had really plush, dig-your-toes-deep carpeting.

"You're going to shred the stuff, and I'll never get my deposit back."

"Huh?" Daphne glanced up at him, then followed his gaze to her feet. Well, paws, actually. She was kneading the carpet. Literally. Claws out and shredding the fibers. Bad kitty.

There was a sudden flash of white, and she froze. Carefully shifting her gaze to the side, she once again saw . . . She jumped. What the hell?

Tail! She had a tail. Of course she would have a tail. No wonder her father went freaking nuts. An accountant with a tail. And she wasn't talking about the tall kind of tale that Duncan might spin for a suspicious auditor. No, this was the fuzzy, wag-it kind.

Did cats ever wag their tails? How the hell would she know? She groaned audibly. Lord, she didn't know much of anything about animals. Like Violet and Duncan Forbes would have tolerated a beast in their pristine palace of a home. So she had absolutely no experience with cats, and yet here she was walking in the prissy little paws of one.

"Easy, Daphne. Just absorb a little at a time. Try face value right now. Just the physical experience. Sorry about the clawing thing. It was just, well, reflex. And seeing as you're an accountant . . ."

"And I deal with money and weigh and prioritize things accordingly? Yeah, I get it. Be kind to the property." Her nose level was below that of a couch cushion. Not that he had a couch—just more folding chairs. "Don't you have furniture? Doesn't your butt hurt after sitting in these for too long?"

He looked nonplussed. "I hadn't really thought about it."

"Right. Nature spirit. You're used to sitting on dandelion heads. Nothing else could possibly compare."

He grinned. "Not exactly."

"Plush things, I'll bet. Soft and velvety, sunny yellow. The puffy white seed things . . . Can you fly away on them, or are you too heavy?"

He sighed but didn't respond.

All right, so maybe she was making fun of him, but honestly, look at the guy. He was not what she'd picture as a nature spirit.

Surely they could come up with a different tag for something as solid and huge as Tremayne was, something more appropriate to refer to chiseled features, totally ripped pecs and biceps, and riveting, nearly black eyes that seemed so flat at first glance.

Look deeper, and the turmoil was there for anyone who searched for it. The depth of those eyes . . . It was hard to look into them too closely or for too long, because they could seduce, lure you in deeply, hold you willingly captive. So hard to look away. She blinked to break contact, taking in the close-clipped hair, almost carelessly shorn, as though he wanted just to get it out of his way. The only softness about him was his mouth. Sculpted and curved, sinfully lush. Honestly. That was a mouth that could kiss—

A small sound had her jumping and looking up into eyes that were wide with laughter and arousal. Oh, lord. To project such thoughts at the guy. She scowled up at him as much as she was able. "Hey, so I'm human. Well, usually. Doesn't mean I act on everything I think. Objectively, you are a work of art. No getting around that. You're also a freaking nature spirit and the guy who might have to eliminate me. That pretty much nullifies all of the above, as far as I'm concerned. All we have left is a reluctant and merely aesthetic appreciation. So, can all the horny ideas."

With a flick of her tail—Oh, she . . . no, never mind. It was time to stop being surprised by this form. Determined, she turned from him to explore the apartment in more detail. The surfaces, the feel of them underfoot and brushing up against her sides, teasing her whisker points . . . Then there was the novelty of a different perspective. Imagine preferring to go under things instead of around them. But there it was. Made a whole lot more sense. Didn't even have to duck.

His bedroom was huge and airy, but spare, with a bed, a sparsely filled closet and a simple nightstand with a lamp. Actually, it was an inordinately large bed, as though he'd sought to fill the room with that one piece of furniture. The man had his priorities.

And what a lush, beautifully carved and dressed bed this was. Not an impulse buy by any means, this looked special ordered or at least lovingly picked out and adorned. He'd swathed the bed in a rich brown satin, with a matching comforter and an inviting mound of downy pillows. If anything, the guy displayed a hedonistic streak in the bedroom—

Not going there. *Not* going there.

"Um, you can go there. Really. Not a problem if you go there. Want to test out the bed? Mind the claws, please, but it's very comfortable."

"Presently I will shred you with my claws. Unless you move out of my way." She exited the bedroom, grateful for fur to cover the flush that would have burned her human cheeks. Good lord. What a position to be in! Could this cat form possibly be in heat?

A snort from behind her told her she was still vastly entertaining. How wonderful.

She stalked down the hallway, her unfamiliar body itchy with rogue energy, and returned to the kitchen. She looked up, pondered her options, then made a leap for the granite-topped counter. Was totally surprised when she miscalculated. She scrabbled for purchase, only to feel big hands under her belly and behind her butt, boosting her up to safety. How mortifying.

"It just takes practice."

She eyed him coolly. "So, I explored a little. But now I really need to go back to human form. Tell me. What do I do? How do I reverse this? I've been calm—oh, many times now—but that doesn't seem to be working."

"Calm is how you avoid shifting in the first place. To shift back, you need to deploy that energy all over again. Just, in reverse."

"Well, that's clear as mud. So glad you could help."

"Daphne."

"Right. Sorry. I'm just a little edgy." She inhaled. And she really felt as edgy as a damn cat, too. Stupid stereotype. "Go ahead. I'm listening. All ears, I swear. You were saying?"

"Remember the energy? You need to call it up, get it zinging around your system all over again, except this time in reverse order and direction."

She blinked, waiting for more.

"No, that's it. Honestly."

"This is your explanation? This is how you teach me to do it? Reverse the energy? Well, so grateful for all the details. Give me a minute and I'll succeed." She stilled, made a show of checking out her paws, claws extended. Then she retracted them and gave him a wide-eyed stare. "Am I human again?" She glanced down. "Nope. Not even close. Gee, I wonder what went wrong?"

"I believe they call that milking it?"

"Can the cat jokes."

"I think that would be a cow joke."

She hissed—yes, *hissed*—at him, which seemed to entertain the bastard almost beyond his ability to hide it. Only a little snort and jaw tensing betrayed his hilarity. She lifted her nose and aimed it past his shoulder to look out a distant window, dismissing him entirely . . . and before she knew what was happening, he'd snatched her and tossed her high into the air, where she yowled, the sound turning into—

—an ear-piercing shriek as she landed in Tremayne's arms. She had one arm hooked around his neck, the other clutching a fistful of white cotton T-shirt. A fistful? Hands! Still trembling, she let go of his T-shirt, worked her fingers to reassure herself of their normal human functioning. Then, breath still uneven, she weakly dropped her head back, gradually letting it droop sideways onto his shoulder. *Oh, man.* Thank heavens for vaulted ceilings, or she would have smashed her face into wallboard and . . . She couldn't finish the thought. Unreal.

"Sorry for the scare. It was the easiest way to get you to shift back on your own. I wanted it to be your own energy doing the shift, not mine. Terror . . . Well, it serves to reverse things for you. Remember what I said about the adrenaline? I wanted you to feel the sensations again so you could mimic them on your own. Without the scare tactic next time."

"From fury and frustration to heart-stopping terror? This is going to be a fun ride. I can already tell." She murmured weakly, "This sucks. Just so you know."

"I can see where you'd think so."

"Great. Put me down."

"Are you sure?"

She raised her head and looked at him. Those dark eyes . . . Whoever said black eyes were cold like obsidian? His were so compelling, drawing her to stare into their glittering depths. Glittering with hunger, interest, jittery emotions. Or were those her feelings reflected?

"Possibly. But some of them are mine." He studied her. "I want you." At her wide-eyed alarm, he grinned just a little. "It only seemed fair to warn you."

"Kind of you. To share it with me, I mean." Unable to completely withdraw her gaze, she cleared her throat. "Could you put me down now?"

With obvious reluctance, he let her legs slide free of his arms, her denim-clad hip dragging down the front of his body. When she glanced up, his eyes were closed, his expression a little harsh. The guy apparently had a hair-trigger libido. No other man she'd known had reacted this quickly to her.

"Then they were all fools. Every one of them." He lowered his voice. "Especially Warren."

Her Druid ex-boyfriend. Well, there was a mood killer. And thank god for that. She pulled away, glancing down to find one foot bare. Again. Impatient with the lack, she kicked off her remaining ballet flat. At this rate, she'd run out of shoes before the week was out.

"Tell me about him."

"Warren? There's nothing to tell. And I don't know you well enough for confidences anyway."

"I thought we were getting downright intimate, what with the shape-shifting and rescuing and all."

She made a face. "So you should be satisfied with what you've learned, then."

"No. Was Warren a Druid or just a wannabe?"

She sighed. "A Druid. But not a very powerful one. Or rather, not a very controlled one. He could perform some powerful spells, in his own biased opinion, but never on command." She paused, remembering. "I thought that meant he was willing to give it up. To be normal. Even law-abiding. Like me."

"You thought you had something in common."

She nodded, remembering. "Yes. We'd be the anti-Druids. The rebels who rejected their heritage. He seemed to agree."

"But he didn't. Not really."

She shook her head.

"He used you, Phil said."

"Yes. But that's not all."

"What happened?"

"We were at that restaurant at my parents' country club. They were holding some function. I forget what. Anyway, I excused myself to go to the bathroom, then when I came back I overheard Warren—all drunk and celebrating, I realized later—bragging to some buddies about his aspirations. More power. From my father. Through me. When I found out what he was up to, I intended to tell my father. I was pissed, and no way was he getting what he wanted at the expense of my pride."

"But he didn't like that."

"Of course not. He grew angry. And then he had one of those rare moments where his powers worked in his favor. He rendered me mute. I couldn't speak. I couldn't write. I lost . . . words." She'd felt completely at the mercy of his power, unable to reverse his spell or communicate. She'd hated the loss of control, the interference in her mind. Remembering the frustration, the helplessness, the humiliation, she glanced away. "It took some doing, but I found my father at the club. Once he figured out what was wrong with me, he . . . well, he had to undo the spell. Once he did, well, I took off in Warren's car. Which I wrecked, as Phil mentioned."

"What happened to Warren?"

"Whatever Druid powers he had were removed. My father saw to that." She gave Tremayne a rueful look. "Duncan doesn't mind using me himself, but he'd be damned if he would let anybody else do it. He's possessive that way and, okay, there's some twisted love and protectiveness there, too. So he took care of Warren for me. I think Warren would have gotten revenge, given the opportunity. Now he lacks anything but normal human functioning. His Druid powers were reduced to . . ." She stifled a laugh.

"What?"

"Well . . . he, um, knits well. Very well. And constantly. He's obsessed with it."

Tremayne looked bemused.

"Dad just channeled Warren's powers and gave them an un-wavering focus. Then he drove him to a craft shop and dropped him at the door. I like to picture him unshaven, sleeping on park benches and knitting while the pigeons watch." She smiled. "Maybe a strand of yarn trailing from an unmarked paper bag to his knitting needles. Anyway, I haven't heard from him since, but I understand he knits a mean cable."

Tremayne tipped his head to the side. "I'm not fond of your father. But I am glad he took care of you in that case."

Daphne nodded.

He moved closer. "I'm not Warren."

"That remains to be seen. You've already proven your ability to render me powerless on a magical level. What else can you do to me? How far are you willing to go to get what you want?" She shrugged. "Everybody has an agenda."

"That's probably true. But for what it's worth, I don't have a 'hair-trigger libido,' as you phrased it. It's you that sets it off, not anything you can do for me or anything I might want from you. In fact, if anything, I have the patience of a saint. Two thousand years, remember? A man who lives that long thinks nothing of waiting just a little while longer for what he wants. I'm used to waiting."

"Spoken like a guy who thinks he *will* eventually get what he wants." She tried to sound cool. Composed. How did a girl reclaim her composure after shifting into a cat in front of a man?

"Composure isn't everything. And you've lost nothing at all in my eyes by shifting to and from cat form. If anything, it's been fascinating. I've learned more about you now than—"

"Than in all the months you've been trailing my parents and me?" She backed up to put distance between them. "With the intent of possibly eliminating us? Great. Just gives me warm fuzzies all over." When he opened his mouth to respond, she grimaced at the roguish glint in his eyes. "And that was *not* a setup for a kitty-cat punch line."

Chapter Six

It was less than seventy-two hours since Daphne had tried to board a plane. Seventy-two very long hours of nonstop . . . stopping. Tremayne had suggested a temporary breather from shifting and magic, a chance for her to settle in, get over her trauma, let her powers return to equilibrium, and blah, blah, blah. So, okay, she wasn't eager to get started again. But in the meantime she was bored out of her mind, while Tremayne stared at his new television set, watching, of all things, *soap operas*? She'd already unpacked, packed and unpacked her suitcase, undecided whether she was better off mobile or settled. Then she'd reluctantly seated herself in a hard metal chair next to Tremayne's hard metal chair and stared at the shiny new television set propped on the kitchen counter. It was pathetic.

"Tremayne." When he didn't respond, she raised her voice. "Tremayne!"

"Hmmm?" He didn't look away from the screen as drama ensued between tender husband and tortured wife.

"Is this all you do?"

With obvious reluctance, Tremayne shifted his gaze from the couple rapidly undressing on the television screen and focused on Daphne. "What do you mean?"

"To occupy yourself. On an ordinary day—just any plain-vanilla Tuesday, for example—what the hell would you do with yourself? Don't you have a purpose? Obligations? Hobbies? Bad habits? Anything?" Hell, the television set was even new. What did he do before that purchase? Daydream?

God. What would *she* do now? Every waking moment of

recent memory, she'd had goals, and a to-do list longer than her arm. Now she had nothing. No purpose other than taking her next breath and exhaling without scrambling her brains. Not killing people? Also on her to-do list. But this was all passive stuff, nothing active about any of it.

Daphne was an active girl. She liked to race toward her goals, not wait for them to shyly approach her. This twiddling-thumbs thing was for the birds.

"Of course I have goals and purpose. That's the only reason I exist—to fulfill my purpose."

She groaned. "Right. To contain the puca powers. Oh, and then there's the ever-popular killing me if I go rabid dog on you. But don't you do anything just for yourself? How the hell do you occupy yourself? You know, just in a mundane way." She glanced at the TV. "Yeah. Soaps. I get it." She reached past his nose to switch it off, to his obvious puzzlement. "You're a true addict, but these shows go off the air at some point. You have to have some other focus in life. Right?"

Leaning back in his chair, Tremayne frowned. "I really only have the one focus. It's mind-numbing to you, I'm sure, but it's all I have. My hope is that there will be something after all of this that will compensate me for my trouble. Something that will truly content me." Then he blinked and said no more.

Ah, but she'd almost gotten somewhere with that question. She sensed further questions might provide illumination. So. How to make the guy talk? Butter him up, naturally. With food, of course.

"How about some popcorn to go with this conversation?"

He looked startled. "Popcorn? Does popcorn make you think?"

"It gives me something to munch on, which yes, does make the thinking go a little more smoothly. Besides, I saw some in the cabinet earlier. It made me covetous." So saying, she strode into the kitchen, located the box, looking lonely on a nearly bare shelf, and pulled out a packet. Less than five minutes later, she was pouring the warm fluff of salty, buttery crunch into a bowl.

She motioned for a curious Tremayne to follow her into his

living room. There she paused before a metal chair. Her butt threatened mutiny; it had seen too many hours in the damn thing.

"You know, furniture would really improve this place. Do you have extra pillows? Or a thick blanket? Just something friendlier and less butt numbing than hard floor or these metal chairs."

He looked nonplussed but pointed to a closet. "I had a hard time finding exactly the right bed pillows. The rejected ones are in there. Would they work?"

No furniture, but rejected bed pillows? Curiouser and curiouser. She opened the closet door he'd indicated, and stared in awe at more than half a dozen pillows, each encased in satin and apparently discarded anyway. "If that doesn't beg a question, I don't know what does."

"What question?" he asked.

"A few, actually. Like, why so picky, and why leave the pillowcase on each pillow when you toss it in the closet? Do you have a supply of dozens? All in brown satin?"

He shrugged with deceptive casualness. "I've been looking for exactly the right pillow. I've tried all these, but they didn't seem right. Still, I might change my mind in the middle of the night and I wanted them all to be accessible."

She was still missing something. "Do you have back problems?" That sounded like one very weird question to ask a magical being.

"No." Ducking, he reached past her into the closet and filled his arms with pillows.

"Then what?" She backed up, letting him past her, before shutting the door of the now-empty closet. "What is so important about having the perfect pillow and being able to grab another on a whim?" She followed him into the living room.

He seemed to debate his response a moment before replying bluntly. "I couldn't sleep before. Now I can. And I like it."

She tipped her head to the side, fascinated to watch his eyes glaze over with something approaching lust just at the thought of sleep. *Look out, Mr. Sandman. Something kinky your way cometh.* Evidently satisfied with his answer, Tremayne dumped the pillows on the floor. He dropped to his haunches to awkwardly arrange them in a love seat–sized space against the wall. As he did, Daphne couldn't help admiring the way his jeans gapped low at the waist, pulling the T-shirt taut across the muscles of his back. All served to emphasize a supremely tight butt, lean waist and some amazing V action widening to mouthwatering shoulders. Oh, to be Mr. Sandman.

"So, why couldn't you sleep before?"

After surveying his work, he straightened and glanced at her. "My duties dictated that I always be vigilant. That I never relax my guard over the puca."

"You mean you served as puca jailer 24-7? Literally? As in, no sleep for two millennia?" Now that would make for one trigger-happy guard. She pictured a cartoon of an exhausted nature spirit, eyes bloodshot and every nerve ending on jittery edge. "And they think *I'm* the one who'll go postal?"

"I'm not human, Daphne. My need for rest isn't like yours."

"You don't need sleep?"

"No. I just enjoy it. I used to crave sleep, even though I barely remembered it as a luxury I couldn't afford. And now, now that Riordan is free and no longer in need of constant vigilance . . . I can sleep. I crawl into bed after the sun goes down and I sleep. Every night." The idea seemed to both delight and amaze him.

She shook her head. "I had no idea."

His smile was sheepish, and all the more appealing because of it. "I like to turn in early now. And sleep late. Getting up before dawn to tail your father on his clandestine outings really annoyed the hell out of me."

"I'll bet," she replied.

"But it was, I thought, a chance to gain something even better than sleep. Total freedom." He gave her a pointed look.

"And that was to be the compensation you mentioned. The thing that would truly content you."

He nodded.

"You almost had it that morning in the grove. A near miss at freedom for you and for me." She nodded slowly in return. "You have my sympathies. It still pisses me off that you're serving as my probation officer, but given the circumstances . . . I imagine if I spent two thousand years wishing for what I couldn't have, followed by nearly getting it and then losing out, I'd be feeling a little violent. I guess I should be grateful you didn't eliminate me when you had the chance."

"I wouldn't do that." He looked affronted.

"Lucky for me, then. So, what about food?"

"What about it?"

"Just . . ." She waved her hands around as though to shape her question. "Did you eat it? Our food, your food, any kind of food? Being a nature spirit and all, I mean. And trapped inside that cornerstone?"

"No, I just sucked the blood of mosquitoes." He gave her a droll look. "Yes, I eat it, then and now. As often as I can, in fact."

"So you weren't deprived as Riordan was."

"Yes. And no." He shrugged, his expression sobering a bit. "When I was in the cornerstone, I ate occasionally, but it was . . . well, the magical equivalent of military rations, I guess. Nothing tasty or fresh. But now that I'm here, fully a part of your world, I've had a chance to realize what I've been missing." He regarded her eagerly. "Do you cook?" They'd been subsisting on fast food and simple sandwiches until now—whatever the delivery guys would bring them in answer to a phone call.

"Can I make anything beyond toast, popcorn and scrambled eggs? Nope. Not even a little. Sorry, buddy, but you cannot sweet-talk, bribe or blackmail me into chef duty. Wouldn't be worth your while any more than it's worth mine."

"So, I guess it's popcorn then, huh?" He eyed the warm fluff with mild interest.

"Orville's best, apparently." She dropped to a knee and, still holding the bowl, wiggled onto the pile of satin-covered pillows.

Once she'd settled herself, Tremayne easily dropped down next to her. Honestly, she felt as if she were reclining in some decadent trysting place to get kinky with a hot nature spirit and a bowl of popcorn. Which was not unlike a dream she'd enjoyed the night before. Her gaze slid past an obviously muscular thigh hugged so lovingly by soft denim—

Time to abandon *that* train of thought. "So, what's it like to live for two thousand years? Aren't you, I don't know, tired of the world or anything? Don't you get bored?" Passing him the bowl of popcorn, Daphne eyed him with honest curiosity.

Tremayne accepted the bowl and carefully selected a perfectly popped kernel. "I was . . . bored before. There really hasn't been much to my life until recently. I was caged with the puca, simply existing. Absorbing, you might say."

"Absorbing what?"

"Words, the experiences of people and animals nearby. I couldn't do what they did, but I could observe and wish. I did a lot of wishing."

"Were you—and this sounds really stupid, but, well—a physical presence? Or were you just . . . abstract. Noncorporeal. Like Riordan was."

"I was a spirit. No body. Senses, yes, but nothing solid."

"Until?"

Tremayne met her eyes, his own dark with emotion. "Until Riordan busted free. When he was loosed, so was I."

Daphne stared. "Just like that? Poof, you get a body?"

"No, I was still a spirit at first. But soon, soon there was more. Like wind picking up dust and mist and energy. . . . You might have experienced me as a ghost early on. The change was gradual, so I wasn't aware it was happening at first." He laughed, his eyes distant with rueful memory. "But then I started bumping into things."

"Instead of going through them?" Trying to picture it was impossible. She couldn't. To be *not* there . . . and then *there*.

"Exactly. And if you thought learning to shape-shift was disorienting, try taking on a physical body for the first time." He frowned. "And other things, too. I didn't have a personal reaction at all when Akker summoned me. I just responded and obeyed. After I was loosed . . . I felt something hot inside of me. Very hard to contain. An energy that wanted to lash out."

"You were angry, you mean?"

He nodded slowly. "That's what I've decided. I was angry."

"Are you still?"

"Probably. But not like I was. Once I had a name for it and an explanation, I could focus better. Instead of concentrating on lashing out, I turned the energy to seeking my freedom. Once and for all. If the spirit somehow grew a body and emotions, isn't he alive? Shouldn't he be allowed a chance at life?"

"Ooh, you're like Data in *Star Trek* . . ." She blinked. "Um, any experience with television?"

"A lot. Riordan's guardians for the past few decades had television."

She nodded. "That explains why you sound like you're from this century instead of one of the past twenty or so of them. You sound modern. Almost normal." At his raised eyebrows, she gave him an evil look. "As normal as a nature spirit can sound, anyway."

"Since I'm the one who's been around for over two thousand years and you're barely a blink in history yet, I think I'm the standard and you're the quirk. *I'm* normal. Makes a lot more sense than the reverse." When she sputtered, torn between offense and amusement—she was a *quirk*?—he spoke over her, obviously extending an olive branch. "So, television. I recognized the quote from before. It was from *The Wizard of Oz*?"

"Yes." She'd loved that movie as a kid and used to imagine the joy of whirling away in the middle of a cyclone, flying far from everything familiar and landing someplace amazing. Although, frankly, she'd always considered Dorothy a little shortsighted. The girl never once appreciated the wonders of Oz, never stopped to explore, just wanted to leave her new friends to get back to her stifling little cornfield where everybody told her what to do. In her place, Daphne would have explored her new world, enjoyed her newfound freedom—and maybe built a more creative, businesslike and effective wizard.

Hell, shortsighted Dorothy would have stayed far away from California.

"But this *Star Trek* . . . Is it a show?"

Apparently Tremayne had been denied Trekkies as guardians.

Poor sprite. Another new world to explore. And it was the best kind of escapism for somebody who felt trapped; there were no boundaries in space, after all. Endless possibilities. "It's kind of a futuristic space-explorer adventure series with some spin-off shows. Anyway, this character Data is a robot trying to be human. He's unexpectedly sweet. Naive, even."

Tremayne's lips quirked. "Sweet? Naive? Ah, yes. Just like me, in fact."

She grinned. "Okay, so maybe a little different. You seem a lot more worldly—and a lot less than sweet—but are on a similar quest. You're seeking life as an individual. Right?"

He nodded slowly. "Yes." Then, seeming to lose himself in thought, he grabbed a handful of popcorn.

Daphne pushed onward. There were many more questions to ask. "So, you went from a purely spiritual form to a physical one sometime in the last few months? And here you are clothed, renting an apartment, and apparently with money to spend. How?"

He shrugged. "It's not that I didn't know about these necessities and how to attain them. I've been eavesdropping on the human world for a long time now."

"But what about resources? Cash. Identity. People generally produce paper trails from birth. But you were born a grown man—sort of—and in need of grown-man necessities, many of which required a supply of cash. How did you get your money? Did you flip burgers? Poof cash out of thin air?"

"No burger-flipping. I don't know how to cook yet." He frowned. "As for cash and documents"—he shrugged—"I conjured what I couldn't legitimately produce."

"Well, that's about as clear as mud. What could you conjure that would fill an immediate need for cash? Cash itself?"

He smiled a little. "You want a demonstration?"

"Sure." Who wouldn't? "What kind of magic does a nature spirit have, anyway?"

Tremayne shrugged. "Depends on the nature spirit. This particular trick came in handy for me." He closed his hand into a fist, eyelids drifting nearly closed, then opened his fist and looked at her.

Daphne goggled. "Are those real? Like, *really* real?" She reached a hand to poke with one finger at the contents of his palm. A rainbow of pure light glittered back at her as a faceted gem rocked gently.

"Diamonds? Of course." He looked offended. "I wouldn't pawn a fake gem. That's illegal. I know that much."

"But where did they come from? Did you steal them off some woman's wedding band? A necklace?"

He frowned down at the sparklies. "No. From a diamond mine. It's still of the earth that way, and less easily missed. Not that I can keep doing it forever. People would notice if a mine went dry after a while."

Her lips twitched as she looked up at him. "So you conjure gems and pawn them for cash?" So, essentially, he performed magic tricks for coin. That was . . . too funny. She wondered if he played the shell game, too.

"Yes, usually gems. Sometimes gold. It seemed simplest."

"Amazing." She absently reached for some popcorn. "You know, with a party trick like that, you would be a major hit with the ladies."

He nodded, his thoughts obviously drifting elsewhere as he pocketed the gems. "I should look into another source of income, though, so I don't have to rely exclusively on magic. When you conjure valuables, you end up with some of those paper-trail problems you mentioned."

"So you'll need a career." She munched thoughtfully on more popcorn.

"Yes. After you're set on your course, that is. I'll need to make my way in life, once I've retired from duty to Akker."

"Hmm," she mused. "Must be strange to work for a dead guy."

"It can get complicated." He gave her an ironic look. "Especially since the rules seemed to change as much as I did."

"Do you suppose Akker planned for this to happen to you? That you would change?"

Tremayne shrugged. "It's possible that it was a contingency plan. He had a lot of them."

"You were a contingency plan? Now *that's* humbling. And arrogant of him. Very arrogant."

"You and I think so. But he would have seen it as his right. I was a tool summoned in anger to exact his revenge."

"Sounds like a nice guy."

Tremayne nodded. "Your father is like him in some ways. Genetics, I suppose."

She started. "Genetics. You're right. I guess I'd forgotten. Akker was some kind of ancestor of ours."

"Yes." Tremayne eyed her speculatively.

"Is that good or bad?"

"He was another man driven beyond rage to madness. Misused power to harm innocents."

"Ahhhh. Yet more evidence that I, too, might one day be drooling in the corner—if not flying into homicidal rages." Recalling her recent tantrum as a goat, Daphne set the popcorn down, her appetite gone. Maybe they were right. Maybe she was doomed. "I really, *really* wish I hadn't followed my father to the grove. Or that I had set my foot just six inches to the left or right, anywhere that would have left me free of these powers. You know, it's not like I *want* to go insane."

Tremayne didn't reply.

"You know what I'd dearly love right now? A do-over. You know, just rewind to the time when I, on a stupid whim, took my dad's journals out that last time. Just because I saw him writing in them didn't mean I had to find out what he wrote. I should have just let it go."

Tremayne assessed her. "I don't think you do wish that. Knowing your father and what he's written before, you couldn't ignore a new entry. You would have considered it irresponsible."

"Why? They were his personal journals. I had no business sticking my nose in them." She avoided the nature spirit's eyes.

"But you knew the subject matter. Pucas. Knew it was important to the half sister you say you claim, and the new friends you'd made. And you suspected your father might hurt them.

What if he'd recorded his intentions in those journals? That's what you suspected, isn't it? You had to look."

She scowled. "Maybe. But I didn't have to follow him."

He smiled. "Yes, you did."

"Much good it did. They didn't need me. I was little more than an eavesdropper by that point. They'd figured everything out on their own without my input."

"But you couldn't know that would happen. Morally, you were constrained to follow him. As for the rest—the foot positioned exactly so, the cornerstone striking exactly there and then—I believe none of this was coincidence. It was fate. There is a reason you have these powers."

"Is that what it is?" Daphne murmured, finally seriously considering the idea. Maybe the Druids were on to something after all. "So I would have some kind of purpose, like you said earlier. Something bigger than a new career or new home. And that's why I was the one who ended up with the powers instead of somebody else."

"The Druids seem to think so."

"Well, not all of them. I'm pretty sure my father didn't care about a larger purpose when he went after the powers, only about his own uses for them."

"No wonder your father was unseated as High Druid. Apparently he makes a regular practice of violating the basic tenets of Truth and Justice."

She blinked at the formality of his words, could practically see Tremayne capitalizing them in his mind. "You believe in those tenets, too."

"Doesn't everyone? Or, rather, *shouldn't* everyone?"

"Two thousand years old and still idealistic. I am impressed." Gran would have been, too. "They made nature spirits with sturdy moral fiber, didn't they?" She studied him a moment. "But, tell me. Now that you have a physical form and probably a few human failings to go with that very human-seeming body, how do you think those tenets of yours will fare?" She eyed him with curiosity, was surprised to see his lips twist.

"That's an excellent question." He raised his eyebrows. "Sort of . . . 'the spirit is willing, but the flesh is weak'?" She saw laughter in his eyes, and he bent closer and—

"Oh, don't." She slid the popcorn bowl between them. "That is just Cracker Jack–box trite, Mr. Nature Spirit. Eat some popcorn and tell your spirit self to pipe down. This human's got a headache for . . . oh, eternity." Even if the weak flesh in question was both ripped and mouthwatering.

The wicked humor in his eyes made her groan. "I need to stop with the whole projecting thing."

"Not on my account you don't. I'm kind of partial to it, if you want the truth."

"Yeah, yeah, Truth is one of those precious tenets. Give me a break, buddy. You're holding all the cards. It's not fair."

"Not all the cards. You're the one with the mind-reading ability, not me. Perhaps you'd like to learn to control it?"

"Well, I already said I'd like to learn how to avoid projecting my thoughts. Is that all tied together?"

"Sure. Sending thoughts, reading thoughts. Same path, different degrees of difficulty." He paused. "But understand first that just because you can mindwalk doesn't mean that you always should. Or that you can walk through just anyone's mind."

"Like, not a two-thousand-year-old nature spirit's mind, just to toss out a random example?" She wondered if he was giving her a warning, or a simple statement of fact.

He glanced at her. "Good example. I already have centuries of experience living with a puca. I know how the ability works and I know how to block it."

That didn't exactly answer her concerns. She lowered her lashes and asked, "Always?"

He raised his eyebrows pointedly. "Well, maybe not always. Perhaps I will rely on your integrity at certain times. If I can."

She scowled at his implication. It wasn't as if she'd really try to read his mind. Even if she wondered at the possibility of it. She was just curious. What woman would pass up the opportunity to be able to read a guy's mind? "I wouldn't do it. It's not like I'm a Peeping Tom by nature."

He shook his head. "Curiosity, desire for titillation . . . Both are weaknesses for many. Humans are fallible."

"Unlike nature spirits." She gave him a snide look.

He grinned. "I never once claimed perfection. You're the one who thought I was perfect. Mouthwatering, too."

"And I'm mortified. Can we just get on with this now? How do I read minds? This could be interesting. I'd love to be able to get inside my parents' brains and—"

Tremayne was already shaking his head. "I should have known that's who you'd try. Unfortunately, Druids have an effective block against puca mindwalking. You would have a hard time penetrating."

"Hard but not impossible?"

He shrugged. "And then the integrity part kicks in, if you're trying to break intentionally set-up protections."

"So when *can* I use this ability, if not then? We both know my parents have enough secret tricks up their sleeves that I could do a world of good by picking out just a few."

Tremayne nodded. "That may be true, but I don't recommend embarking on a mindwalk without a refined purpose. Mindwalking in search of a purpose to justify the mindwalking . . . Do you see the karmic danger?"

"Maybe in some cases, but—"

He raised his eyebrows. "You concern me. Let me just be clear on this one. In the case of a mindwalk, the end has to justify the means, or the blow to karma can be devastating. You don't invade a mind lightly unless you're invited."

She gave him a sour look. "All right, all right. For the record, I'd be gambling on a sure thing by walking through my parents' heads. That kind of end would justify all kinds of means. But just to make your eliminator heart all soft and squishy, I'll resist. Happy?"

"Ecstatic." His tone and expression were blank.

"So, tell me. How do I do it?"

"It's actually part of what those of the faerie world call a glamour. You can ease your way past human defenses, discover their thoughts and . . ." He paused. "You can manipulate them if karma dictates such is the right thing to do."

Daphne raised her eyebrows. "Not just read but also *manipulate* other people's thoughts?"

"Yes."

"So there are faeries wandering around brainwashing people even as we speak?" Her words came out as a squeak. "That's creepy! What happened to integrity? Ethics? And you want me to do it? I don't want to brainwash people. Well, it might be fun to convince Ted Bundy types that serial killing is wrong, but that's one of the rare instances."

"I'm glad you feel that way. I mean, I'd really hate it if you tried to brainwash me into seducing you." His voice was flat. "I wouldn't have any choice except to obey. Probably a few times, in fact. And then I'd feel so . . . used."

"Oh, gag." She managed to control her grin, as he was clearly joking, but she couldn't help the flush rising along her neck. And the heat in other parts of her body.

One corner of his mouth quirked up. "It would be an unethical use of your power. I'd have to . . . intervene," he continued.

"Gee. I'll keep that in mind and try to resist." She shook her head. She was pretty sure what his intervention would consist of. More of the same.

He tapped a finger against his jaw, thoughtful. "But, if the thought was already there to begin with . . . well, that's a different story. I mean, if my intent was to seduce you anyway, and you just happened to read that intent . . ."

She gave him an innocent look. "But I'm not supposed to read minds without probable cause. That's what you said." Oh, now she'd done it. Flirting with this man? Bad Daphne. Especially since she'd already rebuffed his advances.

He didn't seem to take anything amiss. "Any time you need probable cause, you just let me know," he said. His voice was low and rich, like the softest suede half clinging to, half stroking her skin. "I can provide plenty."

She bit her lip, unable to help herself. "And what exactly

would I find if I walked around in your thoughts? Dirty stuff, I'll bet." She hoped.

"Oh, very dirty. Are you curious? Some of it's about you." That grin flashed again and he leaned subtly closer. "Come see."

Reading the challenge in his expression, along with the provocation, she narrowed her eyes. "You're seriously inviting me into your mind?"

"That's what I said."

Teasing and flirtation aside—and she was *so* bad—the idea of walking around in his thoughts still felt weird and creepy and intrusive, even if she did have permission. She felt as if she should protect his boundaries for him, except . . . he obviously knew what he was risking, and he was okay with that.

She also had to admit to some of that lurid curiosity he'd mentioned. He was so handsome, so mysterious; she wouldn't mind wandering around in this nature spirit's head to see how he was put together. But, no, it wasn't all because she was curious about some of that dirty stuff as it related to her in particular. A smart girl just didn't turn down info when it was offered so freely. That was reasonable, right?

"Okay. What do I do? How do I do it?"

He smiled at her demand. "You're going to hate this."

She gave him a sour look. "Why? Because I told you I didn't approve? Well, I approve if I have permission and you just told me I could take a walk all over your mind. Sounds like a short trip to me, but hey, as long as I have permission, why not?"

"I'm hurt."

"I doubt it." She folded her arms. "So, tell me how it works. What do I do?"

"That's just it. You don't 'do' anything. At least, nothing active or aggressive. That's why I think you're going to hate this. You have to be . . . well, actively passive, if that makes sense. Not just neutral, but almost a vacuum."

"Great. We're back to speaking in paradoxes. This is so exciting."

He sighed in mock disappointment. "And here I thought you were ready to be open-minded."

"If I took even a baby step toward open-minded, you'd be all over me," she said without thinking.

He conceded. "True. But this time you really do need to concentrate on literally opening your mind to pick up on what's already there. You would be a receptor, which, by definition, is a passive role. It's easier to read some people than others. Some instinctively bury their thoughts, so you have to move in a little closer . . . but very delicately, so the thoughts don't burrow even deeper." He demonstrated as he spoke.

"Oooh, like shy wood ticks. Fun. So are yours going to be the right-out-there type or the wood-tick type?"

"I can put mine anywhere I like," he said, smiling at her. "With practice, you can learn to do this, too. You'll be able to consciously keep some thoughts front and center and hide others. Learning to better protect your thoughts is a necessary precaution, if you're existing among magicky types."

She sighed. "It sounds exhausting."

"It becomes second nature after you get better at it. And, if you're going to be hanging out with the likes of faerie royals Oberon and Titania—or any magicky type—you need these defenses or you're completely vulnerable to them. Your mind, your intent, your secrets, all are theirs if you're careless enough to project them. With practice, you can defend yourself better."

Completely vulnerable, no secrets, no privacy . . . what had she projected at the grove? What did she project to Tremayne every day that she lived with him? The very idea . . . if she considered it too long. "Okay. I see your point. So tell me. What does *actively passive* mean, anyway? Hurry up and wait?"

"First we'll do the overview. There's thought projection, mind reading and glamouring. You should be capable of all of these. You already project subconsciously. We'll skip that for now, because once you master mind reading and glamouring, you'll understand thought projection as the intermediary step and know how to control it as well. Doesn't mean you'll have total control of it, especially when you're still learning, and at times of stress or while sleeping, but you'll know the mechanics well enough to perfect it on your own. So. Mind reading."

She raised an index finger. "Um . . . question?"

"What?"

"Okay, I get projecting and mind reading—I think—but how does glamouring work into all of this?"

"You're replacing or manipulating somebody else's thoughts by imposing your own thoughts over theirs. You don't necessarily have to read the person's thoughts to impose your own, but it's a more difficult skill to master."

She regarded him with alarm. "Can you do it?"

"No. It's a puca power."

Thank god.

"And you projected that."

"Shut up."

He laughed. "So. You can practice mind reading on me. I'll make myself about as vulnerable as a normal human. Doesn't mean I'll give up all my thoughts, so don't get too excited, but"—his dark eyes gleamed—"I'll make some of them reasonably available. Reasonable for your average human. Deal?"

She stared at him, amused. "Not all of them, huh? Scared I'll see something while I'm in there?"

"Petrified." He flashed her another grin, seemingly unfazed. "Hence the barriers."

"Okay. Give me the instructions. I'm ready." And, to be perfectly honest, she was relieved that he did have defenses and that this really was just harmless practice. She didn't intend to ever use the skill if she could help it, anyway. She just wasn't that kind of person.

"It helps to make direct eye contact. Thanks to the puca powers, when you make focused and prolonged eye contact, you'll present a natural, almost irresistible attraction for the other person's attention. They'll want to keep looking at you. Humans will be unaware of this and mostly undisturbed by it, but still susceptible. Wielders of magic and those familiar with the glamour will be more able to fight it.

"So. Eye contact. Wait for the pupils to widen. This is a

relaxing of barriers, as the attraction distracts and disarms. You'll feel a give, almost a vacuum. You'll just let it draw you in and observe what you see and hear. Naturally, you'll have to tune out the physical world as you do this. Sometimes that's easier said than done."

She nodded slowly.

"Ready to give it a try?"

She made a face. "No, but I will."

"So much for an open mind," he snorted.

"Just a joke. So. Let's do this. Before I think about it too much."

Shoving the popcorn aside, he tugged her to sit facing him.

"Do you feel the pull of my unholy attraction?" she couldn't help but murmur.

"Every second of every minute of every hour of every day."

She blinked, unprepared for this particular deadpan—almost serious?—response. Then, heart pounding, she deliberately labeled it a joke and set it aside. "Excellent." She looked into his eyes. The pupils really did enlarge. Wow.

"Just calm yourself," he murmured. "Let everything you see and hear go unfocused. Blurry visuals, white noise in the background. Now you'll do the rest while I stay silent."

She kept her focus on his eyes, let everything else dim and soften. Deep black eyes, so seductive in themselves, drawing her in every bit as much as she drew him. She could feel the pull, sensed something beyond. A connection. Layers. Boundaries hastily drawn and retracted.

Then, nothing. She blinked. It was gone. Even his pupils had contracted again.

"Anything?" He regarded her curiously.

"I'm not sure. I could sense . . . a structure. Sort of. I think . . . I think I could grasp what you were talking about. But as for actual thoughts, no. Nothing yet."

He nodded. "That's a good start. If you remember that structure—and, yes, it really exists—you can decide where to set your own thoughts. Don't shove them out in front of the structure. Find another spot for them. They won't find their way over to me if you keep them penned inside." He smiled. "Which kind of stinks for me. I'll miss being able to hear them."

"That makes one of us." She gave him a wry look. Lord, she couldn't help it, she had to ask. "You said you made some thoughts available to me and hid away others. Which ones did you make available?" The look in his eyes when he'd said that . . . she wanted to know. She wished she didn't want to know, but she did. "Did you just make something up?"

"No. I picked around and chose some thoughts I didn't mind you knowing."

"Like?"

"Like, how important it is for you to learn these skills."

"Oh, great. Like cracking the code on a boring instruction manual." She rolled her eyes. "Not exactly incentive to keep poking around."

"Maybe there were a few other things, too." He grinned at her.

"Like?"

"Well . . . you might have discovered that I've been fascinated with you since I first saw you. Months ago." His gaze was distant now. "I was after the cornerstone, and I suspected your parents had it, so I watched them. And you. Increasingly, it was hard to stop watching you long enough to keep an eye on them.

"Everywhere I looked, there you were, often one step ahead of me. You were spying on your father, subtly blocking some of his efforts. Aware of your mother's covert activities and secretly foiling some of those, too. Confusing me. And obviously objecting to what they were doing but feeling loyal enough to protect them as long as you could. They didn't deserve it. You humbled and fascinated me."

He seemed almost brooding now. "It was inevitable that they would disappoint you and I would then have to hurt you. I knew one or both of them intended to use the puca powers for selfish or destructive intent. And it was my job to deliver justice."

Remembering past encounters and their implications, Daphne found herself suddenly cold. "Yeah, about that. You being so certain one of my parents was responsible for the cornerstone disappearing. As it turns out, you were right. But what kind of justice were you considering before others intervened?" It seemed a pertinent question.

Grimacing, he pulled back. "You already know."

"I suspected. Death?"

He shrugged. "Only as a last resort. As it turns out, there was no need to kill anyone."

"But you were willing?"

"Yes."

"Well." She gave him a tight smile. "Ask a loaded question. Answer's bound to do damage, right?"

"Would you rather I lie to you?"

Her smile faded. "No. I guess not. At the very least, I've come to expect honesty from you. And likely more information than I can handle. But not lies. Not disinformation." She studied him, saw as his features grew expressionless, and suddenly felt cold. "Or maybe not even that." How could she have dropped her guard? Of course her potential eliminator was prepared to lie to her. Probably *had* lied already.

"I don't want to lie to you. And I will be honest whenever possible." He met her eyes. "But I can't promise full disclosure, given my duty. There will be secrets. And that's as honest as I know how to be. Does that work for you?"

"Not really." She abandoned the popcorn and rolled to her feet. "Guess I'll go to bed now. Nice getting to know you better, nature spirit." *Or not.*

The flicker of his lashes as he winced proved he'd heard her last two unspoken words. Fine. She'd intended him to. Projection should work to her advantage at least occasionally, shouldn't it?

Chapter Seven

Daphne wasn't pouting so much as she was productively panicking. Obsessively analyzing. Okay, so what she was really doing was childishly hiding in the extra bedroom to avoid facing her eliminator and memories of her own stupidity. She must be twisted! There was no other explanation for the fact that she'd been flirting with Tremayne so blatantly yesterday.

How could a man who claimed to be fascinated with a woman almost in the same breath admit he might have to kill her? Could he really do that, as he'd been prepared to do to her parents? And, knowing all of that, how could she still be so attracted to him? Maybe the Druids had a point about her possible insanity.

Oh, and if she weren't there already, she knew what would send her careening down the road to Nutsville. The Druids expected her to learn how to control all of her powers.

She closed her eyes, remembering the feeling of total vulnerability, total helplessness, that she'd experienced with every shape-shift. And now, to repeat that experience, over and over, with Tremayne, allegedly the only person who could help her? Just the idea made her stomach heave. There had to be another way.

Maybe she could skip practice altogether if she promised never to shift again. She'd live an emotionally monotonous life, avoiding joy, terror, rage, sex, all of the extremes, in favor of perpetual tedium. Total emotional management. There must be some class she could take, Extreme Yoga for Bland Living, or something. Now there was quality of life for you.

The ringing of her cell phone interrupted her neurotic mental blathering. Desperate enough even for *this*, she answered. She'd been avoiding it for days. "Hello, Mother."

"Daphne. Thank god. My detective said he saw you go with that Tremayne creature. Tell me you're not staying with him."

"Your detective found me? You had your own daughter followed?" Like she needed that suspicion confirmed.

"Well, I was worried. It's been almost four days since your father or I heard from you. Your old apartment phone number is disconnected. I tried calling your new number in California, but you didn't answer, and I've left dozens of messages on this one."

"How did you get my new number? I haven't given it to you yet." Daphne fumed. It was just this kind of thing that always left her feeling furious and violated and helpless. Could her parents not observe a single boundary?

"I have resources. And you *are* my daughter. I couldn't see you move all the way across the country with no other way of contacting you than a cell phone."

What did *that* mean? Her mother didn't think she could interfere with Daphne's new life, did she? Of course she did.

"So I could only assume that the Druids refused to allow you to leave town. That's what I would do in their place." Daphne could hear the shrug in her mother's voice, along with irritation. It was likely an annoyance that Daphne was under High Druid Phil's thumb instead of Violet's.

"I'll bet."

"That was uncalled for," her mother complained.

"Um, no. It was *very* called for. I'm an adult. You do realize this, don't you? If I choose to move to a new city and take a perfectly legal—not to mention plum—job somewhere other than at Mommy and Daddy's firm, that's my right and my business."

"Of course, dear. But since you're here and not there, why not come back to us in the meantime?"

Oh, there were so many reasons. Like, it had taken all the resolve and fury she could muster just to leave the first time. Where would she find additional reserves to do it a second? Maybe her cat form had some? Or maybe the goat.

"It doesn't have to be a lifetime commitment," her mother was saying. "Just . . . show up. We'll talk. Maybe we can work something out. That's reasonable, don't you think? Negotiation between adults, equal compromise on both our parts. Surely you can grant me that!"

"Mom—"

"Just to chat, then. I will miss you when you're gone. You *are*"—Violet Forbes's voice lowered as she deployed an oldie but goodie—"my only child. The only one I'll ever have. Forgive me for not wanting you to leave on such a bad note. Please. Let's just talk. Woman to woman."

Daphne swallowed. When would this stop working on her?

Not today. "Fine. I'll be there in an hour. But we're just talking," she warned.

"I'll see you then."

Already regretting the concession, Daphne flipped her phone closed. Would she—*could* she—really go back to work for her parents again? Wouldn't that be like sealing her own doom? She was caught up in this adolescent cycle that left her kicking herself and humiliated. They would offend, she would bluster and rebel, and then, out of guilt or a wish to please, she'd go along with whatever they wanted. With anyone else she could state her position calmly and stick to it. With her parents, everything just seemed to stack up against her.

But what else would she do if she didn't go back to her job—spend 24-7 grunting and sweating and proving over and over again that she couldn't willingly morph into an animal? That's how it would be. Some life. When she thought of her life now and the plans she'd been forced to forfeit, thanks to a single encounter in a Druid grove she'd spent most of her life avoiding . . . California seemed like a distant dream now. She knew she had a week, tops, before her new employers rescinded their offer. And then there was that issue of income and paying her own way in life. Relying on a bossy nature spirit for room and board, basically every necessity in life, was galling for any woman who prized her independence. After she endured the fun chat with her parents, perhaps she should start networking again, pursue some new prospects.

Sighing, she stood up. She'd have to change clothes; no way would she be able to meet her mother on equal ground while wearing pink polka-dotted pajama bottoms with a purple tank top, even if they were comfy. So, what then? Not business wear. She was not silently committing to anything with her clothing choices.

With that thought, she pulled out a nice—but not professional!—pair of khaki slacks. She started to remove, but then on second thought retained, the purple tank. Then she pulled on a trim white cardigan, letting the buttons remain casually open. Funky beads, big hoop earrings. Then . . . heeled mules. Yep. Those shouted "grown, independent woman randomly visiting her mother." Not "professional lackey returning with her lips puckered for butt-kissing."

Okay. Now to face the nature spirit. Grabbing her purse, she opened the bedroom door and found Tremayne lounging on the pillows. They'd left them there on the living room floor. Apparently he considered it an acceptably permanent use for his rejects, and now he reclined in sensual luxury, surrounded by metal folding chairs, and drank a cup of coffee. He should have looked ridiculous. Instead, he looked sexy as hell, his yummy hard body sprawled all over sleek satin and smooth downy fill. The image reminded her of the sumptuous treat of a bed he slept in every night. She could picture him naked on those sheets—

Yep, she was nuts. Shaking off the vision, she stepped briskly forward.

He looked up and surveyed her with interest. "Where are you going?"

Recalled to her errand, she suddenly felt too embarrassed to tell him—as though she'd caved to a weakness. Well, she had, in a way. But still, they were her parents. And she was a grown woman, in no way requiring his permission to visit anyone.

She raised her chin and didn't lie. Well, not really. "For a . . . walk. I'm feeling claustrophobic and I need out of here for a while. I promise to remain calm and unshifting, but I'm going alone."

He nodded slowly. "Do you have your phone on you?"

She gave him a startled look. "Always."

"Good. Call me if you need help. I'm here."

Realizing there was a tiny off chance she might need it, she shot him an annoyed look but nodded. "I'll be back."

Standing just inside the doorway of her mom's office, Daphne gave her parents the evil eye. "For the record, I'm here only out of sheer boredom." And that was the truth. Well, mostly. One more hour bouncing off the same four walls as Tremayne, and she was going to prove the Druids right and go bonkers. Maybe she'd shift into mouse form, chew a hole in the wall and make a home. One with actual furniture, for example, would be cozy.

Either that or she'd give in to her lust and rip Tremayne's clothes off him. Then she'd survey every contour of that ripped body. With her tongue.

"Oh, Daphne, you don't mean that." Violet Forbes rounded her desk, high heels clicking.

Oh, lord, she wished she did. But no, it wasn't the boredom that had made her flee. The apartment practically oozed with sexual tension, and the last thing she needed was to do the mattress mambo with the nature spirit who might decide to eliminate her. There was no coming back from that. There was no coming back from elimination, either.

"You're a Forbes. Period." Violet's tone was no-nonsense as she approached her daughter. She wore a pinstriped navy power suit, a flattering cut appropriate for her age, style and ruthlessly trim figure. Her hair was tinted ash blonde, a tasteful shade or two darker than Daphne's, which had been her natural color before age dulled its strands. Her eyes were a darker blue than Daphne's, and she preferred a higher heel to compensate for her slightly shorter stature. All in all, she was an imposing figure and an attractive counterpart to the aging but often charismatic husband she frequently hated, and who stood ominously behind her desk.

"You belong here," Violet continued. "We know you didn't really want to resign. If it's more money, more autonomy—anything—you should have come to us. There was no need for theatrics." She shook her head in disdain.

Theatrics? She'd typed a resignation herself—a formal document for a family firm—and had hand-delivered it in triplicate. Sure, she knew they'd just dismissed it as an adolescent rebellion, but she'd sort of thought not showing up for work and moving across the country would prove her point. Of course, she hadn't actually gone.

The Druids were worried that it was her newfound magic that would drive her nuts? Her family should have done that long ago.

"But that's all in the past now. We're ready to talk and move forward." Violet smiled.

In other words, they wanted to sweep the past under the rug. Daphne stared out the wall-sized picture window by her mother's desk, hoping the view of the courtyard would siphon away some of her frustration. "Mom—"

"I agree." Duncan cut his daughter off, nodding at his wife's words. "And I'm so glad you're willing to hear us out." He frowned, obviously preparing to recite words he detested but felt necessary. "Daphne, I apologize if my actions and decisions complicated your life. I know these powers"—he cast her a speculative look—"must be difficult to get used to. I have Druid training, you know. My magic has been stripped from me, true." He looked enormously pissed about that. "But I have the training to help you learn control. These powers you have . . . can be very useful if you wield them properly."

"Oh, I'll just bet they can be useful." Daphne scowled at her father. "That's really why you want me here. You want to manipulate me into making these powers useful to you."

"Of course that's not the reason, dear!" Palms outward, Violet patted the air in a soothing manner. "You are my . . . our only child." Her lips compressed as she glared at her husband as the implied words, *only child together, at any rate,* went unspoken. Frankly, Violet had always seemed to resent Duncan's contribution to Daphne's conception, as if she would have much preferred to leave him out of it entirely. "We would never use you and never distress you to such an extent. We want only to help. And my powers have not been stripped. I would be so relieved if you would let me help you with—"

"No," Daphne interrupted, the word yanked straight from her gut. "Just do me a favor and keep your powers and your training to yourself." She glanced from one parent to the other. "Both of you."

Violet folded her hands and her manner cooled—which was much better. "Maternal" and "hovering" looked downright unnatural when projected by one such as Violet Forbes. Although, if there were any one person in the world whom Violet loved as much as herself, it would be her daughter. Her marriage was a disaster fraught with power struggles and Duncan's affairs with both humans and, if hearsay were to be believed, even a faerie or two. Daphne had overheard a few arguments about some woman her mother called a "faerie-queen whore."

"So tell us, Daphne. What are your plans?" her mother inquired. "You know, your job is still here, right where you left it. Now that we're heading into the thick of tax season, we could really use your help. We have clients who are very loyal to you and trust you implicitly. They'll be disappointed to see you leave, too. Mr. Ralston asked about you the other day." Her mother smiled. "He was one of your first clients, you know."

"I know, but—"

"*And* I imagine the normalcy of routine might be a relief for you. Given your new and unusual circumstances."

Daphne winced. Honestly, this was the most persuasive argument her mother could use. Daphne would love nothing better than to run whimpering back to her old job long enough to reclaim her identity, sense of self, blessed normalcy. Maybe she could ditch the memory of fur on her face and claws extending from her paws—She cringed again. Make that, *extremities.* She was not an animal. She didn't have paws. She didn't want paws.

No, all she'd ever wanted was freedom. Instead of getting it, she'd gone from parents wanting to control her career and personal life to oversight, if lackadaisical oversight, by a nature spirit deciding her life or death based on her decisions. It would be stupid to return to the job she'd fought to leave. Violet and Duncan practically salivated over the puca powers Daphne wielded. Long term, she would shrivel up and die in this situation.

But for now? Normalcy? A purpose away from Tremayne and his temptation? The reassurance of steady income and her old, familiar identity? A girl sometimes had to take what she could get. Her parents were, after all, a devil she knew.

Unlike that dark-eyed devil who posed a risk to everything that she was now and hoped to eventually be. Sure, her parents were controlling, but Tremayne could do her a lot more damage. She was growing more vulnerable to him, more drawn to him, more dependent upon him as each hour passed. Time to halt that progress. After all, dependence on a nature spirit poised to eliminate her was more foolhardy than she could acknowledge even silently. Distance in the form of employment might help her regain perspective. "I can start tomorrow. Same job. Same office, which I see you haven't given away. Same terms. But no promises regarding anything beyond the immediate future. I still have a place in California and a job waiting for me." At least for now. Time was running out.

"You're doing *what* tomorrow morning?" Tremayne eyed Daphne with disbelief as she sat down across from him in his living room. He'd restrained himself—with effort—from following her on her walk earlier. Given the goat calamity, she needed him too much to run, so he'd thought he was safe offering this small gesture in the hope of rebuilding a little trust. Talk about backfiring.

"I said I'm going to work. I got my old job back." Daphne shrugged, her casual manner obviously feigned. "That's all."

"But why? It's not as though you need the money. You can stay here for free. Anything you need—food, personal necessities, *anything*—you come to me and I'll provide it." The last thing he needed was Daphne back in her parents' employ. He knew she was particularly vulnerable to their influence. It was a bad influence, he was certain.

Daphne was scowling at him. "Because, damn it, I'm not a child. I can provide for myself and insist on doing so. Besides, I need something to do. Something normal to keep from going nuts. Avoiding insanity *is* one of our agreed-upon goals, isn't it?"

"But, to work for your parents? I thought the new life you want so desperately is based on your need to get away from them."

She shrugged. "Nothing's changed on that front. But my new life has been postponed, and I need something to fill the gap. This will do, with no extra effort on my part. They rehired me, no strings attached. I can quit later without giving notice."

"But they want to *use* you."

"Of course they do," she snapped, a quickly veiled flash of pain in her eyes. "I'm not stupid. I've known Duncan and Violet Forbes my entire life. That makes me an unrivaled expert on the Forbes family method of manipulation. I know how to handle them."

Not likely. He'd yet to see her handle them capably. "But that's just it. If you know them so well, know what their intentions are, why wouldn't you find something else, *anything* else, to occupy your time? I know you could find temporary work with someone who wants nothing but your business skills and a decent job performance. Why would you take this risk?" He was incredulous. And he was feeling that damn tightness in his chest again. Different this time, though. It wasn't guilt. It was . . . fear? But not for himself. For her. And it wasn't objective concern over a potentially bad outcome, but a painful, personal discomfort over the idea of someone hurting Daphne in any way.

Daphne gave him a fierce look. "It's no risk. It's *not*. I know their intentions. I know what they want. That makes them a known evil. Correct?"

"I guess. But why choose to work for an evil? Wouldn't you prefer a stranger with no agenda?"

Daphne stood and began pacing. "I plan to be through with

you and this city in as short a time as possible. It only makes sense to just kill time where I left off." She paused, and a hint of fear filled her eyes. "Besides, what other employer will understand if I spontaneously shift into something four-legged and furry?"

"I still think you're fooling yourself." Tremayne spoke slowly but with assurance as the realization stole over him. "I think you have your own agenda, hidden even from yourself." And he began to truly believe that it was a damn shame she hadn't made it to California. She was so open to her parents' manipulation. She wanted something from them—something they couldn't give. She wanted normal, ethical, moral parents who wanted only the best for her, regardless of their own needs and wants. She would hope in vain.

She stared at him. "And you—a nature spirit only recently given a body—realize all this from long personal experience with human families? You don't know anything. Not about me, and not about my parents. Not really. You're just an observer. For one thing, unlike a certain 'eliminator' in the room, my parents would never intentionally do me permanent damage." Her gaze shifted from his slightly, but not before he read uncertainty in them.

Ignoring the defensive jab, he considered her quietly. She knew the truth, whether she admitted it or not. Her parents might not intentionally hurt her, but he bet they'd be plenty capable of flattening her in their headlong rush to get what they wanted. "I think that should be the *least* a person would expect of family members—no permanent damage. You don't actually trust them, do you?"

"Of course I don't trust them." She scowled. "No more than I trust you. But this job will give me purpose and income. Besides, it would be wonderful to maintain contact with the real world while I'm living in weirdo limbo here."

Tremayne sighed. So, Daphne's parents had seduced her with normalcy—a promise they could deliver upon and that he could not. Given her attitude toward 'freaks' and 'weirdos,' he should have seen that coming. Of course she would run right back to her old—normal—life if it were made available to her. He wondered if she saw his only recourse now.

The next morning Daphne ate breakfast, showered and readied herself for her return to work. As she grabbed her bag and reached for the doorknob, however, an equally clean and presentable Tremayne exited his bedroom. He'd even traded in his usual jeans and T-shirt for something more businesslike. Not a suit, but khakis and a freshly pressed shirt. Apparently nature spirits cleaned up well.

"You look nice," she remarked as he strode decisively in her direction. "Are you off to find that career you mentioned? What kind of job does a nature spirit—"

"I'm coming with you."

"With me? Oh, no you're not." She stepped back from him. No way was she taking weirdness to work with her. That totally negated the purpose!

"Why not?"

"You're a nature spirit and I'm an accountant, and ne'er the twain shall meet. What's the problem, anyway? I'm just going to work. I almost never shape-shift on the job," she added as a joke.

He apparently didn't get it. "When you last held this job, you weren't capable of shape-shifting. Now you are."

"But—"

"If you do spontaneously shift," he continued quietly, "money says rage will be the catalyst, and the source of that rage will involve your parents. I'm coming along to make sure nobody gets hurt. I have to. But don't worry, I can be inconspicuous."

She couldn't argue with the possibility of rage at her parents, but still . . . "This just serves your purpose, doesn't it? After all, you've made a career out of spying on the Forbes family. I've just given you free entrée into their inner sanctum. What a lucky break for you."

He pointed out the obvious. "I'm not interested in your parents now, except for their connection to you. The only reason I spied on them before was to find the cornerstone and the puca powers contained within. Now I know where both are, so your parents are incidental."

"Incidental. As in expendable?" she asked.

"No. As in incidental. They no longer figure directly into the equation. You, however, do. So I'm coming with you. Ready?" He swept a hand toward the door.

She shook her head. "Oh, *this* should go over well."

He cast her a wry look and followed, locking the door behind them.

"I'll drive." Snatching her keys out of her tote and slinging its straps over her shoulder, Daphne headed for the stairwell. Four brand-new tires were just waiting for a test drive. Tremayne had provided, and she, as an independent woman, would repay him for towing and tires once she recouped some of her funds.

Tremayne, catching up, deftly took the keys and held the stairwell door open for her.

She halted. "Who do you think you are? Those are my keys. Give them back!"

"I'll drive."

"Right. I'll admit I've seen you at the wheel a time or two, but I seriously doubt they offer driver's education classes and licenses for nature spirits. You want to drive your own car? Fine. Leave mine alone."

"I know how to drive." When she cast him a challenging look, he just shrugged. "I learned when I was in that cornerstone with Riordan. I don't know if it was paranoia, an overgrown sense of responsibility or simple loneliness, but he had more than one guardian who carted the cornerstone everywhere. Using a car. I watched."

"Oh, well, that's reassuring. Or not. Give me my damn keys."

"If I don't, will you lose your temper and shift into a dragon? You could barbecue and then eat me all in one gulp." He smiled, his eyes wickedly insinuating. "Very efficient, but dangerous, driving as a dragon. If you could even fit in the car."

She folded her arms and didn't budge. "Look. I get that you have a job to do. But so do I. And I'm not playing your stupid games to test my control and my temper. I took my old job back to regain a little normalcy in my life. Inside of five minutes, you've taken that away. Where does that leave me?"

"The same as before: a busy CPA attending to clients of Forbes & Forbes Accounting and Financial Services. I can be inconspicuous. Consider me wallpaper. Or furniture."

Right. As if he knew anything about furniture. And there was no way he could manage inconspicuous. The man didn't resemble any coatrack she'd ever seen.

"And what will you do while I'm meeting privately with clients? Their business is confidential, you know. You can't just hang out and listen." She pursed her lips.

"You don't have secretaries? File clerks? Cleaning people?"

"And you are none of those, are you? No, you're a freak, for Pete's sake. 'Sure, come on in. Meet the boss, the clerk . . . and the office nature spirit. Oh, you're leaving? So soon? But we haven't even calculated your karmic—I mean, your *taxes* yet.'" She swept her hand in a negating gesture. "See how that doesn't work for me? At all?"

"It will have to work. Because you're not going back there unless I go with you. Period. I have a job to do, and it's a lot more crucial than some temporary stint at a public accounting firm you want to leave anyway."

"Oh. That's right. You'll be busy deciding my life and death. How could I forget?" Eyeing him with frustration, she pondered her options. She didn't want to have him drive her. She was tired of riding shotgun through every part of her life. "Fine. Give me my keys back. We'll walk to the office." She might have walked anyway, if she'd thought twice about it. Her old apartment was in the West End, but Tremayne's was downtown, just blocks away.

Turning, she strode off. It was a nice day. She might even relish this walk, if it weren't for Nature Boy following so ominously in her tracks. No doubt he was just waiting for her to morph into a man-eating monster. Not a bad idea, actually.

"I heard that."

"I don't care." But she sped up, though she had little hope of losing him, given the length of his damn legs.

Letting her walk a step ahead, drilling her heels with staccato violence into the sidewalk, Tremayne eyed Daphne's swaying behind. The view was fantastic. He could enjoy it. What he couldn't enjoy was being shut out of her thoughts. Whether Daphne realized it or not, she'd made enormous progress in controlling her mental projections. Ever since the mind reading/glamouring tutorial he'd given her, she'd minimized the thoughts that wandered in his direction. Now he was sensing little more than stray wisps of concept, and that only when she was tired or emotional. She was a woman who sought control, so it shouldn't surprise him that this had happened so quickly.

Ah, but the timing couldn't be worse. Why had she done the unthinkable and gone back to her old job? Was she trying to rebuild a bridge with her parents? That would be unwise. He didn't know what she might do in pursuit of such a goal. Betray him? Betray herself? She might, given proper incentive and a load of convincing lies.

Too, he had to remember that she carried the genes and tendencies of her ancestors, conniving Druids one and all, the very shifty bunch cold enough to deploy him on this thankless, endless mission. And now, to have their spawn wielding puca powers, as the puca brothers themselves had done to his disadvantage? It would be a mistake to ever let his guard down. In spite of the very fine behind swaying so seductively in front of him.

"What made you become an accountant?" He asked quietly, hoping the question would qualify as an olive branch. A man couldn't hope to get inside a woman's head if he didn't attempt conversation.

"My accounting degree," she responded.

He grinned in spite of himself. "I had no idea degrees could be so demanding."

"Yep. Get an accounting degree and that's the first thing it makes you do: get an accounting job to go with it. Matchy-matchy, but what can you do?" She stalked up the stairs to the building that housed her parents' offices and reached for the door handle.

Tremayne was there before her, already swinging it open. Startled by his speed, she paused before walking silently past him.

"Daphne! We were afraid you—" Violet Forbes paused in her welcome to eye Tremayne. "What do *you* want?"

Duncan appeared from his office and joined his wife, adding his own glower. "You're not welcome on this property. Leave."

Tremayne eyed the ex–High Druid with curiosity. "Will you have the police come and throw me out?" he asked.

Daphne glanced over her shoulder at him, and he was surprised to see amusement in her eyes. She told her father, "I don't think that would work. I think Spirit Guy here would have enough firepower to counter whatever the cops brought."

"We don't allow firepower in the office, at least not before noon," Violet responded.

It was disturbing in a way, Tremayne mused, how alike mother and daughter were. They exuded the same classy sophistication and discipline, the same personal strength, but the older woman seemed colder. Her manner seemed flatter. Daphne had energy. Zest. It was youth, undoubtedly, but also a straightforward, if not always easily readable, quality. She didn't advertise her goals, but she didn't seem to hide them, either. There was nothing dark in her manner.

Violet was also goal oriented, but unlike her daughter she gave off the vibes one might expect from a predator. Calm, silent, patient—always ready to strike.

"Why are you here?" Duncan demanded.

Glancing at Daphne, Tremayne raised an eyebrow. He was openly leaving the decision of disclosure up to her. While her parents might tell her what to say, do and think, he would limit his demands to those preserving safety and secrecy. He hoped she would realize that and that it would make a difference to her.

Daphne shrugged. "You can tell him, Tremayne. I wouldn't mind seeing what he has to say about it, actually. As a former High Druid, he knows more about this cult and otherworldly junk than I do. I'll consider him a hostile consultant."

"All right." Tremayne turned his attention back to her parents. "I'm here to keep an eye on Daphne and see how she handles her new puca powers." He gave her father a meaningful look. "It's my job to determine if these powers will drive her insane like they threatened to do with you. Oh, and I'm to see if she's inclined toward violence or criminal behavior—also like you." He glanced at Violet. "So far I haven't seen you committing any crimes, but my guess is that you're just better at covering your tracks."

"My, what a sunny disposition you have, nature spirit. You make friends wherever you go, don't you?" Daphne murmured as her parents stalked off to their respective offices. Apparently they'd deemed Tremayne's comments unworthy of replies. Or maybe he was just right.

Actually, this whole scenario could really be entertaining. The world was a stage. She should just sit back and watch, enjoy the dialogue and take nothing, but nothing, seriously. She could do this. She had little choice.

Tremayne turned to face her. "So. Where do we go now?"

"We? I'm going to my office. As for you . . . Well, let's see. We have the coffeemaker in the kitchenette, just beyond the copy machine. We go through a lot of coffee around here. Oh, and there's a big stack of folders next to the file cabinets just waiting for a guy who knows his alphabet well enough to put them in their proper place. You do, don't you? So why don't you make yourself useful? Wendy is the receptionist and can show you around when she gets back from wherever she is." Motioning to the empty reception desk in front of them, she didn't mention that the receptionist was also a Druid neophyte and one of her father's mistresses. Tremayne just grinned and, cheerfully ignoring her suggestions, followed her into her office.

He stood back as Daphne rounded her desk and slid neatly into her chair as she'd done thousands of times before. "It's strange being here again," she said after a moment. "I swore I wouldn't do this. When I left this building last, I expected never to sit behind this desk again."

"But here you are. And by your own choice," Tremayne pointed out.

"Yes. That makes a difference. It was my own choice this time. And I'm here on my own terms. I'm not here forever." She glanced down and grimaced. "How entertaining, that my things—files, supplies and everything—are exactly the way I left them. They really didn't believe I was leaving."

She drummed her fingers on her desk, just staring at the files for a moment. Then, fighting past her resentment, she picked up one of the folders. She really shouldn't feel this way; it was never the work that she disliked, but the environment. The work was supposed to be a blessing now. And the environment, temporary.

Tremayne dropped into a chair on the other side of the desk, silently watching.

Daphne opened the file folder but still felt his eyes on her. She paused and looked up. "Please tell me you don't mean to just sit there and watch me work. That alone will drive me nuts. Not exactly the goal, right?"

"Well, no, but I'm not sure exactly what—" Then he frowned, his attention taken by something behind her. "Maybe there *is* something to occupy me while I'm here."

"Like what?" She glanced over her shoulder. What was he looking at?

He nodded toward her computer. "*That.* Show me how to use it. I haven't had an opportunity to explore one yet, but I've heard of a wonderful new resource, something called"—he frowned— "the Interwebs?"

Disarmed, she forced a concealing smile. Sometimes she forgot he really wasn't from her world. He'd adapted so completely— well, except for the furniture—that she sometimes took for granted his familiarity with all aspects of modern culture. "You mean the Internet? On the computer?"

"Yes!"

"Actually, it's not all that new." She grinned ruefully. "In fact, it's old enough that most workers take it for granted and wander around lost if a server goes down."

"I've seen two thousand years pass. The Internet, by comparison, is a mere babe," Tremayne remarked dismissively.

She raised an eyebrow. "Well, if you view things from that perspective, I'd imagine most dirt is brand new."

He just stared at the computer with naked enthusiasm. "All you have to do is show me how to get started. I can learn the rest on my own. I live to adapt."

She snorted. "That must be a gender thing. Has to be. You barely know what it is, and you can't keep your eyes off of it. Here's a different test: If I say the term *video game*, do you get feverish and jittery? Do your thumbs twitch and your pupils dilate?"

He grinned, his attention still focused some few feet behind her. "They might. Now, don't be a tease. Show me."

An unexplored possibility startled her. "Um, you do know how to read, don't you?"

He raised his eyebrow.

"Hey, up until you asked about the 'Interwebs' with such awe, I thought you were familiar with everything. I guess modern technology would be where we could tell, though. So . . . you *do* know how to read? English?"

He cast her a disbelieving look. "With two thousand years at my disposal and an extremely bored puca who could not seem to shut up? Yes. I can read English. Riordan liked to learn from his English-speaking guardians, and he was constantly demanding answers and information from them. As he learned, I was right there, absorbing right along with him. His guardians had more interest in books than computers, though. Maybe that was their ages speaking."

Daphne shrugged. "Maybe. So Riordan shared his education with you. What did you share with him?"

Tremayne met her regard squarely. "I shared my space and my two thousand years. He saw me as nonsentient, and expected no response." His words sounded bitter.

"You didn't set him straight?"

"I decided it was wiser not to," Tremayne answered after a moment. "He would have bombarded me with impossible demands if he knew I was there and believed I might be able to address them." His manner was momentarily brooding, but it soon lightened. "Anyhow, yes. I read. And now I want to learn the Internet."

And boy, did he. Twenty minutes of rudimentary instruction later, Tremayne was mousing away like an expert. Daphne fought back amusement and annoyance.

Suddenly a chime sounded, and Tremayne's fingers stilled. "Do I have mail? The computer says I do."

Daphne laughed at his excited tone. "No, that would be me. And I happen to be expecting something, so if you don't mind . . ." She watched, amused, as he reluctantly surrendered the keyboard and mouse and stood up.

Dropping into the chair he'd vacated, she clicked into her personal e-mail program, anticipating the regularly distributed bulletin from her professional networking site that—

She stilled. This wasn't at all what she'd been expecting.

"Something wrong?" Tremayne asked from behind her.

On impulse, Daphne immediately minimized the e-mail so he couldn't see. "Nothing's wrong. Although, I could use some privacy to compose a coherent reply. Why don't you help yourself to some coffee. It's in the kitchenette. Um, out the door and to your right. Remember where I pointed? You'll see it."

Tremayne nodded quietly, then left the room, closing the door behind him.

Alone, Daphne retrieved the e-mail.

A little birdie told me you were desperate for a do-over. I can grant do-overs. If you want it badly enough, I can give you your life back.

Chapter Eight

Heart pounding with alarm and excitement, Daphne studied the unsigned message, seeking clues to the sender's identity. Whoever it was must have overheard her conversation with Tremayne. To use so exactly her words and wishes . . . She'd literally wished for a do-over. That was no coincidence, was it? No. He or she had mentioned a "little birdie." That suggested someone had overheard her.

She scanned the e-mail again but didn't see any clues. The return addy was unhelpful. There was no name or affiliation, just a jumble of numbers and letters with a popular Web-based domain name.

She was sorely tempted to jump on the offer, but she needed more information. What did her supposed helper mean by offering assistance "only if she wanted it badly enough"? Obviously, the e-mailer expected compensation or some kind of sacrifice on Daphne's part. But what? The contents of her bank account? Her immortal soul? And it *was* immortal, now. So she'd been told.

Enough already with the mental blathering. It was time to make a decision. Information—she was just gathering information. There was nothing wrong with that. Fingers clumsy and trembling, she typed up a careful response.

I might be interested. Who are you, why do you want to help me, and how would you bring about this "do-over"?

She scanned her reply, deemed it adequate. Hesitating over the send button, she clicked the mouse. A moment passed and it was gone. Too late to call it back.

But why would she even want to call it back? Somebody obviously thought they could help her. Well, maybe. No doubt the e-mailer had had an agenda when he or she made the offer, but then, didn't everybody? It didn't necessarily have to be a *bad* agenda. Besides, what could it hurt to gather information? That was really the only rational course.

Except that she'd kept it secret from Tremayne. She didn't really know why. Just a gut reaction, she supposed. Somehow, a solution delivered via the Internet didn't seem very fate and karma friendly.

"Daphne. You're still here." The sun had already set when her father strode into her office without invitation. "I appreciate your dedication, but it's nearly seven. I don't want to burn you out on your first day back."

She eyed him. Dedication? Is that what he supposed this was? More like she was still waiting—in vain—for a response to that blasted e-mail she'd sent this morning. So far nothing. And she'd already shipped her personal desktop computer to California, so she couldn't do this at home. Maybe she'd bring that commuter laptop she took on business trips back to the apartment. She could use it to check. "I'm almost ready to head out. Just need to collect my things and find Tremayne."

"Where'd he get off to, anyway?" Duncan looked around as though expecting to find the nature spirit curled up in a corner or gnawing on a phone book under the desk.

Daphne smiled humorlessly. "I'm sure he didn't go far. Just needed to stretch his legs."

"He's been hovering over you all day long. Does he think we intend to harm you?"

She gave her father a wide-eyed look. "Oh, no. He thinks I intend to harm *you*. Any idea why that might be?"

"You're still holding a grudge about that cornerstone, aren't you." Duncan looked disappointed. It ticked her off. If it weren't for his actions—his selfish, impulsive need to grasp for power even after he'd been busted for crimes against more than one realm—she would be in California right now, free and clear and fully human and independent.

"I know. How unreasonable of me. It's not like anything *you* did wrecked my life. Oh, but wait, it did. Or ruined my chances at a new career. Oh, but look, it did that, too. Or threatened my very existence. Oh, and look how you managed that one, too. All with one brick! How efficient of you." She powered down her desktop computer and bent to retrieve the laptop from a cabinet.

"Daphne, you know that was an accident," Duncan said.

"I know. You intended to take the powers yourself. So you could kill people. That's much better. I must be as insane as you are to be back here working for you." She tugged the leather-clad laptop free, closed the cabinet and stood.

He shifted uncomfortably. "Um, about that. My head's not . . . I mean, I know my mind wasn't right before, with the warring Druid and puca magic and all of that. But all of that conflict is behind me now. I'm me again."

The two magics warring inside—he'd actually experienced this. To hear it described as reality, not just possibility . . . Daphne swallowed hard and sat back down before her legs collapsed under her. Was that her future? Her fate? Maybe she should just throw in the towel if that was the case. Or blindly take the e-mailer up on his offer.

"I know what it's like, Daphne. I don't want you to suffer like I did. That's why I want to help you."

"How kind of you, Druid."

Daphne jumped at the sound of Tremayne's voice. Her guardian could move way too silently for someone of his size. Did nature spirits walk on tiptoe, or did they glide freely with the wind and recirculated air currents?

"Stay out of this, spirit. This is between me and my daughter. You have no say." Duncan's tone was cold.

"I have every say and you know it," Tremayne responded. "You couldn't control the powers when you wielded them. Why do you think you can help your daughter find control that eluded you?"

"That's a great question. Why didn't I think of that?" Daphne marveled facetiously as she turned a challenging gaze on her father. "So, what's the answer?"

Duncan frowned. "Just because I couldn't control them myself doesn't mean I don't know how they can be controlled. My mind is strong again, and I remember my experiences. I can help you learn from them, Daphne."

"I don't trust you to help me," she replied.

Her father straightened as though she'd slapped him. "And you trust this nature spirit? Hell, he's not even that anymore. There's nothing *natural* about him. He's evolved into something that doesn't belong in this world. He's an abomination. You'd be a fool to trust him."

"Sounds like a bunch of wild accusations to me." Daphne kept her voice even, though she was incensed by her father's accusations. Who was Duncan to be accusing anyone else—anyone at all—of deception and untrustworthiness? The man took hypocrisy to new heights. "Do you have anything to back up your claims, or am I actually expected to take your word?"

"Okay, try this one. He would have killed me if he thought it necessary. Wouldn't have thought twice about it, wouldn't have flinched while doing it or regretted it later. Just ask him. He doesn't feel emotions the way we do. And he's willing to kill you if necessary, too. You know that, don't you?"

"He told me." She spoke slowly, feeling the burn of that knowledge. "But he wouldn't harm any of us out of malice. He would do it to protect others."

"And did he also tell you how he hates everything about Druids and pucas? He blames us for what he endured."

That gave her pause. *Hates?* He hated everything about Druids and pucas? She wondered where her father was getting this information. "Considering what he went through, I guess I can't blame him for holding a grudge. I hold a few of my own. I really hate the thought of my own parents trying to use me, for example. And you *do* want to use me. Don't you?"

Duncan bristled a little. "Well, has it occurred to you that your precious nature spirit wants to use you, too?"

"Use me? How?" She glanced at Tremayne, whose face was suddenly expressionless. Suddenly, dangling right there in the middle of the office was the memory of Warren, the man who'd pretended interest in her just to get to her father. She'd been a simple means to an end, with the end being more power. Could it happen all over again?

"Tremayne? Are you trying to use me, too? You know, that would just really suck." She studied his face. "I thought you said you wouldn't lie to me. But then, you never promised full disclosure. I guess straightforward was too much to hope for. Even with a nature spirit."

"I'm as straightforward with you as you are with me," he replied.

Daphne mentally stumbled. Was he referring to the e-mail she was hiding from him? She'd been careful about not projecting it, and she thought she'd succeeded so far. So, maybe he hadn't meant anything by his words. Just a flip comment. No hidden message implied.

"I suppose that's fair," she said at last. And it was, even if it gave her the creeps.

I can grant do-overs. If you want it badly enough . . . It was just a co-incidence that the e-mail writer had used the same term she had. No one was spying on her. Or maybe a Druid could have been? Maybe it was Tremayne. No, that couldn't be. Or could it?

Alone in her borrowed bedroom with her borrowed laptop and her dithering thoughts, Daphne stared at the computer screen and clicked send/receive. She watched as the screen refreshed itself. New mail invited her to try a stimulating new sex device. *Delete. Send/receive.* Oh, look. Prescriptions half price through various foreign countries. How enlightening. Not to mention healthful. *Delete. Send/receive.*

A new message. Daphne paused, saw a familiar, if nonsensical, Web-mail address, then deliberately clicked to open the message.

In many ways, I am like you. People want to use me. Hurt me. I feel powerless. Your unwelcome powers are a hindrance to you, and my inadequate powers are a hindrance to me. We can help each other. That is what I want.

Troubled, Daphne stared at the message. The other e-mail had sounded like somebody exploring options and offering her some of her own. Networking, almost. This one rang with gut-wrenching emotion and need. Why?

Acting on a hunch, she quickly typed a response.

You aren't the same person who e-mailed me earlier. What's going on?

She hit the send button and waited for what seemed like eons. At last, a new message showed up.

I intercepted the earlier message. My need is greater and I am not evil.

What the hell did that mean? She quickly typed.

I should just take that on faith? Why would you not be evil? And who says your need is greater than anyone's—or even valid? Why should I take risks for you or trust you?

A few minutes later, a reply arrived.

Do you trust a nature spirit so much more? He has no heart. Whatever else you believe or don't believe, this can be verified. The nature spirit will not be moved to pity or compassion. He does not love. Only humans and fully sentient beings feel the emotional range of compassion and love; he's neither. Unreasoning altruism, duty, a weighing of good versus evil, yes. These are familiar and natural to him. But he has no heart to be won over or swayed. Even if you

turn down my offer, remember that much. It may save you
in the end.

"The end of what? The world? My life? This e-mail?" Were
straight answers suddenly too plebeian for the average cyber-
rescuer? Everyone, but everyone, felt it necessary to spout use-
less, cryptic inanities.

Especially Druids. Her e-mailer probably was one of those.
Furthermore, if she was honest, she'd have to admit that it was
probably one of her parents, squabbling still and now, apparently, intercepting e-mail. But the question was, had the person
lied? Or could they really remove the puca powers? She had to
go fishing for the answers.

She typed,

You are a Druid.

Then she hit send and waited. A familiar chime announced a
new message in her mailbox.

Yes, some would call me Druid. I've exhibited a measure
of trust in admitting it, too. Does that help you to trust me
in return?

Daphne grimaced, pondering. What if she was wrong? There
was somebody else who could have sent these. Somebody who
knew firsthand how much she wanted a do-over. Tremayne? Was
he setting her up? He didn't have a computer as far as she knew
and claimed to have little experience with one. Still, he could
have faked that to throw her off.

But if it was Tremayne, maybe she could catch him. The
e-mailer was probably still online, waiting for her response. Carefully, deliberately, she slipped the laptop off her lap, set it on the
bed and slid to the edge of her mattress. Quietly raising her hips
off the bed, she typed while standing and bent awkwardly over
the keyboard.

You could still be lying to me. I mentioned Druids first. Maybe it just gave you something to use in place of the truth. Your response to my question leaves me with no convincing answers and still the same questions.

There. Never let it be said she couldn't be annoyingly cryptic when she wanted. Those latent Druid genes, no doubt.

Glancing at the closed door, she shifted her weight, poised to move immediately, and hit the send button. Then she tiptoed quickly to the door and opened—

She shrieked into Tremayne's chest. He leaned backward a little, eyes twinkling and amused. He peered down at her.

"Did I scare you?"

Panting, she looked up at him. "No. I always shriek when I open doors. It's like my own little warning system for anyone who might be standing on the threshold. Yes, you scared me to death! Were you spying on me?" She peered suspiciously behind him, looking for any sign that he might have a computer hidden, or some other way to send e-mail in the past ten minutes. Nothing was overt, but . . . Well, there were likely still ways, damn it. Probably sneaky, magicky ways she could never guess, too.

"Why, were you doing something I should be spying on? Do you have a guy in here?" His raised brows lifted impossibly higher. "Oh, I know. It's High Druid Phil, isn't it? Is it the purple glasses that turn you on? I can get glasses."

She blinked at him, utterly taken aback. If he only knew what turned her on: nature spirits, too bad for her. *Oh, no!* She hadn't—

Tremayne's smile was humiliatingly wide.

Yes, she had. Damn thought projection.

Carefully, she ratcheted down her emotions and evened her breathing. She'd mostly figured this part out, how not to project. Once her breathing was calm, she latched onto opportunity.

"Tremayne, a little Druid told me something, and I was curious about your take on it."

He shook his head, obviously still entertaining himself. "Phil again? Is he under the bed?"

She let that go. "I was told that, as a nature spirit you lacked"—
she shrugged, and her light tone deserted her—"a heart." She
looked into those dark eyes, so flat at first and yet deeper than any
normal man's eyes she'd ever encountered. Maybe that was it. He
wasn't a normal man.

"You're asking me if I have a heart?" He gave her a quizzical
look.

She nodded.

The question seemed to take him aback. "I assume you mean
in the metaphorical sense, not the physical one. As far as I know,
my anatomy is typical of the average human male."

Only a blind fool would label Tremayne's anatomy average or
typical. And no, she damn well would *not* project that thought.
Testing him, she watched his eyes, which never flickered. Success.

"So, let's speak on the metaphorical level. We can even get
specific. You have emotion, right?"

He blinked. "I do."

"Right. You laugh, you get impatient on the very rare occa-
sion, and you feel lust. I think you feel intrigue sometimes, too.
Right?"

He nodded.

"What about compassion? You know, fellow feeling?"

He frowned. "You want freedom. I want freedom. We understand each other. I would call that fellow feeling, wouldn't
you?"

His reply made her breathe a sigh of relief. She hadn't wanted
to believe what her father said. "Right. Right! I'd forgotten.
That equates almost to compassion, right? Or empathy at least.
Okay, suppose I morphed into a cat and charged into the street,
got hit by a car, probably wouldn't live through it. You'd feel . . ."
She prompted him with raised eyebrows.

He shook his head. "You wouldn't die. You're immortal."

She nearly jumped, reminded of her condition. "Right. Immortal." Not that her immortality was the point.

"You forgot." He seemed to be hiding a grin.

"No." She made a face. "Okay, maybe I did. Or, maybe some
unacknowledged corner of my freaked-out mind remembers

very well, but the rest of my brain—the sane part, the part you're hoping to cultivate, as you recall—refuses to acknowledge any of it, thank you very much. I like to leave the loony stuff in the corner brain bin. Sanity stays at the front. So I am projecting sanity at all times."

"And believing in your immortality is not sane?" He looked confused now.

"Of course it's not sane! Not to a normal human. Think about it. Immortality? The idea of me, Daphne, never dying and living forever? It's not even comprehensible. Here's a little secret for you, in fact. Want to drive a human nuts? Force her to comprehend infinity. By definition, she could never finish the thought. Boom. She's bonkers. See how that works?" She felt her eyes glazing over at the prospect. Shaking it off, she refocused. "So . . . back to that heart thing."

Tremayne nodded, folded his arms and leaned against the doorjamb as though vastly entertained. "What about it?"

"Well, this is going to sound weird."

"Weirder than your take on immortality? I can't wait." He laughed.

"Why do I feel like your personal puppet show?"

He shrugged and winked. "I have no idea. I consider you more like a variety show. One moment you're cool, composed and mysterious. The next, you're a frightened child—"

"Don't you mean frightened farm animal?"

"—and then you suddenly become this whimsical creature I see before me. Very entertaining. I like all the acts."

His smile was genuine, and Daphne caught her breath. Tell her this man did not have emotions.

"So, I think that in part answers the cat question," he continued thoughtfully. "For what it's worth, if you were to become roadkill while in cat form and die . . ." He lowered his voice and his eyes darkened. "I would be unhappy. For many reasons." He canted his head a little. "You make me laugh and you make me think. You make me question what I've always held to be true." He smiled. "So, watch out for cars."

She blinked at the intensity in his eyes, which seemed to belie the casual nature of his words and his smile. The next words out of her mouth were, "Druids lie sometimes, don't they?"

He gave her an odd look. "Of course. You've seen what your father—"

"No, I mean your average Druids. Normal ones not prone to criminal acts or chaotically amoral ones. Regular Joe Druid types."

"Probably as much as a regular Joe Human would. It depends on how seriously they take their philosophy and how strong their moral character." He stared at her. "Or was that a rhetorical question?"

"A little of both," she mused unhappily. Emotion wasn't the right term for what she sought, now that she truly considered. It wasn't specific or strong enough. She pondered her do-over e-mails, specifically the one suggesting Tremayne wasn't fully sentient, that he didn't feel compassion, couldn't feel love as humans and fully sentient beings could. If her own fate would be decided by something with little feeling beyond that of a turnip . . . what chance did she have? She had to know. How much stock should she place in an anonymous e-mailer's assertions? It would depend on Tremayne, really, whether he proved that e-mailer correct or not.

She studied him. Maybe a direct assault was her only option. "Tremayne, have you ever loved?"

His smile faded. "You *have* been talking to Druids," he said.

Her heart pounded but she didn't respond.

"Honestly? No. I've never loved. Not like you mean. I've coveted. My freedom I covet with every fiber of my being, but never have I loved."

"But you know what love is?" She studied him.

"I've been doing research on that, and I do believe I've seen others who loved. It seems kind of nice, actually." He smiled, maybe a bit sadly.

"And you know that you haven't loved. Do you think you're capable?"

He considered. "Maybe. I know I've hated. Does that translate?"

"If somebody hates, does that mean they can also love?" she mused. "I don't know. It's possible, I guess."

He shook his head. "Somehow, I don't think it does. Hate is a learned emotion. You focus on an object causing pain and you hate. It's a simple cause and effect, a reaction you'd expect from any creature. It's just basic."

"Yes, but suppose you focus on something that might bring you a positive change in your life. Like . . . a bringer of justice?"

"Basically, if someone stood up for me in some way, even in some grand way, could I then love him or her for that reason?" When Daphne nodded her support of his interpretation, Tremayne shook his head. "I think it would be easy to feel grateful, or to consider myself in that person's debt. But, love? I don't know. I have no experience with this, so I'm just guessing, but I don't think justice strikes the same deeply primitive chord as pain does. The reaction isn't as immediate, as natural."

"Is that how you evolved to what you are now? By learning?"

"Partly. I've learned to mimic," he admitted.

Daphne paused. Did that work? Children mimicked early on. But they also learned to love their parents before they even spoke a word. She looked up into Tremayne's eyes. He seemed fascinated by the subject, no doubt absorbing information as he had always done. But did he love? Could a nature spirit learn to love?

She latched onto something else. He'd said he knew how to hate. "Who do you hate, Tremayne? My father said you hate Druids and pucas." There was nothing like confronting the issue head-on.

"I think hate might be too strong a word," he replied. "I don't trust them. Thanks to their infighting, I was enslaved for two thousand years." He shrugged. "A guy tends to hold a grudge and stay away from the types who make his life miserable."

That was, Daphne decided, very reasonable. Unfortunately so.

"So, um, speaking as a hereditary Druid—if a nonpracticing one—and a woman who now wields puca powers, totally against my will, am I your enemy? Do you hate me? Do you hold a grudge against me?"

There was a smile in his eyes as he replied. "What do you think?"

"I think you're not answering my question."

"If I hated you, I would prefer to see you as roadkill. No, I don't hate you, Daphne Forbes. Do I trust you?" He shrugged. "Have you given me any reason not to?"

She swallowed and vowed not to think a word on that subject. "What about Phil? You and he seem to know each other."

"We've been aware of each other for some time now, and he's known of my situation, but he still didn't try to help me. He's the ultimate in noninterference. Which, in itself, is the ultimate interference. I hold that against him. I also think he has an agenda. But do I think he's evil? No. Do I trust him? A little." Tremayne's eyes glittered. "Is he useful? Immensely."

Chapter Nine

"Oh, thank god." Mina swept past a bewildered Daphne and into Tremayne's apartment. It was the following evening, and she had called only five minutes before to alert Daphne to her impending visit—and her tagalong. To give the women privacy, Tremayne retreated to his bedroom.

Mina scowled at the older woman who still stood in the doorway. "My mother here has been driving me nuts, and I desperately needed somebody to lend the voice of reason. Somebody logical, sane and at least marginally objective." She turned to Daphne. "So, I thought, who's my favorite accountant? And there you were, top of the list. So, here we are." Mina dropped her purse on the floor and slid onto a folding chair. "Nice place. Interesting decor. Very . . . minimalist."

A little puzzled, Daphne turned back to her other guest, Mina's mother.

The woman eyed Daphne with open curiosity. She was obviously intent on greeting her hostess with more decorum than her daughter had. "Hi, Daphne. I'm Lizzy Dixon. It's nice to meet you in person at last. I hope you don't find it awkward that I tagged along, but I did want to thank you for being kind to your . . ." Lizzy shrugged. "Well, to my daughter."

Daphne returned Lizzy's curiosity. This was the woman her father had chosen to take to bed long enough to conceive Mina mere weeks before he got Daphne's mother pregnant. In spite of Daphne's growing relationship with her half sister, she'd somehow escaped an in-person meeting with Lizzy Dixon. She had actually hired a detective to investigate Lizzy a few years back, but . . . well, once she'd learned about the older woman, Daphne just couldn't bring herself to hate her. Which felt like a betrayal of her own mother.

Lizzy tipped her head to the side. "I'm not sure what you are to me. Not stepdaughter, since I never married your father . . ."

"He was already married when he met you. To my mother." Daphne couldn't muster any animosity.

"Yes." Lizzy said just the one word, naked and open to criticism.

"Oh, nuts." Mina rubbed her face. "Why didn't I think . . . How utterly insensitive can I be? Daph, Mom and I can leave. We can walk out the door without another word. I was caught up in my own personal bridezilla act and didn't even—Ugh."

"No, stay." Daphne was still studying Lizzy. "I've been wanting to meet your mom. I told you that."

"That's just plain weird, then." Mina glanced between the two. "You're really okay with this? Gee, how kind of me to belatedly ask you and all. I should be kicked for putting you in this position." She looked at her mother. "But that was not an invitation."

Lizzy drew herself up, her spine stiff. "I have never kicked my daughter."

"Great. We'll write that on your tombstone." Mina rolled her eyes.

"*Urn*, please. You know I prefer cremation." Lizzy shook her head at her daughter before turning back to Daphne. "If you're sure this is okay?"

"This is great. Come in."

Smiling, Lizzy stepped inside and looked around. "So, this is Tremayne's apartment?"

"Such as it is, yes," Daphne responded. "He's not big on furniture."

"You don't say." Mina feigned amazement. "No biggie. I imagine he considers this place temporary."

Does he? Daphne wondered. "No, I don't get that feeling. I think he just has priorities. And a couch isn't one of them—or at least, it hasn't occurred to him to make it one." She shrugged. "So what brings you by?"

Mina, suddenly recollecting her reason for arriving, moaned piteously, even as her mother let out a world-weary sigh. The daughter spoke first. "Please. Talk some sense into my nutty mother. She thinks I should wear hot pink and get married under the full moon. You know, like I might spout some prophecy as the clock strikes midnight. I think we've already traveled this path and realized I'm as extrasensory as . . . How did you put it, Mom?"

"A brick wall." Lizzy spoke pleasantly from her perch on the edge of a chair. She was dressed in a ladylike pink designer suit and holding an expensive black leather purse in her lap. She wore a long string of crystals where one might expect pearls, and a mood ring in place of a wedding ring. All that, together with her hair styled in a classy, timeless cut, screamed, "Just because you're pagan doesn't mean you dress like a Woodstock flower child."

"Right. As extrasensory as a brick wall. Love you, too, Mom." Mina stuck out her tongue.

"You asked. Would you prefer a polite lie? All right. I'm sure you have hidden talents, darling. Perhaps you'd like to experiment with some of my crystals again? Please don't try to eat them this time."

Mina addressed Daphne. "I understand I was two the first time she handed me a crystal and told me to work the damn thing. Whose mother gives a toddler a bite-size crystal to play with?"

Daphne fought a grin. "Yours?"

"Exactly. A *nutty* one. One who prayed I would grow up to be some psycho psychic able to fulfill caged-puca prophecies and perform other acts of weirdness, all for her vicarious delight. Like I've been trying to tell her for all of my thirty-one years, I just want normal. Give me a white dress, a church, an adoring groom willing to kiss the ground I walk on—"

"Like a foot fetish? Oh, dear. I think I'm too innocent to hear any more. My sensibilities!" Fanning herself, Mina's mother managed to look prim despite the wicked laughter in her eyes.

Mina scowled at her, albeit good-naturedly. "Oh, right, like you didn't try for years to get me to express my sexuality. Yech. Give me normal! Give me tradition! Is that so terrible?"

"Well, when you're wanting tradition with all the trimmings, you generally need just a little more time than you've given us. What's the almighty hurry anyway? Are you pregnant?"

"Mo-*om!*"

"And if you are, what's the big deal? So we reverse the order a little. Haste or tradition. You can't have both."

"I'm not pregnant! Sheesh. I just want to be married as soon as possible, and I want it to be like . . . well, like I want it." Mina shrugged. "It's my wedding day, and I want it to look like a wedding day, not a pagan festival." She turned to her sister. "What do you think, Daphne? Don't weddings just demand tradition? Don't *you* want a few white and lacy bells and whistles?"

"To be honest, I'd rather rip my toenails off and eat them than tie myself to any man for life. I've seen how that works. I've come to the conclusion that I'm too squeamish for marriage. The bloodshed alone . . ." Daphne shuddered.

Mina studied her. "Seriously?"

"You've met my parents."

Mina shuddered. "No comment. Out of respect for you, naturally. But what about Tremayne?"

"Huh?" Daphne gave her a baffled look.

"Well . . ." Mina glanced at her mother for help, but the older woman just raised an eyebrow and let her daughter fend for herself. Mina turned back to Daphne. "It's just that there's kind of a pattern going here: pucas and their guardians pairing off, falling in love."

"That's nice." Daphne gave her a confused look.

"As in you, puca, and Tremayne, guardian . . ." Mina trailed off pointedly.

"Oh, no," Daphne said. "Does not apply. Besides all the usual objections—you know, like free will and logic and how I don't fall in love according to pattern—let me also point out that I am not a puca and Tremayne is not my puca guardian."

"Semantics," Mina argued. "You're a hereditary Druid

wielding puca powers and he's your mentor as assigned by Druids. Same general kind of relationship. Same pattern."

Daphne turned to Lizzy. "Did you never teach your daughter the old maxim about not jumping off a cliff just because her friends did?"

Lizzy smiled. "Hasn't my daughter ever told you about her white-picket-fence dreams? She wanted nothing more than traditional, normal and boring. Just like the other sheep. I personally think it's fitting and entertaining that she ultimately fell in love with a cursed puca."

Mina laughed. "And ended up with my white picket fence after all!"

"So who wins?" Lizzy turned her smile on her daughter.

Mina blinked. "Well, Riordan, of course. Who else?"

Lizzy nodded, her eyes softening. "I completely agree." She turned to Daphne. "Mina does have a point, though, about patterns. I believe in them. And Tremayne's seriously a hottie. You're sure you won't run him to ground, break and domesticate him? You're a pretty girl. He probably won't put up much of a fight."

Daphne choked. "No, I think I'll skip that part, thanks. Like I said, I have no desire to stand at an altar next to a 'broken' man. If I did, I'd have to take him home and try to fix him. Sounds exhausting."

"Bummer." Mina looked disappointed.

Daphne stared at her half sister. "Why? If you like him that much, why don't *you* marry him?"

"Because I'm marrying Riordan, and I was hoping to talk you into being my maid of honor. But if you're opposed to marriage as an institution . . ."

Daphne caught her breath. "Maid of honor? Me? You mean . . . I mean, you really . . ." She swallowed hard, feeling her heart race, goose bumps sprouting all over her arms, spine and the back of her neck. "You really want me? For that?" *Like a real sister.* Sparks of joy shot everywhere, until her consciousness wavered and—

Dead silence, broken only by the clatter of a single shoe falling to the floor. It was a black slingback like the ones Daphne had worn that day.

A few heartbeats later—"Ho. Ly. Cow. Would you look at that. Janelle did *not* exaggerate. But I thought she said cat." Mina gazed in wonder at Daphne. "Can you fly, too?"

Oh, god. Oh, god. Oh, god. I can't . . . I'm a freaking . . . Tremayne, where the hell are you? And right in front of—

The door to Tremayne's bedroom opened abruptly. "Daphne?" Tremayne sounded alarmed. He glanced at Mina as he strode into the room. "What happened?"

"I didn't do anything, I swear." Mina held her hands up in protest. "We were discussing marriage and her total disaffection for the institution. Then I mentioned I'd intended asking her to be my maid of honor, and poof: lovebird. Which is kind of sweet. Unless her powers are making fun of her. They're not, are they? I don't know how the hell this works, but I promise I didn't mean to do anything to her."

He nodded absently, his attention on Daphne.

Tremayne, shift me back. And then just take my head off and put me out of my misery, would you? Please? I swear, this is like losing control of my bodily functions in front of company. I'm so embarrassed.

Grimacing, Tremayne dropped to a knee and set a finger down before her. Daphne eyed it. He obviously expected her to perch on it.

Oh, no. That's not going to work. These legs will snap if I move them. Have you seen bird legs? Just lift me. Please. And get me out of here. The kitchen, maybe? Anyplace but here.

Wordlessly, Tremayne scooped her into one gentle hand. "We'll be back in a moment," he told Mina and Lizzy. "Make yourselves at home."

"I'll just use your bathroom, if that's okay?" Mina's mother asked with a sweet smile.

"Sure. Right through there." Tremayne pointed with his free hand, and Lizzy quickly moved in that direction.

"Daph, I'm really sorry. I didn't mean to hurt you."

Mina sounded upset enough that Tremayne paused. "She's

just embarrassed. This is new for her. I'm sure she'll explain when she's herself again."

"She's embarrassed?" Mina was flabbergasted. "But why? That's so freaking cool! She can turn into a bird! Man, she could probably fly if she practiced. Wow. I had no idea."

"I think it's a control thing for her."

"Control is overrated," Mina said. "When you can turn into a bird, everything else—including control—is secondary."

Unless you're locked in a room with a dozen hungry cats, Daphne thought.

"Seriously, Daph, don't be embarrassed. Hey, you have not seen humiliation until you've been raised by my mom. The woman scared away every boyfriend I ever had, until Riordan."

"I heard that!" Lizzy's voice echoed from the other room.

Mina squeezed her eyes shut. "My mother just spoke to you from the bathroom. See what I mean? She lives to mortify me."

Heart lightening with reluctant amusement, Daphne let Tremayne carry her into the kitchen. She breathed a sigh of relief when they were finally alone.

"Okay, since speed is probably what you're looking for right now, I'll help you do this," Tremayne murmured quietly. "But only if you promise we'll practice control at some point in the near future."

I promise. If I had fingers, I'd even cross my little birdie heart. Please, just change me back.

Closing his eyes and cradling her against his chest, Tremayne stilled. As before, Daphne felt the maddening tingles and rogue energy being drawn from her body. Reality wavered, then realigned, until she realized she was once again clothed in her own skin and supported by familiar limbs. She relaxed into Tremayne's embrace, relieved but still needing the contact. She leaned her forehead into his shoulder.

"How did you know?" she asked.

"That you had changed? You mentally yelled for me. Didn't you do that consciously?"

"Must have been my panic. I had no idea this would happen.

I mean, I figured terror and fury would do this, but joy?" Her heart pounded at the implications, and panic took root all over again. "I have to be afraid of being happy, too? Mina had just said something, and I was so touched—"

"Just take a breath. Calm. Wait for the flickers to slow."

Breathing steadily, she felt—actually *felt*—the flickers of energy slowing and finally fading. Dear god, that was kind of neat. Even better, maybe she really could master these damn powers. Control them instead of letting them control her and rule her life. Could she really get her life back? It seemed almost possible. "Okay. Okay. I could feel that. All I have to do is catch it early?"

"Yes. It's easier for you to catch now, since I drained a fraction of your power. The energy is sluggish. But you did slow the process. And now that you know how that feels, you can practice. Before you know it, halting a shift will be automatic for you. You won't even have to think about it."

"That would be good." Her breath hitched just a little before she evened it out. Then she announced, "Mina asked me to be her maid of honor! You know, stand up at her wedding. I was really, really moved. I mean, she's my sister. I actually have one!" Not since her grandmother's death had she felt this brand of joy. A connection. Family. Someone who cared, someone who didn't judge her, didn't try to use her . . . Her heart leapt all over again. She hadn't realized she'd missed it so much.

"Keep your breathing even," Tremayne said. But he was smiling. "I'll admit I'm not sure exactly what a maid of honor does, but it sounds . . . nice. I think you should do it."

Daphne cleared her throat. "Yeah. It would be very cool. If she still wants me to do it. After, well, *this*." What bride wanted her maid of honor shape-shifting her way down the aisle?

"She does," Mina answered.

Daphne swung around, standing awkwardly with one foot bare, to see her sister standing in the doorway. Mina shrugged a little sheepishly.

"I couldn't stand waiting, knowing you were hiding in here from me. I'm sorry. It was my fault for springing it on you like that. I mean, I could have built up to it a little."

Daphne inhaled deeply. "It's not you. It's me."

Mina widened her eyes and joked, "Does this mean you're dumping me?"

Daphne laughed. "Can we still be friends?" she murmured in a nasal, artificial tone. "I'm serious, though. It looks as though extreme emotion of any kind sends me into a change."

Mina looked sheepish. "So I scared the hell out of you?"

"No. Well, maybe a little, but mostly I was just . . . well, touched."

"Breathe, Daphne," Tremayne whispered in her ear, even as he kept a hand on her shoulder.

Thank you. She hoped he got that message. She didn't need to morph now and ruin the moment. She was already nervous enough as it was. This sisterhood thing was so new. She didn't want to screw things up.

She said to Mina, "I would feel privileged to be your maid of honor, in spite of what I was saying about marriage earlier. From what I've seen of you two, you and Riordan are like a team. Sure, you tease and you taunt each other, but you're always on the same side. That's not what I'm used to seeing. You're good together. So, I'd love to be your maid of honor. And"—she glanced briefly at Tremayne before grinning at her sister—"I'll practice controlling this puca stuff so I don't go waltzing down the aisle as your ostrich of honor."

"Are you kidding? Not everybody gets an ostrich of honor." Mina gave her a fake fanatic look, bridezilla on steroids. "It could be the event of the season!"

Daphne giggled. "It would serve you right if I did morph. I can't believe you went fangirl all over my lovebird impression like that."

"Hey, I was busy counting my riches, like in that cartoon with the guy who discovers a frog that sings and dances to show tunes. We could make a fortune on you!"

"Ugh." Daphne grimaced. "That is exactly the future I'm trying to avoid."

Mina winced. "I didn't mean—"

"Oh, stop, please. Bring back bridezilla, anything. But this walking on eggshells around me will only bring on another morph. One born of pure rage. It could get ugly." Daphne regarded her evilly.

"Really?" Mina looked fascinated. "What do you do when you're enraged? Oh, I know! Can I send Riordan over here the next time he launches into idiotic, punch-Mina's-buttons mode? It would do him good to get a taste of his own medicine."

Tremayne laughed. "Use puca powers against him? Give the puca a puca ride? That'd be great."

"Okay, let's stop punching *Daphne's* buttons now, shall we?" Daphne shook her head. "I don't particularly want to morph at all, if you couldn't tell."

Mina glanced at her. "I know. I just don't want you to be embarrassed by it, either. If you think of any way I can help, let me know, okay?"

Daphne nodded.

"So. Let me go collect my mother and get out of your way so you can practice the whole morph-mastering bit. Deal?"

Tremayne clapped. "I like that plan."

Daphne glanced at him but didn't comment, just followed Mina out of the kitchen. Mina glanced around the still-empty living room. "Mom?" she called.

They heard the sound of a door opening down the hallway, then measured steps. "Coming, dear." Lizzy strode unhurriedly into the room, deposited a lipstick in her purse and zipped it shut. She smiled at Daphne. "Everything okay now? For what it's worth, you know, I'd love to be able to do what you do. Most of the population would."

Daphne shook her head. "You'd love to once you knew you could control it. Until then, it's just unnerving."

"Well, I have every confidence you can master it. You dress so nicely, and I'm sure your good taste is a reflection of your inner self. Mina, do you see? She looks *classy*. In control. You should really go shopping with her and let her—"

"Mo-*om*." Mina rolled her eyes. " 'Bye, Daphne. 'Bye, Tremayne." She led her still-chattering mother—who flashed Daphne and Tremayne a mischievous smile—out the door.

Daphne smiled wistfully after the pair. "See? Now that's how a mom is supposed to interfere. She's supposed to embarrass you, drive you batty with badgering and always be your biggest cheerleader. What do I get? Parents who break laws, assault innocents, consider homicide, and even secretly tempt their daughter to the dark side." She scowled.

Tremayne gave her a surprised look. "They're secretly tempting you to the dark side now? What does that mean?"

"Never mind." She had truly been tempted just a few minutes earlier. Which was bad, because the more she thought about it, the more she believed her parents were behind that blasted e-mail correspondence.

Could they really free her of these puca powers? She could only believe that they could. After all, why bother tempting her if they had no way of taking the powers from her? They wanted them so badly, and she wanted so badly to give them up . . . It was a match made in heaven, right?

Okay, that was taking absurdity to new levels. As if it were even possible to label something a match made in heaven when her prospective matchee was none other than the devil she knew.

"All right, Daphne. What's this about?"

Her mother eyed her as she would any spoiled child making impossible demands, and Daphne decided that was exactly how things must appear. She had, after all, called her parents to a private meeting on an already-packed day of business. They were now seated in her mother's office.

Oh, but she'd struggled with the logistics of this conference. In the end, she'd decided confronting her parents was her job, not Tremayne's, and she would do it alone even if magical backup would have lent her confidence. But including the nature spirit would have required elaborate explanations and guilty confessions, so she'd planned the meeting without telling him and at a time when she knew his attention would be riveted to his favorite soap opera. A Friday cliff-hanger, no less.

To compound her guilt, last night she'd opened the door for a pair of delivery guys carrying a brand-new couch. It was big and welcoming, luxuriously upholstered in dandelion yellow microfiber. Yes, the color was actually dandelion—she'd read the packing slip. Thus the sprite was able to sit on his cushy yellow flower, just as she'd teased him. He'd bought a couch and based it on a private joke between them that was even at his expense. It was . . . endearing in an uncomfortable way. She suspected he'd meant to please her.

"Daphne?" Her father looked sincerely distressed. "Are you in trouble?" His expression darkened and focused—eyes beginning to glitter as though sighting sudden opportunity. "Those powers are too much for you, aren't they. It's good that you came. We can help, you know."

Did he always keep his eye on the goal? Couldn't he just be worried about his daughter for once? "Are the powers too much for me? Why, I'm not sure. I could have ended up at the pound several days ago. I was mugged at the airport and got so upset I turned into a goat and then couldn't shift back to human form. But don't worry, I'm fine. And I'm sure these powers are better in my hands than yours."

She turned her gaze out the window, wishing she were outside in the courtyard or back in Gran's library. Anywhere but here. It was so revolting: not two minutes in their company and already she'd reverted to adolescence. She really needed to get out of town. And she almost had. Almost.

"Have you ever tried to board a plane while in goat form?" she asked. When they remained uncharacteristically silent she added, "I thought about trying, since I was already there, but I decided they might not board farm animals as regular-paying passengers. Of course I could have crated myself and called myself a pet goat, but then how would I buy and work the crate, and of course how could I physically pay for both it and the plane ticket?" She shook her head sadly. "To think I used to take my thumbs for granted."

"It's begun, hasn't it?" Duncan stared at her. "Your mind is beginning to crack under the pressure. Daphne, please. Let us take those puca powers from you and you can—"

Take? So they could take them from her. Damn it, she'd

hoped to be wrong about them. But no, she'd ignored all the evidence, hoping for once, just once, that they weren't trying to manipulate her. This time via e-mail.

Violet had stared in increasing horror while Daphne spoke, then grimaced at her husband's words. Sighing, she concernedly met her daughter's eyes. "Your father's a bumbling fool, but I think he means well this time. And he's right. Since, unlike him, I still retain my Druid powers, I am capable of taking those puca powers from you. As long as you willingly relinquish them."

Daphne twisted her lips, angry. "So I was right. You're the one who wrote that anonymous e-mail offering to relieve me of these powers."

Silence.

"My own mother, deceiving and manipulating me. You even undermined High Druid Phil to do it. I can't believe you'd try to use me like this. No, wait. I can. And that's worse."

"To be technically correct, the tramp out front sent the e-mails." Violet flashed her husband a poisonous look. "At least, the first one. Oh, she claims not to know anything about it, but I traced it back to her computer."

"*Wendy* did this?" Now her father was surprised. "Why would she—And how did you convince her to keep quiet?"

"Blackmail." Daphne guessed with confidence. Not that she had a shred of evidence to prove it.

"Don't take that tone with me, young lady." There was no protestation of innocence, just Violet putting her daughter in her place. That, in Daphne's experience, amounted to an admission of guilt.

"No problem, Mom. But do me a favor and keep the details to yourself. They'll only make me nauseous." Daphne shook her head. "Just tell me this: when would you have told me you were the e-mailer?" How long could the deception have gone on?

"I wouldn't have revealed myself at all." Violet's voice was matter of fact. "We would have arranged an anonymous meeting. I would have shown up in disguise and performed a ritual, and then you would have left, happy and normal. And you wouldn't have known it was me, so you wouldn't be burdened with worries over my motives or intentions. That offer is still open, Daphne. I can't promise you the bliss of ignorance any longer, but I can still give you that do-over you wanted. You could go back to before all this happened."

"I doubt it." Daphne narrowed her eyes. "And that term. *Do-over*. Where did Wendy get that? Were you eavesdropping on me?"

Violet looked amused. "No, actually, and I doubt Wendy is capable of effective eavesdropping. Did you really use *that* term? How about that. Maybe she has enough of a brain to remember your speech patterns, even if she has nowhere near your intelligence. A do-over. It does sound like something you would say."

Her mother had called her intelligent. But how could Daphne react to a compliment in such a context? Warm fuzzies, cold chills? Warm fuzzies, cold chills? It really was a toss-up.

Duncan, who'd been listening with silent fury, glared at his wife. "You never told me about any of this. Why? Were you going to use those powers against me once you got your hands on them? I must be really intimidating, if you need that boost against me with my magic stripped."

Ah, Daphne thought, here we go again.

"Intimidating? Ha! Like I need any help at all to effectively annihilate you." Violet's eyes glittered as she rounded on her husband. "No, I was going to use them against that *faerie* whore of yours."

Now Duncan looked surprised. "You're kidding. I'm surprised you care who catches my fancy. Lord knows you don't share my bed anymore."

"Who says this has anything to do with you?" Violet bared her teeth in a smile. "Maybe it's just between us girls. I needed a wild card. And my reasons and intentions are none of your damn business."

Duncan eyed his wife shrewdly. "With both Druid and puca powers, I suppose you could have met Titania on nearly equal ground. But then what would you do?"

"Titania?" Daphne goggled at her father. "As in, Queen of

the Faeries Titania?" Duncan was sleeping with royalty? And notoriously immoral and poisonous royalty at that?

He shrugged. "She, uh, was the 'faerie chick' at the grove. The one tossing the cornerstone to Tremayne when I intercepted it."

The overblown floozy faerie? That was a *queen*? Daphne, who now couldn't get past the visual of her father and X-rated Titania doing the nasty, wanted to hurl.

Her mother exuded cold fury. "With a combination of puca and Druid powers, I could have met her on *more* than equal ground. You have no idea of the potential!" She gave her daughter a hooded glance.

"I think I need a shower now." Daphne gave her parents a disgusted look. "Let's skip the adultery and retaliation soap opera and the fun slice-and-dice-your-spouse threats. I just want to say this: I'm rejecting your offer. Not so much because I want to keep these powers as because Gran taught me better than to give a weapon to either one of you. If I thought you would use them responsibly . . ." She broke off. "Never mind. I'll deal with my problems without selling my soul to the devil." Or to her mother and father.

Duncan regarded her. "So you're more willing to take your chances with Tremayne—a nature spirit who hates Druids and pucas—than to accept help from your own parents?"

"Did I hear my name?" came a familiar voice.

Chapter Ten

Daphne jumped and whirled around guiltily. Where and how—?

Tremayne smiled at her, though the expression didn't reach his eyes. "You all seemed so caught up in your discussion, I guess you didn't know the door was open a few inches. I was going to close it, but then I heard somebody mention my name."

"You were eavesdropping," Duncan accused.

He probably had been. Daphne winced. She wondered how much he'd heard.

"Yep. Bad nature spirit. Will you punish me now?" He gave Daphne's parents a mocking look, which they avoided. Clearly Tremayne made them more than a little uneasy.

Duncan turned to Daphne. "You can't trust him."

She gave her father an incredulous look. "Wow. I have so many objections to that statement, I don't know where to begin."

"I know. You're upset with me and at how recent events have affected you. You have every right to be angry. But to lose all trust? You're my daughter. I wouldn't willingly hurt you. Can you say the same for *him*? He could just abandon you whenever he chooses, leaving you in dire straits." He paused, and Daphne could almost see the bullshit machine in her father's brain churning out new arguments, new strategies. "In fact, he probably would have done so before now if he didn't think you were useful to him. Remember Warren? How *he* used you?"

Daphne winced. "That's not fair."

"No, but it's a fact. Tremayne wants something from you,

too, and he could do a lot worse than just steal your voice and words."

"Me, useful to Tremayne?" Daphne scoffed. "What could I possibly have that would be useful to someone as powerful as he is? If anything, I'm a burden. Until I know how to use these powers and can prove I'm not a homicidal nutcake—like my *father*—he's stuck babysitting. Fun."

Duncan spoke condescendingly. "Is that what he told you? That's *it*?"

Her stomach knotted. "Yes."

Her father folded his arms and looked disgustingly pleased with himself. "Well, there's a lot more to the story than—"

"Spare me your knowledge and questionable insights," Daphne interrupted. That smug look of Duncan's was so poison-ous. It always, always made her stomach hurt. Even if it meant forfeiting information, no way could she tolerate his gloating. "I'm not taking your word for anything on this."

"But—"

"I'll ask Tremayne. In private. I don't need your fucking agenda polluting his explanation."

"Daphne!" Violet sounded shocked. "How dare you talk to your father like that?"

"Okay, that's enough." Tremayne interrupted quietly. "Daphne's made her decision. And, whether she believes it or not, she's capable of holding her own in a simple conversation with me. She'll be safe."

"I disagree," Duncan inserted, his arrogance undiminished by his lost powers. "You're a seasoned wielder of magic, and you want something from her. Daphne, as a mere novice, wouldn't have a clue how to defend herself."

In no way ready to have Daddy Dearest play Papa Bear, Daphne scowled. "Ever heard of a learning curve? I'm climb-ing it. *Let* me. Oh, and have Wendy cancel any appointments. I'm taking a personal day. To talk to my nature spirit."

She opened the door, spine stiff with tension she was trying to hide, and Duncan tried one last tack. "I see you've thrown your lot in against your father. Never mind that I put a roof over your head for twenty years."

"Can he do that?" Daphne gave Tremayne an outraged look. "A parental guilt trip? After everything else?" She scowled at her father. "Have you forgotten the grove? How, for your own selfish purposes, you made a play for that cornerstone and ended up swatting it at your own daughter? Now there's love. And look at all the extras you gave me, too! Weirdo powers, my plans demolished and even my life at risk? I'm so grateful, I'm choking on it. Guilt? Give me a break."

"Daphne!" her mother objected again.

Duncan spoke over his wife. "I know. And I'm trying to make up for that. Ask the nature spirit. Do it for yourself and save it for later if you must, but ask him. What does he want from you? Hell, ask him exactly what kind of conditions Akker put on his freedom. Ask him how he means to use you. Maybe he'll tell you."

Daphne stared at her father, trying to figure out whom to trust. "Naturally, you suggest all of this with only the purest intentions. Selfless love. Forgive me if I have doubts."

"Daphne," her mother interrupted. "You know I don't often agree with your father, but this time I must. You *talk* to Tremayne. He has an agenda just like everyone else. Make him deny it."

Turning away without responding, Daphne left the office. She heard the door close quietly and Tremayne's even tread behind her.

She eased past Wendy with little more than a glare for the receptionist's part in the e-mail stunt. Why bother getting angry? The woman was dumb as dirt and, since she was sleeping with Daphne's father, was destined to be Forbes roadkill.

"A woman could really get jaded by all this, you know," she muttered.

No response from behind, just a loud thump. She glanced back to find Tremayne leaning a muscular shoulder against the wall. He looked a little dazed, and puzzled.

"Tremayne? Are you okay?"

"Hmm? Yes. I . . . Sure. I'm fine." He shoved away from the

wall and, still frowning, followed her out the front door. "You were saying? Something about being jaded?"

"Well, who wouldn't be? My parents with their giddy enthusiasm to take the freakiness dumped into my lap in that grove—"

"Puca magic," Tremayne corrected calmly. "Calling it freakiness is nothing more than denial."

"Fine. Puca magic. They covet what I don't want and can't even get rid of."

"So, they admitted to writing that e-mail?" Tremayne sounded unsurprised. "One, or both of them?"

She gave him a startled look. "My mom, but . . . You mean you already knew about the e-mail?"

"Was I aware of it before I heard you discussing it with your parents? Yes. I saw it, remember?"

So she hadn't shrunk the message down quickly enough.

"And then you hid it from me."

Fighting guilt, she gave him a defensive look. "I hardly know you. And somebody offered help when I was feeling desperate. So, yes, I was tempted. You'll notice I didn't accept the offer, though."

"Before or after you realized who was making it?"

"Hey, I was suspicious all along. I e-mailed back, but just to get information. Now I've rejected it outright, which I think is good enough. As for not telling you . . . I don't owe you a thing. It's not like you and I are lifelong best friends who share secrets over pillow fights."

"Now there's a visual." His expression lightened considerably.

"Oh, stop." And she refused to entertain any such visual. Absolutely refused. Especially since he had some explaining to do. "Hey, if we're talking secrets, what about you? I assume not telling me you were aware of the e-mail was a test of some kind. So, did I pass? Money says the jury's still out on that one. And now I learn you're hanging out with me not for some noble do-gooder reasons or because you have no choice, but because I'm possibly useful to you. As in, used by you."

When Tremayne didn't respond—didn't *deny* the charge—

her heart sank. "You know, that really throws me. My dad can be a liar, but . . . he's not lying about this, is he? I can't believe I was starting to trust you." She shot Tremayne an annoyed glance. "But I guess you never promised we'd be on the same side in this stupid battle for my sanity."

"You're wrong. I am on your side. Or rather, we're on the same side."

"Now there's an interesting distinction," she muttered.

Tremayne caught her arm and calmly held fast to slow her frantic pace. So, maybe she was a little upset. But it was just possible that she had cause to be upset, damn it. She couldn't count on anyone.

He looked down at her. "You can count on me to coach you on controlling these powers. My motives may not all be selfless, but I think we both want the same thing: you sane, and in full control of your shifting abilities."

"Why? So I don't put you to the trouble of killing me?" she growled.

"You do seem to obsess over that point."

"That you consider eliminating me as a viable and justifiable option? Yeah, I know. I guess I'm just petty that way." She strained against his hold on her, only to find herself tugged to a stop, and turned to face him.

He bent his head to train that dark gaze on her. This close, he was overwhelming. Big, dark, seething with potential energy. Power. She could almost feel the tingle of it radiating from his skin. And he would use it against her.

"I don't *want* to use it against you," he murmured reluctantly.

"But you would, if driven to it."

His brows lowered. "I hope that I would have the strength of will to do what I must if you drove me to it. And so, I think, would you." He bent closer, his breath against her face. "The only way . . . The only thing that could drive me to it would be if you were past redeeming. Past saving from yourself. Insane. Over the edge. No viable return. *Dangerous.* Do you understand what I'm saying? Part of you would wish for an end, and I would be bound to honor that. Both for your sake and everyone else's."

Shaken by the sincerity in his voice, she studied his face. "Insanity. You honestly think that's a real possibility."

"You saw your father. And he only retained part of the powers—and temporarily at that. You have all of them. Permanently." He paused and gentled his voice. "So, yes. I think you are at risk."

Daphne swallowed. "But I feel normal. I mean, okay, life is pretty freaked-out right now, but I don't feel like going postal or anything."

"But then, you're not currently provoked. Like I said before, the real tests are under trying conditions."

"Trying conditions, huh?" Memory pricked at her, pulling her out of the spell cast by his proximity. "Sort of like finding out my mentor is in fact intent on using me? I'd like to hear more on that subject, by the way. And, hey, consider this me, multitasking. I'm getting answers even as I'm putting my powers in a pressure cooker. Let's see what happens, shall we?" She smiled grimly. "So, tell me. How will you use me?"

Tremayne studied her. "All right. I need you at full strength and capable of controlling both puca and Druid powers so that you can perform a ceremony to free me."

She narrowed her eyes. "What kind of ceremony?"

"I'm not sure. I'm told it's something that you will know instinctually once you master your powers." He studied her.

"Well, just for the record, if this ceremony involves yours truly stripping naked and performing ritual coitus, forget it." She shuddered. "I don't play temple priestess for any man."

"No man, eh? How about for a really appreciative nature spirit? I think you'd be great at the temple priestess gig." Tremayne—Mr. Tall, Dark, Sculpted and Occasionally Scary—managed to look wistful and amused all at once.

"Isn't there some rule against you trying so consistently to get in my panties? It just seems so . . . unethical."

He looked thoughtful and didn't smile, but she still had the sense that he was laughing. "I don't think so, but I guess we could ask High Druid Phil."

She snorted. "Why? So you can watch me get so furious I morph into a cat all over again? Speaking of which, I'd better learn how to choose my morphing form. It would really suck to shift into cat near a Rottweiler. I can just see the salivating jaws. . . ."

Tremayne eyed her hopefully. "Are you saying you'd like to practice when we get back to the apartment?"

"Like to? No, I'm saying I *should* practice. I did, after all, promise not to walk down the aisle as Mina's ostrich of honor. And then there's the bit where I need to learn how to control these damn powers so you can sign off approval on me and let me get on with life. That management accounting position in California will only wait so long."

"Damn." Tremayne murmured the word.

"What?"

"I—Well, that was the reason I showed up today when I did. There's a letter for you at the apartment. I thought it was for me, so I opened it without looking . . . but I guess you had stuff forwarded to my address?"

Nodding, she closed her eyes. She'd only given that address out to one party. "Yes."

"I'm sorry. I am. But it's from that company in California. They couldn't wait any longer, so they've rescinded their offer of employment and given the job to another candidate. They wish you luck in all your future endeavors."

Endeavors like shape-shifting and continuing work with her parents. She was worse off now than she had been before she quit her job at Forbes.

Daphne blew the hair out of her face and gave Tremayne a near-violent look across the cardboard kitchen table. "I'm trying, damn it!" And she had been ever since they walked in the door of his apartment three solid hours before. Hey, it wasn't her fault that, as a human from birth, she somehow found it difficult to morph into an animal.

"But you're not concentrating." Tremayne sounded absolutely certain. And calm. Why did he get to be calm while she felt like a freaking idiot? A damn failure at everything. She couldn't even freaking leave town without turning into a shape-shifter, and then she couldn't hold on to the job of her dreams once it had been offered to her. No, she'd had to run whimpering back to Mommy and Daddy and their family firm of happy horrors. They'd known all along she'd never leave. And, look, they were right! She was utterly incompetent. A total failure. If she couldn't even succeed at a real-life, normal career—simply accept an advancement that was outright offered to her—why did she think she could possibly master magic? She was human, not puca. She stood up from that hated metal chair and resisted the urge to smack feeling back into her butt.

A new and welcome thought suddenly popped into her head. "Has it occurred to you that maybe I don't have the ability to shape-shift anymore? Maybe the powers have worn off. Maybe they rejected me and ran off to attach themselves to a corner-stone. Or maybe they went back to the puca they've known and loved for longer than, say, my country has been in existence. Why stay attached to me?"

Tremayne just regarded her quietly.

"You keep doing that, damn it. First my parents look at me like I'm nuts, and now you? Why don't you just kill me and be done with it."

He didn't respond to that, either.

Of course not. She'd been speaking irrationally. She'd been doing that a lot lately. No doubt it served as further proof of her dwindling supply of reason. That and her frustration. She'd known they couldn't hold that job for her forever, but damn it, the reality of her failure still sucked. She'd been replaced—as in, was completely replaceable. No way was she telling her parents she'd already lost the job, either. She didn't think she could stomach the satisfaction and pity and virtual pat-pats on the head as they told her it was all for the best and of course she didn't really want to move to California.

"I suppose we could talk to Kane or Riordan and see if they have any suggestions to offer." He sounded doubtful. "But I really think it would be a waste—"

"Of time? Effort? Energy? Too late." Daphne folded her arms. "This whole experience has been a waste." As was her every attempt to escape this burg.

"It just takes practice. If you would just—"

"No. I'm done." She groaned at his expression. "Yes, go ahead and look at me like I'm a spoiled toddler who's tired and unsure of herself and totally unwilling to cooperate." She turned and stalked off to the extra bedroom. "I've had enough. I'm declaring a break. Why don't you go do some nature-spirit things while I go pretend I'm human for a while."

She slammed the bedroom door behind her and welcomed the undemanding silence.

"Tremayne?" Daphne called a little while later, so timidly she made herself cringe. Well . . . she wasn't proud of herself. She'd stayed in her bedroom for a long time, surfing the Internet and catching up on e-mail and some work she'd brought home, but it was nothing urgent. She'd done nothing that couldn't have been set aside in favor of more critical demands on her attention, like learning how to control her powers and staying on the good side of the only guy who could help her with that.

Tremayne didn't answer her summons, and the apartment seemed quiet. She frowned. The door to his bedroom was mostly closed. She supposed he was in there. In fact, he was probably listening to the MP3 player he'd bought himself the other day, much to her amusement. Apparently the man had spent a little time recently shopping on the Internet—first the couch and now electronics. What kind of music would entertain him, she'd wondered. Classical? Bluegrass? Show tunes? Alternative? Eighties pop? A peek at his playlists had proven her right: he listened to all of those—and more. Evolving nature spirits were apparently voracious consumers of culture.

Before she caved to cowardice, she decided she better beard the lion in his den. She reached for the doorknob and, as soon as the door swung inward, dove immediately into "Tremayne, I'm sorry. You were right. I wasn't focusing, was really fighting because I didn't want to do it. I was just upset about losing that job and . . ."

Her words dried up as she absorbed the view. *God.* No, really, he had to be a god. No lesser being, even a magical one, could look this magnificent. She leaned back against the door, absently closing it so she'd have something to prop up her hormone-beleaguered body.

Tremayne was sprawled on his belly across his lush bed, his big body dwarfing its satin-covered surface. Blanket and comforter were bunched low, as though he'd shoved them down with his bare feet. Right now, his equally bare legs slid restlessly against hot-chocolaty satin. Bare buttocks flexed and tugged the muscles of his back into definition. Heavily corded arms plunged beneath a pile of four pillows—his nonrejects, she could only assume. He'd snugged his face deeply into one.

She should have felt bad for staring, but she couldn't work up even a teeny bit of remorse. Nobody was that big of a hypocrite. She swore she could bounce a quarter—no, a whole freaking roll of them—off his . . .

"Daphne."

She jumped. *Busted!* Her face got hot. "Yes?"

His response was just to mumble into the pillows, tug them closer, and she saw the muscles of his shoulders and upper back bunch. But he said nothing else. He was sleeping, she realized.

He was saying her name in his sleep? Daphne swallowed. Oh. Wow. Shame would reassert itself at some point, right? Or not. Hey, he'd said her name. That kind of gave explicit permission for her to remain within sight—er, *earshot.* Right? In case he said anything else?

As she continued to stare, long legs moved restlessly over satin sheets, slid to the side, and then on a groan he rolled—Daphne squeaked, attempting to turn away—onto his back. Too late.

She stilled in shameless awe. Whoa boy. They grew nature

spirits big. And Spirit, Jr., was . . . well, there was plenty of him, too.

Tremayne lay with his arms stretched overhead. His face was turned from her, but she saw his chest rising and falling with breath. A chain with a small charm glinted from a swirl of dark chest hair that dwindled to a narrow line arrowing—

"Did you need something?" a deep voice rumbled.

She looked up.

Tremayne had turned his head to look at her, his dark eyes blurred with sleep and heat. As he continued to watch, she continued to be too stupid to move, and that lush mouth she'd admired so often quirked at the corners. He seemed to be waiting.

"Daphne? You wanted to see me?"

Oh, man, did she ever. And had she ever.

He shook with laughter.

Projecting. Oh, dear god. "That elimination thing you mentioned? This would be a good time for that."

"Not even if you begged me." Still chuckling, he rolled onto his side and propped an elbow to rest his head on his hand. He eyed her with tender amusement. "You know, you could slide right into this bed with me and I wouldn't question it. Not even for a moment. No awkwardness, nothing but you and me."

Oh, don't even tempt—

"I was dreaming about you."

"Yeah, I heard."

Now he flushed a little, but his gaze never left hers. "What did you hear?"

"You said my name." And if she'd thought about it in time, a mindwalk would have been fascinating, if perhaps contrary to the karma he held so dear.

"I said it out loud, huh?" His gaze traveled down the front of her. After work, she'd changed into faded jeans and a T-shirt, leaving her feet bare, but that cotton felt downright transparent the way he was looking at her now. "In my dream you were naked and under me."

Oh, no, no. He couldn't do this. And why did she let him? Why would her stupid feet refuse to move? The rest of her was on fire. Her nerve endings rejoiced in total, feverish rapture, bouncing with joy all over her body. Like she was nothing more than one long, tangled fuse ready to be set off.

Oh, lord, she couldn't—

Or . . . maybe she'd just shrink. She swallowed hard. Either the floor had just gobbled her whole as she'd prayed, or . . . She looked down and saw cream-colored paws; then she looked up, way up, into amused, dark eyes. Tremayne was peering over the edge of the bed at her.

This was a new low. And not just literally. Annoyed, she turned to leave the room, only to find the door closed. And look! Her with no thumbs again.

"Daphne." Tremayne's voice was low and shaking only a little with laughter.

Why did she always play the fool around him? Normally she was composed, polished, and even intimidating, at least according to some men. Around Tremayne she shifted into cat form, swallowed her tongue—any number of humiliating things. It wasn't fair. Annoyed, she dropped her butt onto the carpet and just stared at the closed door, attempting to will it open. Could pucas will a door open? How about Druids? Or maybe she would need training to do that, too.

"Daphne." Tremayne spoke again, and very patiently.

She didn't respond, just stared at the damn door. Willed it open. Nothing.

If she couldn't go through the door, how about that original plan? After all, it would be much easier for the floor to swallow a cat whole than a human whole, right? A cat had a smaller body mass, so it was—

"Please turn around."

"No." Maybe she could climb out a window. Yeah, right after she grew a couple of thumbs to open the damn thing. She would write an ode to thumbs tomorrow if she ever got some back.

Mortification outpaced nonsense, and she groaned almost audibly. Yes, she was so attracted to Tremayne she'd shape-shifted into a cat. How was that for a dead giveaway? Slightly less than coy, certainly.

"You can't ignore me forever."

"Yes, I can." And she would, too.

"Don't you want to shift back?"

No. She was done with life as she knew it.

"I get it. You're afraid of me. I turn you on. I'm just too much for you to handle, right?"

"That's supposed to work on me?" she snapped. "I'm telling you, nobody but nobody is that juvenile. Well, maybe you are. But then, you stripped naked in broad daylight to nap with the door unlocked."

"And then I forced you to come in and stare at me while I slept." He affected a scandalized tone. "Oh, *bad* me."

A smile tugged at her mouth. A smile in cat form? Was that even possible?

"I really shouldn't do that, should I? Where's my compassion? I'm just too hot for you to witness in human form. Smoke spewed out of your ears and suddenly, *poof*, hello kitty."

Daphne growled.

"What was that? I'm afraid I didn't understand . . . ." He was obviously entertaining the hell out of himself.

"This is just a barrelful of laughs for you, isn't it?"

"What? You proving beyond a doubt that you want me every bit as much as I want you? That's the best news I've had since I gained a physical body." He spoke with bald sincerity. "If you're expecting me to feel bad about it, to pretend I don't understand, I guess I'll just have to apologize. I don't. I can't. I wouldn't even try. I love it that you want me. Now I just have to convince you to do something about it."

"Why? Because you're into bestiality? Sicko."

He chuckled. "That won't work this time."

"It should." She grumbled low, which emerged as a sound that was less than intimidating. Just like her form. If she had to be a cat, why couldn't she be an exotic-looking Siamese, or a black cat with spooky yellow eyes? No, she had to be a damn creampuff with bimbo baby blues.

"I kind of like your current form," Tremayne said. "Not nearly as much as I do your human one, but the cat . . . well, it appeals on a different level. Like seeing the Daphne that lives beneath the business suits."

"Normally I do not look like a cat when naked."

He laughed. "That's not what I meant and you know it."

"I know. You're talking about that whole first-shift and intimacy thing. I get it. But do you think it's fair that I find myself in this position whenever I'm around you? I don't. It's like getting naked with a stranger, which is something I'm not in the habit of doing. Unlike some nature spirits I know."

Tremayne laughed. "Nudity seems like a big deal to you. First you weren't going to do nudie rituals with the Druids, and now you won't willingly get naked with me—physically or otherwise."

"You know, I really don't want to discuss nudity with you when you're wearing nothing but a . . ." She glanced over her shoulder then whipped back around. "Hell, you're not even wearing the sheet, and I've been in here with you for . . ." Hours? Days? Mere moments? She couldn't possibly gauge.

"I don't mind being naked around you," he replied. "You seem to enjoy it. And I enjoy you enjoying it. Why should I deny myself? You do that often enough without me adding to it."

She mocked: "Poor nature spirit. Like you haven't gotten laid a million times. Sex is probably boring for you by now. Is there a single being you wanted but didn't have?" She tossed a glance over her shoulder.

"Yes," he said. "You."

"So that would make me the one holdout. I'm honored."

"Daphne. Do you have any idea what my life has been like for the last two thousand years?"

She thought a moment. "Long?"

"I've spent the majority of that time without a body." He raised his eyebrows pointedly.

She would not blush. "Well. I just, uh, figured you guys maybe do it differently. You know. Spiritually?"

His lips twitched. "Ooh. What a turn-on. Wanna bump auras with me?" His tone was insincere. "No. That's not how it works."

"Oh." She tried to digest that.

"And during the short time that I've had a body, I've been serving an ancient Druid's warped sense of justice."

Another good point. Still, *look* at him. What woman could say no to him and actually mean it? "So, maybe it's only been a couple thousand women?"

"No," he replied.

"Less?" She studied him.

"Less."

"A couple hundred women and only their closest friends?"

He shook his head, his cheek rolling on the hand cupping it. His eyes were amused, yet gently inquiring.

"So maybe a hundred, plus a few steady relationships?"

"Daphne." He spoke with patient acceptance. "There's been no one."

She stared. He didn't mean, couldn't possibly mean . . .

"I've *never* made love to a woman."

Chapter Eleven

Never? He'd never been with anyone? As in, he'd never had sex? No. Not possible. No man as sexy as Tremayne could possibly go without it. He probably meant he'd just never been with a human woman.

Heart pounding, Daphne attempted a joke. "So, maybe a pixie or two and a couple of gremlins?"

He just watched her quietly. Waiting.

Now she was completely flustered. He'd never . . . He didn't mean *literally* never.

"I do mean literally never. I've never been with a woman, human or otherwise."

Daphne cleared her throat. She shouldn't ask, should just drop the subject here and now. "Do you, um, know how it works?" Oh, bad. She should have just left it alone. This conversation could go anywhere now, and she had only herself to blame.

He grinned at her, his dark eyes leisurely appraising the look in her own. "Do I know what goes where? Only too well. You know, modern couples are a lot more inhibited than the ancients were. They used to have public fertility rites that amounted to orgies. Trapped as I was at the stone circle for so many years, I had to witness a lot of them. The puca did, too. He was bored and envious enough to narrate occasionally—much like a modern-day sports announcer."

Tremayne grinned ruefully. "Impossible puca. I couldn't even tell him to shut up. It was slow torture, but very educational." He eyed Daphne speculatively. "I have a lot of theories I'd love to test."

"O-kaaaay, how about we just drop—"

"And what's more . . ." He spoke determinedly over her, though his voice never rose. "I've never wanted another woman the way I want you. Right now, it's you or nobody. That's what I want."

When he paused this time, she didn't have any words left. Didn't have a clue what to say, could just pant like an aroused, amazed, guiltily pleased idiot.

He continued. "I guess it's only fair to warn you that I'm a little infatuated with you. Obsessed even." He tried another smile, but his eyes were hot and intensely focused. On her. "When I think about trying out some of these theories—fantasies—it's always you that I picture. Always."

Her? She glanced down, saw fur, and nearly jumped out of her skin. "Look, I'm a cat right now. This is very weird for me. I mean, you can't just say these things, feel this way. How am I supposed to . . ." She shook her head, completely at a loss.

"Oh, but I already did. And do. And trying to muddy up the issue won't work. *It's you that I want, Daphne.*"

"This is so disturbing. Yeah, I know, you're comfy with the whole cat thing. I'm not. And I really—"

"Come here."

"What? Are you insane?" She backed up, feet tripping over each other in quadrupedal confusion.

He smiled a little. "I would help you shift back. That's all."

"Riiiight." With that look in his eyes? She'd bet every one of her nine cat lives that he had more than mentoring in mind.

"I'm just offering help. Look, I'll even pull the sheet up to make you more comfortable. Anything that happens after that . . . well, that would be up to you."

"See? See that?" She backed up another step, her body low and poised to flee. "I told you you were a pervert. Hot for kitty. Yech. Next you'll be getting me drunk on catnip and taking advantage of my—my feline assets."

His lips twitched. "No, I mean after you've shifted to human form. I'm offering to help you shift back to yourself. Do you want help or not?"

"Well. Shifting help." She approached with caution. "Yes, I do want that. If you'll just . . ." She held up a paw, as though they could do a finger-meets-kitty-toe connection and transfer the power that way. He shook his head and smiled.

"What?"

He slid back on the bed, leaving an obvious spot open in front of him.

"This is blackmail," she growled. "I'm telling a Druid."

"You are a Druid."

"I mean a real Druid. Like Phil," she clarified.

Tremayne's voice was a sexy rumble. "And what would you tell him? That I want you? Do you think he cares?"

"Well . . . doesn't he? I mean, you can't play mentor if we're doing the knee-knocking thing, can you?"

"Knee-knocking?" He raised his eyebrows.

Daphne gave him a wide-eyed speaking glance.

"Oh. *Knee-knocking.*" He nodded wisely. "That's very romantic. I can see how you'd be tempted almost beyond endurance."

She sputtered a moment, then laughed. "You're impossible."

"Since you mention it," he went on, "never once did I hear a Druid tell me knee-knocking was out of bounds." He shrugged. "I think they regard nature spirits as just intrinsically balanced and fair."

"Really?" she said. "Did they account for evolving nature spirits?"

"What, you want me to ask for fine print?"

"Maybe," she said.

"Well, I won't. But I'm also only offering help at the moment." He patted the mattress in front of him. "Hop up here and I'll switch you back."

"But why up there? Why not you—"

He lifted a corner of the sheet barely covering him. "I can do that if you want. But it means losing the sheet and exposing your delicate sensibilities to my nudity, and I know how you feel about nudity: it's as bad as discussing politics in mixed company. Maybe even worse. Offering a rare steak to a vegetarian. I mean, you know if they were honest, they'd admit they really want it, right? Temptation is just cruel." Before she could growl, he interrupted. "A joke. I was *kidding*. But if you want my help and you don't want me to lose the sheet, come up here."

Aaarrrrggghhh. The man was impossible. Not that she had any choice. On a more audible groan, she made a death-defying leap upward, snagging her claws into satin, until a big hand gently boosted her upward.

"Sorry," she muttered.

"Hmmm?" She could feel the rumble of his voice in the pit of her belly.

"The sheets." She stumbled a little, finding it hard to gain her footing on the soft bedding, still warm under her toes from his body. "I know you like them, that whole sleep thing, and I'm afraid I might have snagged—"

"Who the hell cares? I have *you* in my bed now."

"Whoa, buddy. Hold on to your bedsheets. Meow? Remember meow? I'm still a cat."

Smiling, he tugged her close to his chest. She leaned into his warmth in spite of herself, in spite of her misgivings. Then she felt the same draw she'd felt before. A rush of energy reversed itself and left her, to be absorbed into his big body. After a moment, he opened his eyes and stared directly into hers.

"Hi."

"Hi?" She cleared her throat, relieved and yet alarmed to find herself human—thankfully clothed—and snuggled up to his big, mostly naked body. And big was right. Any woman who shared a bed with him would risk getting bounced right off in the middle of the night.

"Not you."

"Hmmm?" A mumble of her own this time. A purr almost. Humans didn't purr. She hadn't changed back again, had she?

"No way would I bounce you out of bed."

She choked and ducked her face but found the evasion less than helpful, since it just gave her a really good view of his marvelous chest. He was—Oh. He really was perfect. He smelled . . . so good.

She ducked ever so slightly closer, drowning in the scent and heat of him. Long fingers tunneled through her hair, massaging her scalp a moment before tightening to tilt her face up to his. She got lost in dark eyes seething with heat. And as aroused as she was, he seemed even more so.

"How I've wanted you." He rumbled the words and she lost her breath. When he moved his face closer to hers, she lifted her own, saw his nostrils flare, his eyes becoming molten darkness as his mouth took hers.

He was hungry and insistent but not rough, just supremely focused and thorough. He consumed her lips, his tongue exploring every curve, surface, texture and expanse as though he could learn and memorize her mouth. She groaned and raked her fingers through his hair as he slid an arm under her. Rolling onto his back, he tugged her on top of him.

She gasped into his mouth at the feel of him pressed against her. All of him, all of her. He was hard all over and so aroused. There was no give to his chest. She could feel the muscles of his belly contract as he instinctively but subtly rocked his hips against hers. He was holding back. Just barely.

The thought of his control and how all of that hard body seemed so hungry for hers was more than she could handle. She pulled back, breath coming fast and furious. She saw his mouth, wet and red, and the heat coming from his eyes. The thrust of his jaw suggested how much he wanted her, yet how much control he was exerting. If that didn't test her, nothing would.

"I'd better . . ." Her voice sounded hoarse, and she saw his nostrils flare. Oh. Her resolve wavered.

Summoning her strength, she pulled back, feeling his resistance for a moment before he released her. She slid off of him. Carefully, she took deep, even breaths. She would not—refused to—shift back into a cat. Not now. No, no, no.

He smiled a little, obviously privy to her thoughts. "You won't shift. I think you're still in the recovery window."

"You know, a gentleman would stay out of my thoughts right now."

"Stop projecting them. I showed you how, remember?"

Sure, she remembered. But remembering while calm and

unemotional was one thing; remembering and staying focused while as horny as a bitch—no, a *cat*—in heat was another. "Let's just say it's not second nature yet."

He sat up, gently tugging her with him and bunching the sheets around him with belated modesty. Then he met her eyes. "So, how about we take it up a notch? If you could glamour me, mind reading would be easier and thought projection would be even more basic."

Shocked, she leaned away from him. "You want me to glamour you? Not just read your thoughts but *change* them? Can I do that?" More importantly, why would he let her?

"Only momentarily, and only if I'm open to it. Being what I am, I can knock out your power without a second thought if that's what I want. Or, I can choose to allow it. Normally I allow you all of your powers, even though you don't use them. When you've shape-shifted and need help shifting back, I call up my powers and they drain you."

She studied him, a scary thought intruding. "You drain magical powers. Are there . . . other things you can drain?"

"Yes."

"Like what?" Maybe she shouldn't ask.

"Like . . . a person's essence. Their life force." He paused. "But I don't do that. Karma, remember? I like my skin too much to give it up easily in so short a time."

She could certainly see why he liked his skin. Although, with effort, she kept her gaze from taking it in.

Seeing the wicked glint in his eyes, she groaned. "I'm projecting?"

"No. Not with your thoughts. Your face is pretty readable, though."

"Gee, there's a relief." She gave him an ironic, probably red-faced look and he laughed.

"So. The glamour. Are you ready?"

"No, but let's do it anyway," she said. "So, it's . . . well, the pupil thing first, right?"

"Yes. You'll begin like I showed you for mind reading, although you don't have to wait for my thoughts. In all honesty, the glamour is easier to initiate, and a lot of times it will bring thoughts forward as you attach your commands to them."

"That's just weird."

"Come on. Keep an open mind, remember? So, you look into the person's eyes . . . That would be me. We'd initiate that unholy attraction you remember. . . ." He grinned as she rolled her eyes. "My pupils will enlarge and then, if you wait, contract and then enlarge even more.

"When you're dealing with a typical human who's in thrall, the person will hold your gaze and be unable to look away. While the person is in this state, you make your commands. If the command fits with the person's natural inclinations, he or she will accept it completely. If it contradicts the person's personality, he or she will likely eventually set aside the contradictory command.

"When you've given your command, pull your subject out of thrall by inviting the person to come back to himself." He shrugged. "And then it's done."

"Okay, back up," Daphne said, and frowned. "How do I keep from glamouring when I'm mind reading, then? Wouldn't that second pupil thing happen if I'm looking too long?"

"It's possible," he agreed.

"Well, that's not good. What if I say something stupid when I'm just trying to read a mind?"

Tremayne shrugged. "Don't."

"Oh. Well, gee, that solves everything."

He grinned.

She shook her head. "This is wrong, you know."

"Only if you use it for criminal or unethical purposes." He gave her a knowing look. "I'll bet you'd never do it, at least under normal circumstances. You'd never use this power at all."

"But these aren't normal circumstances," she mourned.

"Nope." He spread his arms and smiled. "I'm willing, aware and consciously not drawing your powers from you. Glamour away with my blessing."

It was actually really brave of him, she decided. "So, this is like hypnosis, then. Can I make you bark like a dog?"

"Do you really think that fits with my personality?" he asked.

She gave him an evil look. "Sometimes."

"We've talked about karmic retaliation. Did I ever mention nature-spirit retaliation?" His expression was misleadingly innocent.

"All the time. But usually it's directed at my parents. Remember the death thing? No, wait. You called it something more palatable. Elimination. You would *eliminate* them. Or me."

He sobered, though his eyes conveyed understanding. "I'm trying to help you here, you know."

She sighed. "Yes. So. We begin with the unnatural attraction."

He nodded and met her gaze. She looked into his eyes and, after a moment, felt him move marginally closer. As his pupils enlarged, she became aware of a channel seeming to open from her mind to his. That was new. She hadn't sensed it the last time. As she continued to look into his eyes, his pupils constricted, then enlarged until they nearly consumed the irises.

"Oh! Oh." It had worked. She should . . . What should she do? He'd said to give him a command. Okay. But what command? She should have thought of one before.

He seemed to lean closer, in thrall and drawn to her. A command—She needed one now! But nothing horrible.

She caught her breath, and words emerged before she thought twice. "You will not kill my parents."

"I will not kill your parents."

A thought in his mind slipped past, a reluctance to eliminate *any*one. But there was determination, too. Honor. He had a duty that was above her concerns, above his own, above even the reluctance she'd seen. Her command—was it compatible with his personality or not? She suspected not.

Meanwhile, he still stared at her. She tried to draw back, but he followed.

"Tremayne? Tremayne, you're scaring me—"

He blinked, breaking the connection, and inhaled, his gaze moving over her face and around the room. Then he focused inward, seeming to shift a little as though reading a page.

She watched, hesitant and nervous. But why? Should she really feel guilty for requesting that he not kill her parents? No. She would not. Imposing her will and turning him into a robot was wrong, but . . . She hesitated, then cleared her throat. "Did you . . . I mean, could you tell . . . Were you aware . . ." She took a breath. "Did you recognize my command? Did it work?"

He nodded slowly, then met her eyes. "It worked. Or rather, it would have worked on another being. I saw it imprinted before I erased it." He paused. "I do understand. I hope you realize that I would do nothing out of malice."

She gave him a rueful look. "If I believed you would kill them out of malice, I would behead you in your sleep. And it's a pretty head. I'd hate to have to do that."

"I'm touched. And, congratulations on your first glamour!" He gave her a grin. "I believe you may have read thoughts while you were in there? I felt something."

She nodded slowly.

"And the structure you saw before?"

"It was clearer this time," she admitted.

"Excellent. And did you take advantage of my naked body while I was in thrall?" He gazed at her with exaggerated hope.

She laughed, not able to fully squelch her amusement. "I figured you wouldn't need glamouring to allow that."

"So that's a no. I'm heartbroken." He looked more amused.

"Well, if it makes you feel any better . . ." She sobered and met his eyes. "I came in here originally to apologize. And to ask if we can continue working on shape-shifting."

"That's a relief," he replied. "And smart, too." He wasn't rubbing it in, just relaying information. "Now that we've made some inroads on mindwalking, maybe you'll find it easier to open yourself to shifting."

"My paws are crossed," Daphne muttered under her breath.

"This isn't working." Chest heaving with frustration and pent-up tears, Daphne glared at Tremayne. They'd been at it all evening, and this was in addition to that afternoon's morphing disasters. She felt incompetent, foolish and defeated.

Tremayne obviously did not agree. No, the man was unfailingly patient. Unemotional. Calm. The man was so damn *calm*, just staring at her while she sat there humiliated and digging her toes into the rubber soles of her flip-flops. Did he even care about her fate? Was there a heart beating behind those impossibly sculpted pectorals?

At the moment, she really doubted it. She could see why the Druids doubted it. If he did have a heart, he sure knew how to lock it away to get work done.

"Daphne. You're not focusing."

Same damn thing he'd been saying all afternoon and evening. "What's to focus on? Energy I can't see? I'm supposed to focus on my joints and skin and muscle, and change each into that of an animal? I never did study anatomy. . . ."

"You don't need to study anatomy. This is magic, not science."

"Maybe this is news to you, but I actually have a hell of a lot more schooling in the subject of science than in your freaky, good-for-nothing magic. What's the use of having the magic if it doesn't even work? This is pointless."

"You just need practice. It will work." Tremayne. Patient. *Still.* Did he never lose his temper?

"What would be the point in losing my temper? You're frustrated enough for both of us."

There, at last. A crack.

"Why do you want me to lose control?" he asked.

"Maybe so I'm not sitting here seething all by myself? I feel like a rebellious student you keep plopping in the corner for a time-out. I'm a grown human woman who has every right to feel frustrated about not being able to turn into a damn house cat."

"So, turn into something else," he suggested.

"Like what? A mouse?" She raised her arms and affected a mystical tone. "Yes. I can feel the connection now. A soul connection. Why, our minds are flitting around on the same wavelength already. Is that cheese I smell?"

He sighed. "Take a break."

"A break from what? Nothing?"

"Yes. Basically." He grabbed her hand and tugged her around to face him on the couch. Then he spoke clearly, with quiet sincerity. "I don't see you as a child. If I did, it would be sick and very likely illegal, given what I so desperately want from you. No . . . I simply see you as justifiably frustrated."

Her tension easing, she eyed him with some relief. "Really? So we're feeling sympathy and silently wishing to offer reassurance? Because you don't give off sympathetic or reassuring vibes."

His lips quirked. "No? What would those be like?"

"Calm and comforting, not . . . detached. Here, let me put this in terms a magicky, nonscientific type might understand." She widened her eyes mockingly. "If we were to examine an aura as one exudes sympathy and reassurance, it would radiate lovely shades of sky blue or maybe butter yellow. Like breezy sunshine on a spring morning."

He eyed her with disbelief. "And you call *me* strange."

"I most certainly do not. *Strange* would be such an understatement, considering you're a two-thousand-year-old nature spirit with ripped pecs and unexplainable dampening powers."

"You seem fascinated by my pecs," he remarked. "Does that mean you like them?" Tremayne peered down at his chest, which was concealed by a T-shirt.

She grinned. Never had he looked more human than now, preening over his stupid muscles.

"To be vain is human?" he asked, thus proving she'd dropped her guard.

She shrugged, not really minding. "At the moment, it seems so."

"Okay." He smiled. "If I suggest trying this again, but a little differently, will you give it an honest shot?"

She tipped her head to the side and considered. "That all depends."

"On . . . ?"

"Whether you're giving off those sky blue or buttery-yellow vibes I mentioned."

"Ah. Well, picture me striped blue and yellow as I make my

next suggestion. I want you to leave the cat and mouse out of this. And don't even think goat. Try for something different. Something you'd love to be. When you were a child, did you ever wish you could do something you'd seen an animal do?"

"Fly free." She responded without thought, the words startling her. "Yes. Fly away, high over the trees and out of earshot and sight of everyone." She grinned. "And then maybe do some loop de loops."

He nodded slowly. "That's fairly advanced shape-shifting. Not just mastering the change, but also the bird's body and mind and skills. Stumbling while flying . . . could be physically dangerous. I'm not saying skip it. I'm saying, call it a goal just beyond your next. For right now . . . how about something that *runs* free? Something small and quick. Does that appeal?"

She thought, then nodded slowly.

"Do you know what it is yet?"

"I think I do."

"Don't tell me," he ordered. "I want you to imagine it in your head. Close your eyes and really feel it, not as an inanimate picture, but as a pleasure. A joy. It's an adventure. Feel the excitement, the freedom as you outrace your cares and bothers. Leave them all behind and run fast into the wind."

She did so, trying not to be self-conscious, just concentrating on his words, wanting to feel them and experience their meaning.

"Yeah, like that. Now, as you race, imagine the world around you revolving slowly, then faster and faster, as though creating an energy vacuum, sucking it all in, in counterpoint to your mental spin."

She felt the whirl, felt the excitement, the building and preparing energy.

"Now let it race along your spine and shoot outward to all the points of your body. Your mind, your face, your arms, fingers, legs, toes . . ."

She felt the zinging, felt the energy all over and inside of her, heat, excitement, disorientation . . .

"Open your eyes, Daphne." He spoke with soft awe.

She did. Blinked. Glanced down. Her lower half—what used to be her lower half—was a tangle of impossibly slender limbs and dainty hooves . . . curled around a flip-flop. Carefully, afraid she might break, she slid her front legs off the couch. They held. She glanced at Tremayne, who seemed to regard her with quiet wonder.

"I'm doing okay?" she asked.

He nodded.

Carefully, she worked her rear legs off the couch and stretched. She felt light, lithe . . . and restless. Tremayne rose behind her then swiftly moved toward the front door. "We could, if you want, slip out the back way. Maybe head toward the park?"

"Can we?" She itched to find open spaces.

He grinned. "Hey, a gazelle isn't so different from a deer that we'd be risking much. Not at this hour. Why not?"

Her heart pattering with anticipation, she followed. The swift movement of her body was so free. She felt as unfettered as she'd once hoped she would.

Tremayne checked outside, found the hallway of the apartment building clear, then motioned for her to follow. He closed the door quietly behind them and led her down a set of stairs at the rear of the building. From there, it was only a block to the park. Given the hour, the place was deserted. She glanced at him, saw his smile in the darkness, then took off. And she really did feel as if she were flying free, on the dainty but swift legs of a gazelle leaping over bushes and arrowing between trees and under branches.

After the first rush of euphoria had worn down, she found him again, sitting on a park bench. "Thank you," she murmured, feeling odd. Until tonight, she'd spent every shape-shifted moment feeling angry, terrified or sarcastic. Never at peace. Certainly never exhilarated.

"No need to thank me. You did all the work." He paused. "And we're not through yet. You still need to shift back."

She grimaced inwardly. "Maybe we ought to do that inside

your apartment? So as not to alert the authorities to men speaking to strange gazelles on city property?"

"Exactly what I was thinking. Wow, you really have mastered the mindwalk." He spoke with mock awe, rising to his feet.

"That's the other thing you need to finish teaching me."

"I don't think so," he replied.

"What do you mean, you don't think so?"

"I think you can master it all on your own. You've already done a glamour. For the rest to come, all you need now is to practice and, frankly, not analyze so much. You possess the magic and therefore the ability. You want to control everything, always, but that's not always the answer. Sometimes you need to relinquish control and just let your instincts take over."

He rounded the corner of his apartment building, checked the stairwell and motioned her to follow. They climbed to the second floor, but had only opened the door to the hallway, when Tremayne halted.

Daphne looked up. Someone was at the door to Tremayne's apartment. It was Duncan Forbes. And he was determinedly fiddling with the doorknob, trying to break in.

Chapter Twelve

Before Tremayne could react, Daphne sprinted past him in a fury. She couldn't believe her father would try to break into Tremayne's apartment. Why? What did he hope to gain?

Shoving between her father and the door to plant her hooves squarely on the doormat, she turned to face him. She felt almost beyond speech—not unusual for a gazelle, she supposed. "Is there no crime that's beneath you? Theft, assault, attempted murder and now burglary? Or is burglary a repeat for you? It's getting hard to keep track."

Duncan, who'd jumped at the sound of his daughter's voice emerging from a gazelle's mouth, just dazedly shook his head.

"What? You have nothing to say for yourself? No lies to spout? No defense? No 'foiled again' speeches?"

"You're a gazelle." His voice shook.

"That's it? Yeah, okay. I'm in gazelle form. You knew it could happen. You might have even done it yourself a crime or two ago. And yet it throws you to see me this way?"

He closed his mouth, still visibly upset. "You're my daughter. And you're a gazelle. It's . . ." His breath left him in a whoosh. "It's a little startling."

"Like catching your father breaking into an apartment?"

He blinked and glanced at the door, then at Daphne, then at Tremayne striding unhurriedly toward them. "But I just came to apologize. For before. And with everything that's been going on, I was worried when you didn't answer my knock."

Daphne narrowed her eyes. She wished she could believe him, both because he was her father and because she was an idiot.

"Now that you're here, suppose you say what you need to say and leave. Next time you decide to 'visit,' try picking up a phone first. And here's a hint: if nobody answers, it's not a good time. Let's do the bulk of our conversing on the job."

"Okay. What I wanted to say . . ." Duncan lowered his voice. "I'm sorry about earlier. I don't want to make your life harder. I want to help if I can. I'm worried about you and I'm afraid you'll let pride get in the way of asking for help if you change your mind and decide you want to be rid of these powers after all. So I'm making the offer again. And I want you to consider it an open offer, no strings, no I-told-you-so's. Even if I have to beg your mother to save you from those powers, I will. You're my daughter. I won't see you tortured like this. Especially when it's my fault you're in this position." He paused, and when he continued there was a harder edge to his voice. "But I suggest she not be allowed to keep the powers once you've rejected them. She wouldn't—"

"Yeah, I get it. This is where the halfway-decent apology and offer of unconditional help becomes a lobbyist's speech. Can we just leave it here and say we'll see each other in the morning?"

Her father nodded silently and backed up a step. "Just . . . don't be afraid to call if you need me. Any time."

"I . . ." She sighed and shrugged helplessly. "Thanks." Then she stepped off the mat and turned.

"Good lord!" Duncan lunged backward, his gaze trained low.

Daphne glanced down at the floor where her father was staring. The jute doormat on which she'd been standing had black and smoldering marks. Her hoofprints had been branded into the mesh of ropy fibers.

Okay, this was new and badly timed. And really freaking scary. "No, don't tell me. I've taken on the form of Satan himself, haven't I? Is that hellfire I see sparking from my feet—I mean, hooves?"

"That's not hellfire." Tremayne sounded calm but curious. He glanced at Duncan. "Leave, Druid. I'll deal with this."

Duncan, still looking appalled, backed away, then hurried toward the elevator.

Daphne, feeling shaky, didn't know what to do or where to stand. "I'm Fire Girl. No, Fire *Gazelle*. This is out of control, Tremayne. What did I do?"

"It looks to me like your Druid powers are trying to make themselves known."

"Oh. Nice timing." Eyes on the rug, she shifted a bit, watching for more scorch marks on the tile floor of the hallway. "So, this is what you meant before?"

"Before what?"

"At the grove. When I asked if I could make a crater of the clearing. You seemed to imply that all hell could break loose if I blew my lid."

"Yes." He grinned ruefully. "But if it makes you feel any better, I don't think you'll set the apartment on fire."

"Be grateful for small favors? This is so unacceptable," she muttered.

"Just learn to control the Druid magic, too, that's all. You'll be fine. Powers tend to make a little noise when they first make an appearance—which is apparently what's happening here. A few scorch marks aren't the end of the world." He wrinkled his nose. "But you can spring for my new welcome mat."

"Right." She nodded gamely, or tried to, as she glanced around. "As long as you think we're safe from a fiery inferno, how about we go inside?"

He laughed. "Good plan. I'd hate for the neighbors to think I let an African gazelle with fiery hooves run loose in the apartment complex. I could get evicted for that!"

When Tremayne opened the door for her, she stepped docilely past, actually a little relieved to be inside. Until she could shift back on her own, no way would she initiate a shift outside Tremayne's apartment. "So, how do I shift back?" she asked.

He glanced at her, his expression wry. "I tried to explain once."

She sighed. "I remember. I was less than receptive, as I recall. It could be that terror was getting in the way."

He smiled. "All right. I'll try again. How about you try to

hold off on the frustration while I try to channel those yellow and blue stripes."

"Deal."

"Okay. Do you remember how it felt when you morphed into this form? The energy patterns? Can you remember them? Not just in your head, but a sensual memory."

She frowned as she tried.

"Close your eyes, Daphne." When she did so, he continued in a low voice. "Remember the joy of running free? That's what got the energy flowing before. Why?"

"Excitement. Adventure. Freedom," she answered. She shivered in reaction but didn't open her eyes.

"Yes. Good. Remember that excitement. Feel it again. Just a hint of it. That freedom."

She felt the zing, but held off doing anything with it.

"Now, take that flow of energy and reverse it. Same pattern, just backward."

Like a roller coaster crashing to a breathtaking stop, only to surprise its riders by slowly moving backward, picking up momentum and then *whoosh*, she felt the adrenaline rush backward through her at a breakneck speed, rounding curves, darting at angles and targeting extremities—

"Good! Excellent! You did it!"

Daphne popped her eyes open, blinking to look around, up, down. She was back!

Tremayne laughed in triumph.

Smiling, too, Daphne took a step then stumbled. She looked down. One flip-flop. She sighed. "Lost another one to the cause."

"Patience, little human. You're making great progress. I think keeping both shoes intact will be the ultimate sign that you've mastered shape-shifting."

She groaned, mourning all the shoes she'd sacrificed so far. "When this thing is over, I'm buying a brand new pair of red stilettos. I swear."

"Get us both free, and I'll buy the shoes for you."

"Deal," she agreed, and inhaled deeply. "So. We try again?"

"We try again."

Thirty minutes later, Daphne had managed to shape-shift into an animal and back to human again twice. First she changed to a petite white poodle. Out of shame, she morphed back to human form almost immediately, much to Tremayne's amusement. He was actually quite impressed with her efficiency, however.

Daphne snorted. "Why not a sleek greyhound? A sassy schnauzer? But, no, I get puffball cats and poodles."

Then, much to her shock, she morphed into a wolf. Tremayne seemed equally surprised.

"I'm actually . . . a little bit dangerous in this form, aren't I? As in, capable of more than wetting the carpet or shredding furniture or gnawing chair legs." She frowned. "Or branding your welcome mat."

He nodded. "You're progressing. Rapidly. This is good. Fantastic, in fact. How do you feel?"

"You mean, do I feel like my brains are rattling around in my skull and urging me toward violence? I think you're safe. As long as you don't actually say what you're thinking when you really are thinking something like that. Then I can't be held responsible." Cautiously she took a step forward. Then another. She could feel the power in her muscles, the restless urge to run. It was . . . inspiring. No doubt she'd be craving raw and bloody rabbit meat any minute. That part was unnerving. "Okay. Werewolf Daphne is shifting back."

Tremayne grinned. "You're not a werewolf."

She paused and eyed him haughtily. "A woman shifting into a wolf? If that's not a werewolf, I don't know what is."

"*Werewolf* . . . is too limited a term. You do more than that, and you have more control over it. And, unless you go nuts, you probably won't run around biting innocents."

"Okay, I'll buy that. But all the same—"

"Wait. I have an idea. Let's take the return shift a step farther, shall we? How about we try to keep your shoes on this time?"

Daphne glanced down at her paws. "Wolves don't wear shoes."

"No kidding. But you might notice that you didn't leave one behind when you shifted to animal form this time."

Daphne blinked slowly. He was right. She'd actually shifted both shoes for the first time. To gauge her progress, they'd ensured that she was wearing both shoes every time she shifted. Flip-flops, actually—much cheaper, especially if she purchased them in bulk.

"Suppose we concentrate on bringing that other shoe back with you this time."

"How do you suggest I do that? I didn't consciously bring it with me when I shifted to a wolf, so I don't know what I might have done differently."

He frowned. "Suppose . . . just suppose you hold on to that shifting sensation, that energy flow, until it winds itself out. You've been stopping short—out of fear, I think, and probably relief. This time, just let everything run its full course."

"Like letting the phone finish its ring before I pick up."

"Sure," he agreed. "See what happens."

Concentrating, Daphne closed her eyes. She let the energy overtake her again, then, consciously, reversed its flow. She let it surge backward in the same pattern, with the same velocity, let it stream all the way back to its source until it slowed to a stop.

Opening her eyes, she looked down. One. Two. Two shoes. She grinned up at Tremayne. "Well? Am I good or what?"

"Damn good." He nodded, dark eyes gleaming with approval. "Here's the thing, though. You know all the shape-shifting skills now, but you need to keep practicing. I want you to be able to control yourself easily, not just hope for the best every time you attempt a change. That means a lot of practice."

"How much is a lot?"

"I'll assign you tasks every day. Different ones. Assuming I can think of them."

"Every day? You understand I'm working a full-time job right now, right? Then there are the minor inconveniences of eating and sleeping and laundry. You know, *life* things."

"This is important. You'll find a way."

"Slave driver."

His grin turned wicked. "Does that make you my slave?"

She snorted. "Only in your dirty, wet little dreams."

She did as he directed, and later that week Daphne fell into bed exhausted, her head buzzing with all the energy she'd started, stopped, reversed and embraced. A girl could feel like a walking switchboard after a while. A freaking tired one at that.

Groggy, she let exhaustion overtake her, swallow her whole, even as the buzzing seemed to continue into her dreams. It slowed, separating itself out into a rhythmic pattern, repeating until her breathing seemed to flow in harmony with it. Just before she woke, the pattern seemed to slow further, becoming a language of its own, an insistent voice that demanded something from her.

When buzzing became voices in the head, did that mean a girl was going nuts? Was this something Tremayne would object to? She had every right to wonder.

At least it had only been in sleep.

She crawled out of bed the next morning with an uneasy feeling in the pit of her belly. Her weird dreams seemed to want to follow her into wakefulness. Shaking them off, she showered and went to the kitchen for breakfast. There she found Tremayne . . . cooking?

She blinked at him. "What are you doing?"

He was frowning at a saucepan, into which he'd dumped a block of frozen bacon. So, he was making pig soup? "I thought . . . well, I thought I'd learn how to cook."

She nodded slowly. Then she said, "Um, I admit I don't know a lot about it, but that looks very wrong to me."

"It doesn't seem to be doing much except turning black on one side, while the rest stays frozen." He poked the meat with a fork.

Maybe it was the smell that had made her stomach feel weird, not her dreams. "Have you tried a cookbook?" she asked. "If you could forego one of your soap operas, I'm sure you could find cooking shows on the television. Or maybe you could download some cooking info from the Internet."

"Did you bring your laptop home?" he asked.

"Sure. You want to look now?"

He gave her a sheepish grin. "A little later. I think right now this bacon just wants me to give up and put it out of its misery." He dumped it into the trash and she hid a grin.

"Okay. Well, you're welcome to look if you're interested."

"Would you be willing to leave the laptop at the apartment here with me? Would you trust me with it?" he asked. "I plan on staying here."

She gave him a startled look. "Even though it's a workday for me?"

"Sure." He smiled at her. "I have to trust you to resist insanity and spontaneous shape-shifting at some point, right? Today seems like a good time."

Trust and faith. He was offering her that.

She smiled at him. "Okay. And, yes, I can leave my laptop with you. I'm meeting with a client, but he's coming to me this time. I'll use the desktop PC."

"Thanks." Tremayne reached into a cabinet for some cold cereal, which he poured into a bowl. As he was putting the box back in the cabinet, he seemed to trip over his own feet and slam into the fridge. Daphne jumped and automatically reached for him, although his bulk would have just landed them both on the floor, but he caught himself, one hand on the counter, the other on the fridge.

"Tremayne?" She gripped his arm.

"You know, nature spirits aren't normally clumsy, I swear." He gave her a sheepish look that seemed strained around the edges, and she didn't smile.

"I would be surprised if they were. Is there something you need to tell me? I mean, this isn't the first time you've seemed to just . . . well, launch into furniture. It's kind of weird. Not like it's gravity taking you down or your feet tripping you up. Are you feeling okay?"

"Other than stupid and embarrassed? I'm fine. Just hungry." He slid the bowl over on the counter and opened a drawer.

"You're sure? I mean, are nature spirits prone to viruses or anything? Inner ear infections?"

"Yes," he admitted. "Weirdo creeping diseases that make us grow vines out of our ears and roots out of our toes." He waggled his eyebrows then reached in the drawer for a spoon. "I'm fine. Stop worrying. Don't you need to be leaving soon?"

She glanced at the clock and quickly retrieved the cereal box he'd returned to the cabinet. "Soon" was right.

Several hours later, she was looking back on Tremayne's expression of faith as the one bright spot in a hellacious day. And by the time she returned to the apartment, she was dying to ram something sharp down somebody's throat.

She slammed the front door, dropped her tote bag onto a chair and scowled at Tremayne. Startled, he gave her a wary look in return.

"Bad day?"

"Were I to judge the entire world based on my parents and the company they keep, I'd be one disillusioned human being."

Tremayne's gaze sharpened. "Did something happen with your parents?"

"No, with Eli Norton, a seriously arrogant sleazeball of a prospective—no, *much anticipated*—client. I'm supposed to become a fiction writer, it seems, and make up numbers on his behalf. We would begin by doctoring payroll-tax returns, then create worlds of fun-and-make-believe with his quarterly income taxes." She glared into Tremayne's eyes.

"You're kidding."

"I wish. And it's not like Norton's hurting for cash either. He's actually well-off and well-known locally. That's why my father wants his business, although I doubt Dad realizes the extent of this guy's expectations. Good old Eli wants me to do his lying for him and sign off on the paperwork so he can throw my name at the IRS when he gets audited."

Tremayne grimaced. "What are you going to do?"

"What can I do? I'm supposed to meet with Norton again the day after tomorrow, at which time I'll refuse to change his numbers." Daphne sighed tiredly.

"What will he do then? Prepare his own taxes?"

"Heaven forbid." She laughed humorlessly. "He'll find some other accountant, probably apply force and promise incentives until he gets his way."

"So, basically, subject some other accountant to the same treatment he gave you?"

"Basically." She shrugged. "What else can I do? My choices suck. Either I enable tax evasion and assorted other shady behaviors, making me a party to his crimes, or I report him and repel nervous clients who either believe me a disgruntled party to his schemes or fear I'd report honest mistakes. Either way, I come out a loser. I can't afford that. So I'll refuse him and do nothing."

Tremayne nodded slowly. "Does it occur to you that you have other options now?"

"Options?"

"Think outside the box, little human. You are a hereditary Druid who wields puca powers. I think special powers should be used for good, don't you? Does this give you any ideas?"

She gave him a wide-eyed look. "You're saying that I could be the vigilante puca accountant. Batman meets H&R Block, with a tail!"

Tremayne grinned. "That's the spirit."

"So to speak." She rolled her eyes. Still, the idea had taken root and sprouted almost immediately. Oh, to actually use these powers for good, maybe counterbalance all the crap her parents had perpetrated over the years. The idea appealed so greatly, she could feel her throat tightening with emotion. A purpose! To cover the rush of feeling, she tried to joke. "And, hey, don't look now, but I'm pleased about my powers for once. I'm experiencing delusions of grandeur. Maybe it's my childhood addiction to comic books, but I seriously need a fantastic superhero name that wowed kids can whisper in awe."

Tremayne stared at her. "You do?"

She gave him a laughing look. "Yeah, like Batman or Super-man or Wonder Woman. But it has to be something power-ful, modern, sexy and catchy." She widened her eyes. "Oh, and it has to go with the term *accountant*, but it can't clash with my wardrobe or make me look fat. Got any ideas?"

"Speaking of wardrobe, how about we get you a cool cos-tume?" He eyed her with lustful whimsy. "Something tiny, with leather and lace and fishnet stockings. Stilettos? Big hair? Red lips?"

"So I can be Superpuca Ho?" She gave him a quelling look. "Calm yourself, wild nature spirit, or I'll turn a hose on you."

"Spoilsport."

Her anger and then her hilarity fading and leaving her open to her surroundings, Daphne suddenly recognized a different smell in the air. Sniffing audibly, she turned her attention to Tremayne. "Are you trying to cook again?"

He grinned, manly chest expanding with obvious pride in his own accomplishment. "I'm baking, actually. I found one of those cooking shows you mentioned, then went online for the recipe. I had to try three different times—messed up the first couple batches—but I think this last one's going to work. Did you know there's a difference between baking soda and baking powder? And cooking cocoa is different from the kind you use to make hot chocolate. The things you can learn. So . . . do you like brownies?"

"I love brownies," she agreed. And it was damn sweet that her nature spirit mentor was baking them. She could picture that intent look he sometimes got when he searched the Inter-net. He'd bring that same focus to learning how to cook—she just knew it. She sighed inwardly. And he couldn't have picked a better day to offer choco-comfort either. *Good* nature spirit.

He was also very wise, in that he'd long ago made a very good point: if these stupid powers weren't going anywhere, it might be a good idea to learn to use them productively instead of just denying them. And he was so right. This would be the ultimate demonstration of control, wouldn't it?—controlling the puca powers and using them for justice.

Chapter Thirteen

"Good morning, Mr. Norton." Daphne gave the sleazeball a cheery smile as he approached the table she'd reserved for their breakfast meeting. It had been her invitation—and a strategic maneuver. "How are you?"

She'd spent all of yesterday planning this meeting: setting up locations, considering potential scenarios and practicing shape-shifting until she was exhausted. Granted, she hadn't entirely mastered the two-shoe shift. In fact, Tremayne had even accused her of practicing with his shoes because she'd run out of complete pairs of her own. Finally, however, after a few unproductive hours, she'd had to cry uncle last night. A superpuca needed her beauty sleep to fight crime. If she needed to shift, she would just kick her shoes off and store them somewhere discreet. Otherwise, she was ready.

Norton took his seat, and after they'd ordered and exchanged the briefest of pleasantries, he regarded her coolly. "So. I hope you've had a chance to rethink those numbers you quoted me before?"

"I did. My math was correct, and payment, naturally, must accompany the forms we send in. I trust you brought your checkbook with you?" She gave him a professional smile.

"I thought we had an understanding, Miss Forbes. You get creative with the calculator and paperwork, and I write you a big check instead of giving the government a huge one. Back out on me now, and I'll feel compelled to share a version of my negative experience with all my nearest and dearest. And I'm sure your father would be displeased."

Blackmail, too? Goody. "Mr. Norton, I'm ashamed of you. Surely you didn't think I would lie to the government just to save you a couple of pennies."

He lowered his voice and moved closer, threateningly so, and into her space. "I damn well did think so. You knew that."

"Maybe. But I was really hoping I was mistaken. Or that you'd had second thoughts. Since that's not the case, I'll just be turning you down flat. What will you do now? Take your business elsewhere? Find some other poor accountant to bully?" She watched him speculatively.

"No. I have no intention of taking my business elsewhere. Either you do this for me, or I'll somehow discover money missing from my account—oddly enough, right after I gave you my account number for future transfer and rebate purposes. I could easily destroy your reputation in this city," he warned.

It was absolutely a bluff. She knew that. But that didn't negate her own feelings. This asshole had a Napoleon complex so big he was going to either pop his shirt buttons or make a nervous puddle on the floor. The bully.

"Mr. Norton." She met his gaze and held it. As she watched, his pupils enlarged, contracted, then enlarged again. It was now or never. "Mr. Norton, you must pay for your breakfast. Include a decent tip. Then calmly leave the restaurant with me." She pulled money out of her wallet, left it on the table and watched Eli do the same. Then, docile still, he walked out of the restaurant with her and rounded the building to the entrance of the park. She'd planned this location with the park in mind.

"All right, Mr. Norton."

He met her eyes.

"You can return to our conversation as though we'd never interrupted it. Do not think it's strange where we are. Wake up now. You were saying?"

"It's very simple. I will make it impossible for you to find honest work in Richmond or anywhere else in this state. And once word gets out that you stole from me . . ."

Containing her fury—or rather *using* her fury—she let her energy level ratchet high, then loosed it to dart in dizzying slashes, nerve ending to nerve ending. She felt the itch crawl up her spine and travel to her extremities, as her reality seemed to shift sideways then travel up. As did Eli Norton's wide-eyed gaze. Perhaps he would wet himself now?

Daphne smiled inwardly, then was a bit startled to hear it emerge as a quiet whinny.

"You . . . You . . . What the hell?"

"You know, this is not how I usually deal with clients, but it turns out you're kind of a special case. As in a thief, a bully and a blackmailer. How dare you?" She ducked her head low, nosed him where the sun didn't shine—Eli squealed, much like a frightened horse, in fact—and tossed him on her back. She trotted forward as he flopped all over, protesting in a hoarse screech.

"Shut up and hold on, Eli," she warned.

She quickened into a canter, forcing him to hang on or fall off, and felt a tug at her mane as he grabbed a handful. Then he wrapped the other arm awkwardly around her neck. Yech. At least he was hugging a horse and not her actual body.

"Now, Eli . . ."

No answer. Just horrified panting from the man as she took her gentle canter into a gallop, heading for a wooded area. When she'd planned this little jaunt, she'd taken the nearby stables into consideration. It was not uncommon to see people riding horses in this park. They wouldn't draw undue notice.

"Answer me, Eli. Now."

"Yes? Yes, um, ma'am? Horse, ma'am? What the hell. Whatever. Anything."

"That's better. Now let's talk finances. And the law. And what I can do to a man who tries to strong-arm me into thieving servitude. I don't tolerate it. As you can probably see."

"Yes. Yes, I do see." And his voice warbled high at the end. "Look out—"

She veered at the last moment, avoiding a tree he'd no doubt visualized connecting violently with his forehead. Hey, she'd missed it. Might've been a near thing, but she hadn't done it on purpose. Not exactly.

"Good. *I do not fix the books for anyone.* Not the president of the U.S. of A., should he request a warped version of my services; not Napoleon Bonaparte, were he to emerge from his tomb; not Elvis Presley, were he ever to reenter a building alive; and most certainly not a slug like you. You will accept the paperwork I drew up for you. You will sign and submit your tax forms as I requested. You will pay your taxes, correct to the penny, on time and every quarter. You will never again try to con me, the government, your employees or customers."

"But I don't—And not even—"

She leapt over a bush, drawing another squeal out of the man. "Because if I ever, ever hear of you trying to strong-arm me, another accountant, a gullible customer or even a Girl Scout selling cookies, I will report you to the IRS. I will notify the Better Business Bureau. And I will contact any other authority or entity I believe might be interested. The police maybe? The attorney general's office? The media? Your wife? I've never dealt with a crooked client before, but I have resources and I'm creative. Are you listening to me, Eli?"

"Yes. Oh, yes." He clutched desperately at her mane as she proceeded in a bone-jangling zigzag. "I'll do whatever you want. Sign anything. I'll write a check. Who do I make it out to? The Better Business Bureau? I can do that—"

"No. You must pay the *tax man*, remember? That's why we met today. Eli, you'd better be taking me seriously."

"Oh, I am. I am. Just a little distracted." He touched his forehead to her neck, muffling his fear-filled voice. "Willing but distracted."

"That's good. Because if I find out you've reneged on any agreements we're making right now, I will follow through." And she would, too. It would be a headache, but she was committed. And that felt damn good. Instead of working a job she hated, living in an apartment that was not her own and pining for a different life that was now out of her reach, she was focused on something positive: a purpose and a goal that she would see through. "So, pay your taxes and keep your nose clean or you'll have legal nightmares the likes of which you've never dreamed."

"I'll have nightmares. I know that. Pay my taxes. Lots of nightmares," he mumbled.

"So we understand each other?"

"Yes. Very much so. Yes." He gasped brokenly. "I'm going to be sick now. If that's okay."

"I'll be in touch." And on that note, Daphne hurriedly ditched him from her back and retraced her hoofprints, as the unmistakable sounds of retching echoed behind her.

Wincing slightly, she picked up speed. As she neared a group of tall bushes, preparing to shift discreetly, she was surprised to hear footsteps in the brush. "What, wasn't one ride enough for you, Eli?" She frowned, wondering how he'd gotten in front of her.

"I think one was plenty." It was Tremayne, sounding pleased and amused. "Well done."

Daphne slowed at his approach. "You saw?"

"And heard. He didn't stand a chance." His grin grew wider. No doubt her nature spirit had been lying patiently in wait for her and her victim, as he'd known her plan. He had a stake in it, too. "You know, most pucas . . . well, the other two I know, anyway . . . would not have bothered with the diatribe on honest accounting, but would have stuck to the nightmare threats. Simple, effective, straightforward."

"Right. As though I'm anything like them. I'm just a tiny bit younger, and brand new to the puca experience. I think I should be allowed a few eccentricities," she replied. "I am an accountant. A *super* accountant." She grinned. "But I'm still a bean counter and not an ass kicker. As befitting my experience and conscience, I fed the man a little logic, gave him a taste of his financial consequences—"

"And showed him the light. Naturally. I like your style." And he sounded sincere. Even admiring.

Daphne stared a moment then looked away, momentarily grateful for her horsy form: horse hair tended to mask a hot rush of blood to the cheeks.

"Where did you leave your shoes?" Tremayne asked.

"My shoes?"

He grimaced. "Forgot to kick them off, huh? I hope they weren't expensive."

She frowned. "No, I . . ." She looked around. "I'm not sure. I can't remember what I did with them." Like it mattered. With a resigned sigh, she let the energy build again, reverse upon itself to draw the tingles from limb to spine until it centered deep inside her. She felt the warmth encompass her, then fade, and she opened her eyes.

"Daphne."

She blinked, attempting to reorient as she stumbled toward him—and tripped over what felt like debris. He caught her arms and steadied her as she opened her eyes.

"Your shoes, honey."

She groaned. "Yeah, I know. I . . ." She looked down, expecting asymmetry or bare feet, then stared as she saw shoes neatly encasing both of her feet. Not only that . . . The pile of loose "branches" that had tripped her up was actually a tangled mass of shoes—a scuffed red patent leather stiletto, a ballet flat, a sling back, her running shoe, mismatched flip-flops. They were all shoes that she'd lost while shifting from one form to the other. She'd bet any amount of money that the mates for these were all piled on the floor of Tremayne's extra bedroom. She'd managed to shift both shoes she'd been wearing—along with all the others she'd lost in the past. She'd done it! She had, and in a time of great stress. Full control of her shape-shifting power. So where did that leave her?

Victorious . . . and possibly no longer in need of a mentor? She had no idea what to expect. Would Tremayne leave her now? No, of course he wouldn't. He still needed her to perform whatever chant would finally set him free. *Then* he would leave. And she . . . well, what would she do then? What on earth would she do with her life now that she had it back?

"What do you think? Do I look like a wedding cake?" Grinning shyly, Mina patted the skirts of her wedding dress.

Since the encounter with Eli and the bad news about the California job several days earlier, Daphne had been looking forward to this, a day of catching up with Mina and discussing normal things like wedding dresses and fittings and invitations and guest lists. They'd planned it over the phone the day after Mina's last visit. Daphne had already tried on her bridesmaid dress, found it acceptable, then hurriedly changed clothes so she could see her sister's outfit. They were standing together in the common area of the boutique's dressing rooms.

"You look beautiful. Breathtaking!" Daphne stared with unexpected awe. "You know, I've never seen a wedding dress this close-up before. I didn't realize lacy white bells and whistles would affect me this way. But it really is magic."

"Really? Didn't any of your friends get married?" Mina asked.

"Well, a few, sure. But . . . I don't attend weddings if I can help it. Just not my idea of a good time."

"You mean, you don't approve of the institution."

"No," Daphne responded slowly. "Not exactly. It's not that I don't approve. I'm just not sure I believe in what they promise. We talked about this. My parents and all, but . . ."

"But?" Mina smiled knowingly.

"But I could see where it could work for someone like you or Riordan. You both . . . have something different between you. I haven't seen anything really like it before. You make me believe in possibilities I've always discounted." She shrugged. "Not likelihoods, you understand, just possibilities."

Mina gave her a shrewd look. "But that's not all, is it."

"What do you mean?" Daphne narrowed her eyes. "You really haven't known me long enough yet to claim sisterly ESP."

"Doesn't take ESP to see that somebody's given you reason to change your mind a little. You're falling in love with him, aren't you?" Mina sounded sure.

In love? With Tremayne? Daphne stared. "Oh, good god, no. I mean, I respect him. Even like him . . . surprisingly. I mean, we've gone through a lot together. But love? No. Oh, no. We're not even of the same species. Hell, he's the one charged with executing me if I go bonkers and have to be put down like a rabid dog. I'm supposed to *love* that? Get real." Ah, but would she like to twist up the sheets with him a little? Those satiny sheets that looked so good against his skin? Oh, yeah. And maybe, just maybe, that could happen sometime soon. This mentor thing was almost at an end, after all, so the power balance between them wouldn't be weird, and if sex made things awkward between them, they could go their separate ways, no problem. It was a thought to consider. Thoroughly.

"Well, he hasn't even come close to executing you yet, and I seriously doubt he could really go through with it. Not when he looks at you the way that he does. The way he held you when you turned into that lovebird . . ." Mina shivered theatrically. "As for the other . . . I hope you know that 'different species' argument just isn't going to fly . . . um, so to speak. Not with me anyway. I'm marrying a former puca, for Pete's sake!" She turned and looked at herself in the mirror one last time, then sighed and contorted herself sufficiently to unzip her dress.

"But that's a completely different thing. You two love each other. He's known a great family, and your mom and stepdad, from what you've told me, were really happy together. You know what you're doing. I think you'll be really good at it. But not me. I mean, look at my background, my history. My parents' relationship is a deterrent in and of itself. And I told you about the Druid ex. I'm not chancing being . . ." Daphne broke off, not wanting to go there. "Anyway, it's all a moot point. Heck, Tremayne might not even know how to love. Not like humans do."

Mina frowned. "I had hoped . . ." She stopped herself.

"What? Do you know something? Tell me."

"It's nothing." Mina shrugged, looking as though she wished she'd kept her mouth shut. She quickly stepped back into jeans and pulled on a T-shirt and cardigan.

"Oh, you can't leave it at that," Daphne protested. "That's not fair. Tell me what you know."

Stepping into a pair of mules, her sister sighed. "Fine. But take this with a grain of salt and please consider the source."

"So? Who's the source? And what's the source saying?"

"Your father. And mine." Mina carefully arranged her dress on a hanger and slipped a garment bag down over the top.

Daphne made a face. "Pulling out a big old shaker of salt, here. My father and wisdom are two concepts I wouldn't willingly connect these days."

"See?" Mina shook out her dress's train and pulled the hem of the garment bag down over it. Then she turned back to her sister. "So, why should I bother telling you? It's probably wrong."

"Be that as it may . . ." Daphne braced herself. "Let me have it. I need to know what you know."

"All right." Mina sighed and dropped into the settee next to Daphne. "It was just an offhand comment I overheard Duncan make. Remember when Janelle and Kane were trying to figure out who was framing Kane, and then suddenly Tremayne was on the scene?"

"Yeah," Daphne said.

"Well, Duncan was nutso at the time and muttering under his breath and said Tremayne was dangerous. That . . . well, he implied that Tremayne was so cold, he was more robotlike than human. That in a game of twenty questions, he would more easily resemble mineral than plant or animal. And, honestly, Dunky sounded nervous when he said it."

A robot? Seriously? She'd never—Well, she supposed she had at one point compared him to Data, a fictional robot. Maybe she should have taken that sentiment a little more to heart. An automaton. It was possible, she supposed. But then, decidedly, she shook her head. Maybe at one time he was like that, but not anymore. "Tremayne's evolved since then. I know that much. And he's evolved quickly, from a nature spirit with no body to having a luscious body with a sense of humor and patience. I just don't buy any description of him as robotlike or cold. I'll buy dangerous. Or powerful. But Duncan misunderstands him if he thinks he doesn't have *any* emotions. He might not be capable of all of them—I can't really tell for sure—but he does feel."

"Daphne's right." This from behind her. Daphne turned to see Riordan, who had entered the dressing room on quiet feet.

"Hey, you didn't see my wedding dress, did you?" Mina scrambled to her feet and shoved several protruding ruffles back in the garment bag. "You can't see the dress until the church! I insist on that much tradition."

"No, I didn't see the dress." Riordan grinned at Mina as he strode farther into the changing area. Totally at ease, he looked around. Various feminine undergarments, necessities and fripperies, all for sale, were scattered around, complementing a decor splashed with florals and pastels, all muted, soft hues.

Mina folded her arms and regarded her significantly unrepentant other. "And I suppose you know this is strictly a women's dressing area."

He shrugged. "I crashed the ladies' room; so sue me. But Kane and Tremayne will come knocking any minute. They're almost done trying on their tuxes next door. If you want my take on the nature spirit, it's now or never."

He dropped onto a pink couch, propped his boots on a dainty coffee table and folded his arms. Daphne bit back a grin. Rolling her eyes, Mina went to sit next to her fiancé and motioned for him to continue.

"In my opinion, there's a hell of a lot more to Tremayne than Duncan or any of us knows. I think Tremayne purposely lets others underestimate him." The ex-puca grinned ruefully. "I know he fooled me completely—and that for two thousand years." He slid an arm behind Mina's shoulders and she nestled close.

"How did you underestimate him?" Daphne asked. "What exactly did you know of him when you were trapped inside that cornerstone?"

"When I was inside the cornerstone, I didn't believe he was even a thinking being, just some energy force that wouldn't release me. He maintained that fiction for a hell of a long time. Now that I'm out and I've met the guy, I've decided I was damn lucky."

"How so?" Daphne asked, confused.

Riordan shrugged. "It's pretty simple. I'm here, aren't I? I'm not dead or insane."

"Not insane? That's a matter of opinion." Mina ducked away when he tugged on her hair.

Riordan shook his head and turned back to a smiling

Daphne. "To be blunt, I was a royal pain in the ass in that stone. I was in there against my will, totally cognizant of my surroundings but disconnected from them, and trying not to lose my mind. So I talked. I mean, I would not shut up. But he never tried to stop me or silence me. And some of the things I said . . ." He shrugged. "Anyway, I think the guy understood. He put up with it because he . . . well, damn it, I just think Duncan's wrong. I think Tremayne has something naturally human about him. He's no colder than you or I. He has a heart. A *compassionate* one."

Daphne fought the feelings that were growing inside her. Tremayne's humanity had little to do with her—except for his lenience as a guardian.

Riordan went on. "He was entirely honest when Kane was on trial, too."

"That's right," Mina spoke up.

"He doesn't cherish any kind feelings for pucas, but also he didn't lie when he could have," Riordan pointed out. "He was honest and spoke up in defense of someone he didn't like. That shows strength of character and goodness—at least in my book. I say, don't underestimate the guy. As for Duncan, he's been known to misjudge a lot of people and things: Lizzy, Mina, me, Kane. You." He smiled. "Your father's wrong. He was wrong before and he's wrong now."

Daphne relaxed. "I guess it *would* be kind of dumb to take relationship and humanity advice from Duncan Forbes, huh?"

Riordan shrugged, his smile lopsided. "It's not for me to say—but I won't argue."

Daphne nodded. As she pondered what to do with the information, the door opened on a loud knock.

"Everybody decent in here?" Janelle's voice rang out as she peeked around the door. "I found two men loitering in the hallway." Grinning, she strode in with Kane and Tremayne on her heels. "Sorry I'm late. The clinic was crazy with emergencies today. Just be glad I stopped off to shower before I came."

"Hold the details, please." Mina held up a hand. "The bride is squeamish, if you recall. I'd rather not hurl on our imminent finery." She gestured toward the rack of garment bags.

"Ooooh! Which one's mine?" When Mina pointed, Janelle snatched hers up and disappeared into an adjoining room. Riordan joined the men to chat.

Mina murmured to Daphne. "What do you think? I mean, you've been living with him. Do you think he has a heart? Is he like us?"

Daphne stared at Tremayne. Standing between the two puca brothers, who seemed to accept him, he appeared awkward but pleased. He'd been so surprised when he'd been asked by Riordan to stand up in the wedding. Kane would be best man, but Tremayne would be the only other groomsman. "He's a good man, Mina. I think . . . I think Riordan's right."

Mina nodded, satisfied. "I knew you were a smart girl."

Daphne grinned. "Maybe I take after my sister."

Tremayne casually made his way closer, and a moment later he asked, "So, what's up?" He eyed the room's occupants a touch nervously, then Daphne.

Grinning, Riordan strode over. "Why, were your ears burning? I was just telling Daphne that I thought she was in decent hands with you. Never once did you fry my puca ass for stuff I said in that cornerstone. And I talked so much! I figure you're as patient as patient gets."

Tremayne raised an eyebrow. "Your ass needed frying on many occasions."

"I'll buy that," Kane agreed from where he stood.

Riordan shook his head, still grinning. "Man. I still can't believe you said not a single damn word the whole time I was in there. I knew you were there, sort of, just figured you couldn't speak."

Tremayne shrugged. "And I figured letting you believe that was the only way to keep you off my case—and me from frying your ass as a result."

"No doubt." Riordan's mouth quirked. "Speaking of that time, though, and specifically, the cornerstone . . ." He looked puzzled.

Tremayne's gaze sharpened. "What about it?"

"Where is it, anyway? Kane said he doesn't have it."

"Nope," Kane verified. "No idea where it went after the Druid Council meeting."

Riordan turned to Tremayne. "Do you have it?"

The nature spirit stared at him. "It was my job to hang on to it. I take my job seriously."

Riordan grimaced. "No need to tell me that."

Tremayne eyed him curiously. "Why do you ask?"

"Well . . . I was just wondering about the powers it contained. The powers I forfeited on November Day last."

"Daphne has them."

"Yeah, I know she's the one who wields them now. But are they grounded in her or in the stone? Are they volatile still?"

Tremayne frowned. "Again, why do you ask? You gave them up and have no claim on them."

"Oh, I know. I was just concerned. They ended up hurting a lot of people before, including my brother and Janelle and several other innocents. I never really got to speak to you about it, but . . . I feel vaguely responsible, and I'd just like to know they're safely contained."

Tremayne made eye contact with Daphne. "I begin to think they are, actually."

Daphne smiled at him in response.

However, on their way home, the words that had given her such warmth started to leave a bad taste in her mouth. Tremayne believed she was close to mastering her powers. Which meant he would leave her. For so many reasons—all of them unexplored—she wasn't ready to say good-bye. How ironic was that? After she'd been so eager to get rid of him?

Of course, he'd been enslaved for two thousand years. Next to that, her own wishes meant nothing. It was time to release him from babysitting duties, as soon as he and the Druids were okay with it. And when the equinox rolled around—less than a month from now and a mere week after Mina's wedding!—she would set him free for real. He'd earned at least that much.

Daphne's heart raced in protest. Would it be so wrong to wish for a little more time with him? No. Not really. But it had to be his choice.

Slamming the door, she rounded the car and caught up with Tremayne on the sidewalk outside his apartment building. "So, I guess we'll be seeing the Druids soon." She made her voice the ultimate in breezy.

"Hmm?" As he turned, Tremayne's eyes grew unfocused. He swayed into her.

She caught his arm. "Whoa. Are you okay?"

"Yeah, sure." He shook off his dizziness but was still frowning as he opened the lobby door for her. They walked toward the stairwell. "You were saying?"

He still seemed unsteady. Concerned, Daphne just shook her head. "We can talk when we get to the apartment." If he was sick, no way was she leaving until he was better. Not that she was using illness as an excuse or anything. It simply would be irresponsible to abandon a sick man.

In the stairwell, Tremayne seemed to hold the rail tighter than usual, taking each step with a little more care. At the top and through the door to the hall, he swayed again, even more violently. Daphne caught his shoulder, really worried. Normally Tremayne's movements were so deliberate. But lately . . .

She looked at his eyes and narrowed her own. "You're fading in and out, aren't you?"

"Yeah. No, I . . ." He scrubbed his face and stumbled again. "Tremayne?"

"Just . . . disoriented. Off-balance. I can't seem to . . ."

He stumbled again, this time going down hard on the cold tile floor, as though shoved from behind. Squatting next to him, a protective hand outstretched, Daphne whipped around to see . . . But of course nobody was there. She turned back.

"Tremayne?"

There was no reply.

Chapter Fourteen

Groaning, and feeling as though somebody had pounded a rock into his temples, Tremayne rolled his head around the pillow. He parted his eyelids just enough to let in a sliver of light. He was in his bedroom.

"Oh, thank god." It was Daphne, sounding shaken. "What the hell was that?"

"What?" He squinted up at her.

"You passed out in the hallway. At least you were clear of the stairs already, but you hit your head on the tile." She touched a tender spot and he grimaced. Considering his powers of healing, he must have conked his head hard for it to still be painful. "You had a nice egg here. And then I had to drag you . . ." She broke off, and he noticed she looked pale and exhausted.

"I'm sorry. I don't know what the hell . . ." He gazed around, baffled and angry at himself. And mortified. Damn, he'd passed out like a weakling—and then he'd been saved and dragged around by a woman half his size. Big bad nature spirit he was not. That'd seduce the girl for sure. After all his hard time doing research, to be laid low—literally—by an attack of the *vapors*. Wimp.

She gave him an odd look. "Nature spirits don't come with expiration dates, do they?"

"Other than the spring equinox? Nope."

"Spring equinox? What are you saying?"

Scrubbing his face, he tried to shake himself out of his daze. "Never mind. Bad joke." Well, actually it was entirely true. But did the equinox figure into this? Were his recent problems a cosmic reminder of time ticking away?

"Then, what was this?" Daphne asked. "A simple dizzy spell? Do nature spirits have dizzy spells?"

She sounded incredulous—and well she should, he thought wryly. Nature spirits generally did *not* do dizzy spells. It was bad for the image, he amused himself by thinking. Bad for Druids and bad for adoring nature spirit groupies.

"Adoring nature spirit groupies? Oh, gag," Daphne said.

Tremayne glanced up. "You did it!"

"What?"

"I didn't say that aloud. You read my thoughts!" And boy, had she picked a bad time to start reading his mind.

She frowned immediately. "Know what else I read? You're keeping something from me."

"Just my bra size."

"What's going on, Tremayne?" She didn't sound amused.

He mentally reinforced his defenses. "Damned if I know."

"You're still keeping something from me."

"That's entirely possible, but it's not about this." He gazed at her directly. "And don't worry—this is not me headed for almighty death throes and spontaneous reversion to spirit form. If that's what you're worried about."

She frowned. "I *was* worried about that. Like, maybe your body is rejecting your spirit or your spirit is rejecting your body. That could happen, couldn't it? Like a body rejecting a transplanted organ? Or maybe . . ." She took a deep breath. "You know, these episodes of yours started about the same time we noticed my Druid powers awakening." She looked away and shrugged, obviously upset. "Are they related? Am I somehow responsible for what's happening to you?"

"No, of course not." He reached for her hand and squeezed it. "I'm the power vacuum, remember? Your magic can't work on me unless I consciously and specifically open myself to it."

"Oh. That's right." She looked inordinately relieved. "As long as you're sure."

"As sure as I can be." He glanced around and a thought occurred to him. "How the hell did you get me back to the apartment?"

"Sheer force of will. And terror for you." She widened her eyes. "I would have shifted to horse form, but I was afraid somebody would see me. You know, they might be surprised if you have your own pet horse—that you keep in your apartment. And then there was the daunting prospect of trying to hoist you onto my own back and open the door. I didn't see how it could be done."

"I appreciate the thought." Grinning crookedly he added, "And the visuals."

"My pleasure. You know, I really wish there was some kind of nature spirit doctor we could consult."

He shook his head. "There's nothing. A Druid, maybe, but I'd rather not trust any of them."

"Because it's a weakness?" She looked troubled. "I can see that. They've kind of resented or coveted your power up until now."

"Yes, I frighten your average Druid," Tremayne remarked. "And, given how I was manipulated by one for two thousand years, I might have been a little arrogant right back. Didn't exactly foster friendly relations."

"Whoa," she said as he sat up. "Maybe you shouldn't be up yet."

"I'm fine." He glanced around. Really fine, actually. Steady as could be. He swung his legs off the bed and stood.

"For the record, I'm really not in favor of you being upright," Daphne remarked.

"You want me flat on my back, do you?" He turned and smiled. "I've always suspected, but it's nice that you finally admit it."

"You really are feeling better." She gave him an exasperated, if rather warm, look. It was different, and it touched him in a way none of her other expressions had. She'd worried about him. Sincerely. Had anyone ever worried about him before? And yet, he could see her eyes dilating now, and the quiver of a flut- tery pulse. The flush of new warmth glowed in her cheeks.

"Better? Hell yeah. But it sounds like the lady needs proof."

Glancing up at Tremayne—way up, actually, since the man was as big as a truck—Daphne caught her breath at the look in his eyes. She hadn't meant to challenge him, but that was defi- nitely how he seemed to be taking it. And he did appear damn healthy.

Why, even now the nature spirit was metaphorically compos- ing a Stone Age ode to testosterone. She bit back a grin. Appar- ently, nature spirits had egos every bit as tender and cavemanlike as the human male: exhibit illness or weakness of any kind in front of a female and both commenced chest beating.

"Given the circumstances, the lady is more than willing to accept your word on the matter."

"What circumstances might those be?"

"Well, passing out, for one. You poor thing." She gave him an innocent and therefore provoking look. She was *so very bad*. But she just wanted to see the fists beat a little harder.

"Ah." He stepped closer, taking the bait. "So, tell me. Am I the hottest guy who ever passed out at your feet?"

She bit back a laugh. "I can honestly say yes. You are defi- nitely the hottest guy who ever passed out at my feet. Especially since you're the *only* guy who's ever passed out at my feet. Sober, I mean. Warren did it drunk one time. Right before I rammed his car into that building."

Tremayne raised his eyebrows, obviously sidetracked. Whoops. It was possible that she'd sounded a little too happy about that memory.

"You told the High Druid that was an accident."

She shrugged. "I lied."

"Do you hate cars?"

"No, I find them very useful. Er, and not just as punching bags. I like to drive them places that are too far to walk," she added.

He gave her an amused look. "So why do you keep hurting them this way?"

She narrowed her eyes. "You don't care that I lied about the accident?"

He shrugged. "No, not really. If I'd known you at the time, I would have rammed Warren's head into the wall. You were relatively kind."

"So you don't consider it evidence that I'm bonkers—or doomed to be?"

"Nope." He grinned and stepped closer. "You see, I couldn't ethically try to seduce a mentally unbalanced woman. So it's in my best interest to categorize you as sane. I'm just hoping you're limber, too."

She laughed, but then he took a step that brought him within a whisper of touching her, and she lost her breath. "You, um." Then she lost her train of thought.

"Yes?" he breathed, looking down at her.

She felt the warm air against her temple and cheek, could see the stubble on his chin, the sheen of moisture where his lips met. They parted. Strong, white teeth glistened as his lips pulled back in a lingering smile.

"You wanted to say something?" He spoke low, the look in his eyes making it obvious he knew he'd scattered what remained of her wits.

Say something? She supposed she had wanted to say something. She licked her lips, rewound her memory. "Limber. You fantasize about limber women?"

"I fantasize about *you*," he said. "I would love it if you were limber as well. You see, I've had these images in my head of you with your legs . . . So, anyway. Are you?" His voice was provocative, a gleam in his eyes. "Oh, and let's not forget naked. In fact, naked is more important. I can totally forego limber if naked is the other option. See? I'm not inflexible."

"But are you limber?" she replied.

He laughed. She felt the muscles of his abdomen move against hers, a slight, very welcome jostling, and couldn't help but bring her hands up to touch that hard belly, seemingly for balance.

She could feel the rumble of his mirth deep in her own belly. Ridges of muscle flexed beneath her fingers.

"Would *you* settle for naked?" he whispered, so low she might have imagined it.

She stroked the soft cotton of his T-shirt, wanting to tug it out of her way and touch skin. She wanted to find that line of dark curls and lightly rake her fingernails—

"Daphne."

She opened her eyes. Why had she closed them? Ah yes, to feel him better. But now they were open and she was looking dazedly into his. They were so hot, so close, and getting closer.

His warm mouth took hers, her lips already parted and hungry. There was no preliminary plucking or light tasting; this was strictly devouring. She dug her fingers into the hard flesh at his waist. Oh, he was so good at this! She found it impossible to believe he'd never—

Daphne jumped as the doorbell rang. Steadying her, Tremayne glanced up. "Expecting someone?"

"No," she replied.

A furious pounding on the front door soon commenced, along with a distant, commanding voice.

Daphne closed her eyes. "Coming, Mother," she muttered in an annoyed singsong.

Tremayne winced. "Must we answer?"

"Only long enough to tell her to stop making so much noise. She's disturbing your neighbors." Oooh, she talked big. But could she follow through?

Checking her outfit for signs of disarray, Daphne took a steadying breath. Then she finger-combed her hair and cast Tremayne a wry look before exiting the bedroom.

Violet was still pounding away when Daphne unlatched the door. When she pulled it open, the woman stumbled inside, hands reaching for Daphne's arms. Daphne steadied her, even as she leaned backward in surprise. "Mom?"

"Daphne? You're okay? Your father—that idiot man, waiting until now—told me you shifted into a gazelle with fiery hooves! Are you okay? You have to give up these powers before they consume you like they did him. Are you feeling okay? Are you hearing voices? Did you hurt anyone? I have an attorney. I can keep you safe. And that damn Phil can just keep his magic off my baby!" She was patting Daphne almost frantically.

Violet was sincerely upset, sincerely worried. Daphne's own irritation abated. "Mom. I'm okay."

"She really is fine, Violet," Tremayne added. He'd appeared quietly behind them. "In fact, she's learning how to—"

"You just keep your hands and thoughts and words to yourself, you, you . . . you abomination! You freak of nature! Look what you did to my baby. If you'd contained those damn powers like you were supposed to, she wouldn't be in this position."

"As I recall, Mrs. Forbes," Tremayne said with icy formality, "your husband was the one who stole the stone and toyed with the powers. Correct?"

"Yes. The idiot man—"

"Given the opportunity, you would have stolen it first and done exactly what he did," Tremayne interrupted.

"Except I'm stronger than he is, in every way. I wouldn't have done the things he did."

Daphne stepped back, feeling as though she'd lost something all over again. "No, but you would have done other things, equally hurtful. I appreciate your concern, but I'm fine." All positive feeling had leached from her.

Violet shifted her shrewd gaze to her daughter, scanned her, seemed to buy some of the truth Daphne was offering. "I still think you should give up those powers. This is too much of a risk."

"And you are transparent, Mom." Daphne was just tired now. "You want the powers just like Dad. Sure, you worry about me, but you keep your eye on the goal, don't you? A new weapon in your arsenal."

"Every wife should have something to hold over her husband's head," Violet replied. "It's the only way to retain power. Forfeit your power and the relationship crumbles." And she actually believed that, Daphne realized. In some whacked-out manner, maybe her mother believed this power would rebalance her marriage—or even rebuild it.

It would never succeed.

"Go home, Mom. I'll see you at work."

"Daphne."

"I'm fine. Go home." Daphne held open the door.

Violet shot Tremayne a warning look but reluctantly went.

Closing the door behind her mother, Daphne was left with a reminder of the scars of her parents' marriage, the destruction such a relationship could wreak. It was kind of a buzzkill for the moment Violet had interrupted.

Her mother had had impeccably bad—or good—timing.

Holding her breath for just a moment, Daphne hopped to the edge of the roof, to the edge of the gutter. Then she spread wide her wings and flew!

She was soon soaring over the city, briefly following the river, just because she could, just for the sheer joy of it. She sought out wide expanses of green. The green imbued her with peace for some reason. She liked the green.

Also, there was a place that drew her. She could feel it calling, a voice. It was like hers, and yet not. Murmuring softly at first, then rhythmically, it coaxed her to join. She knew the rhythm. Could feel it deep in every cell of her body. She had heard it before in her dreams, but not as clearly as now. She knew it was not time yet, but she would learn the rhythm. And she would remember it for later.

When she was awake.

"You're quiet this morning." Tremayne glanced at Daphne the next day. The heat from their encounter of the evening before, ruined by her mother's interruption, still hung unacknowledged in the air. "Is it because I cooked? I'm still learning. If I did something wrong, if it tastes weird, you have to tell me. I'm a big boy. I can take a little criticism."

Big boy, indeed. Daphne couldn't help but smile at the picture he made. Bare chested, barefoot, Tremayne wielded a spatula as if it were a foreign object. She'd never dreamed a man as intimidating as Tremayne could also be endearing or utterly charming. And so sexy. A butt that rounded out denim the way his did would send a weaker woman into cardiac arrest.

"Nope. The eggs are great." So saying, and still enjoying the view, she forked up another bite of omelet. Hard to believe the man hadn't known how to crack an egg two months earlier.

"And the ass?" Dark eyes wickedly teased her. "It's great, too?"

"Fabulous." She gave him a bland look, this time utterly unfazed by her accidental projection.

He laughed. "Fabulous, huh? And you freely admit it? That's one for the books. Although you only admit it now because you think I won't interrupt cooking my own breakfast to come seduce you."

"I know you won't. You like those eggs too much." Ever since the block of bacon and his brownie-baking adventure, Tremayne had been downloading recipes and obsessing over cookbooks and cooking utensils. Generally, she just left the laptop at home these days so he'd have access whenever he wanted. Not a bad move, either, given that she was eating home-cooked meals nearly every day now. She was also finding the eager but amateur cook nearly irresistible. The man knew how to focus when he found something that interested him. If her mom hadn't interrupted them . . . She frowned.

"Don't count on it. I might just . . ." His teasing smile faded and his gaze grew alert. "Something's bugging you. Are you okay?"

"No, I'm hearing voices. They urge me to kill." Her joke actually wasn't funny, given her dreams. The first step to insanity? Just as the Druids predicted? She shook her head, rejecting even the thought of it. "I'm fine. I just thought . . . well, I thought I should talk to Phil. About things."

"Things like?"

She gave an impatient sigh. "Druid stuff. I need to know what nature of weirdness I'm harboring. Magic, heritage, potential for insanity . . . Now that I have a little more experience of my own for context, I want as much information as he can give me. I want to know what I have and what I should fear. And, honestly, if there's anything I can do about any of it. Does that make sense?"

He nodded. "It does."

She set down her fork. There was no helping it; she had to tell him. "I already called. I'm meeting him in the grove today. And . . . I think I should do this alone. It's hard to concentrate with you around."

He nodded sympathetically. "It's the butt, isn't it?"

Yes, she thought. "No. It's just that I would feel self-conscious."

"I knew it was the ass. No problem."

The guy was incorrigible. No doubt it was just part of his evolutionary process: nature spirit to . . . ape, a teasing ape. It just figured that *that* would be his progression. But she was smiling, as he'd no doubt intended.

She would never have believed she could be so completely charmed by a heartless nature spirit assigned to eliminate her. But there was no question—she was.

Standing alone in the grove later, Daphne began to wish she'd let Tremayne accompany her. Six months before, this would have been just a pretty clearing in a rustic park. Now . . . now she knew what it was. Had felt the energy. She'd even wielded some. And the place echoed with that power. Daphne felt lingering traces of magic, fate, good, evil, anger, love, hate, malice, vengeance, justice. All mingled here, waiting to be called forth.

"No, not really. I mean, sure, there are echoes of all that energy, but for you and me it's just a reminder of the real thing. Most of us can't access that." Phil was striding down the path toward her.

She stared at him. "You can read minds?"

"Just a minor and crudely executed ability, something I can do as High Druid. But you were helping me a little. I believe your nature spirit calls it projecting."

"That's not good," she muttered.

"Oh, don't worry. I'm aware you can usually control it. Of course, it requires discipline and constant vigilance, and you're not a woman used to constantly being on her guard. You've lived in the human world, where people don't believe in the things that you and I must now discuss. They don't believe in the powers you wield, in your potential."

The High Druid strode up to her, looking for all the world like a man anticipating a simple round of golf. He wore neat khaki pants and a striped polo shirt, a navy-lined yellow jacket draped over one arm. This was a pagan?

"Do you always speak to people before they see you or before they know you're reading their thoughts?"

"No, but you seemed spooked. There was no need for that. This is a safe place today." Phil smiled at her, his eyes kind behind his glasses. "I'm a nice guy. Really. Powerful and omniscient and all that good stuff, but fairly easygoing. We'll do fine. So, tell me more about this disturbing dream you had."

She grimaced. "It wasn't the dream, exactly. That was, honestly, something I should have predicted. I was just . . . well, I was a bird, flying free. I had been thinking earlier it would be fun to shift to bird. No surprise that I would dream of it."

"Yeah, a bird *would* be fun," Phil agreed. "You let me know if you need help. I'd love to see you fly free one day."

He meant that, she realized silently. "Um, thanks."

"So back to the disturbing part. Not the flying, but . . ." He coaxed her onward.

"Well, I heard this voice in the dream. I've heard it before in other dreams, more faint. It's my voice that I hear, but not. And I don't understand the words. I just know I feel pulled by them, pulled to this grove and pulled to focus on the voice and the words."

Phil smiled in encouragement. "What exactly can you remember about the words? Were they threatening in any way? Enticing? Why were you compelled by them?"

"The voice was almost hypnotic. There was a rhythm, and the words were repeated over and over. Like I was memorizing or something."

"Ah." Phil nodded, his smile fading. "I expected this."

"You did?" Obviously he hadn't felt the need to warn her. That kind of ticked her off. "What exactly did you expect? And why does it scare me?"

"What did I expect? I expected a shift in your Druid powers. I think this is part of that. More, I really can't say. Why does it scare you? That's something you have to answer yourself."

"Just tell me what's happening!" She exhaled heavily, feeling completely creeped out. "What is this voice? What does it want? What is expected of me?"

Phil regarded her patiently. "Again, I can't answer these questions. That's for you to find out."

"But why must I figure everything out for myself?" she complained.

The High Druid shrugged. "That's just the way it is. It's part of a progression you must make. A journey, if you will. Don't worry. You're doing great. One thing I *will* do . . ." He dipped a hand into his jacket pocket and pulled out a chain that gleamed between his fingers. Was it a necklace? A charm? An amulet? Maybe it was something amazing and mystical that would help her—

"Here." He poured the chain into her hand.

On its end was a thumb drive. Daphne looked up in disbelief. "What is this?"

"Exactly what it looks like. A wealth of information. Or . . . homework." Phil smiled at her. "I think you need to learn about your Druid heritage. Whether or not you choose to do anything about it is up to you, but this is untainted information."

"You mean, my father hasn't touched it?"

"Well, I wasn't going to put it that way." He pursed his lips. "Look. I should admit that we're cheating a little here. Sort of. Do you know anything about Druids?"

She gave him a droll look. "Well, there's Mom. And Dad. And all their freakazoid buddies. You might say I've learned more than I wanted about your kind."

"Maybe. Or maybe you've just learned about your parents' kind. But here's the deal. Technically, we're not supposed to write anything down. As a matter of tradition, Druids have always passed on their experiences exclusively through the spoken word. Students learned through listening, repetition and committing information to memory."

She frowned, remembering her dream and the chanting voice.

"Technically," Phil continued, "I didn't write anything down. I typed it." He gave her a triumphant grin. "Hey, Druids have to keep up with the times, too! And we've accumulated a lot of data over the past few millennia. More than can be memorized. I believe in efficiency."

"I'm kind of a fan of it myself." Daphne closed her fingers around the thumb drive and chain. "Thank you. You think this will help in understanding my dreams? The voice?"

Phil shrugged. "It might. I think you'll notice a difference of some kind after you've studied the information a while. You'll be accepting your heritage on some level. And you can begin separating fact from fiction. That nudie thing? And orgies with neophytes?" He grinned and shook his head. "Not my style."

"I can't tell you how that relieves me." And creeped her out a little. So her parents had chosen rather than been required to—*Yech. Let it go.*

"Glad I could help. So why don't you check in with me when you make a connection, or if something disturbs you. I can't give you answers, but I'm always here to help you consider what you find on your own."

She studied the thumb drive as though she could read its secrets just by looking. "Is this something I should keep from Tremayne?" she asked after a moment. She didn't know if she was testing Phil or not.

"That's up to you. Read it. Decide for yourself." The High Druid smiled. "He's coming down the path right now."

Daphne heard footsteps, and shortly thereafter Tremayne emerged into the clearing.

"Druid," he said to Phil.

"Nature spirit. Good to see you."

Their words were stiffly formal, and maybe a bit contentious. Maybe they'd exchange crushing handshakes followed by a magical pissing contest? Daphne glanced from Druid to nature spirit and back again. Then Phil broke out into a big smile.

"No worries. You're doing fine, spirit," he said. "And you'll find your own answers soon enough."

He glanced at Daphne. "Well, if we're through here, I have a date." He grinned. "She's hot, too. Rotten at golf, but then, that just means she needs tutoring. You know how that is." He winked at Tremayne, then gave a cheery wave and strode away. "I'll have my cell. Ring if you need me or have questions, Daphne." Following the path, he rounded some trees and soon strode out of view.

"You know," Daphne muttered. "I never pictured Druids as preppy golf types dating hot women. Do you suppose he plays Barry White to put her in the mood, or weirdo chanting? And the robe! Do you think he ever wears it while . . . you know. While doing the wild thing?"

"Please! The visuals. Have mercy." Tremayne rubbed his eyes and followed her up the path.

Chuckling, Daphne fingered the thumb drive Phil had given her. She couldn't help but wonder about its contents. And their consequences. What sort of change in her powers would she see? And mightn't the increased knowledge drive her that much closer to insanity? That voice in her head. What would it tell her next? And would she be able to resist? Should she? Would she know the difference?

Chapter Fifteen

"Shouldn't I feel some kind of connection to all this stuff? An affinity or something?" Daphne scowled at the screen full of Druid teachings and leaned back in her chair.

"Not necessarily." Tremayne shrugged.

"And how would you know?"

He gave her a look. "True power is rarely obvious at first glance."

"Really? Where were you when I very obviously morphed into Felix the Weirdo Cat in a grove we both know and dislike?"

He smiled at her almost fondly. "Well, that's what was so wondrous about that experience. The drama of it. Normally, power is something one subtly takes on. Overt displays are usually a sign of weaker powers. People with lesser talent make a lot of noise to distract onlookers and compensate for their meager results. Think of all the pagan dilettantes with their love for costumes and elaborate props and ceremony. They go through the motions, but do we really see anything happening at the end? What are the tangible results? Often, nothing at all. Their elaborate displays are all crutches and decorations. True power needs nothing but itself to make an impact on observers."

"So, maybe my puca powers are really weak, and—"

Tremayne was already shaking his head. "I've felt your powers, Daphne. You have yet to realize their full potential. I say, keep studying the Druid stuff. Absorb whatever you can. Something will be important."

"Goody," Daphne muttered. "I'm a metaphysical sponge waiting for the squeeze."

She was just yawning over another dry section—imagine, someone making Druidism and magic boring!—when a subject heading caught her eye. "Tremayne," she murmured. "Come here."

"What is it?" He rose from his chair and set down a book he'd been reading, an Internet instruction manual she'd slid into his hands to keep him from reading over her shoulder. "You connect with part of it?"

"I don't know about connections, but I think this part might apply to *you*." She pointed to a section on curses.

Tremayne read, frowning, then shook his head. "It wouldn't work on me. This isn't it."

"How do you know? How can you be so definite?"

"Curses in general do not work on me. No magic does."

"Not even Druid magic? I know what you said about puca magic not working, but didn't Akker summon you?" Daphne stared at him. "Doesn't that count, the magic he used against you?"

"That was different. He called me to consciousness, a consciousness he defined. But I used my own powers and energy to willingly follow the path he opened. I knew there was potential to pursue, and that's what I did. By choice."

"So, he pointed the way, and you used your own magic to follow," she mused.

"Basically."

"But others' magic is powerless against you."

"Well, directly, yes. Indirectly . . . If, say, you used magic to hurl a car at me, the car could hit me and damage me. But direct magic won't work. A curse would be considered direct magic."

"Well, so much for that. Man." She slumped in her chair—a hard metal one she'd resorted to out of desperation. If she'd tried reading this stuff on the couch, she'd be unconscious by now. "I thought I'd be plowing through this stuff like a thriller, but it's all very . . . well, pedantic. Like an old man chastising a child and teaching him manners. Respect for nature. Love for the living. That kind of thing."

Tremayne shrugged. "All very important." Then he narrowed his eyes. "Why is the text blinking?"

"I'm not sure. Maybe it's the computer?"

Carefully, Tremayne touched the screen. The blinking stopped. When he pulled his hand away, it resumed.

Daphne blinked in surprise. "What does that mean?"

Tremayne's lips twisted. "It's charmed. Magic. It's *more than what you're reading.*"

"What are you saying?" she asked.

"You are absorbing more than you know. That's probably why you feel so sleepy. It's encouraging you to relax, so that the flow of information can be increased. It's covertly transmitting secrets!"

"Secrets?"

He nodded. "Druidic secrets. I didn't sense anything malevolent, but it's pretty underhanded for them to convey things this way without warning you."

"What, I'm being brainwashed? Hypnotized?"

"*Subliminal suggestion* is the term you're looking for."

"The 'get some popcorn' message reputedly embedded in movie trailers at the theater?" She gave him a dubious look.

"If that means somebody's influencing you subconsciously, then sure."

Her humor faded. "So, you're serious?"

"Yes."

Uneasy, she glanced from him to the computer. "Is this . . . I mean, should I . . . Man, that's just sneaky." Frowning, she grabbed her cell phone and dialed.

"Hello, Daphne."

She frowned a moment. Caller ID. That had to be it.

"I do have caller ID, but your phone isn't listed."

She blinked. He was right. "Is this Phil?"

"You did call me, so I assume you knew who you were calling?" The High Druid was teasing now. "Relax. Your nature spirit is telling you the truth. There is more to that program than the text you're reading. I swear to you that it's merely passing on Druidic teachings in a quicker manner than you could absorb otherwise. Our formal instruction usually takes about twenty years. I thought you might prefer an accelerated version. I would have explained this to you before, but an unbiased, unprepared and unaware mind more readily absorbs at the accelerated rate. There's less mental resistance to it that way. Your defenses are down."

She pulled the phone away, looked at it, then cautiously put it back to her ear. Then she motioned for Tremayne to listen in. He moved closer and pressed his ear to the phone as well. "Are you doing the subliminal thing now to make me believe you?" she asked.

Tremayne's lips twitched at her question, but she stubbornly refused to stop requesting answers.

"No. And good evening to you, nature spirit."

"Druid," Tremayne greeted him in return.

"I don't lie, Daphne," Phil said. "You have no cause to believe this, but I think the nature spirit will back me up."

She glanced at Tremayne, who nodded. She nodded in return, and he pulled away. "I'll do it this way, then. Assuming it will still work?"

"It will, but you might tire more easily."

"Bummer. Well, I guess I'll get back to it then."

"Excellent. Call if you need me. Oh! And remind Tremayne that you're to come by the grove tomorrow for a divining. Bring the nature spirit with you. He needs to hear, too."

Baffled but curious, she agreed; they set up a time and both hung up. Then she focused on her computer. "This is still eerie."

Tremayne, staring at the blinking screen, frowned. "Yeah." Then he brightened. "I wonder if I could talk Phil into planting a few suggestions on that thing for me. Something like 'Daphne, do a striptease and seduce the closest nature spirit.' That would make it all worthwhile."

"No. You are not to tell the High Druid about my stupid malady. Whatever it is." Tremayne scowled, looking every inch the wild, chest-beating warrior. Never mind that his battlefield was a Druid grove in the middle of a state park and that his opponent appeared as civilized and savvy as any college professor. Nature spirits could be so darn stubborn.

"We have to do something, and I think Phil is our best option," Daphne argued. In the time since she'd last seen Phil, Tremayne had experienced two more violent dizzy spells. Now that Tremayne had accompanied her to meet with the High Druid, she'd suggested using this opportunity to pick Phil's brain. "Come on. What if this is just some wacky nature spirit virus and Phil has a cure?"

Tremayne raised an eyebrow. "You can't be serious. A nature spirit virus? We don't get sick. We simply exist or we don't."

"Yeah, well, you're an *evolved* nature spirit. I'm thinking you're going to get some disadvantages along with the advantages. Doesn't that make sense? Phil would know."

"Don't tell him. We're here for a divining. Period. And to report on your progress."

"A progress report? You didn't say anything about that."

He shrugged. "You didn't ask."

"That's low."

"Would you have done anything differently if you had known? Other than worry?"

"I just don't like having that stuff sprung on me. Accountants are organized. We like to plan and schedule, to fill out tables and input meeting details on our electronic calendars. This needed inputting."

Tremayne gave her a harassed look. "Consider it inputted."

"Only if you don't tell Phil about the flaming hooves." Daphne made the request impulsively.

Tremayne folded his arms. "Silence on the flaming hooves in exchange for silence on the malady?"

Daphne grimaced. "Deal." Better than nothing.

"Hi, folks!" Phil was striding down the path toward them, robe flaring out behind. "How's it going with the shape-shifting?" he asked. "Gold stars all around?"

Daphne gave him a startled look. Tremayne responded, "She's making excellent progress."

"Er, no dead people yet," Daphne said with cheerful anxiety.

"Excellent." Phil beamed. "Now, Daphne. As I mentioned before, this whole situation is awakening the Druid side of you, and that's to be expected. It's the next step of dealing with your absorbed puca power. There will likely be a few more surprises in your very near future. Your job is to make sure all your powers continue to play nice." He smiled knowingly. "You don't need to elaborate on the details to me, just let me know whenever you're feeling mentally strained. I'm here to help."

"Um, what kind of surprises are we talking about?" she asked. Was he referring to the fate of Tremayne's doormat?

"You'll see soon enough," Phil replied. Eyes twinkling, he clapped his hands then folded them. "So. Consider this part of our meeting over. You've reported back and have been approved." He bowed smartly.

Daphne blinked in surprise. She'd hardly reported anything aloud, and she'd consciously avoided projecting anything. Had she failed? Had he heard something she didn't realize? "That's it? That was all the progress report you need?"

"Am I supposed to draw blood?" Phil looked equally startled, then flashed her a grin. "Yep, that's it. And now that we have that business checked off our list, how about some fun?"

"Fun?" Tremayne eyed him doubtfully. Daphne shared the nature spirit's skepticism.

"Yes! How about that divining session? Anybody curious?" Phil sounded like a schoolteacher hoping to intrigue a class of bored adolescents into learning. "I've felt tremors. Something wants to emerge. So . . . I brought my props with me. Shall we?"

"Props?" Daphne echoed.

Phil doffed his purple-rimmed specs, tucked them in a pocket of his robe and pulled out a leather case. From that, he plucked a pair of black Wayfarer sunglasses. His movements not without flair, he slid the sunglasses precisely into place without disturbing his coiffure.

Daphne watched in disbelief. The whole scene was too cheesy

to be real. *The future's so bright* . . . "You can't be serious," she said.

"You didn't really think that was just a pop eighties tune, did you? A trite turn of phrase? Timbuk 3 was really—" He tried to look stern and mystical, but his lips were twitching. "Oh, all right. That's what it is. My shades are little more than exactly what I just called them—a prop that entertains me.

"Actually," he continued, "a Druid blessed with the talent of divination can see the future in nearly everything around himself: cloud shapes, wind movements, insect chatter, birdsongs . . . the peculiar entrails of a disemboweled but still writhing sacrificial victim." He made a face. "I prefer inanimate objects and dark, uncorrected lenses. It's more practical."

Daphne, hearing logic in that statement and really disturbed by it, turned a wondering gaze on Tremayne.

"There's just no telling with Druids," he muttered. "Especially this modern bunch."

"Shhh. I'm concentrating." Phil muttered to himself a little bit, then was silent. Daphne and Tremayne watched quietly as the High Druid faced them, his hands seeming to clench and relax, not quite convulsively. Daphne couldn't help wondering if that was a good sign, a bad sign or just the way this worked. She also couldn't believe she was waiting for a white-robed Druid in black Wayfarers to predict her future.

After a few moments, Phil removed the sunglasses. His eyes remained distant. They were almost translucent. "I see hail. Lots of it. Pelting you. Then a rain of mammoth stones. And more. A pervasion of evil and a perversion of good. A battle. You will both face choices and challenges. Whether you are equal to them"—his eyes cleared and he focused on Daphne and Tremayne—"is yet to be determined."

"So, who determines that kind of thing?" Daphne asked.

Phil smiled. "You do. In part. The other part has been decided for you. Fate interweaving with free choice and energies already set in motion. You can avoid some eventualities, deflect parts of others, and set your own energies in contradiction to any or all of them."

Daphne studied him. "And all of this means . . . what exactly?"

The Druid shook his head. "You will see when it's time. Just know that there are battles ahead of you, one for your soul and one for your very existence. In the final confrontation, you will be tested on a painfully primitive level, your powers used against you in an attempt first to devastate and then to destroy you. And, no, it's not my test." He paused, his expression softening. "There are things you must learn, things you must free within yourself to accomplish your goals. Come to me when you realize what they might be. I will help."

Daphne eyed Phil doubtfully. "This is all really vague. I don't deal well with vague."

"No, an accountant likes numbers." He smiled sadly. "Numbers are safe for you. But none of what's ahead will be safe on any level—for either of you. Just accept that." He turned to Tremayne. "You will have a battle of your own to face. But it's not the sort of battle a strong man is comfortable fighting, which makes it that much harder. So you will battle yourself as well as your enemy." He smiled. "Ah, but you're evolving rapidly, spirit. I think that will win the day for you. Just trust in that ballooning heart of yours." Checking his watch he remarked, "And now I have to go. I have an appointment with my therapist. Just call me on my cell if you need anything." With a wave of his hand, he turned and strode back up the path.

Daphne just watched until he disappeared behind a veil of green. Then she muttered, "He's seeing a therapist?"

Tremayne was smiling. "What do you think they discuss?"

"It could be literally anything. Stress management. A bad potty-training experience. Or maybe some minor issue, like the fate of the world." She shook her head. "You know, if he's even remotely honest in these sessions, they'll lock him up and throw away the key."

"Spoken like a woman who doesn't shift into animal shapes." Tremayne motioned her toward the path Phil had taken.

"To a guy who didn't evolve from a formless nature spirit," she countered ruefully. "Such is life in Weirdo Central."

Their pace slow and thoughtful, Daphne and Tremayne headed up the path to the parking area. "Hail and a rain of stones," Daphne murmured after a few moments. "Do you think he's predicting the apocalypse? And me with only my puca and Druid powers to fight it. I guess I could shift to cat form and meow. That should solve everything."

"For all we know, those phrases referred to bad weather and kids' pranks. You can read a lot or a little into every word. That's the trick with prophecy and divination. You have to take every—" Tremayne stumbled.

"Whoa!" She caught his arm. "You okay?"

He frowned, looking annoyed. "Not again . . ." He dropped suddenly to his knees, bringing Daphne with him.

"Oh, crap." Panting, Daphne fought to support Tremayne's weight as he sagged, unconscious, to the ground.

What the hell was going on? Was it something to do with Phil? Granted, the Druid seemed pretty benign, but that could all be illusion. The guy did divining, for Pete's sake; he could totally be a nutjob. And look how he'd stuck her with abilities she didn't want and leashed her to a guy she didn't know at the time. Maybe he really was the reason all of this was happening to Tremayne.

Or it could be one of the other Druids, she supposed. Or worse, her parents. She couldn't bear to think of any Druid seeing Tremayne in a state as vulnerable as this. One had taken advantage of him long ago, and she had no idea if any of the others were cut from the same cloth. She imagined they were.

She had to get him back to the apartment. Ugh. To be bigger, stronger, and possessed of a few more limbs than these four wimpy ones would be—

A familiar buzzing darted along her spine, shooting off toward her limbs. On impulse, she didn't halt the spontaneous shift. Still, she noticed it was different this time, more deliberate, as though following a blueprint instead of just veering off in hysteria. A moment later she was looking down at Tremayne. Way down. He lay next to a pair of hooves—her hooves!—attached to slender white legs leading up to her powerful chest.

Great. She was a horse. Four legs and no arms to boost this grown man onto her back. Damn it!

A ruffling from behind distracted her. Oh, no. Had somebody seen her shape-shift? She glanced to the side and saw something fluffy out of the corner of her eye. No, not fluffy. Wispy. Feather-like? She turned, muscles cramped, and . . . stretched her wings? Oh. Wow. A winged horse. How was this even possible? And, gee, wouldn't it be fun to explain it to the park ranger?

She supposed she had asked for more limbs. "Might as well make use of them and get the hell out of here."

"Daphne?" Tremayne frowned up at her, even as he winced and clutched his head again. Agony. She could tell he was hurting.

"Yeah, it's me. And don't ask. Let's just get you home before somebody sees me."

Kneeling next to him, she managed to wedge a wing under his body. Lord, the wing was strong. Amazingly strong. Wow. With only minor assistance from the woozy Tremayne, she managed to get him astride and rose to her full height. "Okay. So now . . . I don't think we want a flying horse on the national news, so we're just going to tuck those babies away. You hold on. And, um, maybe . . . Yeah, tuck the wings under your legs. Like that."

She took off at a run for the parking lot. Once there, she knelt by Tremayne's car. She helped him slide off of her and onto a nearby park bench. He still looked green. Concerned, she let a shift overtake her, energy swooshing through her body, remolding, restructuring, resizing, then easing to a slower rhythm. She opened her eyes to meet Tremayne's. Now he looked dazed. And dazzled.

She glanced away, oddly self-conscious. "Let's get you in the car before you collapse again."

She managed to raise him off the park bench, his arm draped over her shoulder. Accepting his weight with a grunt, she staggered determinedly toward the car. His recovery seemed slower and his movements more sluggish this time. Why?

As they hobbled along, Daphne wondered how she'd get

him in the car. He was trying to help, but she barely had a hold of him. "Tremayne? I'm going to have to set you down or prop you up so I can get the car door open."

He didn't answer, just raised a hand. The driver side door opened.

Daphne stared, then said, "You're not driving."

The driver side door closed and the passenger door opened.

"Oh." She blinked. "That's better." If disarming as hell. He really hadn't used any overt magic in her presence before—apart from summoning those diamonds. She wondered what he'd done with them.

Tremayne seemed to have lapsed into semiconsciousness, as though the trick had burned the last of his energy. Reeling under his bulk, Daphne managed to wrestle him close enough to the car that she was able to control his fall and shove him backward into the seat. Panting heavily, she rested a moment before lifting his legs into the car and fastening his seat belt. Then she closed him in, rounded the car and slid behind the steering wheel. Rattled, she sat and stared out the windshield.

"A winged horse." Tremayne was apparently conscious, if exhausted. "You're getting fancy on me."

"You're back." Her voice was shaking. "I was worried."

"Yeah. Tell me about the winged horse. Did you plan that?"

She shook her head. "No. Well, maybe I made some specific wishes for strength and additional limbs, but . . . a winged horse? No." She glanced over at him.

Eyes slitted open, he was smiling crookedly at her. "Why do I get the feeling you're trying to apologize? To a nature spirit, about changing forms."

She reluctantly grinned. "It does sound ridiculous when put that way. I just . . . well, you looked surprised."

"I was." He closed his eyes. "Beats feeling sick and dizzy, though."

"I'll bet," she agreed. "Let's get you home before you hurl all over your nice upholstery."

Tremayne tipped his head back on the seat, eyes closed. "Sounds like a plan."

Twenty minutes later, Daphne was rounding the car and helping him out. He moved cautiously but seemed less woozy. Unfortunately, as they were climbing the steps he seemed to freeze and then, in slow motion, drop like dead weight.

Panic congealing in her throat and hair abruptly standing on end, Daphne grabbed for him. Six feet away. And pulled him back to her.

She caught her breath. Six feet away? *Six feet away?* How—?

Naturally, Tremayne was staring at her arm, which was presently morphing back into its normal shape. What, was she Rubber Woman now? A walking, talking joke? Maybe they'd both found their way into a radioactive field and were paying the price: She, as a mutant. He, sick and possibly dying.

They made it into the apartment without further incident, and Tremayne, apparently exhausted, dropped into bed. At least he was safe there. She touched his forehead, felt for his pulse. He seemed to rest easier. If past experience was anything to go by, he would sleep for a while. And she would get answers for him.

Grimly, Daphne retrieved Tremayne's cell phone and placed it on the nightstand within his reach. Making sure she had her own phone, she quietly exited his apartment.

She walked to her parents' office, anxiety ratcheting higher with every step. Was it because of her? Was she somehow to blame for whatever was plaguing Tremayne? This duty of his to keep watch over her, did it take some mysterious toll on him that she didn't know? Or was it something to do with his evolution? The very source of it?

A Druid might know. But she wouldn't endanger Tremayne by asking—at least, not by asking the wrong person. She had to ask a Druid she knew, and one she could lead around without revealing truth. So she'd stay far from her wily mother, skip Phil and his followers, and discreetly pounce on the remainder.

She entered the building and strode purposefully down the hallway to a familiar office, closing the door behind her as she entered.

"Daphne?" Her father gave her a startled, if pleased, look. "Did you need me for something?"

It pleased him that she might need him. It did not please her.

"I had questions. Of a Druidic nature."

"All right. I'll help if I can," he replied.

Doubtful. But he might be persuaded to help in spite of himself. Daphne knew he had a bit of a blind spot where she was concerned.

"I'm worried," she admitted. And that was nothing but the truth.

Frowning, he stood and rounded the desk. She backed away and turned to the side so he wouldn't get any paternal huggyhuggy ideas.

"What worries you? The puca powers? Are they overtaking you? I would take this burden from you if—"

"Tell me something I don't know," she interrupted. "No, that's not it. I'm not nuts yet, and I'd like to stay that way. So I'm here gathering information about this pattern of mental imbalance that Phil mentioned. I already know what happened to you when you had the powers. What I'd like to do now is check out some of the older branches on the family tree. Especially the twisted ones. Say, Akker, for example. He was nuttier than a fruitcake, right? What do you know about him?"

"Well . . . you know about his daughter, how she betrayed Kane by sleeping with Riordan? To save her own butt, she lied to all three of them about the true circumstances. With Kane's help, Akker avenged her by summoning Tremayne to help him imprison Riordan's magical half inside that cornerstone."

Daphne was nodding. "I know what happened to Kane, Riordan and Tremayne. But what was Akker's fate? Did he die angry? Did he consider himself avenged? And what of the girl?"

"The girl died in childbirth less than a year after Riordan was imprisoned. The child was stillborn."

"Whose child was it?"

"They don't know."

She winced.

Duncan nodded. "It was a long time ago."

"Not to them," Daphne returned fiercely. "A lot happened during that 'long time' you mentioned. Two brothers and a nature spirit suffered for a long, long time. I want to know if Akker suffered, too. Did his curse backfire on him at all? What about this precious karma everyone rants about? Didn't it apply to him, too? Wouldn't he get whammied righteous for doing what he did?"

Duncan sighed, his gaze distant. "I don't know if it backfired. I think everything he intended came to pass. And everything that came to pass . . . he accepted as necessary."

"What are you saying?"

"Akker died during the ceremony. The curse, and its karmic retaliation, I suppose, cost him his life. Some say he couldn't endure and was vanquished by it. I think he surrendered his life willingly, and for reasons known only to himself."

She stared. "He acted as his own human sacrifice just to give punch to his curse? That is *angry*."

"Well, as Phil mentioned, it was understood that he had kind of lost it at that point. His rage consumed all of him that was good. Any worth he had left . . . he fed into that curse."

"Into the stone?" she questioned quietly.

"If you prefer to call it that, yes."

She swallowed. Was that how Akker had forced a nature spirit to evolve into a man, by offering up his own humanity? And, if so, what did that mean for the nature spirit involved? Akker was an archdruid, true, but he'd been mortal. Did that mean Tremayne's evolved form would end mortal as well? Did he have an expiration date, after which he would revert to his lesser self?

And then . . . would he die?

Chapter Sixteen

Only a little over an hour had passed before Daphne unlocked the apartment door and strode into Tremayne's bedroom. "How are you feeling?" she asked.

He was sitting up, his back propped against several of those wonderful pillows he owned and his dark eyes still blurred with sleep. "I feel fine. Back to normal. I just woke up a few minutes ago and realized you were gone."

She studied him. He wasn't pale any longer, but—"Are you sure you're okay? You scared the crap out of me. Maybe you should rest more. Shoot, tomorrow's Friday. Mina's wedding. Maybe I should call and make excuses for you or something so you can—"

"Honestly, I'm fine now, Daphne. Tomorrow night won't be a problem. So tell me where you went."

"I went to see my father."

Tremayne's gaze sharpened. "Why?"

"I was trying to find the cause for all of these episodes you're having, so I decided I should begin by learning more about the source of our current situation. The Druid who summoned you, imprisoned Riordan and instigated your evolution. Akker. And . . . I think he's behind what's happening to you now."

Tremayne's face smoothed into an expressionless—and therefore quite telling—mask. "Daphne, tell me you didn't—"

"No, of course I didn't tell my father what's been going on with you. I just framed my question as relating to worries for my own sanity. You know, how Akker apparently went bonkers all those centuries ago? And then how my father did."

Tremayne relaxed and nodded. "So, what did you learn?"

"Enough to form a couple of theories." And both of them sucked. But keeping them to herself wouldn't do Tremayne any good, so she took a deep breath. "Is it possible that your evolved form, your physical body, is mortal?"

Tremayne looked skeptical. "You think I'm aging? Do I look elderly?"

No, he looked damn good, actually. So good, in fact, that she was relieved he'd napped fully clothed. Of course, his nap had really been him passing out, but . . . Still, he was right. He looked fully recovered from his episode.

"No, I don't think you're aging, but just hear me out."

She repeated what her father had told her about Akker's death, his theories, and her own steps of logic. "So, I wondered, what if your evolution has a different end than you expect? What if your physical self is mortal and able to exist only a finite period of time?" She lowered her voice. "And what if that time is almost up?"

He frowned. "I guess that's possible, but if I were dying or losing my body, don't you think I'd feel sick all the time, not just pass out and fully recover afterward? I feel great right now. Like I had a nap, which I did."

She pursed her lips and discreetly allowed herself to breathe normally again. The idea, just forming it and thinking about it, had made her queasy. Inhale. Exhale. She refused to think about why she was so upset.

"Okay. I want that theory to be wrong. I'm willing to be convinced," she said.

"So you're not ready for your nature spirit to give up the ghost?" He grinned at her, his eyes warm.

"Don't even joke about that," she snapped. Her voice caught. Looking away, she took a deep breath. "I do have another theory."

Nodding, he drew up his knees and wrapped his arms around them. "What is it?"

"Well, Akker apparently prepared for all kinds of eventualities, right? That's why you're nearly human now instead of a barely conscious—"

"Barely *sentient*." Tremayne looked annoyed, obviously reminded of his recent unconsciousness. "There is a difference, you know."

More chest beating. Daphne fought back a smile at how male he really was. "Okay, barely *sentient* being. Well, it sounds like Akker poured his all into cursing Riordan and making sure everything happened according to Plan A or, failing that, Plans B through Z, subscript twelve. If you know what I mean."

"Did I know that he was thorough and a wiz with the fine print? Yes," Tremayne admitted. "Could he have set in motion some kind of self-destruct or corrective mechanism that would punish me if, say, I failed at my duty?" He paused, thought a moment. "I guess it's possible, but unlikely. I think he would have seen to it I was taken care of in a more obvious or more permanent manner, if that were his aim."

"Not if his life force sputtered out before he could finish writing that fine print. Maybe you were a half-done curse." Hmm. That sounded hokey even to her own ears.

Tremayne's eyebrows shot up, and his eyes twinkled with dark humor. He clearly agreed. "Not that you're reaching or anything. Twice-baked potatoes and half-done curses, with a side order of eggs over easy. Are you sure you can't cook?"

"If anything is completely cursed around here, it would be my cooking," she said, folding her arms. "But I think the half-curse idea has merit in your situation."

Tremayne shook his head. "Like I said, curses don't work on me."

Daphne nodded. "I remember. But try this, then. What if his curse's fine print was part of this path you mentioned? The one he forged for you, but which you willingly followed on your own steam. By implying approval of Akker's path when you followed it, maybe you were also saying okay to the attached fine print that could destroy you. Maybe he tricked you into allowing the curse as part of that path."

Tremayne frowned thoughtfully. "I think this is probably closer to the truth. It sounds like him. If anything, it could be that his plans were even more complicated than they already appear—and the worst is yet to be realized."

"You think there might be more in store for you? Oh, fun." She wasn't even sure how to address *that*.

He shrugged. "Not much to be done to change the past. We can only go forward," he replied. Then he eyed her significantly. "What concerns me is you."

"What do you mean?"

"The way you shifted. Halfway."

She winced and nodded. "Like I'm not already freakish enough, now I'm creating mutant forms."

He studied her. "I think . . . I really do think we're seeing your Druid powers awakening."

"What, because I can shift into freak forms? I thought pucas could shift into nearly any form."

"As long as it exists in nature, yes. But what you did—" He shook his head, obviously amazed.

"Totally unnatural, I know. Likely out of control. The Druids will croak me."

He held up a finger. "Not necessarily. I think they might see you as useful—and in some ways, it was totally *in* control, as you did what you needed to do. Also, I'd be surprised if Phil didn't already suspect this was happening. This might be what he meant by a shift in your powers. Which means you must be careful, as he recommended."

She frowned. "Because I can morph into mythical creatures and hybrids?"

"Well, think of the potential. If you can shift into shapes and have abilities outside of natural occurrence, there really is no limit to your power." He paused, studying her closely. "Some would see you as either a tool or a weapon, to be used for or against them."

"But . . ." She shook her head. "I don't want to be used for or against anybody. Except maybe muggers and rapists in airport parking lots. And I think that's justifiable, by the way—in case karma might be eavesdropping on this conversation." She glanced over her shoulder.

Tremayne smiled. "Karma's not a Peeping Tom or gossipy old lady."

"I'm picturing a gossipy old lady, if you want the truth. Or at least a judgmental and interfering one." She stopped on a horrified thought, her stomach dropping. "Oh, no. Please. Tell me I'm wrong. My mother isn't karma, is she?"

Tremayne laughed. "I think your mother is a force to be reckoned with, but no, she is not karma."

"Thank god." Nudging her patient to scoot over, she plopped weakly down next to him. "Do you have any idea of the fate of this world should my mother be in charge?" Daphne shuddered.

"Oh, I don't know." Tremayne eyed her with an amused smile. "Maybe we'd have more people like you in it. That's not so bad, if you ask me." His dark eyes glittered. "In fact, it'd be pretty damn wonderful."

She stilled. Oh. Oh, that was a *good* one. She honestly had no defense against it. She'd expected funny, sarcastic or unfazed. Instead she'd gotten unpretentious, genuine, sweetly irresistible.

"You know, if you're not careful . . . a girl could really fall for you. Really."

His expression rapt, Tremayne studied her. Utterly focused. "A girl like you, maybe?"

She cleared her throat. "It's, um, terrifyingly possible." And entirely true. Heaven help her.

His eyes darkened in full comprehension. "Heaven help me, too," he whispered, his voice hoarse. He cupped big hands gently around her face. "Because if I weren't so damn sure it was still impossible . . ." He gazed at her mouth, his fingers lightly caressing cheekbones and lips before he looked into her eyes. "I'd swear I . . ."

He didn't finish his statement, but she was shaken nonetheless.

"You know," he murmured, almost against her mouth, "if anyone or anything in this world has made me feel like so much more than what I once was, it's you. You've opened a new world for me, the world inside of me. I never dreamed that such a world could exist. If I could, I'd have you live there, so you were always with me, no matter what. You could be the heart people swear I don't have. Would you?"

Oh. Oh, how could he . . . How was a girl supposed to resist . . . "I think—" She swallowed hard, her heart in her throat all of a sudden. "I think I might like it there," she said. Nature spirit or not, human or not, there was no going back. She cared. More than she wanted to care about any man, much less an evolving nature spirit. Maybe she really was nuts. Was it kinky to have strong feelings for someone not quite human? It didn't feel kinky. Well, not bad kinky, anyway. The guy was certainly hot enough to inspire kink in even a very grounded woman. And she felt very *un*grounded these days. In fact, there was always that possibility that she was on a one-way trip to Nutsville anyway. Even if she didn't feel nuts. Phil didn't think she was nuts. Although, she'd suddenly taken to babbling fruitlessly in her head.

Tremayne smiled, his dark eyes gleaming with what could only be wicked thoughts. "And did I mention that nobody but you has ever morphed into mythical creatures or grown six-footlong arms just to save me?"

"I'm special that way," she muttered.

"Oh, but you are. One of a kind." He tunneled his fingers into her hair. "And not just because you're a freak of nature."

She couldn't help a small flare of annoyance. "What? Who are you to be calling *me*—"

With a smile, he consumed whatever she was going to say with his mouth, parting her lips with a hungry and exploring tongue. He pulled her hard against him, leaned back on the bed, tugging her on top of him.

She scrounged up every last bit of will she could find and pulled back. Straddling his belly, hands flat against his chest, she spoke in between breaths. "Tremayne. Are you sure? That you . . . That you're up for . . . this?"

"You're worried about my health? *Now?*" He gave her an incredulous look.

"Well, you did pass out . . ." She ran her gaze all over his body, the ripple of muscles beneath his clothes, wanting to believe only good things about his current health. She couldn't deny that he seemed damn healthy.

"I already told you I was fine. Back to normal. Well rested. More than up for every bit of this." His eyes glittered with his intent to prove it.

"If you're sure . . ." *Please be sure. Please be sure.*

His lips twitched, no doubt because she'd projected that breathless wish. "How's this? I'm going to expire right now—you'll have a dead nature spirit on your hands—if you don't deflower me immediately."

"Oh, that's right!" She gave him a wide-eyed look. "I'm in bed with a virgin! How many women can say that? Even better, a two-freaking-*thousand*-year-old virgin. None of them can say that. Why does it sound like a fetish? I feel so depraved."

Laughing, he was already tugging at her clothes, ruthless in his quest to uncover skin. Shoving her blouse high on her ribs, he slid hungry palms across her belly. She sucked in a frantic breath and felt his fingers climb higher, raking bra and blouse upward. Cupping her breasts, he reared up and buried his face in her cleavage.

Between the cupping and the nuzzling and the feel of some hard abs rippling beneath her, Daphne thought her eyes might be rolling back in her head. "Okay, you're healthy," she gasped. And then she grabbed his wrists and—not without reluctance—peeled his hands away. She leaned her weight forward until she had his arms pinned to the bed above his head, and when he gazed up at her, eyes hot and blurred, she grinned down at him.

His dark brows lowered slightly. "What are you doing?"

She gave him a smile full of teeth and promise. "This is *me* deflowering *you*. Remember? That's what we're doing. And this is how a deflowering works. You're the naive little virgin. And I'm the more experienced, ruthlessly sensual creature who's set on drugging you with my hands and lips and mouth and tongue and, er, other parts. How does that sound?"

"Yes. Good. All of it." He tripped over his own words in laughing eagerness.

"Excellent. A willing victim." She ducked her head and nibbled along his jawline. Such a square, manly jawline. This close, she could see the muscles bunching, stubble rippling across tanned skin as though he was grinding his teeth, fighting for control. She grinned and gave that muscle a swipe of her tongue. "Your deflowering can now begin with seduction."

If she could herself last that long. So saying, she patted his wrists to silently demand they stay right where she left them, then dragged her nails down sensitive flesh along his inner elbow, underarms, ribs. She pulled back just enough to yank at his shirt, dragging it above his belly, above his ribs, then over his head, where, with an inspired smile, she left it twisted and bunched like manacles around his wrists. She met his eyes, where she saw heat vie with humor. "Do you feel victimized yet?" She blinked down at him.

"Oh, horribly. More, please." He grinned up at her, his eyes intense, his chest rising and falling with quickened breath.

"Begging is always encouraged," she replied. Ducking her head to kiss his throat, she saw the Adam's apple bob as he swallowed, felt his chest rising and falling erratically as she worked her way down.

Oh, this was a good chest. A really good chest. Sure, she'd seen it before, but it was even better up close. Broad and hard and hot. Not hairless like some girly guy, but then, no ape either. Just enough dark swirls to remind her that he was every inch a man. She paused to nuzzle the crisp hair and nibble at the subtle peaks.

Tremayne groaned. "Uncle! Does that work here?" He hadn't moved his arms, but the rest of him was writhing.

"Nope." She grinned against her sensitive quarry, pausing long enough to hear another groan. Poor little virgin. Then she found his ribs and nibbled until he arched his back, obviously fighting the urge to free himself and take control.

Kissing every curve of a nicely defined six-pack, she dipped a tongue into his navel. It quivered with his broken laughter. "Are you enjoying yourself?" he ground out.

"Immensely."

She found her way suddenly barred by denim. That wouldn't do at all. Pulling back a little, she ran a fingernail down the fly and watched Tremayne nearly leap off the bed. Then, carefully, she tugged the button free and rattled the zipper tab down its track.

Then she just stared. "You know, I just never guessed, but I suppose I should have. Of course a nature spirit would go au naturel. Commando?" And of course, she'd already marveled over Spirit, Jr., who really deserved senior status.

"It's . . . freeing." His voice was hoarse. "I like freedom. So do you. Maybe you should . . . go commando."

She cocked her head in mock wonder. "I never thought of it that way. It bears considering." She blinked. "Did I say 'bares?'"

"Yeah." His voice sounded strained. "And about that deflowering? I think my flower is going to explode—or will wilt and die, unless you *de-* it sometime soon. You will, won't you?" It was definitely a plea.

Biting back laughter and seeing the tendons in his neck standing out, Daphne took pity on him and backed up to tug his jeans—carefully at first—down his legs and off. Then, after quickly shucking the rest of her own clothes beneath his hot gaze, she paused to do some admiring of her own. After all, she had a naked nature spirit sprawled across cocoa brown satin, and this time he was all hers. Every ripped, straining inch. And those were a lot of inches. They looked magnificent when straining.

Grinning, she climbed back on the bed, back on top of Tremayne, her knees on either side of his hips. "Are you ready for a little *de-*?"

He freed his hands and grabbed her hips. Yes, she'd been purposely taunting him by dangling the goods so close to his, but now he held her body steady while he slowly, deliberately thrust inside. She inhaled, felt utterly incapable of exhaling, as the penetration seemed to go on and on forever. His gaze held hers, so hot she could feel the warmth radiating to every part of her. Slow burn, quick sizzle. Oh, no!

She wouldn't shape-shift. She wouldn't shape-shift. That would be horrible!

He stilled. "I've got you. And, no, I don't think you will. You have more control than that now." He lowered his voice to a more devious, if ragged, tone. "But just in case, keep your body against mine, okay? I think all of you should be touching all of me at all times. Especially the hot and slippery parts. I really like—I mean, I really think it would be *best* if—"

Made helpless with laughter and frustration—but not panic anymore, thanks to his joking—she growled. "Oh, hush. My own flower is going to bust if you don't—"

"You're a virgin, too?" he asked.

Giving him an evil look, she let her hips drop, seating him suddenly and wholly inside of her. She heard him groan deep in his chest. Then control snapped. First his and then hers.

He tilted his hips to thrust hard and high into her, and then he rolled until she was under him, her back sliding against satin bedclothes warmed by his body. Hard warmth above, sleek satin beneath, fiery heat thrusting deep inside and rocking her hard. Sensual overload. Arching her neck back, head sliding everywhere, she felt her body explode, climaxing and gripping him deep inside.

As she started to come down, body loosening like rubber, Tremayne dropped onto his elbows, face right above hers. Then, his eyes open and watching, he gently took her mouth, inhaling her panting breaths as he rocked slow and deep. Gradually, she felt her body catching fire all over again. She'd never . . . It couldn't possibly . . .

He varied his thrusts, catching her body by surprise. He was experimenting! His eyes avid as he watched her face, he gauged her response to every sally, absorbing and filing away everything he learned. A taunt, a tease, a possession, then again, until he started thrusting in earnest. As she found herself flying off into oblivion all over again, he joined her this time, bucking hard into her body and stealing her breath as he groaned out his own release.

He let his face drop into her neck, his breathing still harsh.

After a few moments, he rolled off to the side, tugging her with him until she lay half on top, half next to him.

Daphne couldn't move. She would swear that every bone, every scrap of her flesh had liquefied into a gelatinous goo that threatened to flatten and ooze into a puddle of total infatuation. No, it was more than shallow infatuation, but she refused to label it. Not even silently. Not yet. Oh, but there was *so* much there. She could laugh with him, play with him, tell him anything, be at her most vulnerable and trust that he would keep her safe. Never in a million years had she dreamed she would find something like him, someone so wonderful and perfect. She smiled against his chest, her happiness escaping in low chuckles.

"Something amuses you?" His voice rumbled in his chest and teased her sensitized flesh.

She shivered. "It's just that we did it wrong."

"Wrong?" He opened his eyes. "That was wrong? But I thought . . ." Alarmed, he lifted his head to frown at her. "Hell, you seemed to like what I did. I might lack experience, but I had an awful lot of knowledge stored away. Tell me what was wrong," he demanded. "I'll make it right."

She cleared her throat, fighting laughter. "All wrong. *I* was supposed to deflower *you*. I was supposed to seduce you, scared little virgin that you were, until you reluctantly surrendered and accepted my advances. You did it all wrong."

"Oh." He affected regret. "I see what you mean. Damn. Well, you know how I feel about practice. I guess we'll have to try again, and just keep trying. . . ." Tightening his arms around her, he rolled her onto her back. "Except I'm not a virgin anymore. How about you be the shrinking novice this time?" And then he nibbled her neck while she squirmed with giggles and gave in.

As his very satisfied deflowerer snuggled up to his side and, to his amusement, snored just a little, Tremayne watched the darkness outside give way to dawn. It was true: If a being like himself could love, then he most certainly did love Daphne. If he were to ever win her love in return and prove his own love real, he owed her the full truth. Whatever the cost. And the cost might be great. Why, that cost . . . could mean surrendering up everything that he'd so painfully gained. He could revert to nearly mindless, passionless spirit. *Loveless* spirit. How could he bear it?

And how could he bear it if Daphne refused to accept what he told her? She might. God knew he was every bit the weirdo she once suspected him of being. And, frankly, worse. She had no idea of the extent of the secret he was keeping from her. How could she love what he was? But one thing he'd learned from his research was that love should be unconditional. He wasn't sure that directly applied to a situation as extreme as this . . . but he would hope.

Yes, he had Phil to thank for his foray into the world of televised soap operas. Emotional research for an emotionally evolving nature spirit. He'd had to learn how to go about it, hadn't he? And if there was a better source illustrating the full range of human emotion than daytime drama shows, he had yet to find it.

But now he was just postponing the inevitable. His time was up.

He kissed her cheek until she moved restlessly against him. He kissed her again, this time on the lips, and watched as her eyes blinked open sleepily. She smiled up at him but seemed puzzled by what she saw.

Tremayne let a mental barrier drop. The haze in Daphne's love-fogged gaze cleared, and those crystal blue eyes peered at him, into him, as deeply as he silently invited. Then her eyes widened. "Tremayne?" She pulled away, taking the sheet with her.

He slowly sat up, watching her as he slid backward to lean back against the pillows.

"I dreamed that. I must have. There's no way . . ." She shook her head slowly, eyes narrowing. "You know, I see it there. It registers, just as you apparently intended. But . . ." She bowed her head.

"You're not seeing things that aren't there, Daphne. Go ahead."

Slowly she looked up at him, clear eyes searching. "You . . .

you're not just some euphemistic nature spirit, some wind-blown sum of ideals and purpose and . . . well, as you said, mat-ter and will. You're . . . My god, you're the spirit of the Sarsen stone itself. Some rock in the stone circle at Avebury called the Warrior stone. A rock. You weren't just trapped inside that cor-nerstone with Riordan. You were the cornerstone itself."

He eyed her quietly. "Yes."

"Dear god. I'm falling in love with a rock."

Chapter Seventeen

"I'm not just any rock, if that makes you feel any better." Tremayne eyed Daphne warily. She'd clapped a hand over her mouth as if to call back those unexpected words. But he would remember them, however this turned out. He had a feeling she'd be recanting soon enough, though, and that hurt more than he could say. "I'm not as well-known as the Obelisk, maybe, but the Warrior stone is pretty damn impressive. Or it used to be. It's mostly gone now."

Daphne barely heard his words; she was too busy talking. "You're not just a nature spirit, tied to the stone, but literally the spirit of the stone. You are the spirit of a rock. Hell. *You're* a rock. At last Akker's bad genes make themselves known. Instead of homicidal maniac, I'm something much more pathetic—a woman obsessed with her pet rock. I need therapy."

She was totally dumbfounded. Never had she seen this coming. "You know, this is something to which I have never, ever aspired. Falling for a rock. Just imagine. I've even daydreamed about—a little nervously, mind you—actually being married to you. A rock. Making love to and having babies with a rock. Would we have pebbles? Man, that would hurt. I . . ." She shook her head, her foolishness collapsing in on itself. Tremayne just studied her.

"What? You just look at me and say nothing as I have my little breakdown. I think I have a right to a little shock, don't you?" He looked like a man. Made love like a man. And he was a rock? How? Had she just been kidding herself when she regarded him as nearly human? How does an inanimate rock evolve into a thinking, feeling, possibly loving man? It just couldn't be. She knew what she'd thought she saw and felt in him, and it just didn't fit with what she now knew. The gap was too great. She was a self-deceiving fool.

"You have every right to be shocked. Even angry with me, if you choose. I'm just waiting to see what's left after shock wears off. Do you still want to be with me?"

Damn good question. She was apparently in love with a *stone*.

"I don't know what's left. I hardly even know what I'm dealing with. Why didn't you tell me what I was getting into? We slept together! I was falling for you! Surely you could see that." She shook her head dazedly, feeling hurt and angry now. "So, let me get this straight. I'm supposed to sacrifice my new life, everything about it, stay with you, trust you, bare all to you as I shift from one form to the other. Totally vulnerable, totally trusting in every way." She glanced at the pillows that had cushioned them while they made love and slept in each other's arms. "Meanwhile, you can pick and choose which secrets I might discover?"

He was shaking his head slowly. "I didn't choose to keep this from you out of spite or reserve. I don't think you understand the gravity of this secret—one I willingly shared, just to keep the record straight."

"So, tell me, then." She waved a hand. "Everything."

"All right. I am a nature spirit. Specifically, I am the spirit of the Warrior, derived of Sarsen stone that once stood in the circle at Avebury. As the spirit of the Warrior stone, I have certain specific powers. I have power over minerals and some magnetic fields. My dampening force basically reverses energy fields, including magnetic ones. I can reverse gravity when I wish and reverse the energy flow of magic as well, negating its effects, as I've done with you. But a nature spirit's greatest weakness is its physical manifestation."

She frowned, losing him a little. "What do you mean?"

"I am tied in all ways to my particular stone. The Warrior stone."

"Meaning . . . ?"

He shrugged, his face and manner expressionless. "Whatever happens to the stone, happens to me. I feel it. Pain, trauma. And if the stone is destroyed . . . then so am I." His eyes were open and pleading.

Daphne paused. "That's one hell of a vulnerability. No wonder you chased that cornerstone all over. Oh, my god." Her eyes widened. "If that brick is all that's left of your stone . . ."

Her mind whirled with images. A mammoth stone, called forth into service, sealing a puca within. Then it was busted into small pieces by an enraged Kane, chiseled and hammered into brick shape. She winced as it was hollowed out to perform duties as a cornerstone, cemented to the corner of a house and subjected to who knows what. Then it was removed and probably banged up even more while being sent to this country. Then it was busted in Mina's house. An explosion. A nasty game of keepaway . . .

"Oh, my god." She grabbed his arms. "You felt everything? All of it?"

He sighed. "I know what it is like to be broken into pieces, yes. I didn't know if I would survive the battering, especially that original one when Kane took my stone apart. But I did. Somehow, in his fury, the puca managed to keep the heart of the stone intact. Thus, I am intact." He pondered a moment. "Most likely it happened because he subconsciously feared his brother's fate, should the stone be completely destroyed."

Daphne stared at him. "That must have hurt like crazy. Assault and torture." She shook her head. "And in spite of all that, you still didn't kill anyone out of vengeance. How have you remained sane?" A sudden, horrifying thought struck her and she jumped off the bed. "No. Oh, no! Tell me you're not Akker reincarnated. That'd make you my great, great—however many greats—grandfather or uncle or whatever."

He frowned. "Why would you think that?"

"My father said that Akker died making that curse happen. He invested his . . . his humanity in it. Put it in the stone. And, along with a curse—poof!—we suddenly have a newly evolving nature spirit. Wouldn't that make you Akker? Some form of him? He seems to have . . . spawned you, for lack of a better word."

Tremayne looked annoyed. "He didn't spawn *me*. I've always been me, since before Akker's time. I'm just a smarter, more complicated me. It's as though a chemical reaction took place, except with magic instead of chemicals, and fueled by Akker's powers and sacrifice. I have never been Akker. And I am no longer just a rock or just the spirit of a rock. I am more. I am *Tremayne*." When she still stared at him, eyes wide, he sighed. "We're not related. Is that clear enough?"

"Oh, thank god." She dropped weakly back onto the mattress. "I mean, my family life is twisted and all, but . . ."

"To have sex with—"

"Don't even say it. Don't even. So. Back to the stone. The many-times-shattered, chiseled and otherwise-abused stone. *You*. Why did you not go postal when you found yourself with a body? The puca brothers still live. No Druids were massacred. You even made love to me, and I represent both groups in a way." She felt vulnerable all of a sudden. "Why didn't you seek revenge once you could?" She froze. "This . . . This wasn't your way of . . . ?"

He glanced where she pointed to the pillows with a trembling hand. "Revenge? No. That wasn't revenge. That was me making love to you. And then me baring my soul to you. I swear it. I don't need revenge. I need you."

Ignoring the last statement, she averted her eyes and folded her hands. "Okay. So. No revenge. And yet . . . how is it possible that you didn't go insane?"

"I'm not human." He smiled a little. "I keep having to remind you of this. I'm stronger than you in nearly every way. Magic-wielders fear me because I can disarm them with a touch. That's great power. To balance . . . well, there is the stone. That keeps me in check. Harming the stone harms me."

Daphne froze, her thoughts coalescing. He'd just entrusted her with the secret of his very existence. Sure, he'd been less than forthcoming up to this point, but given how much he'd suffered, could she really hold it against him? To make himself so vulnerable to her. Willingly. That was huge. If anyone knew . . . "To get at you, one needs only to get at the stone."

He nodded. "That's why I keep it in a safe place now. I'm damn glad to have it back. It was like having my nuts in a vise before. That's as close to insane as I want to get."

A thought struck her, and she narrowed eyes. "Where is this safe place? Is the stone *really* protected?"

"As far as I know." He frowned. "You're thinking about my mysterious malady."

"It seems only logical to wonder. Where's the stone?" Could it be as simple as that? No intricate plan spun by an ancient, long-dead Druid, just a huge but natural vulnerability and someone taking advantage?

Frowning, Tremayne went to his closet and pulled out what looked like a large shoe box. Inside the box was a fireproof safe. He touched the lock. Daphne's eyes widened as the dial spun by itself, pausing and reversing into specific positions, until a click announced that the lock had opened. Tremayne opened the safe and pulled out a soft bundle. Setting it carefully on the floor, he began unrolling.

The material, Daphne couldn't help noticing, looked similar to the satin sheets on his bed, but quilted. Watching him take such care, she couldn't help but marvel over what he'd suffered in the past. And all without going berserk. They had no idea. Honestly.

He finished unrolling the bundle and folded back the top half, then the bottom. But it was already apparent from the shape of the bundle that this was no brick. No, instead Tremayne's boot was nestled in the cloth—one of the boots he'd laughingly accused her of sacrificing instead of her own during a shape-shift. The work boot had been heavy enough to fool him with the box closed.

Eyeing the boot, Tremayne dropped back onto his heels and lifted his gaze to meet Daphne's. He said, "It looks like you hit on the answer. I should have realized. But this . . . Obviously, this is not the cornerstone. Somebody must have taken it. Whoever has it . . ." He frowned. "If someone was bent on hurting me, I think I would have experienced more than simple vertigo by now. The intent must not be violence toward me, but there must be something else."

Daphne was feeling just a little violent herself. Sure, it was a bit of a shock to discover she was in love with a rock, but damn it, he was *her* rock. And no one, but no one, was inflicting any more pain on this man, intentional or otherwise. Not on her watch.

Tremayne was thinking aloud, his gaze distant. "I remember . . . Riordan has, in the past, asked about the magic of the stone, about what was inside. I told him it was empty, but maybe he didn't believe me. I wonder if he swiped it to experiment, believing his old puca powers were still grounded there, though manifesting in you."

"Do you think so?" Daphne asked, though her thoughts discreetly raced along other paths.

"It's possible." Standing up, he reached for his jeans. "I want to question him alone. No offense, just . . . maybe I'd like to preserve a few illusions for you after all." He tried to smile. "I won't hurt him, but I might have to force the issue."

Daphne watched as Tremayne dressed, and she absently started gathering up her own clothes and pulling them on. Of course he wouldn't hurt Riordan. Not really. "All right." It was an expression of trust.

Fully clothed, Tremayne turned and smiled at her. "If a rock can love, Daphne . . . I *do* love you. I promise you."

She studied him. Yes, if a rock could, then he damn well did. But that still begged the first question.

He reached for her, but she, fearing that she would project her thoughts in her weakness, just smiled and backed up. "Oh, no you don't. Find your rock. No more dizzy spells. We'll figure the rest of this out later."

He studied her a moment, obviously reassured by whatever he read in her eyes, then nodded. "Deal." And without another word, he planted a hard kiss on her mouth and strode out of the apartment.

She watched through the peephole as he walked to the nearest stairwell, then watched out the window as he left the parking lot. Once he was out of sight of the building, she exited the apartment, too, heading in the opposite direction.

Twenty minutes later, she was storming up steps, through a door, past the unmanned receptionist's desk, and stomping into her mother's office. Conveniently, both her parents were there, no doubt in the middle of their usual Friday morning meeting. Which she was crashing.

She slammed the door behind her, trapping their little family inside together.

"Give it to me. Now." She gave her father a cold look.

"Give what to you, darling?" Violet Forbes strode unhurriedly close, her manner inquisitive and concerned.

"The cornerstone. It was stolen again. Give it back."

"Now, Daphne . . ." Duncan approached. "Just because the thing's gone missing again doesn't mean I—"

"You just can't be happy, can you? Either one of you." She glared at one and then the other, her voice trembling with fury as her heart hammered away in her chest. "You can't be satisfied with a marriage, successful business, reasonable comfort in mind and body. No, you have to always have more. Why? Why not work on what you already have? Work on your marriage. Perform random acts of kindness. Hell, just let other people live their lives!"

"You don't seem well, Daphne." This from Duncan. "Is it happening now? Your mind—"

"Oh, stop with the patronizing insanity talk! I'm not losing my mind. I'm angry. A rational emotion, given the situation. I'm fed up with both of you. You insisted on running my life, and now you insist on hurting the man I love." There was something freeing about declaring it aloud, regardless of her doubts and heartache.

Duncan frowned. "Man you love? But you haven't been seeing . . ." His eyes seemed to bulge. "You can't mean the nature spirit."

"And why can't I mean him?"

"Because . . . he's an abomination!" Her father sounded truly revolted. "An evolved nature spirit? One that mutated from a neutral, natural entity into something dangerous? You'd be insane to get involved with him."

"Thanks to you, everybody believes I'm bound to go nuts anyway." Daphne bared her teeth in a parody of a smile. "I might as well have fun in the meantime."

"Is that why you're doing this?" Violet asked. "Some attempt to get back at us? A rebellion of some kind?"

Daphne laughed. "No. Strangely enough, my falling in love with Tremayne has nothing to do with you. It probably has everything to do with insanity. I'll only be hurting myself in the end. I can't imagine a love more doomed." A woman in love with a rock couldn't be destined for anything but heartbreak, could she? As far as Tremayne had come, as far as he'd evolved, she still couldn't fathom the spirit of an inanimate rock evolving so far as to be capable of love. Even Tremayne himself doubted he was capable. That would make him the more rational of the two of them. Nice irony. Lord, if she told anyone she'd fallen in love with a rock . . . any normal, intelligent being would send her straight into therapy. Perhaps that intelligent person would have a good point, not that it seemed to matter to her. She focused on her parents. "Doomed or not, I can't seem to help myself. *I do love him.* That's why I ca—" She clamped down on the rest. What an idiot! Tremayne, whom she professed to love in spite of all rational thought, handed her the greatest weapon to use against him—trusted her with it—and at her first opportunity, she nearly went and blabbed it to his enemies, her parents.

"You love him, so that's why you 'kay' . . ." Violet eyed her daughter shrewdly. "That's why you came here?" She raised her eyebrows. "Demanding that we give you back the cornerstone?"

Shit.

"You're so concerned about retrieving that cornerstone. If it's empty of the puca powers, and you have them, then why is it so important you get it back?"

"Because it's been stolen, period," Daphne brazened out. "I figured the two of you had some new scheme. Maybe to mine the rock for any lingering magic?"

"That would be pointless. I know that rock is empty." Duncan sounded sure of himself. "There's no puca magic in it anymore."

"And how would you know that?" Daphne glared at her father. "Unless you're the one who stole it. Tremayne grabbed that stone before we ever left the clearing. You never should have had contact with it, not after you threw it at me."

"I didn't throw it at—"

"Tremayne grabbed it? *He* had it? What claim does he have on it?" Violet's eyes widened. "Wait a minute. A nature spirit . . . a dampening force . . . implying a connection with gravity fields and minerals and stone . . . That's it! He's the spirit of a rock. *That* rock. The one that became the cornerstone."

"No!" But it was too late, Daphne could see. There was no taking back her words. Damn it. Why couldn't she keep her trap shut? She never should have come here.

"A rock?" Violet was incredulous. "My daughter's in love with a rock? You can't be in love with a rock, human body or no. And you!" Violet turned on her husband. "You knew this, didn't you! And you kept it from me. Of course you would, if it meant hurting me. But I can't believe you'd put our daughter in harm's way just to get at me. Where is it? Where did you put it?" She advanced on him.

He held his ground, his expression stormy. "I said I don't have the damn thing, and I don't."

"But you knew what it was to Tremayne." Daphne glared at him. "That's why you tried to break into the apartment. You really did break in there, didn't you? And you took it!"

"No! I didn't. It . . ." He scowled, his eyes furious. "All right, I did break in. Later. But it was already gone, damn it. I thought your mother had it. Do you?" He glared at Violet, but her previous fury had been all too real.

"No. I don't."

Daphne glanced between them. Maybe her parents didn't

have it. But then, who did? And now what? "You just stay away from Tremayne," she growled. "And don't even think about hurting him."

Duncan turned to her. "You need to stay away from him, too. He's not right, you know. An abomination. A freak of nature. The spirit of a rock? He's a rock! How could he feel anything for you? I don't care how supposedly evolved he is. A rock can't love you back. He's not human."

Daphne shook her head. "If you're the shining example of humanity, thank heavens he's not. I'll take a nature spirit over a weak and conniving cheat any day."

"Daphne! Is that any way to talk to your father?" Violet asked.

Daphne had to fight hard not to laugh at her mother's hypocrisy. "This is the way I talk to anyone who would destroy someone I care about."

"But he's not someone. He's a rock." Duncan couldn't seem to get past it, and Violet was nodding vehemently, too. The pair was in complete accord. Nice timing.

"Tremayne isn't just any rock, any more than he's just any someone. He's who I love—and therefore he's deserving of your respect. He's the spirit of the Warrior stone, which once stood in the stone circle at Avebury," she said proudly.

"And so he's tied, utterly, to that cornerstone." Violet's eyes glittered. "That's all that's left of it, isn't it? The cornerstone that once contained the puca, and then puca powers." She turned on Duncan. "So tell me, husband of mine. What were you hoping to gain by stealing that stone? Did you want to destroy him? Or me?"

"Maybe both." Duncan shrugged and gave his wife a bitter look.

"*You*. Oooooh, I can't believe . . ." Daphne fisted her hands in impotent fury. "I swear, if you use that rock against Tremayne, I will not be responsible for my actions. I will not."

For once, she'd caught both of her parents' attention. "Daphne, please. Calm down." Her mother made shushing gestures even as she shot Duncan a poisonous look.

Duncan nodded. "Yes, let's sit down and discuss all of this rationally."

"No. You will just give me the stone or tell me where it is or could be, then I will leave. Period. Where is it?"

"We don't have it." Violet cast her husband a grudging look. "But . . . I also don't think you should give it back to Tremayne when you do find it. Give it to me. You won't regret it. He can be controlled with that stone. Daphne, you and I could . . . Why, we could do anything! If he can render the powerful powerless, and we control him, then *we* can render the powerful powerless. Through him. Do you understand?"

"Oh, sure. I understand plenty. You are two of the most morally bankrupt people I have ever met. And I've inherited my share of your tainted gene pool. I'm completely screwed, aren't I? Well, maybe you two should remember that when you start pushing me!"

Violet shook her head. "You're so angry. Already, you've sided with that rock man over us. I can't believe it. You don't even know him. He's a *rock*! He doesn't have a heart or soul, and that ceremony . . . Daphne, we can't let you perform that ceremony he wants you to perform. If you think your life is a mess now . . ."

Daphne recognized true fear in her mother's eyes. "Why? What will it do—free Tremayne? Yeah, and I know. It will prove once and for all that I can control the powers I was given, thus freeing me to live normally. I don't know. Sounds good so far."

"But, Daphne, do you know what happens if you fail?"

"No freedom for Tremayne? Yeah, I get it."

"No, it's worse." Duncan looked grave. "This is no straightforward spell or charm, honey. This is a true exchange of magic. You're drawing upon everything that you have and are, opening yourself to old powers and new. If you don't perform it properly, or if you can't control what you're wielding . . . Your mind can't withstand such a failure. It has no defense."

"What are you saying?" A sudden chill drew goose bumps along the back of her neck.

"Failure for him means he reverts. Failure for you means

complete insanity. Everything everyone was worried about. It could break your mind."

Daphne squeezed her eyes shut, wishing she could reject her father's every word as a lie. But she knew he spoke the truth for once. He sounded too sure of himself to be lying. But, why? Why would Tremayne keep something like that from her? If he truly loved her . . .

"What happens if I don't try to perform the ceremony?" she asked.

"He reverts and, assuming you haven't achieved what you need to, you'll be assigned a different mentor. But you'll remain sane—or at least have no new chance of being afflicted. He told you none of this, I see. None. And yet you are so loyal." Sensing weakness, Duncan moved in for the kill. "Give *me* the cornerstone when you get it. Tremayne doesn't deserve your loyalty. Let me deal with him. Let me make him pay for what he's done to—"

"No, it should be mine! You don't even have your powers anymore, you stupid man. What could you do with it?" Violet sneered.

Duncan glared at his wife. "And you don't know the first thing about grounding and manipulating powers like these."

"Well, you've been deemed unworthy and incapable. I have not." Violet turned to Daphne. "Bring it to me, daughter. You and I together can—"

Her parents both continued yammering away, hammering at her and at each other, even as Daphne's heart shattered. Tremayne hadn't told her. He'd said he cared, might even love her, and yet he would risk destroying her this way? This was worse than risking physical harm to her. He would risk breaking her mind? He had no soul and no heart. It was all a sham. He didn't love her. He couldn't.

She'd known of this possibility, of course. She'd fallen for him anyway. She was a fool.

"—if I'd had a cornerstone to use against my husband, you can bet I would have made him beg and plead for—"

Her fury and hurt consuming her, Daphne let loose the energy inside. It raced through her body, seeking pathways to each extremity. Feeling the strength, the potential of the magic coursing through her, she opened her eyes, embracing every bit. Power. It was so seductive. No wonder her parents craved it like chocolate-covered drugs.

"Daphne?" cried her mother, sounding horrified. Her chin rose slightly as her widening eyes, tracking Daphne's own, focused several feet higher. "You stop that right—"

"Shut up. Both of you." Daphne bared her teeth. "And climb on." She lunged toward them, a horse much taller and larger than any domesticated equine, fully large enough to carry two bickering humans on its back. She nosed low and reared high until, with both of them yelling and clinging to her, she galloped forward. Yelling for her riders to duck, she crashed through the wall-sized picture window—*Geronimo!*—to land in the courtyard beyond it.

Damn, that had hurt, but she'd wanted to do it forever. And it was only the first of many overdue experiences that were right around the corner.

Her next destination was a distant park—not the one she'd enjoyed as a gazelle, but the one where it had all begun. She ran faster and faster, wishing to outrace her rage and her hurt, but the relentless pleas and demands from her parents only fed both. She had to silence them. One way or the other, this constant pounding would end.

Chapter Eighteen

"Hi, Tremayne. Come on in. Lucky for you, we're all early risers this morning. Even the bride-to-be. So where's Daphne?"

Tremayne entered carefully and looked around. "She's at the apartment. I wanted to do this alone." He turned back to Riordan. "Look. I'm going to be blunt. I can't afford diplomacy right now. You are no longer a puca. Your powers will not return to you. You renounced them and it was permanent. Obtaining the cornerstone will not return them to you."

Riordan stared, nonplussed. "Okay, I get it? Is that what you want me to say?"

Tremayne studied him closely then sighed. "You don't have it, do you." It wasn't a question.

"The cornerstone? Hell, no. Did you think I wanted to bring my jail cell home with me? Man, that's creepy."

"You did ask me once whether I thought the powers were still grounded in it. They're not. So if you took it in some misguided attempt to regain your former—"

"Whoa. Stop right there. I didn't take it. I believe you. I don't have the rock. Only reason I asked before was out of curiosity and concern. I wanted to know it was stable. Those powers were used against my brother, remember?"

Tremayne frowned. "Somebody has it."

"Riordan? Who's at the door?" Mina's mother, sounding mildly irritated, walked into the room. "You know, you really shouldn't be here," she continued. "It's your wedding day. And of all things for the girl to ignore as tradition, this is the worst. She wants the white dress and the flowers and the church, but the good-luck charms? Oh, no. I can't even get a blue garter on the girl! Now she has the groom waiting in the living room?"

"Oh, Mom," Mina called from the other room. "I'm not getting married until tonight. What am I going to do? Kick him out of his home all day just so we can avoid looking at each other? Talk about illogical! I thought *I* was supposed to be the sloppy traditionalist around here, not you. I'm sure Kane will come by later and drag his brother out while I get dressed. That will be plenty of mystery to preserve tradition." Still speaking, Mina entered the room and smiled. "Oh, hi, Tremayne. I don't suppose you brought Daphne, just to introduce a little sanity into wedding prep?"

"No, I came alone."

"This sounds serious." Mina dropped onto the couch. "What's up?"

"It is serious," he admitted. "Life or death, to be honest."

"Life or death?" Riordan frowned. "Why would the whereabouts of the cornerstone be life or . . . ?" His expression cleared even as his eyes widened, and his mouth rounded into an O of comprehension.

Tremayne shifted and scowled. He supposed it had been bound to come out sooner or later.

Riordan was studying him with fresh interest. "Well. Nice to meet you, Tremayne. I honestly had no idea."

"And if you had known?"

"If I'd known you aren't just some *random* nature spirit"— he eyed Tremayne—"but are actually the spirit of the stone that served as my jail?" Riordan stared at him a moment, then simply shook his head. "Nothing, I hope. It's not like you were the guy who acted against me."

"I followed orders," Tremayne agreed.

"You had no choice."

Tremayne sighed, then nodded slowly. "I underestimated you. My apologies."

"No harm done." Riordan shrugged. "So, we need to get the stone back for you, eh? Somehow."

He'd just said "we," taking on Tremayne's cause as if it were his own. "Why would you help?" he asked.

"Call it a friendly gesture. Or maybe a peace offering."

Tremayne just stared at him.

Mina glanced back and forth between the two men. "What I want to know most—and trust me, I have a whole lot of questions, so this one's a doozy—is where the hell is Daphne? I can't believe she'd willingly miss out on something so important. You must have tied her to a chair."

"No, actually, it was pretty easy to . . ." Tremayne froze.

Mina eyed him shrewdly. "So, it was easy to convince her to stay home like a meek little woman while you had your manly, life-or-death confrontation? No, I wouldn't be suspicious."

Tremayne groaned. He was an idiot. "I have to go."

Mina sobered. "Do you think she's in trouble?"

A strange buzzing filled his head—stress, maybe? Shaking it off, as he had no time for a damn episode of illness, he strode quickly toward the door. "No telling. I'll be back."

"Do you want backup?" Riordan offered.

Again, there was no hesitation, and Tremayne glanced up in surprise. "Thank you, but no. I'll call if that changes."

He cursed himself as he left their house. How could he have been so blind? Daphne wouldn't believe this of her friends and sister. No, she'd suspect her parents. And, naturally, her parents' office was some thirty minutes' drive from here. Damn it! And damn himself for a fool. No doubt she thought she was protecting him in some way. Or her parents, he supposed. It could go either way.

He cut the drive to twenty-two minutes by standing on the gas the whole way. The ringing in his ears had grown worse. It didn't feel like the other episodes, but maybe he was picking up on something from Daphne. If she was projecting, that could only mean she was very upset, not quite in control.

He jogged up the steps and burst through the door of her parents' office, where he found Wendy doing her nails. "Is Daphne here?" he blurted.

"She was. Her parents took her to lunch, I think."

That didn't sound right. "Why do you think that?"

The receptionist looked confused. "Because it's lunchtime and they're not here?"

No wonder Daphne wanted to kill her some days. Ah, but she'd restrained herself, so maybe he could as well. "So, they're *all* gone?" he asked.

The receptionist gave him a *duh* look. "That's what I said, isn't it?" When he just stared at her, waiting for more, she sighed impatiently. "How should I know where they went? I took the morning off for a dentist appointment, so I just got here a little while ago myself. I've been enjoying the quiet. Until now anyway." She raised her eyebrows in obvious invitation for him to leave. Sounded like a plan to him, he decided, and left the building.

Where would he go if he were a hereditary Druid wielding puca powers, encountering parents he believed had betrayed him and also someone he loved? But did she really love still? Could she? He believed she did. Which would only make matters worse, at least in this case. She'd be out for blood.

The buzzing in his mind grew louder, for the first time separating itself into words, concepts, images: Horse hooves, and Duncan and Violet. Druids. Puca powers. Grass, trees, a path and a return for judgment.

Judgment? The grove! She was headed for the grove!

Sprinting back to his car, Tremayne climbed in and pointed it toward the park. At the same time he tried to listen for her thoughts. If she was projecting, maybe she'd hear him, too, either on purpose or by accident.

So angry! I want them to just shut up, want to shut them up no matter what it takes, but the slippery blood—

Daphne!

Startled silence. The flow of images and words cut completely off. There was no buzzing, no ringing, no garbled language.

What could it mean? Was he too late? He couldn't think that. But she was angry—no, *furious*—with her parents. Completely enraged. He'd heard it in the tone of her thoughts. She wouldn't take crap from them anymore. Right now, she was confident enough in her powers and frustrated enough with her parents that she could snap. It would be so easy.

The drive was fast but not fast enough. Nonetheless, he was soon parking the car, shutting off the engine and racing along the park pathway down to the grove. Tremayne batted branches out of his way, straining for sight or sound. Then he saw colors and slight movement, and he slowed to a stop.

Daphne sat on the ground in the middle of the clearing, her clothing uncharacteristically mussed. Her head was bowed, her blonde hair hanging in a tousled curtain around her face. More horrifying, there was a great deal of blood smeared on her sleeves and hands. She didn't move; she just sat as though waiting for him. For this. She seemed so small and . . . defeated?

No. Oh, no.

He knew his duty. It was a duty he'd been given long before this part of the world was discovered, long before the birth of civilization. Puca powers, unchecked, were dangerous. His duty was containing those powers. If a being who wielded them proved insane, a danger to humanity or the faerie world, he was charged to dispatch that being. Or, as Daphne had once phrased it, he was charged to put the being down like a rabid dog. It was his duty to destroy—

"Daphne." He choked out her name. She didn't move, didn't even acknowledge his voice, probably couldn't handle what she'd done. No doubt she'd shut down emotionally, mentally, refusing to accept horrible reality.

But damn it, this wasn't her fault! Not entirely. Why should she be held accountable? It should be all on him. If he'd succeeded in containing the puca powers as originally charged, Daphne never would have been burdened with them. She never would have faced the danger to her sanity, to her very soul. In the end, the blame was all his. He would not, could not, hurt Daphne. She would not be punished for this, whatever bloody deed had occurred.

Set on his course, Tremayne moved quietly into the clearing, approaching the woman he adored and knowing it might be one of their last moments together. Even like this, however, she touched him—even disheveled and covered in blood. She was brilliant and beautiful, and strong. And she was good. Even if she had proven herself capable of performing the ceremony to free him, he knew he could never have asked it. In the same way, he could not now dispatch justice.

He dropped to his knees beside her, murmuring. "It's okay, Daphne. This isn't your fault. You won't pay for this. It's my fault. I'll take the blow. I earned it. I should have contained those powers so long ago. They should never have been foisted on you, to torment and test you. You deserve better. You neither asked for nor earned this burden. It's all mine. I will ensure that the blow comes to me."

She was silent for a strained few moments and then whispered: "Blow?" Her voice was shaking just a little as she tilted her head in his direction. A swath of hair still concealed her features. "Is that supposed to be a dirty joke?"

Damn. The woman had completely lost it. God, that hurt. "I . . ." He paused to clear a tight throat. "Let me find you help first. Then I'll take care of everything. Maybe Janelle can recommend . . ." He broke off, unable to continue.

Daphne tipped her head, combing the hair back from her face, to eye him quizzically. "Oh, don't stop there. Give it to me straight. What can Janelle recommend?" Her lips quivered just a little, even as she raised her eyebrows in a prompting manner.

Tremayne studied her cautiously. He didn't quite know what to think.

"Well, you . . ." He glanced around. "Your parents. They're not here. You shifted and took them on a puca ride, didn't you?"

"I did." She blinked. "And now you think I ate them?"

"Well, not necessarily *ate* them—"

"Ah. You think that I removed their arms and legs and fed them to each other."

Tremayne gave her a repulsed look.

"And wouldn't that invite karmic retaliation, or at least some serious, possibly even fatal, hand-slapping from some Druids we know. And you were willing to take that kind of, um, blow,

I think you called it, on my behalf." She ended on a husky note, her eyes just a little too shiny. They were welling with tears, in fact.

Tremayne only stared.

Daphne started laughing even as the tears spilled over and ran down her face.

"Whoa. Honey. Just let me call Janelle." Appalled, he patted ineffectually at her shoulders, tucking her hair back when it fell forward. "It'll be okay, I promise. It's not like they didn't deserve a little terror. Okay, maybe a lot of terror." He frowned. "This is my fault. You just remember, those puca powers clashed with your Druid heritage, and the conflict pushed you over the edge. It was beyond your control."

"No, it wasn't." She spoke quietly, smiling at him through her tears.

"It wasn't? How . . . wasn't it?"

"God, I adore you," she said. Her smile slowly faded. "I really do. You would have done this for me. You, a man who didn't think he had a heart, would have forfeited everything he's wanted for two thousand years and taken a mortal blow for me. And to think that I wondered if you even had a heart. You do. And it's a huge and generous one. You, Tremayne, a brave being evolved from the nature spirit of the noble Warrior stone, are so much more than a rock." She smiled, sounding utterly confident, if a bit awestruck.

He still wasn't sure what had happened. "So, you're saying . . ."

"That I want to be with you, of course. Isn't that what you wanted to know earlier?" She gave him an innocent look, then, grinning, put him out of his misery. "And, no, I didn't dismember my parents. That seemed a little extreme. Although I might have taken obscene pleasure in scaring the hell out of them. They'll have a bit of a hike to get back home, but they're fine. No permanent damage—which, as someone once told me, is the very least you should expect from a family member. So, I think I'm in the clear still."

Tremayne was shaking his head. "But the blood . . ." He

touched her sleeves, her hands. It was dried now, but still a gory sight. "You were so angry."

Daphne looked at her sleeves and turned her palms up. "That's my blood. I'm pretty sure I did that when I went through the window. It appears puca magic, combined with empowered Druid magic, heals me very quickly. I can't even find the cuts anymore." She glanced up, clearly surprised. "You thought that was my parents'?"

He shrugged. "In my shoes, what would you have thought?"

She tipped her head to the side. "Okay. It's not what happened, but I could see where you might make that leap. For the record, though, I didn't draw any blood but my own."

Tremayne slumped in relief. "Dear god. I thought—"

"Yeah, I know. You thought I went rabid horse and you were going to have to shoot me dead—or take the shot on my behalf." She shook her head. "Why didn't I believe in you, then? A man who would self-destruct on my behalf would never, ever ask me to perform a ceremony that might break my mind. Not even for his own freedom. Would he?" She studied him with lucid eyes.

He looked away and shrugged. "No. I gave up on that. I—I can't bear the idea of you with a broken mind. It just shatters my thoughts, shatters my everything, to picture it. So, no. There will be no ceremony. Come the spring equinox, I will undoubtedly revert, but you will be fine. What will keep me happy will be spending every minute until then with you. If that's all right." He gave her a hopeful look.

"I wasn't joking about wanting to be with you," she murmured slowly, staring at him, "so, of course it's all right. Better than all right. But I only object to the secrecy, the idea of trickery, not the risk itself. We *will* perform that ceremony. I just need to—"

"No. I won't risk it. And it's my decision to make, my life on the line, not yours. I would never pay the possible price."

She eyed him stubbornly.

He just smiled, treasuring her face, her smile, her stubbornness. Her everything. She brought him peace just by existing. "I am proud of you. You know, for not dismembering your parents. I'm sure they made it an awfully attractive option."

She sighed. "Oh, boy, did they." After a moment she added, "You know, my life has really taken a turn for the weird. You should have seen the size of me. I was a humongous horse. And I jumped right through that huge picture window in my mother's office. What a rush. But imagine explaining *that* injury in the ER." She shuddered, rubbing her bloodstained hands along the thin sleeves of her blouse. "So weird."

Tremayne unbuttoned his shirt and doffed it. Dressed in only an undershirt, he draped the other garment over her shoulders and helped thread her arms through the sleeves.

She tugged the shirt close and shook her head. "I'm telling you, life as a simple accountant is much easier than that of a magicky type. Predictable days, great benefits, regular salary, straightforward office policies—no sticky karmic ambiguities—and even a discount at the gym!"

"A discount at the gym, too?" Tremayne raised his eyebrows in pretended awe. "Why did you never tell me? I've been working there not knowing. . . . Do you think they'll let me keep my job? I mean, I know *you're* out in the cold after that puca ride, but hey, I'd do a lot for a discounted gym membership."

Daphne shook her head sadly. "Self-sacrifice and intended martyrdom, you've mastered. A sense of humor? Still needs some work."

"Can't have everything, I guess."

Standing, he reached down and tugged her to her feet. She seemed a little wobbly at first, but then steadied and smiled at him. What composure! Carefully, he swung her off her feet and into his arms for a happy spin.

"Hey, wait—"

"Just deal. And, how's the shoe situation?"

"One-two." She kicked up her feet. "Both accounted for."

"That's my girl. So. Shall we drive home, or would you prefer to fly?"

She grinned and her eyes lit up. "Fly, please. It'll make me feel better. I guess you'll have to tag along in the car, though."

"Somebody has to drive it back." His nerves jangled at the prospect of her flying now, alone, but he refused to give in to them. She'd earned his respect and belief, and she would keep them, damn it. Still, he couldn't help a caution or two. "You're ready for this, right? I will tolerate no freefalling from the sky. Remember that any kind of adrenaline surge can start a spontaneous shift and—"

"I remember. And I'll be careful," she promised.

Reluctantly, he set her on her feet.

Gazing up at Tremayne, Daphne smiled, knowing her heart was in her eyes. He might be afraid of saying it—obviously fearing that he wasn't really capable of it yet—but she knew her own heart. She loved him. Given what she'd witnessed today, she knew damn well now that he would eventually give her similar words of love. She would wait for them, wait until he knew himself well enough to realize that he did indeed love. God knew she owed him so much. For the concern, the respect, the faith in her now, if not before. Okay, she'd even admit to feeling a little dangerous before, so he'd had reason to believe she might perpetrate more than indignities upon her parents. Couldn't blame a guy for jumping to reasonable conclusions.

"So, um, wanna race?" She smiled at him, watching his eyes narrow in mixed warning and intrigue. With a laugh, she closed her eyes and called up her energy, let adrenaline course through her blood, felt the sparks flit around, build with excitement. When she opened her eyes, the ground was much closer. She looked up.

Tremayne shook his head. "You know, a simple robin would have been sufficient."

"Or a lovebird even?" she asked pointedly, recalling the terrifying moment when she'd uncontrollably shifted to one in front of Mina and Lizzy. "I was too afraid to walk, much less fly, back then. I'm ready now. And I felt the need to make a statement with this first flight." She spread her wings—a considerable expanse—and peered at him through eagle eyes. "Better make tracks, little sprite, or I'll win."

He backed toward the path to the parking lot, his eyes concerned and watchful, but not censorious. She was glad.

Carefully taking a step or two to get the feel of her body in this form, she soon found her balance. Instincts she didn't normally possess whispered to her of skills she didn't normally have, abilities she'd wanted, but never possessed—abilities that she now felt she could tap. Trusting those whispers, relinquishing her hold on traditional beliefs, she let her wings and body do what came naturally. Moments later, she was gliding several feet off the ground.

"*Up*, Daphne! Damn it, will you watch where you're going?"

Oops. She missed a copse of young pine trees by inches, then rose above them to look down at the upturned face of her very own nature spirit. Wheeling in a wild loop just to goose him, she then let the joy of total freedom guide her wings and direction. Every part of her exulted in the experience.

She glided, eventually, back to the familiar apartment complex that she would freely consider home if given the chance. She'd need a new job, since in her opinion that puca ride and busted window constituted a resignation, but she was through running from her parents and confrontation.

In fact the puca rides with Eli and then with her parents had given her an idea on that subject. While she was sitting there in the clearing, thinking about all that had occurred, she'd decided that she liked the role of good guy. In some ways, she supposed, she wanted to make up for the wrongs her own parents had committed. Not to prove herself better than they, but to ease some of the frustration she'd experienced over the years and maybe add some weight to the balance on the side of good. So. She really would be Batman meets H&R Block—and she could do it with *or* without a tail. She smiled whimsically. She'd be Super Accountant—or, rather, a forensic accountant. Somebody who caught all the cheating bad guys, not just Eli. She could find a lot of purpose in that.

And, she could do it all right here in Virginia. She'd arrange to break her California apartment lease and have her things shipped home—and this *was* home—as soon as possible.

An excited young voice startled her from her thoughts, and she darted awkwardly behind some bushes and quickly shifted back. Thankfully, she saw that Tremayne's shirt was still draped around her. Its overlong sleeves hung past her fingertips, concealing the dried blood.

A child rounded the bushes, eyes huge.

Daphne gave him a big grin. "Hi!"

"Did you see it? It was so cool! Where did he go?" The child looked around.

"See what?"

"An eagle! A real eagle. I saw it land right—"

"Tommy!" A woman's voice was sharp behind him, and the boy jumped guiltily.

The woman, taking the boy by the hand, gave Daphne an apologetic look. "I'm sorry. My son thought he saw something that he clearly didn't. He gets excited. . . ."

"No problem." Daphne smiled at the boy. "Eagles *are* pretty cool. I think I'd get excited about seeing one, too."

The boy looked perplexed but let his mom tug him around the bushes and away.

"Well, that was a little close." Tremayne's voice was dry. Daphne whirled to see him leaning against the wall of his apartment building, so he had to have broken every speed limit in town to get there. But he just grinned at her, shaking his head.

"Yeah, it was close . . . but I did it! And you have to admit I was good, both with the bird and the covert shift back. Did you see me up there?" She raised her arms to the sky, celebrating.

"I did. And you were damn good. Except for a bobble or two." He closed his eyes, no doubt reliving her spin.

She laughed. "Yeah. Well, I guess we'd better clean up and change clothes so we can make it to Mina and Riordan's wedding." Starting for his apartment she added, "Afterward, we have a cornerstone to find and a spring-equinox party to crash. That's less than a week from now, you know."

Tremayne grabbed her hand and pulled her to a stop. "No."

"You don't like weddings? I'm not fond of them, either, but—"

"Daphne. The equinox ceremony is not going to happen. I already told you, I won't risk you that way. I can't."

"Tremayne—"

He stopped her words with a long kiss. When he pulled back, she was breathless and a little dazed. The man could kiss! Honestly, those sensuous lips made no empty promises.

He smiled wordlessly, dark eyes speaking volumes.

Returning the smile and the unspoken volumes, she had to blink back the muzziness in her head. "But that equinox ceremony is the only—"

"And do you realize," he interrupted, "that we have to be at the church in an hour?"

Daphne looked at her watch and then took to her heels. But the subject of the spring-equinox ceremony was in no way closed. Not as far as she was concerned.

Chapter Nineteen

"So Tremayne mentioned you flew home?" Mina's eyes sparkled with curiosity. They made a great accessory for the glowing rest of her. She was beautiful, happy—a traditional, but not cheesy, bride. And now that the ceremony was over, they had moved the celebration to a local restaurant. Mina had pulled Daphne into an alcove off the party room to grill her for details.

"Literally flew? As in, you did the bird-morphing trick and put it to good use?"

Daphne allowed herself a grin. "Yep."

"Not a lovebird, I hope." Mina pressed her lips together, obviously fighting laughter.

"For my first flight? You've got to be kidding. I wanted big and beautiful and impressive!"

Mina nodded. "You turned into an ostrich, didn't you? A flying ostrich on my wedding day, and I missed it."

"Brat." Daphne laughed. "I was an eagle."

"An eagle?" Janelle, who'd leaned closer to listen, looked suitably impressed. "Were you scared?"

Daphne frowned. "No, not really. It was exciting. I felt like I could accomplish anything at that point, though. Would I be nervous if I did it now? Probably."

"Okay, what are you three whispering about over here? Will it burn male ears to a crisp, or can we join you?" Riordan walked up, Tremayne and Kane next to him.

"Eh, you can join us. Given the vows and all." Mina gave him a smile, which he kissed. "Have you seen Mom? I thought she was talking to you."

"She said she had to get something from the car." Riordan shrugged, and Mina nodded.

Janelle slipped her arm through Kane's. "We were discussing Daphne's eagle impersonation. It sounds most impressive."

"Eagle?" Kane smiled. "Sounds like a celebration to me. Is it because you got the cornerstone back? Did your dad have it?"

Daphne met Tremayne's eyes for a moment, but then she shook her head. "He didn't have it. My mom didn't, either. I'm not sure where to look next. One of the other Druids, maybe?"

An awkward clearing of a throat interrupted her. Lizzy Dixon stood in the archway of the crowded alcove, and she looked pale and uncertain.

"Lizzy, are you okay?" Daphne asked.

"I . . ." The woman walked into the room, glancing with odd uncertainty at her daughter, at the puca brothers, at Daphne, and lastly at Tremayne. "I find myself in a strange position. One I didn't know I occupied. Maybe I should have wondered? My motives weren't entirely pure." Her nerve clearly wavered.

Tremayne, who was nearest Lizzy, reached out to steady her, but Lizzy shifted to take his hand in hers, clasping it tightly as she peered up into his face.

"I didn't mean to hurt anyone. I swear. I honestly . . . just wanted a piece of the action, for lack of a more honorable way of phrasing it. I thought I'd just hang close, wait for lightning to strike, or whatever the puca equivalent might be, hoping that it would strike me if I were the nearest available vessel. Mina was touched by magic. Janelle was, and now Daphne. Why not me, too? I really wanted to be the hero for once, to have the power to do good beyond what an ordinary human could do. To help people. I'm past worrying about my own fortune and future, but I'd love to leave the world a better place. After I'm gone, I mean."

"Why? Do you plan on checking out soon?" Mina spoke, a hard edge of worry marring her joke.

Lizzy smiled. "No. Although the young man here might kick my butt into a hasty exit once he hears what I've done."

"Oh, nuts," Mina said. "Just spit it out, Mom. Did you sic Duncan on him? Some other crooked Druid?"

"No. Nothing that simple. And yet . . ." She sighed and set down the tote bag she carried with her. From it she lifted a terry cloth–wrapped bundle, which she offered to Tremayne. "I had no idea the connection was so—I swear, if I'd known . . ." She seemed to run out of words.

Tremayne accepted the bundle from Mina's mother, but he already knew its contents. He unwrapped it carefully, revealing the cornerstone. A hot mix of emotions welled up. Controlling them, he looked at Lizzy. "You know what this is to me?"

"I heard you all talking. That's when I knew. Before, I thought it was just a rock, albeit one tied to power. I thought that it couldn't be hurt."

Daphne closed her eyes. "Dear god. You could've—"

"I know that now. And I swear if I had known then, I would never have . . . I mean . . ." Lizzy gave Tremayne a quick, sheepish look. "I guess I should have bought an ordinary doorstop."

Mina cringed. "Mom!"

"And used the flyswatter on that damn spider." Lizzy shuddered dramatically at the memory. "Oh, but he scared the living daylights out of me. I thought it was a brown recluse, and I just thunked the horrible creature into oblivion."

Daphne flinched.

"And it probably would have been more appropriate to use a hammer to rehang that picture after the nail popped out."

Tremayne winced, feeling each blow all over again.

Lizzy brought a hand to her mouth in embarrassment and shock. "I'm so sorry, Tremayne."

He nodded. Then carefully rewrapped the stone.

Daphne rose quietly and went to stand behind Mina's mother. "At least we know it's safe now. And we know you never would have destroyed it."

Lizzy's eyes widened. "Oh, no. Never! Destroy the cornerstone? I couldn't! Even if it never amounted to anything more than a piece of rock, I wanted it as a memento. It played such an important role for Riordan and my daughter. Destroy it? No, *never*."

"I believe you." Tremayne spoke with quiet gravity, his eyes meeting Daphne's. The relief alone was as disorienting as any of the stomach-churning nausea he'd experienced, but he turned back to the older woman, who wrung her hands. "I'm glad you gave it back to me. That's all that matters."

"Oh, I don't know. I think a few other things matter." Mina eyed her mother shrewdly. "Just how did you get your hands on the cornerstone?"

Lizzy looked a little shamefaced. "We-ell . . ."

"Oh, Mom." Mina covered her face. "You didn't snoop!"

"Well, it was just the once." She drew herself up defensively. "And I didn't snoop everywhere. I . . . Look, it was on impulse. I was on my way to the bathroom and just happened to peek into the bedroom. There was this intriguing lockbox on the bed and . . . okay, I picked the damn lock."

"You picked a lock?" Mina sounded horrified. "In somebody else's home? Does that not strike you as criminal behavior?"

"I was curious! And I was just going to look." Lizzy bit her lip and avoided Tremayne's gaze. "Then, when I realized what it was, I thought maybe fate was leading me to it."

"Did fate also lead you to replace the cornerstone with my shoe so I wouldn't get suspicious?" Tremayne couldn't decide whether to be entertained or angry.

"Well, sometimes fate needs a little help." Lizzy raised her chin.

"Yeah, but back up. You said you picked the lock? A combination lock?" Daphne asked.

"Yes!" Lizzy allowed herself a little smile. "I was so surprised it worked after all these years. It's a trick I learned from an old boyfriend. Now *that* was an interesting man to know. I had to return all of the fabulous jewelry he gave me, of course, but he was fantastic in bed. You know, he never, ever cracked safes for the money, either. Just for the challenge. He loved puzzles." She looked dreamy for a moment. "He said I was like a puzzle to him. One he never, ever solved."

"Ick?" Mina made a face.

"Daughter, you just aren't a romantic."

Tremayne raised his voice over theirs. "So you took it when you came with your daughter to visit Daphne. Daphne shifted into bird form, and when I came out of the bedroom to help her . . ." He raised an eyebrow. "Yeah, I left the safe out on my bed. Locked. Call me crazy, but I thought a locked safe was a sufficient deterrent."

"Against any visitors in your home but my mother"—Mina gave her mother a shaming look—"it probably would have been."

"Or my father," Daphne said. "Not that I think Lizzy's like him. It really could have been worse, Tremayne. He told me he broke in to steal it, but it was already missing. Because Lizzy had already taken it. If it weren't for that . . ." She shivered. "And you know Lizzy didn't intend to hurt anyone. I don't condone snooping and theft, but . . . no harm done?"

After a moment, Tremayne sighed and nodded. Daphne smiled at him.

"I really am sorry," Lizzy whispered. "Is there anything I can do to make up for it?"

Daphne cleared her throat. "Mina told me you cook." She glanced at Tremayne, her eyes twinkling a little.

Lizzy blinked. "Yes, I do. Not as much as I once did. Another boyfriend, a gourmet chef . . . Ah, now *that* man could appreciate luxury. And share it. Dating him was better than attending chef school." She shook her head, smiling a little. Then she refocused on Tremayne. "Can I cook for you? I could be your slave chef every weekend for, say, six months? Oh, and without snooping. You can even keep me on webcam if that would make you feel better. Would that work for you?"

Tremayne eyed her but shook his head.

Lizzy looked disappointed. "Something else, then?"

With a glance at Daphne, he let his lips twist into a smile. "How about giving me lessons instead? I'm trying to learn, but cooking shows and the Internet only get me so far."

Lizzy's face lit up. "I'd love to! Just say where and when, and I'll be there."

Tremayne grimaced. "It would probably have to be soon." *Before the spring equinox*, he didn't say. But he knew Daphne heard. He didn't expect to exist beyond that date, not in any physical form.

Mina was shaking her head but smiling. "I can't deny that Mom can cook. Just keep her out of the organic and health-foods sections when she's buying ingredients. That's one cooking detour she should have foregone."

Lizzy raised her brows. "I did that for you, young lady. I was nurturing genius—or so I thought."

"Yeah, yeah." Mina rolled her eyes.

"Oh!" Lizzy turned to Daphne. "And if you want lock-picking lessons, I can give you those."

Mina cringed. "Just when I thought we were getting some-where. Let this be a lesson to everyone in this room. If you ex-pect a visit from my mother, dead-bolt and booby trap your bedroom doors, and never ever put anything but decoys in your medicine cabinet."

"Well, I like learning about people." Lizzy cast a defensive look at her daughter. "Is that so wrong?"

"Where do I begin?" Mina rolled her eyes, and Daphne laughed.

Later that night, Daphne watched as Tremayne carefully rewrapped the cornerstone and tucked it back in the lockbox, which he stashed under the floorboards of the closet. Using his powers, he'd reset the combination and added a few tricks to the mechanism. It would be difficult for anyone unauthorized to open in future. Tremayne stared for a moment before carefully replacing the boards and turning back to catch Daphne's eyes. She was every bit as glad as he when it was safely tucked away.

"So." Tremayne cast her a speculative look. "I read on a dat-ing Web site that bridesmaids are always horny after weddings. Is that true?"

"Dating Web site? What were you doing on a dating site?

Cooking Web sites, I'm in favor of. Dating Web sites? No. After all, you have *me*. I'm more than enough for any man. With me you get a human female with hereditary Druid powers and wielding live puca powers. Honestly, what more could even a nature spirit want?"

He grinned. "Well, he wants a horny bridesmaid, of course. Now, keep that dress right where it is. I have plans for you in it."

"In this thing?" She lifted frilly skirts and dropped them. There was weight there. And frill. And scratchy fabric from hip to knee. "Oh, that's sick. You do realize that bridesmaid dresses are universally ugly and uncomfortable, don't you?"

"Is that what you told Mina? I thought you tried it on before."

"Of course I didn't tell her that. She's the bride. I was trying to be nice. So let me just get this thing off—" She reached behind her back to search out the zipper tab.

"Freeze, woman."

She did so, biting back a grin as she dropped her arms to her sides. "What?"

"Now put those hands where I can see them. No touching that zipper. Good. Now I want you to fold your hands in front of you and hold them, like you did with your bouquet. And lift your chin as though you have a rusty little halo tipped over one eyebrow." He grinned when she laughingly complied. "There. That's perfect. You look downright virginal in that dress. It's been giving me ideas all day."

"Virginal? Me? Hey, as we recall, I wasn't even a virgin when we first did the deed. You were. Not that you ever looked the part." Although his open appreciation for her bridesmaid dress reminded her of a deprived thirteen-year-old. So naive, so funny and adorable.

"What can I say? I'm manly enough to overshadow thousands of years of inexperience."

She rolled her eyes but fought a grin. His stride toward her was every bit as predatory as she might like, not a bit virginal.

"You know"—he nodded, eyes wide—"the ancients who erected the stones at Avebury were really, really concerned with fertility. Protecting it, encouraging it, proving it. In fact, those stones were all considered either feminine or masculine, based on size, shape and, er, presentation. Warrior was definitely masculine."

"So, what you're saying is that the guy stones were all ancient phallic symbols? Well, out of curiosity I did look up your stone on the Internet. I couldn't find any mention of the Warrior, much less an illustration, but I did see a sketch of the Obelisk. I will admit to being mildly impressed."

He shook his head. "You thought that was impressive? You should have seen the original Warrior. Talk about masculine glory!"

"Really?" She pressed a hand to her heart. "I'm even more impressed. Assuming function follows form."

"You doubt me?" He was a mere stride away now.

"Well, I mean, you're a lot smaller these days. I know size shouldn't matter, but, well, there's a big difference. Huge." Slanting a glance low, she affected concern.

"I'd be more than happy to demonstrate."

"Well, don't hurt yourself or anything. I heard those old stones were tough to erect. Do you need any help? They make these little blue pills now. . . ."

He smiled slowly, eyes glittering. "Your little blue pills mean nothing to me."

Choking on laughter, Daphne took a step backward for every one he took forward. It was shades of their first encounter, right after he became her mentor and invited her into his home. This time she welcomed his advances, though, teased him with her retreat. Then again, was that so very different? She'd always wanted him.

Except she saw so much more in him now. Rock, man, nature spirit, warrior, lover, friend, mentor. All of him, whatever he claimed, whatever he denied, she accepted him as he was. And all of this she projected to him.

"You forgot stud."

"Stud," she repeated obediently, though she could barely say the word over rising laughter.

He closed in, his hips crowding hers until she was backed against the wall. Leaning a forearm over her head, his shoulders impossibly wide and shadowing her, he dipped his head to look into her eyes. "Better. Much better." Then he grinned. "I had fun tonight."

"I saw." She'd watched him relax with the others and had smiled as he sipped champagne all evening, wrinkling his nose at the unfamiliar bubbles. She suspected he was the slightest bit tipsy even now. Which was too cute. A big, bad nature spirit tipsy on bubbly pink champagne!

"That doesn't sound very manly," Tremayne remarked.

"But you're the Warrior," she responded. "How could you fail to be manly? I thought manly was second nature to you. Or, as a nature spirit, would that be first nature?" She blinked at him, watching him narrow his eyes with suspicion.

"You're laughing at me."

"Well, yeah. Why wouldn't I?"

"Maybe for fear of retaliation?"

"Ooooh. Like what?"

"You're giggling at an ancient fertility symbol," he explained gently. "What do you *think* will happen?"

She widened her eyes in awe. "That you'll talk a really good game, bragging and promising and threatening. Oooh, I'm all aflutter." She sighed. "Come on. The least you could do is prove it. Fix a car or flex a few muscles!"

"So you're craving a mating ritual?"

"You might say that." A laugh escaped, but she choked it back. "Time to strut around and wiggle your tail feathers?"

Lips twitching, he raised his free hand to trail fingertips along her jaw. "Close."

"Ooooh, I can't wai—"

Dipping forward, he caught the rest of the word in his mouth. Long fingers tunneled through her hair. Then he cupped the back of her head, angling her mouth for maximum enjoyment.

She could feel his smile around her lips as he devoured them, slanting and caressing, breath hot and mingling with hers. When she hummed a trembling appreciation, he trailed his lips to her cheek, nipped at her chin, then slid lower on a nibbling, devastating trek down her throat.

Tipping her head back against the wall, she played her fingers through his hair, which was so soft and thick and short that it flipped beneath her moving fingers like crushed velvet. He paused to appreciate her collarbone with his lips, tongue and the edge of his teeth, brushing a hand teasingly at the lace along her bodice.

"I love this dress. Textures and sparklies and curves. Pure tease, I swear."

"Obviously . . . you've never had to . . . wear one!" She ended on a squeak as a nibble traveled low in her décolletage. There he dallied and casually devastated her. For a recent virgin, the man had too damn many skills.

His fingers slipped to her waist and back, then skimmed the length of her spine. On a whisper of sound the material loosened, gaping away from bared breasts to slide low and catch on the curve of her hips.

"Oooooh. Sly fingers." When he flashed her a mischievous, very smug grin, she laughed. "You are a quick study."

"Not quick at all. I've studied for a long time. Actual practice, however . . . only with you. Always only you."

She smiled at his words, even as they raised a few doubts.

"No. I will not be curious," he answered. "I've already seen enough women to know none of them are like you. I don't want them. Why would I? Like you said, I have you." He smiled at her with open confidence. "What more could I want?"

"For what it's worth, you have me. All of me." She met his eyes, conveying her own sincerity. "I would do anything for you. You know that, right?" The lacy white bells and whistles, the pledges . . . For him she might even take that leap, no matter how terrifying it once seemed. But first . . . "I want to do the ceremony to free you."

"That's not something for you to worry about. It's my problem."

"But Tremayne, the spring equinox is less than a week away. I'll need time to practice and prepare—"

"No." All amusement vanished from his face. "I won't risk that. And . . . I ask that we not spoil this evening by discussing it. Please?"

Reluctantly, she nodded and was pleased to see the smile return to his face. The man deserved his moment. His evening. She would give him that.

And much more, she vowed silently.

He buried his face in her cleavage again, seeming to revel in the textures and warmth, and she felt a breeze. Then his big hands clasped her thighs, the silly frills of her skirt flaring wide. She caught her breath just before his dark eyes flashed wickedly at her. "Garters? Oh, boy!" Then all she saw was his dark hair and her frilly skirt. Even that quickly blurred, as nimble fingers teased at lace and elastic, then found bare, way-too-sensitive flesh.

A masculine hum of satisfaction reached her ears as her panties were slipped aside and she felt an exploring touch, wandering, learning, knowing. She couldn't see what he was doing past the concealment of her skirts, could only feel—

Broad shoulders nudged her thighs farther apart, and then she felt breath on her. Soon she was keening softly as a wicked tongue and demanding fingers explored ruthlessly, driving her higher. She slipped lower as her knees weakened, but a shoulder and clasping hand held her ruthlessly open to him until she surrendered to the pinnacle of pleasure. She fell forward, only to be caught in his arms as he rose to his full height.

His arms full of pouffy skirt and dreamy woman, he grinned wickedly at her. "You look utterly ravished, little bridesmaid."

She felt dazed and, yes, utterly ravished.

"And you look utterly depraved," she replied. She flicked a finger at his dangling necktie and smiled at his unbuttoned collar and the tuxedo shirt half tugged from his pants. But mostly it was the look in his eyes. Intimately knowing, confident bordering on cocky. Triumphant even. "It's a good look."

"Yeah?"

"A really good look." She gave him a little push backward, gaze drifting past his shoulder to the bed behind him.

Obviously following her thoughts, he backed toward the bed until he dropped onto the mattress. She settled astride his thighs, frilly skirts flaring wide, even as the bodice dipped below her rib cage.

Having deviously distracted him by his position at eye level with her breasts, she launched a little retaliation of her own. She reached for his dangling tie and pulled it free of his collar, then she unbuttoned and unbuttoned as fast as she could . . . but it took so long. And what he was doing with his mouth made her fingers clumsy, so she just pulled and yanked, startling a laugh out of Tremayne, who finally held his arms wide and let her do what she wanted. At last she had his chest bare.

"Much better," she said. And she yanked the tails of his shirt out of his slacks and peeled the crisp white material down past his biceps. "Mmmmm, now this is what I'd call a monument to studliness."

With a wicked glance into his eyes, she ran her palms over his broad chest, scraping her nails in the triangle of dark curls that narrowed to a line she irresistibly followed. Muscles contracted and quivered at her touch, and he moved in to nibble behind her ear. Tucking her hair back, he trailed teeth down her neck even as she busied herself with belt buckle, button and . . . *zzzzip*!

Then she backed off to grin at him. "Is this the part where you start talking about fertility symbols again?"

His eyes darkened with promise. "Don't need symbols if you have the real thing."

"Ooh, *bad*." She was laughing, just a little breathlessly, knowing the guy had a very, very good point. She dropped her gaze low. Who the hell needed a symbol with this much reality?

He laughed.

She glanced up. "I'm projecting?"

"That's okay. I like it."

"Oh, me too." She took the object in question into her eager grasp. Tremayne leaned back on his hands, giving her better access, and while she kept her gaze mostly on her new toy—honestly, who wouldn't?—he trained hot, dark eyes on her face. Oh, the promises that gaze made whenever she looked up at him!

Then, his breathing harsh, he was tugging her hands free and settling them high on his shoulders. He grasped her hips—or, rather, the great poufs of material covering them. Eyes glinting with quick humor, he tugged at the frills, lifting layer after layer to finally find skin. Then he guided her hips until, his eyes meeting hers, he lowered her slowly onto him.

She caught her breath as he drove deep, then settled into a rhythm. Never once did he let her gaze free of his. Those dark eyes held her hostage, watching, heating, demanding, even as he guided her hips while rocking his own in a devastating counterpoint. She felt possessed, body, heart and soul. Totally open to him, even as he opened himself completely to her. She'd never felt closer, never felt more bound to another. Nature spirit, Warrior, mentor, man, lover . . . he was all of those to her and more. A miracle in every sense of the word. Her miracle.

"As you are mine," he murmured, his eyes reflecting her own feelings back.

Her heart hitched along with her breath as he slid his fingers low to tease her. He thrust more deeply, quickly. She felt his eyes on her, felt him watching her, watching her face, meeting her eyes, and soon he'd managed to rock her into another climax. Only then did he let himself go, thrusting once, twice more, before coming with a groan deep in his chest. Then, his breathing harsh, he slid his arms around her and lay back on the bed, with her resting on his chest. They lay there in silent contentment until Tremayne chuckled.

"What? It's the dress, isn't it? You finally see it for what it is—a practical joke played on all of womankind."

"Nope. I still like the dress. We're keeping it. Consider it a sex toy." He rolled their bodies into a more comfortable position.

"You're so twisted." But she was grinning at him. "So, why were you laughing if it wasn't at all this silly satin fluff?"

"I just realized, all those pillows I tried out—"

"The rejects in the closet?"

"Yeah, those. And these on the bed, too." He lazily smacked at one. "They don't matter. Best bed in the world isn't complete unless you're in it. But I'm good now. It's all good."

She pulled back to look at him, but he'd closed his eyes, utterly content.

"Does that mean I'm your chosen pillow?"

Grinning lazily, he tugged her close. "Yep. No way am I stashing you in the closet."

She laughed. "Thank heavens for small favors!" But oh, the man was sweet for being a freaking rock. And smiling, she tucked her head under his chin and decided he made a damn good pillow, too.

Chapter Twenty

Early the next morning, while Tremayne showered, Daphne picked up her cell phone and dialed a number.

"Hello?"

"Mister . . . Um, I mean—"

"Daphne?"

She sighed. "Yes."

"Just call me Phil." There was a smile in his voice. "What can I do for you?"

"You said to call if I needed help, with Druid or other stuff. Well . . . I need help. How do you feel about tutoring an untrained Druid? In secret."

"What do you mean?"

She glanced over her shoulder, relieved to hear the water still running. "I don't want Tremayne to know about it. At least, I don't want him to know I'm trying to figure out how to conduct the ceremony to free him. Can you do this?"

"We can meet. I won't say anything to him about it, and you can make your explanations however you wish."

"Thanks." They set a time and place, and she hung up the phone just as the water shut off.

The bathroom door opened. "Did I hear voices?" Tremayne poked his head out. He looked adorable, his hair slicked back like a seal's. She grinned.

"I look like a seal?" He sounded offended but also distracted— as she'd intended. Although she projected none of the latter.

"Hey, I can't help it. You do. It's cute."

He growled, but his dark eyes twinkled with humor as he ducked back into the bathroom.

"Hey, I need to meet with a client a few mornings this week. Any chance you trust me to be on my own? The guy's older and, well, he seems paranoid. I said we'd be confidential." She kept her voice breezy, her eyes distant.

He peeked back out. "You're meeting with Phil."

She straightened so fast that her spine popped. "Hey! You can't do that."

"No, I can't read what you don't project, but I can make some guesses. Daphne, we're not doing the ceremony."

She shrugged. "Okay, so you say. But meeting with Phil can only help my control, right?"

He looked less than pleased but couldn't really argue. "I guess, if nothing else, it will set his mind at ease that you've mastered your powers. Just don't get any other ideas."

"If you can make guesses, then I can get any ideas I want to get."

So, later that morning she met with Phil. He led her in a down-and-dirty session of concentrated meditation and chanting.

Days. Mere *days* and it would be the equinox. She knew it. Tremayne knew it. But he was being too damn stubborn. No way would she let him revert to nature spirit form—a barely sentient being, as he'd described it. What a waste. Even if she couldn't have him for herself, no way would she see him reduced to that.

Inhaling deeply, she closed her eyes, concentrating on the mantras Phil had taught her. One way or another, she'd find the words locked somewhere inside. The ones to free Tremayne.

Unfortunately, the only rhymes ringing in her head right now more resembled a dirty little limerick about nature spirits and their Warrior stones. She groaned.

"No. Concentrate. Close your eyes and picture it."

Daphne almost snarled at the Druid. "I can't. I can't concentrate. There's so much noise in my head—"

"Noise?" Phil's gaze sharpened.

"Y-yes. Not voices telling me to kill, if that's what concerns you. I'm not insane—although I'll admit I was a little concerned at first. But now I know this is something more. There's an echo. Like in those dreams I told you about. You know, the ones that I thought meant I was going crazy, like everyone was predicting. The thing is, I hear that echo when I'm awake now, too. It sounds like my voice, but it's speaking another language."

Her breath hitched and she finally spoke her hope and fear. "That's *not* me going nuts. I think the fear that I was losing it kept me from really hearing it until now. Honestly, I could almost swear that echo is teaching me the chant I need to learn. For Tremayne, I mean. I think the words would pour out of me at the right time and place, if I let them. But Tremayne won't cooperate. He's afraid of what will happen to me if I do it."

Phil nodded gravely. "He truly is a man now, isn't he? Kind, caring. Whole, but for the technicality. He protects you."

"He's a wonderful man. And whether he believes himself capable of it or not, I think he loves me. I'm just waiting for him to realize it himself." Daphne gave the Druid a direct look. "And don't start spouting ridiculous crap about him being incapable of love because he's the spirit of a stone, either. Calling Tremayne a rock is like calling me a chimpanzee. No, an amoeba. Or whatever the hell would be at the root of my family tree."

Phil smiled, kept his own counsel and just listened.

In no need of his input on that subject, she continued defiantly: "Tremayne is . . . Tremayne. And I will save him, damn it."

"You're determined?"

"Yes."

He nodded happily. "Sounds good. Let's do it then."

No argument? She blinked. "Why, do you have an idea?" She eyed him hopefully.

"Well. Nothing earthshaking. Frankly, I'm surprised you haven't thought of it yourself."

"What do you mean?"

Phil shrugged. "The leverage you have over Tremayne—other

than your emotional concerns—is his vulnerability. And you already know what that is."

"Vulnerability? Oh!" She met Phil's eyes. "His cornerstone."

Could she do this? What if she screwed up and Tremayne paid the price as a result?

So she wouldn't screw up. In the few days since her session with Phil, she'd worked her tail off, successfully enlisting a veritable army to help. She'd planned this event so carefully, projecting not a damn thing. She wouldn't screw up.

Heart pounding, she carefully unlocked Tremayne's safe using the combination she'd seen several times now. He'd made a ritual of checking on the cornerstone every night, ever since he'd gotten it back from Lizzy. Demonstrating a full measure of trust, he'd unlocked that safe so many times with Daphne watching that she'd memorized the combination.

Now she felt a bit like a heel.

But she was a well-meaning one, damn it! She reached into the safe, carefully lifting out its satin-covered contents. She unwrapped the stone with the care she'd show a newborn infant, cradling it once it was free of the quilted material.

She glanced over her shoulder, just to make sure Tremayne hadn't reentered the bedroom. That one moment made her feel like a traitor all over again. The man was sitting on his dandelion yellow couch mixing up a batch of cookies, damn it all, and he reeked of testosterone and sex appeal. How she loved him. He was sexy, adorable, witty. One of a kind. Everything she did now was because of her love.

She turned back to the stone. Touching it, she could hear that voice again, the one from her dreams. The murmuring was almost coherent. Banishing it for the moment, she closed her eyes and concentrated. She recalled the words Phil had given her and carefully chanted them aloud. A few moments later, she heard a loud thump from the other room and flinched. Carefully, she set the stone on the bed, then rushed into the living room.

Sure enough, Tremayne was lying on the carpet, out cold. Wincing again, she checked for injury, but he looked fine. She tucked a pillow under Tremayne's head, put the mixing bowl in the fridge and turned off the stove. Then she retrieved the cornerstone, rewrapped it and dialed Mina's number.

"Okay. Mission accomplished. I'm going to need that help now," she relayed.

Twenty minutes later, Riordan and Kane were at the door, as promised. Neither was empty-handed.

"Janelle sent along some supplies to get the big guy here on his way." Kane rolled in a loaded-down wheelchair, while Riordan was burdened with technical-looking tanks and hoses. With all of this stuff attached, Tremayne would resemble a man on his last gasp of life.

Daphne regarded all of it with doubt. "How in the world will I get this stuff past security?" Maybe she hadn't explored all of the obstacles thoroughly enough in her haste.

"Glamour," Kane and Riordan chimed in together.

"Right." She nodded, feeling mildly unsure.

"Don't worry. We're not abandoning you." Kane smiled reassurance as Riordan busied himself with readying their supplies. "We'll be the med techs helping you get him on the plane, and I'll start the glamouring for you to ease your way as well as ours. Everyone will believe we have permission from every doctor and bureaucrat necessary to make this happen. Are you packed?"

She nodded hesitantly. "I guess. This is a go, then?"

"Yep. We can get you on the plane. Bringing him out of it without incident and getting him to the stone circle will be your job, though. I can't glamour a nature spirit like Tremayne. He can block that, unconscious or not."

She winced. "I just hope he stays in this sleep state until we get him across the pond."

"Did Phil say how long it would last?"

"He seemed unsure."

Kane nodded. "Well, best we can do is get Tremayne on that plane and hope he'll see reason later." He flashed a grin. "I will just be grateful that you're the one in range when he wakes up, and not me."

"Or me." Riordan gave Daphne a wry look before reaching for Tremayne's shoulders. "Grab his legs, bro."

Together, the brothers wrestled Tremayne into the wheel-chair, and Daphne stowed the wrapped stone—which could raise all kinds of security eyebrows—in an emergency care-like metal tank. She didn't want to know what the tank was or what Janelle and the brothers had done to get it; she was just grateful they had. "Okay. I guess we're ready to go."

Together, they wrestled the chair into a van they'd borrowed— more of Janelle's contacts—and transported everyone to the air-port. Kane eased their way with terrifying simplicity past the ticket counter, past security screening and onto the plane. Once Tremayne was settled in his seat, Daphne turned to Kane and Ri-ordan, who were on the brink of deplaning and returning home. "Thank you for this. He would thank you, too, if he weren't so damn stubborn."

"Given the circumstances? I'm not so sure of that. But we owe him. And you. Take care and be careful." Kane hugged her.

Riordan handed her the satchel containing the tank, the hid-den cornerstone, and the proper cording that attached to part of the wheelchair. She'd packed a few other necessities, both magical and practical, in a bag she'd checked. "Keep the satchel and stone close," Riordan murmured.

"No worries about that." Daphne shuddered over possibili-ties. Looping the satchel strap over her arm, she cradled its bur-den close. Then she looked up at Riordan. "Thanks."

"Like Kane said, we owe him. But don't scramble your mar-bles while you're out there, okay? If anything happens to you, Mina will kill me. And you've never seen anger until you've seen a middle-school teacher lose it. They're tough and it takes a lot to blow their lid, but when they do . . ." Riordan shud-dered. "Scary shit."

Daphne smiled and hugged him. "I think they need you two to leave so they can finish boarding everyone."

He nodded, smiled at her, then left.

Sighing only a little shakily, she settled into the seat next to her patient and opened her mind to his.

Just what in the hell are you doing?

She jumped then turned, slowly, to look at Tremayne. He was fully conscious. She'd thought he would sleep for a while yet, that she'd get a little warning as he started to awaken. But he was awake now? He hadn't moved, hadn't opened his eyes.

No, I can't move a damn muscle, thanks to whatever you did. What did you do?

I charmed your stone. Phil taught me how. It's temporary and not fatal, I promise. I just needed you cooperative. Daphne eyed him warily.

And why is that? Did you turn on me already? I thought you cared about me.

She swallowed hard. She'd really hoped she could postpone this moment. *I do. So much. That's why we're here.*

Where is here?

She sighed and acquiesced. He'd find out anyway. *We're on a plane bound for England. We're going to Wiltshire County to visit the stone circle at Avebury.*

What?

She could swear she felt his muscles bunch next to her. Damn. Not already. He couldn't possibly already—

You tricked me!

Somebody had to. She glanced up in relief as the stewardess launched into her passenger-safety demonstration. Soon they'd be airborne and she would have half the battle behind her.

Daphne—

I'm doing this. No way am I letting you revert to your little less-than-sentient life-form. What an awful waste of studliness, you know?

This isn't a joke.

No, let's all sing dirges instead. She glared at him. *Because Daphne is bound to screw up. She screws everything up, remember? Reverts to wishy-washy adolescence during parental encounters, morphs without planning it, can't even keep her new job and new apartment because she can't control herself.*

That's not true.

Well, apparently, that's what you still believe. You think I'm not capable of conducting this ceremony without scrambling my brains. You think I'm not strong enough.

I didn't say that.

It's what you believe.

And she definitely felt his muscles bunching this time. *I think you're the smartest, most beautiful, most capable—if infuriating—woman I've ever met. And I'm in love with you. That's why I can't risk you.*

She blinked back tears. Dear god, but he'd finally said it. No conditionals, no uncertainties. He really believed it. He felt it. And damn it all, but she'd incapacitated him and he had to mindspeak it to her when he said it the first time. It was so unfair! Oh, but he'd said it.

I love you, too, you stubborn, infuriating, gorgeous man. I love you so much, in fact, that I'm willing to risk alienating you completely just to save your Warrior ass. That's why I pulled off this stupid farce just to get you on a plane. The least I could hope for in return from you is a show of support. You've said in the past that you believe in me, that you believe I can control these powers well enough to lead a productive, normal life. You say I'm smart. That I'm strong. Resourceful. Capable. And now you finally say that you love me—and your timing sucks by the way—but I'll still give you the chance to make up for it. You say you love me? Prove it. Trust me.

She saw his eyelids flickering even as the stewardess buckled herself into her seat and the plane began taxiing.

Daphne's heart pounded. Almost in the air. They just had to be airborne.

Tremayne slowly turned his head to look into her eyes. "I love you," he said. Though softly spoken, his words were only a little slurred. "And I believe in you."

With obvious effort, he lifted a hand, palm up, in invitation. Biting her lip as tears overflowed and streamed down her cheeks, she took it, holding tightly and silently as they taxied down the runway and lifted off.

"I swear, you are so lucky that stewardess didn't call security and have us arrested and strip-searched on the spot. Rising up like that!" Daphne closed her eyes, torn between horror and hilarity.

"I'm healed!" he'd rasped, in full hearing of the woman, who'd turned a bug-eyed gaze on both of them. Then he'd risen on shaky limbs, weakly but so bravely holding his arms out like a zombie. Daphne had immediately and quietly had to glamour the woman into believing Tremayne's was a mental infirmity. Then she'd had to repeat the same glamour on everyone who'd seen him wheeled aboard the plane. Lord, when the man entered his fully sentient phase of evolution, there was just no stopping his "development."

Tremayne grinned at her now. "I was just expressing my belief and trust in your abilities to glamour. You perform a gorgeous mindwalk when you set your mind to it."

She groaned. "You're impossible."

"But you love me."

"I must."

"So. Where to now? A cozy bed and breakfast for a round of hot monkey sex before the ceremony?" He gazed at her hopefully.

"You get more and more incorrigible." She eyed him askance. "Are you evolving again? Maybe they have medication for that."

He grinned. "I don't know if it's evolving or just being hopeful. Thanks to you, we just might have a chance."

She sighed. "You're still hoping we can have the hot monkey sex before the reversion and insanity, right?"

"Yup. I just want the hot monkey sex."

She laughed. "I hate to disappoint you, but I don't think we'll have time for the monkey stuff. We're stopping at the inn only long enough to ditch our bags. After that, the stone circle at Avebury."

"Killjoy."

Chapter Twenty-one

"So," Tremayne began delicately, "I take it you didn't call ahead? You know, to make sure we'd have *privacy* in the stone circle?"

The circle was crawling with tourists and pagans of every order. All were there to celebrate the spring equinox in a show of furs and simple robes, face paintings and floral wreaths, wooden staves and exotic musical instruments. They clearly anticipated all manner of miracles.

Daphne watched the group and felt downright mundane. "Well, I was a little concerned with just getting your butt across the Atlantic against your will. So, no. I assumed there would be a magicky helping hand in this somehow. You know, from whatever charm Akker cast over that rock of yours. From what Mina told me, it sounds as if the cornerstone likes to see to smoothing its own way when in transit. At least, that's what Mina said happened when she inherited it. No red tape at all—and even an unheard-of twenty-four-hour delivery time from England to the U.S. All she'd had to do was sign on the dotted line and the thing was hers. Way too easy to be coincidence, right? I was hoping that same luck would continue. I figured all I had to do was direct you and your stone in this general direction and everything else would work itself out. Opportunity would present itself and we'd take advantage of it."

He surveyed the crowd doubtfully. "I don't know. This could be tricky."

"Don't worry. I'm not completely without a plan. The nice lady at the museum said there would be a lull between ceremonies; another group is coming in or something. We should be able to sneak in a little private time then." She looked around. "Good thing this place is open to the public, or this would be impossible."

As they watched, the diversely attired group appreciated poetry and song and some reverently executed pagan rituals. Then the visitors performed what appeared to be a closing ceremony. Only, after that, not everybody left. Sure, some drove off or headed inside the pub for drinks and celebration, but others stayed outside to take pictures and talk.

Daphne and Tremayne exchanged glances. What now?

Well, *hail*, of course. And lots of it. No warning, no gradual beginning, just horrifying showers from above that soon had everyone running for shelter. Everyone but Tremayne and Daphne, whose cause was a little more dire than seasonal celebration. The pair trudged their way through the storm. However, just as soon as the area had cleared of other people, with the crowds retreating to the pub, the hail ended.

Heart pounding, and with Phil's dire-sounding prediction fresh in her mind, Daphne glanced at Tremayne. "It could be a coincidence. Maybe."

Tremayne just raised an eyebrow.

"Right. So what do we do here?" Daphne murmured under her breath.

"You're asking me? You're the Druid."

"Fun-*ny*. Funny guy. Like you're not the weirdest thing this circle has ever seen."

"You think I'm weird? Look at you—a hereditary Druid who renounces her Druid powers but then adopts puca powers rejected by a puca! Only to find the two sets of powers commingling." He shook his head sadly. "You're weird enough to merit guinea-pig status even among magic-wielders."

"The nature spirit has evolved into a comedian. Truly hilarious."

Daphne glanced around, taking in the mammoth rocks situated on the grassy expanse. No trace of hailstones remained. And now that they were here, literally inside the circle, it felt odd that this was open to the public. Anyone could just walk into the circle and touch the stones that had mystified humanity for centuries. Locals had even built a village inside.

Perhaps more surprising, one could commune with local sheep! There were actually many sheep. And, as though the hailstones had not even affected them, they were grazing on hallowed ground. Well, sort of hallowed.

"Would this be considered hallowed ground?" she asked Tremayne.

"Depends on who's speaking," he replied. "If you're heathenish like us, then sure, why not."

Daphne did a little hop-skip, her eyes on the various aromatic piles situated all around. "Watch your step. Sheep leave their own holy relics." Then she glanced up. "I assume you know where to go. Since this is your turf, not mine."

"I do." Tremayne squinted into the setting sun. His gaze took in everything before settling on a specific point on the perimeter of the southern inner circle, one of two smaller circles inside the larger one. "There." He pointed. "That's the spot where . . ." Breaking off, he dropped his hand to his side. "That's where it used to stand—the Warrior." His hand tightened around the strap of the satchel Daphne had brought, the one containing his cornerstone.

She looked up at him. "Are you okay?"

He nodded, silent, then strode purposefully toward the spot he'd indicated. The sheep had deserted this section, no doubt due to the steady stream of traffic it had seen.

At the center of the circle was a cement marker they'd heard a guide call a plinth, denoting the Obelisk. Additional markers dotted one side, indicating other stones missing from the ancient monument. The plinths weren't flat, but rather short pillars to remind everyone that mammoth Sarsen stones had once risen here. Still, the plinths did not entirely complete the circle. And not every stone had been memorialized.

Tremayne slowed as he approached the spot where he'd pointed. No plinth, but a subtle indent in the ground marked the footprint of the Warrior. He gently set the satchel down. Dropping to a knee, his eyes never leaving the earthen indentation, he opened the bag and pulled out his carefully wrapped bundle, then unrolled the cloth, revealing the cornerstone. It seemed at home here, if . . . well, mutilated. Sort of. The original rock had been reduced to a mere cornerstone the size of a large brick.

Daphne eyed the stone, her throat tight all of a sudden. It was strange. Until now, the whole situation had all been so abstract. Sure, she'd seen the cornerstone. Sure, she knew it was all that remained of a mammoth Sarsen stone, the Warrior stone missing from the circle at Avebury. And she knew its personal importance to Tremayne. But to think of its age and its origin and the mystery it represented to humanity, to history . . . Maybe she'd keep her smarty-pants trap shut from now on about nudie Druids and weirdo rituals. Tremayne deserved that much respect.

"So, do you have an appropriate nursery rhyme handy?" Tremayne's voice was wry.

Daphne nearly jumped. "Yeah? I guess?"

He flashed her a grin. "Well, let's go. I'm okay. Memories kind of intruded for a minute, but then . . ." He simply shrugged. "I'm not the same as I was. Not anymore."

She couldn't, wouldn't make a joke about him still being rock hard—at the right times.

"Oh, come on. Take it. That opening was nothing short of a gift. So just insult me or say exaggerated things about my manly parts. Distract me. I'm begging you." Forcing a grin, he looked at her with naked fear in his eyes. Fear for *her*.

She softened. "I promise this is going to be okay."

"You can't promise that. You know I believe in you, but this is for keeps. This is you risking your sanity in who knows what kind of battle just to save my sorry ass. And I can't even do a damn thing to help you. Just stand back and watch. What man wants to—" And he broke off, meeting her eyes in mutual comprehension. They recognized another of Phil's predictions: *It's*

*not the sort of battle a strong man is comfortable fighting. . . . You will
battle yourself as well as your enemy.* Lord, but Phil had nailed that
one. A sneaky, underhanded test.

"This isn't all just for you. A lot of it's for me. Do you think
I'm ready to give you up?" She shook her head. "I just found
you. I'm keeping you. And this is the only way to do it."

"But if it means sacrificing you . . ."

"Who's sacrificing anything or anyone?" She scowled. "I
plan to succeed. Where's all that faith in my strength of mind,
in my integrity? The trust you said you were placing in me?"

He gritted his teeth. "I think they call that dirty pool."

"If that means the damsel gets to save the rock in shining ar-
mor, then you bet it is. Now, keep it down while I conduct a
little Druid ceremony. It's my first time, and I'm a little nervous." She knelt before the footprint and looked up with a silent
request that he kneel as well.

His movements stiff with reluctance, he dropped to a knee
and briefly met her waiting lips with his own. "I love you."

"I love you, too." Carefully reaching into the satchel that had
contained the cornerstone, Daphne pulled out a few crystals
and other objects. As Phil had explained, these would be her
props, helping her focus. But actual power would have to come
from her.

Satisfied with the arrangement, she took a slow breath to
calm herself. Then, gripping the cornerstone, she closed her eyes
and opened herself to words that wanted so badly to emerge.
She felt them whispering in her throat and then in her mouth,
coaxing lips and tongue to mold into proper position for proper
sound. They formed meaningless syllables, words in a different language with an intent she neither recognized nor understood.

By the stiffening of his body, however, Tremayne betrayed
his own comprehension. "Daphne, no!"

But she was already caught up in the loop, speaking the chant
faster and faster. Speech winged free, no longer hers to control.
She felt the energy darting throughout her body, like a shift,

and yet not. More than that. An inverted shift, if such was possible, and the power gathering was so addictive. It was extraordinary. And it wasn't hers.

Realizing the trap too late, Tremayne watched in horror as Daphne shifted. It wasn't her body as much as the essence inside. Then she stiffened and seemed to yank back from the stone as she rose to her feet and stumbled backward a few steps.

Tremayne cautiously followed suit, his eyes never leaving Daphne's face as he edged closer to stand between the cornerstone and the figure of the woman he loved. Daphne. She was there and yet not, and her features, suddenly harsh and less focused, were not quite her own. Neither was the madness in those crystal blue eyes. He recognized it.

Akker.

"You. What did you do to Daphne?" he snarled.

Daphne's features, eerily not her own, shifted into a misfit smile. "I helped her fulfill her function. She is the vessel. My vessel. And here I am."

"So I see." Tremayne kept his voice carefully controlled even as his heart galloped with fear. "But what happened to Daphne? Where is she now?"

"She is indisposed for the moment. She won't get in our way. Forget her. She is incidental."

Is. He'd said *is.* Daphne still existed. Somewhere. "No. She is not incidental. She is human. An individual. You can't push her aside and inhabit her like this."

"Tremayne." The freaky eyes regarded him with satisfaction. "How far you have come. To care about a human woman's rights. You have evolved, my brave soldier. We have succeeded."

"I've evolved all right, but what's the point? I served no purpose in the first place. Your curse was placed on an innocent man's head. Do you even realize that? Did you know it, then?"

What the hell had happened? The chant. As far as Tremayne could tell, the chant had acted as a catalyst to call up Akker instead of breaking Tremayne's bonds. And it was a chant Phil had coached Daphne into recalling. So, was Phil involved? Did he follow Akker? Was he a pawn, too?

"The curse was inconsequential. Just a tool," the Druid pronounced.

"A tool? For what? Revenge against the man who didn't really wrong your daughter?"

"Do you really think I care about a silly curse? Do you really think I believed my daughter's defensive tales or bought the ravings of a jealous, betrayed fiancé?"

"Um, just a guess, but I'm thinking the answer is no?" Tremayne eyed the being before him, gauging its strengths and weaknesses. He had to do something, damn it, but what?

"Of course. They were tools. All are useful to me. As were others before and since. Yes, even your High Druid Phil. Although powerful, he's not exactly battle-tested. He's easily influenced through visions."

"But, how are you here?" And what would send him back where he came from?

A gruesome smile. "Through a combination of Druid and puca powers. I used my Druid magic and jealous Kane's puca magic, both enhanced by the sacrifice of my life force, to preserve my spirit in stasis within the stone, along with Riordan and you. I needed the same—puca and Druid magic combined in Daphne—to release my spirit from stasis and . . . reinvest it. The wait was long, as I knew it would be, but at last I'm back."

Apparently, it had been damn crowded in that cornerstone. "How did I not know you were in there with us?"

"As I said, I was dormant. Preserved in stasis. You would not have recognized me as a living being." Crystal blue eyes, familiar yet foreign, glittered feverishly. "But now, at long last, my efforts are rewarded. Daphne Forbes, daughter to a hereditary Druid and wielder of puca magic, the two commingling into the ultimate combination of Druid and puca, provided me the final key. Once I tie my spirit to my vessel's life force, I live on. And, even better, once I combine Daphne's powers with my own, I will wield powers no Druid or puca has seen before."

Reincarnation. Akker had reincarnated himself inside

Daphne's body. Now he would seek to destroy her or permanently suppress her as he made a grab for her powers.

"No!" Tremayne lunged forward and grabbed Daphne's shoulders. He felt the same shape under his hands, but a different person, the body totally unresisting and barely responsive. "Daphne? Daphne!" It wasn't her. He refocused on the evil haze over Daphne's face. "You can't hijack her life like this. I won't allow it."

Exhaling long and low, Tremayne let his powers consume him. He felt the energy, the magic crackling as he drew it into him.

Akker laughed. And it was indeed Akker's laugh, even if it emerged from Daphne's lips. "Your dampening powers won't work on me! Don't you see? All you can do now is draw some of Daphne's power. Daphne is a shield between you and me. The only way you can get to me is to go through her. To destroy her. Which, I suppose you could do, if you drained the rest of her magic and then took her mortal life."

Tremayne stared, horrified. He would *not*. He stopped drawing power, but he didn't let go of her shoulders, as if somehow he could connect with her still. She didn't respond.

"So, will you? Could you kill her to get to me?" Akker taunted quietly. "Maybe we should see how far you've really evolved, nature spirit. You want to save Daphne. And yet, to destroy me—whom you believe dangerous to both the magical and mortal realms—you would have to kill her. Do you have the heart and compassionate soul of a man, or the ruthless practicality endowed by nature in all her lesser beings?" It was part taunt, part raging curiosity. Akker considered Tremayne his creation and clearly wanted to gauge the success of his little experiment.

Tremayne didn't respond.

Akker continued in a confident, very satisfied tone. "Calm yourself, Tremayne. There's an end to all this. And you've earned your own considerable reward. That part wasn't a lie. You can be free with my help."

Barely hearing Akker's words, Tremayne wracked his brain for solutions. Obviously, he couldn't physically shake Daphne free of the old Druid's spirit. He had to find some other way. He let go of her shoulders. He refused to draw any more power from her, and she'd need a few minutes to recover the small measure he'd already drained. If she could somehow access her own magic to expel Akker, he wanted her to have it.

But that would take the superior control and strength of a seasoned, well-schooled Druid. He didn't think even Phil could handle it. Daphne's powers were infantile in their development, unpredictable. How could she be capable? But what choice did they have? All Tremayne could do was distract the Druid long enough for Daphne to recover from the shock of Akker's possession.

"What's your plan?" he asked. "You don't belong in this time period, you know. You can't stay here."

"Why not? You're here. Just because I was born human doesn't give me any less of a right to immortality."

"Is that what you're after? Simple immortality? But you've essentially been nonexistent for the last two thousand years. What kind of immortality is that?"

"A quiet one, certainly," Akker allowed. "Quieter even than your last two millennia have been. Or Riordan's or Kane's."

"So you've had all the quiet time you need to hone your mental imbalance to a razor-sharp insanity."

Akker laughed, a sound truly disturbing coming from Daphne's mouth. Skin and flesh stretched taut across bone and joint to accommodate an expression not suited to her features. Akker's spirit wasn't comfortable in Daphne's body, whether he admitted it or not, Tremayne realized with growing hope. Akker had not yet managed to bind himself to his new vessel. He was a volatile presence; his occupation was a tenuous one.

"No, simple nature spirit. I'm not completely insane. My Druid training saved me from that fate. I know discipline. I simply clung to my beliefs, my inner world, my goals. And now I have a future spread out before me all over again." He refocused on Tremayne. "And you. My creation. The Warrior who fought by my side for millennia."

Boy, did that churn a certain warrior's stomach.

Akker paused then lowered his voice for significance. "You don't need Daphne. Her job was to summon me and invite me in, so *I* could break the bond between you and the stone. She could never free you herself."

Akker still watched him, his fervor distorting Daphne's beautiful features. He seemed to be waiting for something? Why?

Because he needed something! From Tremayne.

Therein lay Tremayne's weapon. He couldn't kill Akker without killing Daphne, but apparently Akker needed his cooperation to fully bind his spirit to her life force. Akker was hoping to buy Tremayne's cooperation by offering precious freedom, Tremayne's goal now for two whole millennia.

Tremayne abandoned that prize in an instant. His freedom wasn't worth such a penalty, even if Akker could be trusted to follow through. His only goal now was to help Daphne regain control of herself and expel the Druid before he reverted to simple nature-spirit form. So he needed information that Akker would never give up without a little deception.

"You can do this thing?" Tremayne murmured in mock wonder. "Break the bond between the stone and me?" He stared at the figure before him, trying to see only Akker, and not Daphne. The sight of her would lead him to betray his anger.

"I can. And freedom is important to you, right?"

"Freedom," Tremayne mused quietly, "has been my goal for a long time. Ever since I gained a first taste. You say you can give it to me. I believe you. But you haven't yet. Why? Haven't I served you well? What's lacking?"

Akker's mien took on a cast of triumph . . . and greed. "I need you to do something for me. Just one last minor task, but one that's necessary to my existence—and your freedom."

Great. What vile task might cement such an evil bargain? Maybe the old dead Druid needed Tremayne to sacrifice a sheep so he could jump rope with an intestine? Weave baskets with the entrails? Druids were so bloodthirsty sometimes. At least, the original ones had been. The newer ones had evolved, he supposed. Phil hadn't seemed so bad, if Daphne's parents were a bit sketchy. "What is this task?"

"A sacrifice, of course." Akker smiled.

Of course. Tremayne eyed him wearily and sighed. "What kind of sacrifice?"

"You must drain Daphne Forbes of all her powers: Druid, puca, human, immortal, spiritual, physical. Draw them all into yourself, but don't let them disperse as you normally do. At that point, I will take her over completely. Once I do, release the powers back to me, after which I will bind them all to my spirit, and my spirit to her life force. Understand that the combination of her powers and mine is necessary for me to release you from your bond to the rock."

"You want me to drain her completely? Even if it's only temporary, such a draining would destroy her." Tremayne could barely contain his rage. Daphne's sanity, her soul, her life. All would be vanquished by Akker.

Like hell. No way would Tremayne help him do this. But he felt sure, knowing Akker, that there was a Plan B that might succeed without his help.

"No, the draining wouldn't be entirely fatal. I would need her body alive so I could function in this world."

Gee, what a fucking relief. The psychopath. *Daphne. Daphne!* His only hope was that she could pick up his thoughts, that somewhere, some part of her was reaching out, seeking, and would find him. *Damn it, if you can hear me, wake up, babe. You have to eject this guy before he ejects you. Do you understand? Fight for your life, your sanity, your body, your very consciousness. He's going to steal all of them from you unless you give me a little help here. Are you hearing any of this? Daphne!*

Her body jerked and her eyes widened. As did Tremayne's own. Akker had not initiated that movement; he would have sworn it.

"Come. Do it now, Warrior," the Druid commanded.

Tremayne frowned. "I don't know, Akker. How's your karma doing? How would mine fare if I were to do this? I wield magic. If I hurt an innocent . . ." He shrugged, conveying uncertainty, but not necessarily opposition. In their world, it was a rational, completely expected consideration he mentioned. It also served to buy his beloved time. *Come on, Daphne.*

Tremayne?

It was she! *Daphne! I'm going to break his concentration. Somehow, some way. When you feel his hold on you lessen, you have to move in wherever he retreats. Take control of your powers and fight him. It's the only way to survive.*

There was no response. But he had to believe she'd heard him and just needed to conserve her resources. He had no idea if she was hurt, if she was reeling, completely there . . . anything. But he'd said he believed in her. He would. Honestly, he had no choice now: he could not do this for her, could not eradicate Akker without destroying her. Akker had been right about that.

"Do as I say, Tremayne. Dampen her powers. All of them. Now." A great tremor rumbled the ground. "Or I will crush her myself. Slowly." The Sarsen stone nearest them shifted and, as Tremayne watched, the mammoth rock pulled free of the earth until it hovered inches above the ground. "She would suffer that way." Akker did all of this without shifting his focus from Tremayne.

"If you crush her body, don't you forfeit your chance at new life?"

"If you refuse to help me, I forfeit it anyway. If I forfeit my chance at life . . ." The spirit Druid forced Daphne's lips into a grim smile. "Well, at least I'd gain the satisfaction of taking her with me. Vengeance. I do like it, you know. When it's my own. And, of course, she would be the one to lose everything. What do you lose if she dies, my evolved friend? Much, I think."

Surely the Druid knew that a nature spirit, the spirit of a Sarsen stone, would have dominion over minerals. Especially those so similar to his native form. Maybe Akker was counting on it. Akker wasn't ready to commit suicide any more than Tremayne was willing to let Akker kill Daphne.

Tremayne called up his powers. He watched the Sarsen stone hover silently before rising, approaching. . . . But Tremayne halted the stone short of Daphne's body and sent it back to earth. Gently. So gently. He remembered the pain of his own stone shattering long ago, could relive every blow. He wouldn't drop this stone now unless he had no choice.

But another was uprooted, and another, each floating toward Daphne's body. Two! He concentrated, sent both back to their origins, to lie on their sides. Then three and four. More quickly, a fifth . . .

Daphne! Damn it, you have to help me. I can juggle stones all day, but I can't get rid of Akker for you. You have to do that. Come on! Fight to come back to me.

Daphne's form shook and moved a step forward.

Yes! That's it. Come back to me.

Another stone shot up from the ground like it was blasted, aimed like a missile. Tremayne halted it with effort, sent it back, even as two others shot up from the outer circle. He fielded those as well. Tremayne found his attention divided between the massive stones and Daphne's struggle.

As her face distorted, Tremayne saw alternating flashes of Akker's madness and Daphne's terror, but he could do nothing but intercept the damn rocks. They were coming less frequently now, though. Was that a good sign? Or was it bad?—was Akker focusing his fight inward to batter away at his host's mind? Would Daphne emerge sane if she even emerged at all?

Alien flashes of triumph crossed her features. Dear god, she was losing! And all he could do was spar with stones. Damn it, he was helpless. Helpless in the bigger fight. He could do nothing to save her.

No, wait. Not nothing. Tremayne's gaze lit on his cornerstone, the one thing within reach that Akker could not safely touch. Akker's spirit wasn't grounded yet. Just as the unbound puca powers had leapt from the stone to Daphne upon impact, so would Akker's spirit—unbound yet to Daphne, and volatile—return to the enchanted cornerstone if it were accessed. Daphne, her Druid powers dormant, had been as an empty vessel, magically speaking, when the puca powers attached to her, binding instantly. Lucky for her, Druid and puca powers had grown and braided together, rather than fight for occupation of her. Now she was an already fully occupied vessel that Akker would have to forcibly and unnaturally overtake.

There was a risk—to Tremayne's very existence. If one Sarsen stone dropped on top of his cornerstone, he was toast. It was a risk he would take.

"I love you, Daphne. I believe you can do this." Determined, he picked up the cornerstone and lobbed it at her. For at least a brief moment Akker would have to retreat, assuming the stone hit.

Surprise registered on her face, then panic. He was pretty sure the first emotion was Akker's, the second Daphne's. Her hand instinctively flashed out, snatched the rock . . . and then a sharp crackling fire started low, then built, expanding into a heated, multifaceted orb around Daphne's body. A sharp noise sounded, and billowing smoke obscured his vision. Tremayne simply waited.

There was only silence.

Chapter Twenty-two

Smoke drifted everywhere, huge clouds of it floating higher as Tremayne squinted into the haze. What would he find?

He saw a foot. Or rather, a paw—a large one—soon joined by a few others. And a long, lean body with creamy fur. The smoke drifted higher and he caught his breath. A lioness! Beautiful. Majestic. Predatory. And with unlikely but triumphant blue eyes sparkling up into his. The wild she-cat was curled protectively around his cornerstone.

His legs weak, it was all Tremayne could do not to fall to the ground and weep like a child. "Daphne?" he asked.

Who else?

She stood. Then she closed those beautiful eyes, raised her nose to sniff the air, and filled the near silence with another crackling noise that was low and efficient. Moments later, Daphne's true body appeared. She opened her eyes and smiled at him.

"One. Two." She showed him her feet, tennies intact. "I did it." Then she picked up the cornerstone lying between her feet and held it out to him.

Dazed, he accepted the stone, but then nearly dropped it in surprise. Usually he felt something upon connection, like two weak magnets meeting and faintly clinging to each other. But not this time. It was . . . just a rock.

"The bond is broken. But how?" He looked into her eyes. He saw the shine of sweet satisfaction, just before a smug grin crossed her face.

"I ate him."

"Ate?" A smile tugged at his mouth. "You *ate* Akker?"

"Well, in a manner of speaking." She shrugged. "Why not? He would have gorged himself on my powers. I just took his instead—and grabbed some info while I was at it. When I took Akker's powers and combined them with mine, it automatically broke the bond between you and your stone. All was part of Akker's evil plan, no doubt, except *I* was supposed to be devoured, and not him. As for you, his offer of freedom was a lie. Sure, you'd have been separated from your stone, but he intended to enslave you as his warrior forever. Fun times, huh?" She grinned evilly, but it was the very welcome Daphne brand of evil, and not the other. "Hey, does that make you *my* warrior slave? I'm getting ideas."

Distracted by some seriously hot visuals, Tremayne felt a few brain cells go up in flames. He quickly shook off the feeling and held up an index finger. "Hold that thought. It needs revisiting, but first . . . what happened to Akker? Is he gone, or do we need to dispose of him further somehow so that he's no threat to you?"

"I ejected his ass from the premises," Daphne said. "Well, from me, anyway. I can only assume he's taken up residence someplace hot and fiery. Or the pagan equivalent, whatever that might be. Reborn as a slug, maybe?" That seemed to please her. "Anyway, the point is, that cornerstone really is just a rock now. You're free." She flashed him a toothy grin. "I did it!"

"Yeah, you did." He returned her grin and gathered her into his arms. "I'm so damn proud of you. Not just for freeing me, but for all of it."

"Yeah, well you took a hell of a risk there, throwing that cornerstone at me. He could have demolished it."

Tremayne shook his head. "Not with his magic, he couldn't. He would have had to physically destroy it. I had a feeling you wouldn't let him do that." Pulling back a little to look into her eyes, he grinned admiringly. "I'll admit you surprised me when you caught it, though. I was braced for an impact, but . . . there was nothing bad. Just you. Soft hand, light touch. Amazing dexterity." He smiled.

"Pure reflex, trust me. My hand caught it before my brain

could register anything but terror." She shook her head. "I saw it in the air, knew what it was . . . I was so afraid he'd destroy it. You would have been gone! So I guess that last little bit gave me the shove I needed. That surge of terror—or *adrenaline*, as certain nature spirit tutors would point out—got all my magicky sparks whizzing around. And then . . ." She raised an eyebrow. "Hello, kitty?"

He laughed. "I've never been so happy to see a wild feline in my life." He shook his head at the memory. "You should have been in my shoes, watching the battle for your skin and sanity. I was so afraid I'd lose you. I thought—"

"Aw, come on, nature spirit. I told you we could do this thing. Granted, Akker was a nasty surprise." She shuddered.

Hugging her close, he bent to rub his cheek in her hair, inhaled the familiar scent of her shampoo. "When did you know?"

"That the whole thing was a trick so psycho could play squatter in my skin?" She shivered. "It took a few minutes. I was just stunned at first, like somebody had dropped one of these stones on my head. But then I heard an echoing voice. The same one that's been whispering to me for a while now, building as the equinox approached. And the voice I heard, I knew it was coming from me this time . . . only not really." She shook her head.

Glancing down at herself, she gently broke his hold and backed away from him. She avoided his eyes as revulsion twisted her delicate features. "Then I realized . . . I couldn't believe it, but he was here. With me. *In* me. Yech. I feel gross. Filthy. Get-me-the-hell-out-of-here-I-need-a-shower kind of dirty. Nasty." She scrubbed at her arms and then wiped her hands on her thighs, then scrubbed at her thighs. She cast Tremayne a thoroughly repulsed look. "Some dirty old man was in my skin. I hope you kicked his ass for me."

"No, I think you did that all on your own." He knew she'd kill him if he so much as smiled right now, but it was damn hard not to, she'd impressed him so much. "Besides, I couldn't kick his ass. He was wearing yours—and I like your ass way too much to bruise it."

She flinched and wailed, "*He was wearing my ass.* I really, really need a shower now. Blech. Yech. The man hadn't bathed in two thousand years, probably not much before then, either. Eeeeewwwws. Plus, he was a psycho—" She broke off a moment, glanced at Tremayne, and he could see the flash of terror in her eyes. "That was . . . um, that was the ickiest. In my head, you know? Tainted. I could feel how crazy he was. *I'm* not, am I? I'm here and sane? You're here? I'm not crackers?"

He caught both of her hands in his. Forcing her to meet his eyes, he fiercely focused on all his love and respect and desire for her, just plopped them out there for her to read in familiar big, block letters. "You're here, you're sane, and you're so strong you humble me. And best of all, you're Daphne. My Daphne."

Squeezing his hands, she smiled at him. "So, we won?"

"I'll say you did." This was a new voice, this time from behind them. Daphne and Tremayne turned together to see Phil striding forward, his purple specs, sneakers and robe intact. To express his spring-equinox spirit he'd added some swirly face paint and a garland in his thinning but elaborately styled hair.

Daphne bit her lip. Sliding a protective arm around her, Tremayne watched the Druid suspiciously.

"What, are you Akker's backup?"

Seeing his look and hearing Tremayne's less-than-friendly tone, Phil slowed and eyed him quietly. "No. I am whatever fate decides I should be. Just a conduit."

"Akker seemed to believe that you were *his* conduit, that he was influencing your visions." Tremayne studied the High Druid. "He said he was using you."

Phil cocked his head with interest. "Did he now? And how's that working out for him?" He smiled pleasantly.

Tremayne glanced at Daphne, who seemed equally unnerved.

Phil continued quietly. "Apparently fate decided that a battle had to be waged and that Akker had to be returned to his own time and state. It seems that you two were the ones who could accomplish this, so fate set it in motion—in ways obvious and not so obvious." Phil looked around him in amazement. "Although I'll admit I didn't expect this level of drama."

"Actually, you did sort of predict it," Daphne pointed out.

"Remember? Waves of hail and raining stones, the pervasion of evil, the perversion of good. Any of that ring a bell?"

"Sure. But prophecies are capricious and deceptive." Phil shrugged. "I did what I was intended to do. It wasn't my own will, but a will greater than mine. It was a will that believed in the two of you. Apparently with good cause." The Druid beamed at Daphne. "You know, it sure did my heart good when you refused that do-over I offered you."

Daphne shook off her shock. "That was *you*? You sent that first e-mail? What, as some kind of test?" She glared at the High Druid. "Like I wasn't conflicted enough already?"

"It was tough for you, I know, but I had to make the offer. Both, as you said, to serve as a sneaky test and . . . well, okay, so I felt bad for you. Fate can be such a bitch sometimes, and she gave you a raw deal. There were loopholes you didn't know, and I considered it only sporting to offer you a choice. Granted, there would have been a price you had to pay to use any of them, and I hoped you wouldn't be willing . . . but you had the right to a choice."

"There were loopholes?" She gave Phil an annoyed look. "You couldn't just tell me that without going through all the smoke and mirrors? And how did Wendy and my parents get their paws on your e-mail anyway?"

He gave her a sheepish look. "Well . . . that was part of the test. I did hack into Wendy's computer. She was clueless, but I knew her computer was monitored by your mom's private detective, so your mom had access. And Violet reacted as I expected. I was pleased to see you handle that situation so well. You rejected their offer, maintained your control, and even gave them an effective puca ride. You did great! I have to admit I was kind of hoping you'd do that to them."

"Yeah, okay. Wonderful." It *was* all okay, honestly, but nobody liked to be manipulated. Still, Phil was regarding her with such open pride, she couldn't hammer him for it. But she just had to know. "The loopholes you mentioned. What kind of price would have been attached to a do-over?"

Phil blinked, then slanted a meaningful glance at Tremayne.

Daphne recoiled. "No! I wouldn't have paid it. Not even early on."

"I'm glad to hear it." Phil nodded, his relief obvious. Then he glanced between them. "And now I see before me two whole, immensely powerful individuals. Intact. Sane. Immortal."

After a moment he remarked, "You both had a question before, one I really, really wanted to answer. I *hate* not being able to interfere sometimes. But, anyway. You were wondering if and how a nature spirit or any evolving being could learn to love. Well, the answer is yes, of course, he can learn—and the easiest way to learn how to love, is to *be* loved." Phil nodded at Daphne and smiled at Tremayne. "And it looks like you are and do." He shook his head and lightly thumped a fist to his chest. "I just love a happy ending. It gets me every time, you know?"

Tremayne looked both baffled and reluctantly grateful. "That's great."

With a last nod, Phil turned his attention to their surroundings. "We do have a mess now, don't we?" The distant sound of raised voices reached their ears:

". . . vandalized the circle! Look at all the stones! Moved! How could they possibly . . ."

". . . if it's the *apocalypse*?"

"God, no, Marge. That's Christian faith. This here's Buddhism. Where'd you put that brochure?"

"Is not."

"Is too."

". . . paganism? Don't pagans, like, eat people?"

"No, they *kill* them, stupid. Like a sacrifice, with . . ."

Sighing, Phil waved a hand, which froze all the tourists in place. He glanced at Daphne and Tremayne. "I trust you'll keep to yourself what you see here? It spoils my image, you know. I'm supposed to be the brains, not the brawn." Then he waved another hand, gave just a flick of his wrist, and the displaced stones all stood on end. They replanted themselves as though no one had touched them. "Much better." Lightly clapping his hands, Phil turned back.

"Um, if you can do all of that"—Daphne waved a hand to

indicate the few hundred tons of rock he'd just moved like chess pieces—"why didn't you take care of Akker for me?"

Phil shook his head. "It wasn't for me to do. If I had stepped in, things wouldn't have turned out the way they were supposed to. Really sucks for me, too, I have to say. It's one of the hardest things, stepping back and letting others fight battles while I watch and wait." He glanced meaningfully at Tremayne, who nodded. "But sometimes that's what we must do. And see how well it turned out? This is cause for celebration."

Phil flashed a bright smile and spread his hands wide in sudden inspiration. "Hey, since you're here, why not celebrate with us? It is the spring equinox, after all." At his happy tone, activity had abruptly resumed around them. Tourists seemed completely unaware of their previous awe and dismay. "We always have such a good time," Phil continued. "Tons of rituals and music and poetry. Oh, and I think there's a sing-along at a neighboring pub later, if you'd like to join us."

Tremayne just raised his eyebrows.

Feeling the need to smooth things over, Daphne cleared her throat. "Thanks for the invite, but I'm afraid we'll have to opt out. I don't think nature spirits can sing—or at least not this one. It's probably a magnetic or mineral problem . . . like, they interfere with the voice box or something? Everything's gratingly off-key."

At Tremayne's confused look, she just shrugged. "Hey, I've heard your shower warbling. It's not pretty."

"Oh. Well, okay. No problem." Phil gave them a sunny smile. "Come by if you change your mind, though. Congrats to the two of you on your successes, and let me know if you need someone to officiate for the handfasting."

"Handfasting . . . ?" Daphne repeated.

"It's a pagan marriage ceremony," Tremayne muttered, obviously embarrassed by the Druid's presumption. But the look he slanted at her was both intent and speculative.

Now it was Daphne's eyebrows rising, and her cheeks reddening, even as a grin tugged at her mouth. Now that she thought about it, a pagan handfasting might be exactly what she needed. Except, maybe . . . maybe she'd want all the lacy white bells and whistles to go along with it. Pagan handfasting plus lacy white frills. Followed by some nudie wedding night rituals conducted strictly in private. She might be on to something.

" 'Bye, kids!" Phil started toward a group forming on the edge of the circle, obviously preparing for another ritual.

"Magnets clashing with voice boxes?" Tremayne muttered. "And warbling? I don't sing in the shower. Nature spirits have more dignity than that."

"What, you *wanted* to play sing-along? I had other plans. Life-affirming and sanity-challenging ones. And maybe some monkey stuff, too. Interested?"

"Ooh, baby."

"Oh, kids?" It was a distant but familiar voice: Phil, again. He'd retraced his steps and was carrying a familiar-looking tote bag. "You still have to ground the cornerstone before you leave. Daphne can do it. Remember that charm you composed?"

"Right. I forgot." Daphne sent him an ironic look. "You know, what with all the possession silliness."

"Distracted, huh?" Phil nodded in casual sympathy. "So, here's the deal. You charm the stone, tie it back to the circle, and you'll rebalance the magical world for everyone. Birdies will sing in harmony, bees will buzz along to their appropriate hives, and evil, denied its last foothold, will surrender and return to its origins. Okay?" He smiled.

Daphne and Tremayne were nodding in a relaxed, mildly amused manner until the part about evil, when both abruptly sobered. Daphne cleared her throat. "Given the nature of the imbalance—as in, we need to eliminate a foothold for, um, *evil*—maybe you'd like to handle this part? Being the more experienced Druid and all."

Phil waved off her concerns with a smile. "Babe, you're as experienced as it gets now. I know *I've* never battled a millennia-old Druid spirit for possession of my mind and body. But you fought that battle and won. A simple charm like this? It should be a snap. Oh, and here." He handed her the small tote bag, which looked very like one her mother treasured. "This is from your parents. They asked me to give it to you. You'll find talismans, candles, crystals, all kinds of things. I checked and they're both pure and more powerful than the ones you brought." He smiled gently. "Your parents sincerely wanted to help you. In other words, I think your puca ride worked."

Daphne accepted the bag as her stomach flipped with mixed emotions. She cleared her throat. "Thanks."

"Okay, so why don't you get started. I'll do my best to keep the crew busy with bylaw talk until you're done. But you've only got a few minutes. Chop-chop!" He clapped his hands in an encouraging motion, then did a neat pivot and briskly returned to his group.

"That guy's just not right," Tremayne murmured.

Daphne studied the tote bag a moment longer before his words registered. She glanced up with a rueful smile. "A few weeks ago, I'd have absolutely agreed with you. Now . . ." She shook her head. "I think Phil's about as right as it gets. Can you imagine being dour and ceremonial 24-7, just because you can move humongous Sarsen stones with a flick of your wrist? Man. Now *that* would compromise sanity and moral character. But he's struck a balance." She shrugged. "One that seems to work without breaking him or upsetting the universe."

Tremayne nodded. "Maybe you're right. So, how about we finish this thing, chain that rock where it belongs and head back to the inn. I promise I'll run you the frothiest damn bubble bath you've ever seen. Then we can explore some of this life-affirming and sanity-challenging stuff you mentioned—and the monkey business."

"Hmm. I was thinking some warrior-slave fun, too. Decisions, decisions." She sighed dramatically. "So." She fumbled with the tote a moment, accidentally dropped it and nearly leapt out of her skin. As she picked it up, she gave him a sheepish smile. "I'm a little shaky. Sorry."

He laughed. "You're entitled to some shakiness. It's been a helluva day. But we're almost done. Just this one last little thing—closure, really—and we're gone. You can do this."

She eyed him with grim humor. "It's great that one of us is sure. Look what happened the last time."

"What? That you vanquished an ancient, powerful Druid in a battle for your own sanity? Or is it that you performed a ceremony freeing me from the rock and two thousand years of enslavement? Yeah, I can see where you'd feel inadequate. Eesh. Come on. You can do this! I believe in you. A powerful, if strange and highly groomed, High Druid believes in you. Why can't you have faith in yourself?"

She took a breath and voiced her fears. "All the other stuff—you know, fighting for my sanity and my life—that was all instinctive. But this . . ." She shook her head. "This is a charm that I had to compose myself. Sure, I had a little guidance from Phil, but the words are all mine. What if I screw it up?"

Tremayne shrugged. "So, don't."

She slugged his shoulder, but his carelessly blunt tone made her grin. Part of her was beginning to hope. Hadn't she pretty much gotten everything right so far? It was time to start believing in herself. "All right, all right. So I guess . . . Hell, let's do this thing. Now. Before I lose my nerve." Kneeling, she gathered up the implements she'd spread out and carefully replaced them in her satchel. Then she unzipped the tote bag her parents had sent and pulled out crystals, candles and other implements, some natural and others symbolic. With meticulous care, she arranged them. Last but not least, she set Tremayne's cornerstone at the very center of the indentation where the Warrior had once stood.

"A little that way," he murmured.

"Hmm?"

"To your left. The stone shifted when it fell all those centuries ago. It blurred the footprint. So, a few inches over."

The man knew his rock. Couldn't argue with that. Daphne shifted the cornerstone and looked up to see him nodding in satisfaction. "Ready?"

"Damn." He slapped a thigh. "I forgot my tambourine. Music seems appropriate."

Daphne snorted, her tension easing. "Sprite humor is so juvenile." Closing her eyes, she began chanting the words she'd composed with Phil's help, along with a few that came straight from the heart. She paused before saying the last line.

"Are you done?" Tremayne inquired gently.

She jumped as though he'd goosed her in the dark. "Oh!" She clutched her chest. "Don't *do* that. I was in the zone. Rallying the faeries, pixies, gremlins, all of you magicky types. And you have the badly timed urge to just bust in like . . ."

A shower of sparkling lights interrupted her words and sent them both onto their butts in the grass. "Whoa! What did I do?" Alarmed, Daphne extended both hands, palm out, as though she could pat the lights right back to where they'd originated. She *sucked* at charm casting. Then she saw . . . "What is *that*?"

"I think it's a faerie." Tremayne murmured.

"A faerie? So we'll have pixies and gremlins next?" She goggled with mixed awe and horror.

Out of those sparkly lights had appeared a gorgeous woman with red hair curling luxuriously to her waist. She immediately whipped her arms wide, and was bobbling them as though seeking equilibrium. After a moment, she opened slanting green eyes to blink dazedly around, then finally stared down at them. She flashed a smile that dazzled.

"Hi!"

"Okay, just give it to me straight. What have I done?" Back at the inn, Daphne had finished with her necessary bubble bath—those evil Druid-possession cooties had made bathing a top priority— and now she desperately needed answers. Granted, she'd managed to finish the charm once their unexpected visitor left, and Tremayne was pretty certain they'd bound the stone to earth properly, but what about that faerie? What exactly had happened when she misspoke the first charm?

"Karma's going to kick my ass, isn't it?" She groaned.

"I didn't recognize her at first, but unless I'm mistaken, that was Breena, faerie half sister to Kane and Riordan." Tremayne smiled. "But, no. I've been thinking, and it wasn't your charm or the words you said that summoned her to us. There was something else there, some other kind of magic."

"Faerie magic?" Daphne asked.

He frowned. "Maybe, but more a combination of different magics . . . with a talisman or conditional attached? I'm not sure, to be honest. It was odd. But powerful."

"Well, thanks for clearing that up. You know, it might be refreshing if every once in a while your explanations actually made sense."

He grinned at her and slid his arms around her waist. "How about now? Is this explanation clear enough?" He lowered his mouth toward hers.

She dodged his lips. "I'm serious! She just poofed in like that, said something weird about turning the ancient stone circle into her own personal merry-go-round, then *poof*, faerie all gone again!"

"I wouldn't worry too much. She's young and probably on some wild adventure. Faeries do that kind of thing."

Daphne snorted. He sounded amazingly tolerant.

Tremayne smiled. "You're just upset because she left without an explanation."

Oh, man, was she! She'd been trying to picture what the faerie meant, but just couldn't wrap her mind around the possibilities. "A personal merry-go-round? Can you imagine? Would she raise the stones that are still buried? Would it be the one big circle, with two little ones inside? Would they spin independently? Could we ride it?"

Tremayne laughed. "That would be a question to ask faeries and pixies and magicky types. I'm just an ordinary man now— though I'm in love with an extraordinary woman with a few tricks up her sleeve."

"Ordinary man? Ha! Aren't you immortal? And last I heard, you were something from a horror flick. You were Akker's *crea-tion*," she intoned in her best creepy voice. "Like Frankenstein."

"Yeah, well, speaking of Akker and scary stories," he said, "I'm feeling seriously traumatized."

"Traumatized? Really?" She tried to feel sympathetic but saw humor dancing in his eyes.

"Hey, I saw the woman I love possessed by an ancient dead guy right before my eyes! It was terrifying." He glanced down. "I'm afraid my . . . fertility might suffer, just from the memory." He was obviously fighting back laughter, and his fertility was clearly not going to be a problem. She could see his interest, um, rising.

"The only thing that can cure me is if some hot and powerful woman replaces that memory with a better one. Using her lips for something better than speaking some dead guy's evil words."

She shuddered but couldn't help laughing. "You think I should plaster those lips all over something else? Like what?"

"I could give you some suggestions. . . ."

He made a grab for her. Giggling and dodging, she tried to look equally traumatized. "Yeah, well, what about me? Seems like I did all the work today, while you just sat around and played with rocks. I'm feeling a little stressed. Once upon a time, a nature spirit promised me a massage." She projected evil thoughts. They were deliciously evil, and just what they both wanted.

"You're right." His dark eyebrows knitted with concern. "I really need to take care of you. How about some hot stone massage therapy?"

"Oh, *bad*." Giggling, she dodged another grab.

He affected sincerity. "Really. I saw it mentioned on the Internet, and it gave me ideas. A guy like me . . . I think I was made for a career as a hot stone massage therapist. Don't you? I have just the rock for it."

"You're going to use it on someone besides me? Over my dead body." She play-tackled him, and he fell willingly on the bed—which was, after all, where he'd been steering her. Straddling his belly, she bent to glare into his eyes. "And I have it on excellent authority that I am a very hard woman to kill."

He wrapped his arms around her. "Thank god for that. I do love you, Daphne Forbes. With all of my heart and soul."

The fact that he could say that, so proudly and so sincerely, brought tears to her eyes. "I love you, too, sprite."

He grinned back at her, those dark eyes glittering with fresh deviltry. "So, now that I have your attention, I'd like to teach you this nudie love ritual I learned. It's called 'between a rock and a heart place,' and it goes kind of like . . ."

She interrupted with laughter and some evil intentions of her own.

"Oh, you know this one, too? But that's no—Oh, hey, that's good. Damn, they'll be building sandcastles out of me tomorr—Oh . . ."

Author Notes

Legend and historical accounts suggest that the ancient Druids believed in reincarnation, divination and sacrifice. I'll admit, however, that I took outrageous liberties with those concepts (and probably dozens of others) for my story.

It's also said that Druids believed everything in nature has its own spirit, and they called upon these spirits when working spells. Did any Druid claim to have enslaved a nature spirit or forced one to evolve? I don't have a clue. I never saw anything suggesting as much in my research, but as Phil mentions, Druids didn't resort to the written word; they taught and learned strictly through word of mouth and memorization. That's great for keeping secrets—forever.

Erected millennia ago, the stone circle at Avebury is still a mystery. Yes, there really was an Obelisk stone, and from what I've read it still existed as of the late 1600s. It was destroyed sometime in the century following. Many of the stones are destroyed, actually, and others remain buried deep in the ground, waiting to be discovered and replaced in their original footprints. People do indeed characterize these stones as male or female, and some believe the circle was related to fertility in some way. The Warrior stone is my own creation. Wouldn't it be neat if one of those buried stones was resurrected and named the Warrior?

Linda Thomas-Sundstrom

Time to go wild.

Barbie Bradley was swept off her feet—literally. One moment the twenty-something was traversing Forest Lawn Cemetery in the dead of night with her best friend, the next she was thrown like a sack of potatoes over a man's shoulder. True, she and Angie had come to this odd locale for a singles party, but this wasn't quite how she'd planned to get picked up.

Darin Russell found "Ms. Right" at work, which was surprising because girls in the cemetery were usually a tad, in a word, stiff. Not that this one couldn't stand to loosen up. She seemed particularly sensitive about being named after the Mattel toy, and before he popped the question he had to know how she'd react to his furry little secret. You see, though he had a tuxedo and a Porsche, he had more in common with the residents of the Miami Zoo than Ken. And if things went according to plan, Barbie was going to see his animal side.

Barbie & The BEAST

ISBN 13: 978-0-505-52813-1

To order a book or to request a catalog call:
1-800-481-9191
Our books are also available at your local bookstore, or you can check out our Web site **www.dorchesterpub.com** where you can look up your favorite authors, read excerpts, or glance at our discussion forum to see what people have to say about your favorite books.

JENNIFER ASHLEY
JOY NASH
ROBIN T. POPP

A lone werewolf defies his entire pack and everything he's ever known to protect a demon woman from the "Wolf Hunt." ♠ A vengeful vampire thirsts to claim a "Blood Debt" from the two beings responsible for his eternal nightmare: the Old One who turned him—and the beautiful Sidhe muse who killed him. ♠ Haunted by her past and reeling from her sister's murder, one woman turns to a sexy spirit-walker on a ghostly cruise ship that takes them "Beyond the Mist." ♠ Together, three *USA Today* bestselling authors pool their vast talents and fantastic world-building to bring you...

IMMORTALS:
THE RECKONING

ISBN 13: 978-0-505-52768-4